MW01141578

Nightengale
by Carmi Cason

Eight paperback edition February 2023

 Book designed by Carmi Cason

Independently published by Carmi Cason on Amazon

Nightengale scurried to the window, gazing out at the beautiful world that lay just beyond the tips of her wings. She knew that she could paint a masterpiece from the wonder it held, if only someone would teach her to fly.

Prologue

It's all about drawing lines. People say that you cause the problems because you refuse to work on their terms. You don't concede? You draw a line. And that is something they can't abide. Then they blame you for the consequences they choose to inflict. But it's not on you. You didn't choose anything except to draw a line and refuse to step over it. Your line versus his line. Yours preserves people, gives them freedom, choices, hope. Theirs serves their own interests and sacrifices others to the god of ego. Your line must stand. And theirs must fall. – Felicity's journal, April 4

I used to think that there were two sides to every story, but now I realize that's not always the case. In some stories, there is a bad guy. Because this is all on you. You had a thousand chances to make the right choice, to take care of the people you claimed to love, and you consistently fell back to your default – self-worship. And where, exactly, did your family fall in all this? It was apparent to me that you didn't love your children; you loved your progeny; you imagined your legacy. And your children were on the way to being sucked into the vortex of your vanity. – Felicity's letter to Brendon, April 12

March 20

As Felicity grew aware, the memory of a frigid pulsing pain evoked the helplessness of her last thoughts before she had lost consciousness.

Memory robbed her of her ability to process her surroundings.

A grey fog clouded her vision.

Sounds echoed distantly, a muddle against the cacophony of her misery.

Even the sandy pebbles that had pelted her skin, whipped up by the tempest around her, had barely registered their sting.

Not that the fall from the truck bed had physically injured her.

Not that her body throbbed from the drug that had laced her wine.

No, Felicity's whole being ached with the betrayal of her husband, and Felicity hadn't known or seen anything but agony from the moment she knew.

That was why the blackness initially had come as such a relief.

A week before, Felicity would have judged a person who craved darkness.

Hell, I would have judged someone twenty-four hours ago, she mused.

Not anymore.

Twenty-four hours ago, Felicity had been stupid.

Twenty-four hours ago, Felicity had been naive.

Now, Felicity didn't want to open her eyes, didn't want to know what lurked in the shadows cast from the light filtering into her hotel room.

Now, Felicity saw too much – that light was actually just an illusion.

What lurked in the shadows…that was real. All the agony of the unknown and how it could destroy everything she had thought was her life. How could she predict from one moment to the next? How could she keep going forward?

Despite squeezing her eyes shut so tightly that the corners ached, Felicity still sensed the pattern of light that seeped through the geometric print of the flimsy hotel curtains. Her chest grew tight and her breaths shallow. She could picture the door – she could feel it across the room – and she knew the locks on the windows. How she wished she could forget their existence! The points of weakness that could allow him access. If she listened to her denial, she would turn her back to the door, imagining it away. Instead, she knew that she needed to keep it in her sight. Even when she closed her eyes for a few transient seconds of sleep, she had to preserve her line of sight to the door. Felicity wondered if she would ever walk into a room again, unaware of the exact location of the exits.

I won't see it, she forced herself to believe, slowing her respiration. *I'll just will myself back to sleep.*

But even as she suppressed her vision, another sense tore her out of her lassitude.

The sound wrenched her lids apart, sent her heart hammering

into her chest, and left her staring blindly into the darkness that hovered between her eyes and the dingy, smoke-sullied texture of the Sheetrock ceiling.

The only thing worse than seeing what lurked in the shadows was not seeing it.

Knowing it was there.

Knowing it could hurt her, cause her so much agony that she actively wanted to die.

That was worse than seeing it coming.

With her eyes open, maybe she could prepare herself or step out of the way – or jump in front of a bus so she could choose her own pain.

When the noise ricocheted off the night-distant walls again, she recognized the gentle clattering of a doorknob as someone tried to trick his way through the cheap hotel lock.

Felicity scooted up in the bed, her back pressed against the particle-board headboard, the covers pulled up tightly under her chin. Her eyes riveted wide as she anticipated the opening of the door, her heart pounding in her chest.

Thanks to her late-afternoon encounter yesterday, she could easily visualize the "tan man" – lightly tanned skin, pale brown hair, khaki pants and shirt – every part of him bland and unimpressive. And everything about him terrifying to Felicity. Especially the fact that he worked for her husband.

Yesterday, the tan man had followed her through the roads of Quido. Yesterday, he had spoken on his phone about nabbing her from the street.

If she'd had her phone or access to the web, she could have dug up her brother's number – asked him to come get her. She kicked herself for not memorizing it. And she no longer had a husband she could ask for help.

Brendon! her mind sobbed before she could stuff the lament back into the realm of oblivion.

"Absolutely not!" she reprimanded herself aloud. Not now. *He doesn't deserve a passing thought.* Letting her mind go back to that vacuum of torture would completely incapacitate her, and though she had wished to die several times over the past day, she didn't particularly want to be stabbed or shot – or kidnapped again.

When the sliver of dawn broke around the edges of the door, all thought ceased, her mind arrested in anxious anticipation. She groped blindly on the nightstand for a pen, something to stab into the eyes of an unwanted guest.

As the fissure grew larger, a broad masculine form slid into view, cast in deeper shadow by the light behind it. Felicity held her breath. It was Brendon. He had found her. Even when he had passed through the opening and closed the door behind him, she could not budge. Finally, she found her mind swimming, and she realized she had to breathe.

That's when the scent hit her, and images began to flash rapid fire across her vision like an old-fashioned movie. Not terror. Not her husband.

A late-night party, the air hanging with a spicy mist that obscured her senses.

A blue, low-cut dress with a slit that ran to her inner thigh.

A drink-sodden series of moments when Brendon had disappeared and left her alone - alone with the smell that now filled her dim, dingy hotel room.

A helplessness as Felicity felt herself lowered into the back of a running sedan.

An overwhelming scent when the man who now stood before her had leaned over her and inexplicably caressed her cheek as he laid her in the back seat of the car.

A series of strange and confusing words. And that sense of comfort. "Don't panic. You'll be okay. I'll come and find you. I won't let them hurt you."

And now in the doorway of her hotel room.

Jase had come.

Chapter 1

March 10

"When they arrived at the village of El Calvario, Dr. Miller was greeted by a slew of smiling faces." The voice of the journalist rang warm with admiration. "Dr. Miller's campaign to bring internet to the struggling village, long subject to the stagnation brought on by the manacles of the heroin trade, gained him international recognition.

"Dr. Miller believes that, as people gain access to more information and to healthier cultures from around the globe, they will rise up and refuse the sickness involved in so much of the culture fed by drug trafficking – and all the evils that accompany it, such as weapons, human, and sex trafficking. As vice president and CEO of ProtoComm, the world's second largest communications company, Dr. Miller is in a unique position to offer the infrastructure necessary to set up communications in such a remote location. And as one of the foremost experts on management and negotiation, Dr. Miller had no problem utilizing the necessary techniques to prevent interference by the local drug lords. As he has proven time and again, Dr. Miller can work magic where few others can."

Sighing noiselessly, Felicity clicked off the television, internally rolling her eyes at the usual fawning over her husband and his pats on his own back. Such benevolence, such brilliance, such success! She stood to her feet, politely declining the offers to help with cleanup – Brendon would be horrified if his coworkers thought he considered such menial tasks as cleaning.

"No, Janice. It's fine," Brendon assured. "The help will take care of that."

Felicity snickered to herself. "The help" was herself and Briel, neither of whom was paid for cleaning. Not that Brendon would care if he gave a completely different impression. *Gotta maintain the proper image,* Felicity sighed. Before the party, Felicity and Alex had spent the whole day trying to get the house in order while Brendon ran off to whatever "business" appointments he deemed indispensable on a weekend. Now Felicity and Briel would clean up after while Brendon engaged in his "necessary" hours of sleep, whatever he determined that to be on a given day. Well, the alternative was the house stayed littered with leftovers, so Felicity would do it and not complain. She had gotten over that in the first couple of years of marriage when she realized that complaining just brought rage.

"You look lovely as always, Felicity," Jack Buckley interrupted her thoughts, oozing his customary signoff with Felicity. The words of the executive VP never played as a compliment in Felicity's mind – more like an observation to an end. Even if she had not suspected Jack of questionable activities, she would have read the words and the body language as suspect.

Still, as he leaned to grip her elbow and place a kiss on her cheek, she did not recoil. Brendon dismissed her suspicions of Jack, and the VP was to be shown the respect his office deserved. *I'd rather show the man the respect he deserves,* Felicity reasoned as she plastered her fakest smile across her face until the last of the guests had made their exits.

"I don't understand why they say things like that," Brendon Miller was insisting as he accompanied several of the ladies, associates or their wives, to their cars. "I just do what makes sense."

A few deep voices replied, and the collective of men broke into a rumble of laughter before dispersing to their wives with waves and adieus.

"The kids are asleep, Felicity," came the voice of Briel Cortes, the young au pair Brendon had hired a couple of weeks before. At first Felicity had balked at yet another extravagance, but she had grown attached very quickly. Besides the pleasure of having someone to talk to on occasion, Felicity could not process how much more mental space she had now that she wasn't solely responsible for the physical and emotional needs of three children – sometimes, literally keeping them alive. She could not have predicted the difficulty of motherhood, and she could also not have known the relief that would accompany an extra set of hands. Certainly, Brendon had never really provided that assistance. Now he could just pay so that he didn't have to feel guilty about it.

"You don't have to clean, Briel." Felicity suddenly became aware of the clattering of dishes. As she glanced around the room, she realized that most of the dishes had been moved off the coffee table and to the sink.

"No, but I like to be helpful."

Felicity smiled gratefully, but then her eyes were pulled back to the door by the rumble of conversation just beyond the threshold. At the door stood Jack with her husband, and Felicity found herself glaring at the unctuous VP of her husband's company.

"Are you okay?" came Briel's voice from beside Felicity, the young woman gliding into the adjacent space and joining Felicity in staring at the two men.

Breaking her eyes away, Felicity sighed a smile and turned to take the saucer out of Briel's hand.

"I'm fine," she insisted as she moved to grab some stray silverware from a sidetable.

"That man looks…interesting," Briel prompted.

"Ha. Yes, that is one word," Felicity nodded, pursing her lips. "There have been things Brendon said over the years. A little accountant went missing a couple of years back; Brendon had told me a few days before that Jack had blown up in a meeting over accusations made by the man – John Mitchell. You're going to tell me that's a coincidence? There were meetings with lawyers, a couple of big-name politicians showed up at the office. This was back when Brendon was still excited by those types of things, and he thought he would impress me by throwing around names. All he did was make me question the character of his coworkers."

The tension that emanated suddenly from Briel drew Felicity's gaze, and when her eyes met the smaller woman's, anger resided there. Briel shook herself. "I am sorry. In my country, the politicians and corporations are less clandestine about their corruption, but in some ways that makes it better. You go into situations with your eyes open. In more civilized countries – Western Europe, United States – there is a pretense of civility, and most of us live by it. But to reach levels of importance, from police chief to President, people have to accept the hierarchy. The extremely wealthy are beholden to no one, except those who hold their secrets."

A chill ran through Felicity's skin as she glanced back at Jack. "And Brendon has stepped into this hierarchy."

"Brendon is not like that," Briel reassured her, placing a comforting hand on her arm.

"Of course not," Felicity smiled. The conversation drew to an end when the door shut and Brendon turned to them with a smile.

"Quite the adoring public," he grinned. "That will last until they see what a mess our lives are, right, Fel?"

King of the humble brag, Felicity quipped to herself. He knew very well that the execs at ProtoComm worshipped him – he instinctively knew how to impress people and make himself look good. It wasn't calculated exactly; it was almost unthinking, pheromonal.

Like the new house; intended to impress. When Felicity had seen the specs of the home – the layout, the lot size, the area of town, the quality of the build – she had balked at the potential expense.

"You know I had a promotion, Felicity. We are going to have to entertain more, and we have to have a venue that meets the expectation of the type of guest. Bill took that into account in the compensation package."

As usual, she deferred to Brendon on the money issues. She cared little about superficial trappings, and she certainly didn't desire to impress people with the extravagance of her house or clothes or any other possessions. Since it was so important to Brendon, and he made the money, she didn't imagine she could have too much say. He tended to bring the stress home whenever he overtaxed himself, but Felicity had never taken his overly sensitive reactions to heart. As long as she was able to deflect his more vitriolic tendencies off the kids and toward herself or someone else, she could endure what she needed to keep the peace.

For everyone else in the world, Brendon donned the necessary level of charm and ease, and Felicity deceived herself that the charmer was the real Brendon – that everyone got tired or frustrated or stressed. In public, his self-interest restrained him.

It was the subtle, manipulative phrases that really groomed people, broke them down so he could lead their thoughts. And most of the time, they had no idea he was doing it, molding their minds to his way of thinking – about him, about themselves, about the world. For Felicity, dodging his attempts to manipulate her had become second nature and had resulted in a lot of major fights. Felicity knew it wasn't healthy. Still, she had made herself stick with him for enough years to have three children and a vested interest in finding the best qualities about him.

Honestly – though she had not seen his kindness in more years than she could count – before the accident, he had treated the kids with as much generosity as he gave the rest of his "adoring public." They had learned to skirt his moods, not to trigger the yelling or random punishments, and Felicity had figured out how to redirect his frustrations and criticisms from them to her.

After the accident, he had disappeared from the house, but since he still had to maintain his image, he poured money on the problem, upping the quality of the house, the cars, the clothes that represented how he wanted the world to view him and his family. The world saw what Brendon Miller wanted them to see, and they bought it because he bought it. First rule of Brendon Miller: be believable by believing your own sales pitch.

Even the greatest pretender had a core, though, and Felicity managed to blind herself to the pretender. She chose to love Brendon for his vulnerabilities, those times when he didn't quite get the facade up. She saw him try so hard to be structured and responsible, but he found himself frustrated at his own weakness.

He wanted people to love and admire him so badly that he would push himself to inhuman limits, and Felicity watched him crash when he failed. It tore her up inside. It softened her to him despite his actions. She saw the broken heart that fueled the machine. It had been enough to keep her vulnerable to him.

Until recently.

Recently, Felicity had begun to realize that he had caught the children and her up in his drive for acceptance and success. Any way he judged her, he decided that others would judge her, and therefore they would think less of him. She messed up his impeccable image.

And then there was the accident. That had ruined his perfect image, too.

A beautiful head of curly blonde hair, atop the most cherubic face imaginable.

Attached to a tiny, weak body strapped into a wheelchair.

Even worse, his oldest daughter had done it, condemned that angelic little boy to a life of handicap and disability. From childish selfishness and frustration, Alex Miller had caused an irreversible injury to her little brother, Noah.

Alex, of course, carried the guilt of her actions, and had become a much more somber and self-aware child as a result. But her father couldn't see it. All he could see was the damaged little boy, and the closest thing Brendon ever felt to compassion: righteous anger at his son's injury and hatred for the one who had caused it – and the one who had let her.

Felicity understood anger. From the moment she had met him, he had needed to work hard to rein in his reaction to upset, but he had usually done so. Only after they had married had she realized that his irritation typically stemmed, not from some external stimulus, but from his own inability to control things. He blew up at the kids when he was stressed, not because of a true offense, but because they had pricked his frustration on a day he needed peace. A man like that – she could hardly expect him to grow suddenly mature in the face of a grave tragedy. Because she had known him as a youth, she had explained away his actions as youthful immaturity for too long. Once he needed to grow up, Felicity realized he didn't have the capacity, and she did not know how to compensate.

If he had directed his anger properly, she probably would have said nothing, let him rage at Felicity and God and anyone else he could blame. But not his child – not Alex. Felicity knew that there were a hundred people they could blame as much as they could blame Alex, because Alex had been a child. Perhaps old enough to know better, but still with childish impulses and sensitivities.

Felicity could still see the glint off the lake as she had turned around to the unexpected splash. It had only taken a few seconds. In a few seconds, everything around her came to a halt. She couldn't make herself move. How could she not make herself move? Only when she felt the sudden gush of wind as Brendon rushed past her, his yell, his accusations...somehow then Felicity could move. And somehow she outstripped Brendon, made it to the water, and managed like a magnet to find the blond curls where they waved softly with the motion of the water.

And when she had broken the surface of the lake, her son in her arms, Noah had lain unmoving.

Despite her terror, the instinct to save her son brought buried memories to mind. Memories of high school lifeguard classes, rolling Noah on his side for a moment to empty his mouth of water, placing her mouth over his mouth and nose, the gentle puffs of breath she forced into his lungs, the rapid pulse of pressure against his tiny sternum. Finally, the coughs and the rush of water out of the tiny mouth. Then, Felicity finding her own breath for the first time in what seemed an eternity.

Short-lived relief.

From 30 feet away, Felicity could hear Brendon's screaming at Alex. Even without turning around, she knew exactly what was happening, and even as the paramedics dragged tiny Noah's exhausted body from her arms, Felicity felt torn between which of her children she should save. Alex, Felicity decided, would have to be the big sister, would have to deal with her father. Once Felicity knew that Noah would be alright, she would wrap Alex up in her arms and tell her she was okay. That it was Felicity's fault. That Noah would be alright. That they would all be alright.

Only, looking at Noah where he lay in the ambulance, Felicity knew it wasn't true. Noah was not alright. He seemed off, somehow, and when she saw the doctor's face an hour later, her fears were confirmed.

"He may walk again," the doctor insisted. "With a lot of physical therapy and some emerging new treatments, we have seen more progress than has been possible in past years. Merge that with the fact that Noah is so young, and young bodies are so much more efficient at healing themselves, even nerve damage."

Felicity heard every word, suspended her hope on each of them, but she was what she called a defensive realist. Knowing her own tendency toward idealism, she imagined and processed the worst possible outcome, dealt with it in her mind, and then went forward hoping for the best. If Noah never walked again, Felicity would figure out how to make his life as amazing and fulfilling as possible. And she would make sure Alex did not bear the guilt for anything that happened, regardless of what Brendon had laid at the shoulders of a 10-yr-old girl.

After two years, Noah had made little progress and Alex rarely spoke, almost never smiled.

Brendon had retreated further from Felicity, seemingly more convinced that she was a sore on his otherwise perfect image.

Not that Felicity was unpleasant to look at, or even an obvious screw-up, but she just couldn't be enough to make up for Brendon's own shortcomings. She couldn't eradicate her own faults so how could she fix his? Felicity knew she could never fill that infinite void of what drove Brendon Miller to such manic depths. She had never planned to choose her kids over her husband, but he had chosen himself over any of them, and Felicity had to save the only people she could.

When she came back to herself, Briel still holding dishes and Brendon still basking in the glow of adulation, she didn't quite restrain her irritation. "I don't think anyone at the company cares about the mess in our house. They only care about the mess at the company, and as long as you keep that contained, they'll love you."

"Easy for you to say," Brendon countered. "You're not the one who had to get everything ready for the party today. I've worked on this for days, and then you didn't even have the house ready when I got home? I'm sorry for leaving this to you, Briel, but I cleaned so much today that if I don't get sleep tonight, I won't make it to work in the morning."

"It's fine," Briel shrugged, throwing Felicity a glance.

Though Briel fumed, she had found one comfort in Briel. The woman always seemed to notice when Brendon's comments didn't line up with reality, and so for the first time in years, Felicity had support in believing that she wasn't as crazy as Brendon made her out to be, both to herself and the kids. Apparently, as brilliant as Brendon was, he had serious memory problems.

Brendon would still make Felicity pay for her sarcasm once Briel had left, but the nanny's earlier words had shaken Felicity. *The extremely wealthy are beholden to no one, except those who hold their secrets.* She had always reassured herself that Brendon's striving for success was a natural part of adulthood in the business world, but the words gave her pause. Had Brendon reached the level where he was manipulating his bosses' secrets? Had he reached the level where someone else was manipulating his own? Felicity did not know. Though she prayed he hadn't, she worried that she was courting her own ignorance. He had never felt the need to restrain himself unless it was necessary to impress the people who promised a reward. Why did she think he would restrain himself now that he was the one to impress?

Chapter 2

"When there are kindnesses, if I can call them that, they are much more like boxes he is checking off so he can prove how kind he is. No spontaneous expression of affection, just another tool in his arsenal of self-stroking. - Felicity's Journal, March 3

I appreciate your concern, but I assure you that I am fine. A conflict has come up on my schedule, and I'm not really sure when I will be able to make it back. Tell everyone hello for me, and if you email me the name of the new book, I will read it in hopes that my schedule will change. - Felicity's email to the Paradise Valley Women's Book Club, March 7

March 11

"We have to be there in 30 minutes, and it's halfway across town."

Brendon strode into the bedroom, his hair slicked and parted to almost plastic proportions. Not that anyone would complain. First of all, no one would dare, and secondly, he managed to make the look work. His navy suit with subtle pinstripes tailored to perfection, the Venetian loafers, the spiced sylvan scent of his cologne, the infallible smile. Even Felicity – even with all of his judgments and criticisms against her – still found him charming.

As if in answer to her thoughts, Brendon wrapped his arm around her waist, trailing his lips down the back of her neck. He knew exactly the effect on her, and she blew out a slow breath.

"We're not going to get there tonight if you keep that up," she squirmed, turning around to face him. He lowered his lips to hers, vising the back of her head so that she couldn't pull away. "Hmmm…" she complained weakly, and she felt his posture stiffen – he didn't like her to resist him. A moment later, the cool air where he had stood left her with a chill.

"Well, I'm not going to let you blame me for that," he leveled.

"I wouldn't – "

"I only had thirty minutes to get ready after work, and I managed it."

Felicity restrained her glare. "That's because you weren't managing three children, dinner, and a babysitter."

"Yeah, I know. Your life is so hard."

"That's not what I said, Brendon. I'm sorry."

"Because you sit around here all day on that stupid laptop. While I'm off killing myself at work."

"Maybe you could take off a few hours earlier. No one else stays at the office as late as you." She had meant the words as a suggestion for his benefit, but he had taken them as a criticism.

"What, you want to look through my text messages and see what I did today? Besides, you were gone for at least two hours today. What were you even doing?"

"Grocery shopping, and getting shoes for tonight."

"I'm sitting up at the office, working my ass off, and I'm watching your location on the phone and getting more frustrated because I know about the party."

"I thought you hated that I never left the house? Now you're monitoring my location?" She had meant the concession for convenience, so he could call her if he were coming home and have her meet him, or so he could know where she and the kids were when the kids had events. Now he was monitoring her in the middle of the day for no reason? He would explode if she had even asked where he had been in a day, let alone if she had called him out for it. *I'm always at the office,* he claimed on a regular basis, though Felicity knew it wasn't entirely true.

He took his bosses and coworkers out for drinks, played politics, met with other corporate executives. In fact, he usually stayed gone for more than twelve hours every day, sometimes as many as eighteen, and she knew better than to ask him about it. A good portion of his evenings was spent sipping scotch and smoking cigars with his fellow executives. At least two or three times per week, he would share some story that his coworker had entertained him with over drinks. For him to notice she was gone for two hours in the middle of the day for a perfectly justifiable reason? He was a huge hypocrite.

"Don't pretend that this is a normal day," he countered. "You knew about the party. You should have done your shopping before today. Then I come home and have to wait on you to primp when you could have started half an hour earlier?" he accused. "It doesn't make sense. Maybe I should be monitoring your location more closely. Maybe I'm not getting the whole story here."

Flustered, Felicity tried not to rise to his accusation. It was ridiculous – she had not managed any major activities outside of childcare for at least a decade, once she realized that taking care of Alex was more than she could manage and have a social life. What did he imagine she did with her time?

"We don't have time for this right now," he groused. "Come on."

Slipping on her right heel, she grabbed her handbag and followed him to the car.

"We'll be back around one," Felicity called to the nanny who had followed them to the door.

"Bueno!" the petite woman replied in her native Spanish, and Felicity felt a small release of tension as she walked out into the freedom of the night air. Brendon might be a selfish bastard most of the time, but he believed in spending his money on fancy things. Fortunately for Felicity, this fancy thing came in the form of a nanny, at least for the past few weeks. Despite the stress that Brendon's hurry pressed on her, Felicity broke into a smile as she turned back from the door.

"Are you excited?" Brendon smirked as he pulled her down into the limo, completely misinterpreting her motivation. If he didn't know her better than that after 15 years of relationship, he would never know her.

"Right," she quipped. "Always up for a party!"

"Me, too," Brendon murmured, leaning over her and running his hands down her arms and toward her hemline. As if he hadn't spent the ten minutes before they left castigating and accusing her. *Not that he has ever let a fight keep him from pressing for sex.*

"I know you ride in a limo several times a month, and the details fade together, but I can't block out the fact that there is a man sitting a few feet in front of us who can see everything we do back here."

Brendon chuckled, lowering his lips to her neck. "He is well paid to notice nothing and forget everything."

Even though his lips were hot, a shiver ran up Felicity's spine, and she recognized that it had nothing to do with his touch.

"I can't, Brendon," she insisted, struggling out of his arms into a spot a safer distance away. "Not when we're going to a party. You know how these things stress me out."

"God, Felicity. Don't be a child. This party is for my job, and that job pays for your nanny and your car and your clothes. You might learn a little gratitude."

As if I spend money on clothes, or anything else for myself, Felicity complained internally. Not that she denied herself from any great sense of martyrdom, but she genuinely was a simple woman who liked simple things – she didn't need to buy fancy toys. No, she just resented the implication by Brendon that she indulged herself at his expense. Then again, Brendon tended to use whatever half-truth he could utilize to accomplish his purpose, and in this case, he wanted to make sure Felicity behaved at his oh-so-important party. *Message received.*

Before he could delve too deeply into her faults and shortcomings, the car slowed into a long, curved driveway, and Brendon sat up straighter, a part in his routine of what Felicity called "getting his game face on."

She hadn't meant to reject him – she hated how he treated her when she rejected him. He just seemed to have no sense of propriety in general and of what made her feel uncomfortable, specifically. If he had known anything about her – had cared anything about her – he would have known she couldn't play around with an audience.

As if in response to her thoughts, Brendon pulled her out of the car and into a very public kiss, lighted by the ambient glow cast by the high-rise and its nightlights. The limo pulled away, and Felicity suddenly stood completely exposed except for the circle of Brendon's arms. Of course, he knew she would do the only thing she could – cling to him. His image was established, his dominance visualized to the stream of swankily dressed visitors entering the building. Felicity grabbed his hand, letting him drag her through the massive front doors, past the muted gold and grey of the lobby, and into a crowded elevator. Hiding in the corner, Felicity stared from behind Brendon's back at the charmed visages of her fellow riders as Brendon managed the miniature venue.

A few minutes later, the doors slid open into a much grander space. Black and white and tan scattered atop an industrial cement floor, where the varying hues of the women's dresses provided the only splashes of color. She could feel the beat in her legs before she heard the music, and she sucked in a fortifying breath as she stepped directly from the elevator into the posh haunt. Felicity glanced around at the myriad faces, recognizing only a few: David Farnham, VP from New York; Carol Minder, VP from Minneapolis; Amy Mercier, Brendon's assistant; Dan Dominic, CFO. Not one friendly face. Then one particularly unfriendly: Jenna Whitfield, operations manager for Brendon's company.

"Felicity," the gravel voice scratched across the air like nails on a chalkboard. Brendon immediately abandoned her.

Why, God? Felicity lamented. *Why did she have to notice me when I need to be good?*

One thing Felicity never managed was pretense, and the thoughts she had in response to Jenna Whitfield's snarky drivel were rarely acceptable for polite company. Still, Felicity plastered on her best smile before turning and forcing herself not to glare. For just a moment, Felicity found glib satisfaction in her feat. Then Jenna spoke again.

"Oh, Felicity. I'm glad you're hear. My friends and I are deep in the most controversial discussion."

"Jenna," Felicity drawled, barely keeping the bite out of her tone. *Like Jenna and the universe are colluding against me,* Felicity complained. "Do tell," was all she said aloud.

"None of us has really lived a life…like yours, and so we hated to speculate and just quote what all the 'experts' say. What a coincident that an 'expert' happened by just when we needed one!"

"Um, expert?"

"Someone who has stayed home to raise children. Never held a career – I just can't imagine! What is it like not to have a life of your own?"

Felicity paused, trying not to let her mouth fall open.

"What I mean is," Jenna continued, "you have done nothing but raise children for a decade. Do you lose yourself without a life? How do you bear it?"

That's me – zombie mom… Felicity bristled at the stupid and demeaning question. Still, there was enough half-truth in it that Felicity couldn't formulate a ready response. Instead, she fell to her natural state: sarcasm. If the foreign tongue intimidated Jenna, all the better. "*Quel dommage!*" Felicity crooned. "MIEUX VAUT ÊTRE SEUL QUE MAL ACCOMPAGNÉ." BETTER ALONE THAN IN BAD COMPANY…

A deep voice behind her rumbled a laugh, and Felicity cursed as she recognized that she should probably have restrained herself. Still, she wouldn't turn to find out who had eavesdropped on her conversation lest she draw too much attention to herself.

"I'm sorry?" Jenna looked truly perplexed, and Felicity felt a moment of pleasure before her mind reminded her that she had to be polite.

Damn. "I'm sorry," Felicity struggled. "I fell into French."

"I guess Brendon likes French girls," one of the women murmured from behind Jenna, and Felicity couldn't miss the exchanged look between the woman and someone Felicity suddenly recognized as Brendon's assistant. *Great,* she lamented. Would the assistant report bad behavior back to Brendon?

For a moment, Felicity had reveled in flustering Jenna, but the catty woman recovered quickly. "What I meant was, motherhood can be so…oppressive. I've never met a woman who stayed home with her children who didn't lack some – I don't know, mental acuity."

"You mean being a bitch," came a deep voice from behind Felicity, and a guffaw burst from her mouth. Before she could process what had happened, she grew aware of a spicy scent that, like a blanket of mist settling over the hills, radiated from the air behind her, and a burst of heat spread through the thin crepe of her sheath across the small of her back. When she recognized the brush of fingertips on her curve of her waist, she sucked in a breath, and when she turned toward the sensation, her heart stopped.

Deep cocoa eyes surged in connection with her own blues, and the man's chiseled jaw framed his high cheekbones and gently aquiline nose. Who was this man who had come to her rescue? She shook herself.

"I'm sure she didn't mean that," Felicity murmured, her tone strangely enervated.

Jenna's smile beamed at the man behind Felicity, completely ignoring Felicity's words.

"Jase Hamilton," Jenna purred, gliding like a dancer through the space between her and her target. Felicity took the opportunity to breathe deeply and recover her equanimity. Without hesitation, the man – Jase – stepped back, creating a triangle with Felicity rather than the tete-a-tete Jenna had obviously intended.

"I assure you," Jase smiled warmly at Felicity. "Jenna isn't offended. *C'est impossible.*"

For a moment, Jenna's own grin resembled a shark, but the experienced politician reigned in her irritation almost immediately. "Of course, I'm offended," Jenna corrected, not sounding remotely sincere.

"You mean you have offended," Jase countered, sliding his arm so it almost threaded around the back of Felicity's waist. Her breath hitched, and she glanced in shock to see if anyone had noticed. Certainly, Jenna had. The avaricious woman leered at the hand on Felicity's back as if it were a morsel to consume.

Felicity stepped away from the hand, suddenly glancing around to find Brendon. To her relief, Brendon was ensconced with a group of C-level executives from three different divisions, too busy entertaining them to bother noticing Felicity. For once, she was glad to be overlooked.

With a sigh, Felicity turned to smile both at her rescuer and at Jenna, determined to escape. "I'm sure Jenna didn't mean anything by it. But to tell the truth, I don't really have anything to add to the conversation. I mean, I have a life that I love." *And a life I don't.* "I hope you'll excuse me," she coughed gently. "I need a drink of water."

"I'll show you the way," Jase began, but Felicity cut him off.

"No, I'm okay. Thanks." With a slight genuflection, she squeezed between two very tall gentlemen who stood with their backs to one another in separate conversations – the move scraped off any intended pursuer. Breathing deeply, she made her way to the refreshment table and turned back to look for Brendon once she had filled a glass. After the strange encounter with Jase, Felicity felt an unusual urge to reconnect with her husband, a need to fill the cold left where Jase's hand had rested on her back.

Not that she would go talk to Brendon. He had made his entrance with her, but he would spend the rest of the night playing politics. As if to underscore his importance, his assistant walked up to him and nodded imperiously at the roaring fireplace. A moment later, Brendon disappeared around the back side of the double-sided brick structure, and Felicity huffed in irritation, making her way to where she had last seen him.

Felicity heard the voice before she saw its owner, and it reined her up short. Bill Henry, the Chairman and CEO of her husband's company, ProtoComm, spoke to someone in elevated tones. Once she rounded the corner, she realized the target was her husband.

"I'm not going to let this blow up in my face," Bill reprimanded. "This is far outside our SOP."

Brendon stood erect, his body strung tight as if in anticipation of a fight.

"You realize," Bill continued, "that I have gone out on a limb for you. I have toyed with this idea because you are valuable. This is a little more than I ever intended, though."

"Just...I'll take care of everything," Brendon urged. "You just provide the infrastructure."

"Bill," a faintly accented female voice soothed. Felicity realized that the woman stood situated just in front of Brendon, facing Bill. Most of the woman's form was blocked by the larger men, but Felicity could clearly hear the voice. "You know Brendon can do anything he decides to."

TELL US WHAT YOU REALLY THINK, Felicity seethed, and her mind wandered back to the statement by Jenna's friend. Did this woman have some deep-seated need to defend Brendon? Felicity reined in her imagination and stood in indecision. Did she walk away, which might draw attention to herself? Or did she stay still and risk eavesdropping.

Bill leaned in to rivet Brendon with his gaze, ignoring the woman's reassurances. "Just know that there will be repercussions," he leveled. "If this comes back on us, we will throw you to the dogs."

At that moment, Bill glanced up and saw Felicity. He raised his eyebrows at Brendon who followed his boss's gaze to Felicity's confused countenance. Shock and something like anxiety flashed over his face, but he immediately replaced it with an angry glare. His own face eerily reflected that of his boss, and Felicity quickly dropped her eyes to the ground.

Maybe she shouldn't have listened to their conversation, but Brendon at least should have feigned some pleasure at seeing her – for appearances' sake. Instead, his expression screamed, "Not your business." Felicity felt her breath speed, but she didn't know if it was from embarrassment or anger.

ISN'T YOUR LIFE SUPPOSED TO BE MY BUSINESS? she scoffed bitterly.

Yet he had looked as if he wanted to throttle her. Did he think she was five years old? She knew better than to interrupt a discussion between him and his boss, and she knew better than to try to judge the content of a conversation she knew nothing about. Of course, it would have been nice if Brendan had seen her and had instinctively read her distress – rather than creating more. But Brendon was in some ways slave to his impulses, even with all his superior reasoning ability, and his fear of displeasing his boss would suppress any weak natural instincts toward her.

And it wasn't like she could tell him why she wanted to be with him, couldn't even hint about Jase. Whether he overreacted or didn't care, Brendon's response could hardly be pleasant for Felicity.

Felicity knew she had done nothing wrong with Jase Hamilton, but she had felt something wrong. His imposition should have upset her, but something in his protectiveness endeared him to her. Since when had anyone felt the need to protect her?

Apparently not Brendon.

In the beginning of their relationship, Brendon had seemed so compassionate, sharing her irritation with all the little quirks of her family – the greatest source of her stress in life. Felicity had mistaken annoyance for understanding or empathy or protectiveness. No, it hadn't been empathy. Instead, it had been Brendan's innate need to purge the world of stupidity. He had shared her frustrations, but not carried them.

Annoyed and confused, Felicity stalked away, her mind whirling. In only fifteen minutes, her night had devolved to depths even her general loathing for social occasions could not have predicted. Desperate for distraction, she headed back to the refreshment table, threw a few cheese cubes and grapes on a plate, and snuggled up to a window to stare down at the toy lights and cars several stories below. Life was simple from so high. *Maybe that's why God doesn't seem to get how hard things really are from the ground level.*

As she gazed forlornly out the window, a familiar voice interrupted her thoughts. Jase, she realized. She glanced covertly, almost eagerly, toward him only to discover his eyes directed toward her. Why had he looked – why did he look – protective when he stared at her? It was odd, and exhilarating. Her heart thudded in her chest. Trying not to appear self-conscious, Felicity smiled indifferently at him and turned away. He had definitely been staring at her. Why would he do that? Maybe he just had a thing for married women. Felicity tried unsuccessfully to calm herself with the thought, dismissing him, but her mind didn't believe it.

For one, nothing about the man spoke lowlife, from his disarming authenticity to his ready wit. Too, Jenna would not have pursued someone unworthy of attention; she was too ambitious. Of course, Jenna would admire power in any of its forms, and while Felicity could not discern the nature of that power, Jase definitely held power. He expected recognition, he demanded respect, but on what basis? A man could more easily wield power for self-interests than for a more noble cause, and Felicity tried to keep that in mind as her thoughts pulled her repeatedly to Jase Hamilton.

In the reflection of the glass, Felicity could make out his form, so consequential and impressive compared to those around him. Broad-shouldered, tall, a confident stance, attentive expression. Jase had deep chestnut eyes, she had noted, almost black in their depth, and his hair, also a near-ebony brown, waved gently across his forehead.

He wore no facial hair, but one could tell that he had trouble keeping an afternoon shadow from breaking out on his chin. A perpetual smile adorned his face: not the artificial smile of a charlatan, but an amused vitality that spoke internal contentment and wit. Strangely, inexplicably, his eyes met hers in the glass, and she turned her gaze to the floor at her feet. No, Jase needed not settle. Jase could have had any woman he wanted. Yet, he continued to stare at Felicity. She forcibly turned away from Jase's gaze, once again hoping to find Brendon.

Instead, she felt Jase's presence before she saw him.

"I'm sorry Jenna scared you away," Jase intoned, leaning an elbow casually against the window ledge beside her. The motion hemmed Felicity into a corner, and she felt the window behind her when she stepped back. A teasing smirk stood firmly in place on his dark face, and as she stared up at him, she couldn't imagine how he had moved so close to her without her noticing. Though she tried to maintain her composure, her normal casual stance brought her face too close to his.

Flustered, she glanced nervously at the ground, and she felt him move even closer. Felicity's heart fluttered like a trapped bird as her heels scraped the mirrored glass behind her.

"I wasn't scared off," she feigned bravado, but her voice quivered infinitesimally. "I've known Jenna too long to be scared by her. I just wasn't enjoying the conversation and wanted a drink."

With the words, Felicity inched toward the nearby table and its colorful display of beverages. She prayed that she could gain some breathing room.

"Was it Aimée that sent you running then?" he wondered, keeping step with her.

"Amy?" Felicity queried, turning to glance sideways toward him as she set her plate down and grabbed a cup. She took a sip as she waited for the explanation.

"The young redhead who was talking to Jenna when you came up. Have you not met Brendon's assistant?" Jase crooned, as if the words were beautiful instead of slightly terrifying. Still, he seemed to wear an expression that confused Felicity. Like pity and longing melded into one thought.

It made Felicity want to cry. The sentiment didn't last long.

"Aimée has proven quite indispensable to your husband over the past year," Jase explained. "Really longer than that, though she didn't formally work for him last year. She's just a really competent, intelligent woman."

Felicity tried not to read too much into the word "indispensable," but Jase seemed intentionally to infuse the word with meaning. Unfortunately, the contrast with Brendon's opinion of Felicity herself could not be missed. Competent, indispensable, intelligent Amy. Forgetful, forgettable, brain-dead Felicity. Even Jenna had seen it.

I TRUST BRENDON, she reassured herself.

Of course, Brendon wasn't the only one who mattered. Felicity thought of Amy: not particularly beautiful, but kind of a plain pleasantness. Even more, Felicity thought of how Amy looked at Brendon, with undisguised admiration. Of course, lots of people gave Brendon that look. But those people didn't travel with Brendon; they didn't follow him around and see to his every whim; they didn't gush constantly about Brendon's brilliance. "It wasn't Amy," Felicity insisted, a bit harsher than she intended.

Smirking, Jase seemed to take in her intensity. "Well, if it wasn't Aimée, maybe you were just trying to escape me..."

"Oh, no," she replied guiltily, turning to face him. "I wasn't trying to get away from you."

As soon as the words left her mouth, she regretted them. She had meant only to undo any incivility she had communicated to him. Once she had said them, though, the glimmer that returned to his eye told her that she had somehow offered him encouragement.

His warmth should have repulsed her. If she valued her marriage, she should have despised him for his audacity, but she instead found it irresistible. Especially playing on the insecurity brought on by her thoughts of Amy. Drawn to his attentiveness, Felicity peered up into Jase's eyes. They pierced through her for a moment before relaxing and glancing over her shoulder.

The voice knifed through the air, punching Felicity in the gut and sending her reeling. A second later, Brendon's form forced itself into the narrow space between Jase and her.

"Felicity," Brendon commanded, though he looked only at Jase. Her husband quickly placed his arm around Felicity's shoulders, rather more possessive than affectionate, and said, "You have to go, Sweetheart."

Felicity felt herself torn between fury and guilt, trying to ignore her new insecurities about Brendon while holding herself fully accountable for her own weakness.

Turning quickly to Jase, Brendon pressed Felicity behind himself. "Good evening, Jase," he proclaimed in a terse, powerful tone. A dismissal, not a greeting.

"Brendon," Jase replied with equally pained restraint, and Felicity couldn't escape the impression that the dark, brooding man had cast more aggression into that glare than the situation called for. Still, as Brendon pressed her toward the door, she dare not turn to examine Jase's face for an explanation.

"Briel has a family emergency," Brendon claimed coldly. AND OF COURSE, YOU'LL BE STAYING FOR THE PARTY, she silently chastised. As Brendon led Felicity from the room, his arm firmly encircling her waist, Felicity seethed with a confusing mix of anger and regret. Any suspicions Brendon had were at least somewhat justified, she knew, but somehow it riled her to know that Brendon trusted her so little. MAYBE A GUILTY CONSCIENCE, she accused herself. Too, he could easily have picked a less confrontational method to deal with the situation, one that didn't humiliate Felicity quite so completely. THEN AGAIN, she realized, MAYBE HIS JEALOUSY PROVES THAT HE CARES ENOUGH TO INTERFERE.

"I guess I can't take you anywhere," he murmured.

Or maybe not. His words sounded like teasing, but his tone and his expression belied Brendan's true opinion. Felicity had embarrassed him. Again.

She tried to suppress the thought, to feel gratitude for Brendon's attentive concern. She couldn't quite manage it, though. Not this time.

On the heels of Brendon's judgment, somewhere in the back of her mind, a seed had taken root - one that terrified Felicity, if she were honest with herself. It told Felicity that she had a choice. Just because Brendon couldn't appreciate her qualities, someone else might. Even as the thought bubbled from the ugly depths of her heart, Felicity suppressed it. If every married woman listened to her own dissatisfaction – if she compared her husband to other men – no one would stay married for long. What if there really was a problem, though? What if her discontent revealed a deeper crack in the structure of the foundation? Felicity did not know how to determine the truth. And above all, she was the queen of maintaining the status quo. An ironic skill, she knew, for someone who had always prided herself in her defiance.

As Brendon led Felicity to the car, she blinked away the tears that might have exposed her new struggle to her husband. She would have to figure out what to do with her brewing uneasiness because it promised a storm inside her that she had never thought possible.

Chapter 3

I am his to possess, and he is mine. So why does his possession of me
    feel more like demonic dominance and less like the
    cherishing care that every person needs? - Felicity's journal,
    March 9.

I made my choice – 1,000 times a day in a 1,000 moments – and I
    chose you. You didn't return the favor. – Text from Felicity
    to Brendon, April 10

March 12
    Time froze. Felicity couldn't move, she couldn't breathe.
Every tangible thing in life sped away from her to a single, intense,
black hole pinpoint of pain. She was under the water, fighting with
everything within her to surface. Her lungs burned, her stomach
filled with a deep throbbing, and the tears that should have flowed
melted away in the flood of horror and despair.
    'Nightengale!' the voice commanded. She raised her eyes to
the surface of the water, and the words rippled just past the surface.
'Nightengale, wake up...' they read, monuments erected against her
fear,

    Felicity lunged up from the bed, her breath shallow and
desperate, as she settled the nightmare back into the dark past where
it belonged. For a moment, she worked to recover her equilibrium
then twisted to glance at her husband. Brendon still slept soundly,
unaware of his wife's moment of terror.

    Fortunately, she had trained her mind when she was a child,
suffering from the intense nightmares brought on by a vivid
imagination. She had trained it how to wake up, calling to her by her
childhood nickname, wrenching her from slumber by the misspelled
word from her favorite book. Sometimes Nick's voice, sometimes
her mother's, sometimes her own.

    Felicity forced herself to breathe, infusing calm before she let
herself move. Only once had she ever dared remind Brendon that he
had given the kids permission to play on that pier – had silenced

Felicity's protests.

Only when he and she had driven Noah home from the hospital after loading his new, mechanized wheelchair into the handicapped van they had purchased. Brendon had, tears in his eyes, hardened his face into a bitter glare, staring out the windshield as they drove home. "You should have watched them closer," he had censured quietly, gripping the steering wheel with knuckles white with strain.

With the breath punched from her, Felicity had sat silently for a moment before lashing out in her pain, "You never should have let them play there in the first place!"

She had regretted the words instantly, even if she had thought them a thousand times before. Lashing out against Brendon always backfired. But the stabbing agony; it had blinded her for a moment.

Of course, he blamed her – blaming himself was not an option for his fragile psyche. Felicity, though, refused to engage in unproductive thoughts. She would have enough to deal with taking care of a child who couldn't walk. Repairing what Brendon had done to Alex. And, of course, making sure baby Nicholas didn't get lost between his wounded siblings.

Yet the words had come out, and the battle lines seemed to settle between them - Brendon versus Felicity, whether she wanted a war or not. Brendon's vision of their little world had come crashing down, and his love for Felicity had crashed with it.

Still, Brendon protected his image. His image of himself, his image of his marriage, his image of his family. He never looked at Alex the same way again – his first-born child, his pride and joy. No longer. Alex, the selfish child who had destroyed her father's image of perfection, a child's lack of restraint turning into a life-altering catastrophe.

In the present, as her fog of pain dissipated, Felicity shook off the dream, the subconscious memory that hummed as a constant background to her day-to-day thoughts. Anxiety consumed her whenever Felicity looked at her children – the stifled fear that if she looked away from them, if she slept too soundly at night, if she took a break, something else catastrophic could happen.

Maybe something caused by a child's natural selfishness and thoughtlessness. Or maybe something caused by an evil outsider. Or maybe a true accident. If she failed at her job, something else could happen to Noah. Or Alex. Or Nicholas. The possible dangers overwhelmed Felicity every moment of her life.

She stood to her feet, sleep fleeting as a wisp of smoke on the breeze. Her pulse pounded in her head, a combination of standing up too fast and hating life. Pulling out her phone, she shielded her husband from the glare before illuminating the screen. 2:34 a.m. *Ugh!* she complained. Undoubtedly, Felicity would not sleep again for a while, not after the dream. She grabbed her laptop from under the bed and tiptoed toward the living room.

As she glimpsed herself in the cascading hallway mirrors, she sighed in disgust. The small swell at her waistline did not predict a coming bundle of joy, just a monument to the past ones. So much she had given up to become a wife and mother, so many visions of herself and her dreams. Jenna's words rattled in Felicity's head - *Do you lose yourself without a life of your own?*

Felicity pushed the thought down. This was the life she had chosen by having her children. Nothing that the grown-ups in their lives had to deal with was the children's fault, and Felicity wouldn't let them suffer for it. Three years. Three years had passed, and Brendon had drifted farther and farther away. Not that he had ever been easy to reach out to, not since high school and dating and hormones, but he had tried. He had smiled and charmed and bought presents.

He hadn't exactly connected with her, but she could see that he wanted to please her. After the accident, though, he had found more to do at work, he had said yes to all of his friends' social invitations, he had joined a club to relax and unwind. On the rare occasions when he came home, he planted himself in his chair and watched the news – rarely engaged with the kids, kept conversation with Felicity to a polite discourse – when he wasn't complaining or belittling her - closed himself off completely.

If she let herself think about it, Felicity wavered between furious and hurt and lonely and miserable. But her kids needed her to stay positive. They needed her to maintain a calm and laughter-filled home. Despite her frustration, she could get herself up in the morning to see their smiles.

Her family had grown – little Nicholas had brought his mischievous grin and infectious giggle to lighten the sometimes-somber reality of the disheartened Alex and the struggling Noah. Even with all that had happened, even with Noah's disability, Felicity found that she loved her life – not every aspect, certainly not the distance between her and Brendon, but the little niche of beauty that filled her every waking moment.

As her eyes clouded with sentiment, almost an hour after her dream, an unexpected clatter ripped Felicity out of her reverie. Squelching a moment of near panic, Felicity talked herself down. *Stupid toys,* she complained silently. No matter how many times she picked up the clutter, a child inevitably made more, and no doubt one of her brood had just found the offending object with his foot.

As if all the children had slept through the entire night even once in the past 12 years! Felicity glanced back at the clock. 3:27 a.m., enough time to have settled her mind and forgotten the dream. Felicity shed her blanket, walked through the kitchen, and rounded the corner into the hallway to attend to the child.

It was just a child, she reassured herself repeatedly as she approached the dark hallway. Fortunately, the porch lamp illuminated a quartet of squares on the entryway floor, and Felicity spotted a toddler's toy car at the edge of the light. She breathed easier for a moment, certain that she would hear one of her children any second, but the silence did not cease, and when a shadow flitted across one of the window panes, her earlier nervousness ramped up to fear.

Her heart leapt into her throat as her breathing ceased. From the sides of her eyes, she assessed the doorway, slowly turning her head to take in all four squares. She inched backwards, away from the door until she could gain a better view from a less exposed position. Nothing. No more noise, no more shadow, nothing unexpected. Suddenly, she realized that she hadn't breathed in a few moments, so she drew in air through her nose. She had no idea why something so innocuous had ramped up her nerves so instantaneously.

Calming herself, she tiptoed to the front door, forcing her eyes to scan the entirety of the porch, including the shadows. Nothing. *Of course, nothing,* she mocked herself. It made her feel better to dismiss her fears, but she stood glaring at the night for several minutes before she could drag herself back to earth. Certainly, she couldn't wake Brendon. He tended to dismiss any of her fears and concerns as irrational, even after the accident, not willing to inconvenience himself to think hard enough to chase down insecurities.

Finally, relief came in a child's voice. "Mommy, I'm

thirsty," Nicholas's whine interrupted the thought, and Felicity took a moment of shock to register that the sound had come from her phone – a monitor app keeping track of the kids. *Bless your thirst,* Felicity giggled at herself, her relief flushing her system with near euphoria.

"Be there in a minute, bug," Felicity answered her little boy. "Let me go back in the kitchen."

The noise had been Nicholas, toddling around looking for her. The shadow had been a passing bird. Everything was fine.

Reversing her direction, Felicity glided calmly back toward the kitchen, ostensibly to fulfill her son's request - not that Nicholas would stay awake long enough to get the drink. Felicity paused once again at the door to the outside, checking all the locks and peering into the dark. She would check the cameras in the morning. Cameras Brendon had installed a few weeks before, claiming that he wanted to be more involved in the kids' lives.

Involved from afar, her bitterness asserted before she could suppress it. Swallowing the sensation, she peeked into the boys' room and heard the steady rhythm of sleeping breath. Felicity let the pleasure of hearing the sound push down her frustration with Brendon and the tension of her fear, and she forced herself to trek down the hall and climb into bed beside her husband. Always alert, even in sleep, Brendon lay his arm over her and settled back into deep slumber - while she fought the hollow listlessness that seemed constantly to pervade her thoughts about him.

After nowhere near enough sleep, the ringing of the telephone crashed through the stillness of dawn, as if someone had suddenly unmuted the day. Disoriented, Felicity stumbled out of bed and sprinted from her bedroom to the back of the house to the house phone. *Stupid dinosaur,* she accused the phone, uncertain of why she even owned the outdated thing. She looked at the clock. 6:25 a.m. ...

"Hello!" she almost yelled into the phone.

"Oh, pardonnez-moi!" an unknown voice replied. "J'ai le mauvais numéro. Excusez-moi, s'il vous plait!" A click preceded the familiar thrum of a dial tone.

Bemused, Felicity stared at the phone. *How strange*, she pondered, intrigued. Though Spanish speakers abounded in Phoenix, Felicity had rarely encountered someone who spoke French. Of course, they could have called from literally anywhere in the world.

As Felicity climbed back into bed, Brendon fumed. "I hope you reminded your mother about what time she's allowed to call," then reining in his irritation, he turned the reprimand into a joke - Brendon defaulted to a pretense of charm, even with Felicity. "What was it this time, a cute little girl singing on Lawrence Welk?"

Felicity laughed, choosing to be charmed as he had intended rather than irritated at his disrespect for her mother. "Even my mom doesn't watch Lawrence Welk anymore." Felicity grew thoughtful. "Actually, it wasn't my mom. It was a lady who only spoke French. I think she said she had the wrong number."

Unexpectedly, Brendon sat up in bed. "Strange," he replied with a stiff shrug.

Not as strange as the look on your face, Felicity noted, turning to see why he had sat up in bed so suddenly. Instead of his usually confident nonchalance, Brendon looked oddly tense. If she could have found any explanation for it, she would have said he looked nervous. But why would a random phone call make the ever-confident Brendon nervous?

As if to distract from the odd behavior, Brendon jumped out of bed. Nothing unusual about that. Brendon rarely sat still while conscious.

"No use wasting the day," he smiled with no hint of the tension. He held out his hand to help her up. Forcing a smile – she would have slept another hour – Felicity accepted his assistance and rose to her feet. "Since I'm up," he continued, "I might as well get a little extra work in."

Sighing, Felicity acknowledged him with a weak smile. *Of course you will.* Unfazed by her lack of excitement, Brendon, in typical enthusiasm, swept her up into a kiss, a short kiss, but nice, encircling her with his arm and pulling her close before touching his lips briefly to hers.

"Or maybe I need to stay for half an hour?" he simpered, and Felicity forced herself to smile. Brendon's overt sexuality had grown to mean little to Felicity, though she let herself interpret it as affection. Certainly, he had ceased all other expressions of love outside of his own gratification gestures. Still, in her desperation to believe in her domestic vision, she lapped at every feigned attempt. In her deepest thoughts, though, she knew better than to believe them. Standing in the closet, though, enduring his overtures, she apparently hadn't managed the requisite enthusiasm.

He grew rigid and stepped away, quickly releasing her. "You know, you might do something about that giant pile of my laundry that's been growing in the closet," he accused. Like a child, he had interpreted her lack of excitement about him as judgment, and he had to lash out to belittle her before he could feel rejected. Without another word, he hurried to the closet, threw on his suit, and rushed out the door, leaving her disheveled and irritated. She quickly suppressed her frustrations under the demands of her day.

She started off immediately, prepping breakfast for the kids, and since the kids weren't awake yet, she used the extra time to prepare some things for lunch. Then, having gotten as much ready as she could, she started cleaning, a futile exercise in her house where a child could, as a whirlwind, turn a room from order to bedlam in a moment. Now Felicity faced another day of mundane chores and responsibilities, and she steadied herself with a breath.

A wasted breath, she soon realized. As if the past twelve hours had not held enough excitement for her, Felicity found herself suddenly thrown into an unexpected moment of drama. She had just passed the front door on her way to the kids' rooms when the peal of tires on the road beside her house preceded the telltale crunching of chrome upon chrome. Glancing in the rooms to make sure her children still slept, Felicity crept out the front door and strode quickly to the end of the pathway toward the street.

Without preamble, the vehicle that seemed to have caused the crash suddenly slammed into reverse and headed off to the highway where it abruptly sped out of sight. Shocked, Felicity made a quick mental note of the car's description and license plates and rushed over to the other vehicle to see if anyone needed help.

As far as she could tell, no one had exited the car, and such a deep ditch could have caused serious injury. To her surprise, however, when she reached the site of the crash, though only fifty feet from her front door, no one was inside. How had anyone gotten out of there without her seeing him? It had taken her less than two minutes to exit her house and walk to the car, yet the car stood empty with no sign that anyone had driven it into the ditch.

Glancing helplessly around, Felicity wondered that no one else seemed to have noticed the accident. No neighbors rushed to the site of the noise, no police sirens blared in the distance - a particularly tranquil and quiet dawn. She climbed slowly out of the ditch, taking in her surroundings with a new anxiety.

Above her, the early morning sky stretched expansive and clear, and the warm breeze that brushed through the cool air spoke spring. Everything appeared beautiful and poised with promise. Still, though nothing exactly catastrophic had happened to her in the past few hours, Felicity couldn't escape the idea that her life had changed. Somehow, the clattering of her child's toy in the night portended ill, and the other strange occurrences had confirmed it. Despite the outward normalcy, Felicity sensed that beneath the calm veneer of the dawn brewed an unforeseen disturbance.

She shook herself to disperse the thought. *Paranoid?* she wondered, relegating her nerves to sleep-deprived delusion. Though a chill hung around her, Felicity had begun to perspire, and since she could do nothing about the wreck, she headed back inside to call the police. After she reported all that she had seen, including the license plate number of the fleeing vehicle, the police thanked her, and soon a tow-truck removed the physical evidence of the wreck. As soon as it did, Felicity returned to the usual tedium of her life, wiping the morning's events from her mind with a willful determination to remain ignorant as long as possible.

As if to punctuate the normalcy of her day, Felicity had just started chopping some garlic to sauté for an omelet when, on cue, she heard the, *ring, ring* of her cell phone. Eight-thirty, Friday morning. *Time for the weekly call,* Felicity smiled. For once, she felt comfort in the irritating predictability of the ritual. Still, she couldn't help rolling her eyes when she saw the caller ID: Miranda Carlton.

"Hello?" Felicity forced a pleasant tone.

"Good morning, Felicity. This is Miranda Carlton." Felicity mouthed the words with the voice on the phone. "I'm calling to invite you to our weekly book club and playgroup."

"Why, thank you Miranda," Felicity deadpanned. "I'll try to make it."

"We'll be looking for you!" Miranda assured Felicity sincerely. "In fact, we have a new attendee who I think you would like to meet."

Despite her usual ennui with the group, Felicity couldn't hide her interest at the unexpected deviation from the usual conversation. "Really? Why is that?"

"Well, I remember that last year when you joined our group, you spoke of an interest in learning French."

"Yes..." The coincidence piqued Felicity to full attention.

"One of our new members moved here recently from Quebec. Though she joined to practice her English, she would probably appreciate the chance to speak in French on occasion."

Felicity began to laugh at herself. Had she devised a conundrum where none existed?

"Have you already given the woman our directory?" she queried, a sudden idea springing to life.

"Why, yes," Miranda admitted, sounding confused by the seemingly incongruous question. "Why do you ask?"

Felicity sighed an internal sigh of relief, one mystery seemingly explained. "Oh, nothing, really. I just received a phone call from a French speaker this morning. I had thought it extremely odd considering the sparsity of French speakers I know."

"Oh, understandably. She must have dialed the wrong number from the directory."

"No doubt," Felicity nodded, relieved that Miranda had agreed with her own hypothesis. "You've cleared up a real mystery for me."

"My pleasure," Miranda gushed, and Felicity could hear the anticipation in Miranda's tone.

Rolling her eyes again, Felicity predicted the next sentence, and her levity dampened slightly.

As if Miranda's small contribution to Felicity's peace of mind would compel Felicity to accept an invitation! "So, can I expect you at the meeting? You can meet Lizette."

"Certainly," Felicity agreed offhandedly. "I can't wait. Until tomorrow, then."

"Until tomorrow! I'm looking forward to it."

Felicity didn't like to lie as a matter of principle, but she allowed herself this one indulgence with Miranda. She had no desire to sit around and listen to everyone blather about which Baby Einstein skill her child had mastered.

Though Felicity adored her children, she knew she was lucky to get shoes on her kids before she walked out the door, much less have them cleaned and wearing matching clothes, and though she read to her children regularly, no, her two-year-old had not yet mastered all the math facts. When she had first joined, Felicity had anticipated going, excited by the book aspect of the little group. Once she arrived though, there was much more "mom-bunch," and since Felicity had intended the group as a few moments of escape from her everyday life, that didn't really fit the bill.

I swear, she complained internally, *I think these groups are more for parents' egos than for real relationship building.*

When Brendon had found out about the group, Brendon had pressed her to attend. He had claimed disinterest at the pressure, concern for Felicity's well-being, She needed to get out more, engage with other moms. "It's not good for you to be such a recluse," he asserted every time she complained about the weekly call. "You should go."

In reality, Felicity suspected him of another, more utilitarian end: the local ladies were a good source of networking. "You never know when their husbands or families or friends might offer access to something that we need," he had admitted in a candid moment. Felicity considered such reasons a rather Machiavellian intent for establishing friendships, but Brendon saw no conflict. In fact, he tended to judge Felicity for her idealism, labeling her sentimental.

Even with her excuses, though, Felicity felt terrible about lying to Miranda - she genuinely liked the woman. It took a lot of courage for Miranda to continue calling Felicity when every week garnered a new rejection. Regardless, Felicity's guilt would not compel her to subject herself to the tedium of the group – Felicity had enough tedium of her own, thank you very much. Replacing the phone on the receiver, Felicity turned back to enjoy her omelet.

After another half hour, Noah awoke and wheeled into the kitchen from the hallway, rubbing his eyes with his dimpled hands. His yellow ringlets bounced idyllically up and down, framing his face in a golden halo. Felicity loved those golden curls, so incongruous with his parents' straight, brown locks. For the first year of his life, people would often comment on Felicity's adorable "nephew." Little did they know that Felicity's hair, though straight, had rivaled Noah's golden hue for the first eight years of childhood. Only as an adult had Felicity's hair darkened to its current brunette shade.

"Hi, Mommy," Noah greeted his mother, almost knocking Felicity over by wheeling into her legs. Felicity had to laugh at the enthusiasm. Of course, Noah wouldn't stop until Felicity had reached down and extracted him from the chair and offered the obligatory morning hug.

"Hello, buddy," Felicity reached down and scooped her son into her arms, kissing his silken skin and inhaling the powdery scent of his hair. "Are your brother and sister awake?"

"Nicholas is standing in his bed, but Alex is still sleeping.

You need to go get Nicholas before he wakes his sister," Noah insisted administratively.

"Well, yes, sir," Felicity saluted, and rose obediently, Noah on her hip, to retrieve the toddler who had just begun to squeal in protest at her inattention. Though he as yet had little hair, Nicholas seemed destined to wear a deep russet brown coif, and the thin wisps seemed to promise at least a gentle wave. Alex, on the other hand, had a shock of straight brown tresses, plain by comparison to Nicholas's.

Alex had other assets in her favor, though. Like Felicity's brother, Nick, Alex had large, round, soulful eyes that twinkled with a somber amusement – too wise an expression for a child. No one who saw Alex would notice the unremarkable hair on her head, so enraptured would they feel with her cerulean eyes.

Felicity's children filled a part of her soul that almost made all her other dissatisfaction fade to the background in insignificance. Almost. *Though it feels empty without my partner,* she couldn't help lamenting before she shoved the void down into the depths of her heart.

When she had married Brendon, he had played the part well, but Felicity soon realized that his initial fascination with her had melted into disappointment. The soulmate had been an illusion of her own fantasy, and he judged her for wishing it. The accident had just completed her descent into uselessness. Now, Felicity had decided to refocus on her children since her husband had left her every way but physically.

As Noah had predicted, Alex began to stir, and Felicity glided over to her room, Nicholas on her other hip, to persuade the eldest sibling toward breakfast. The rest of the day proceeded as usual, and when Briel arrived at noon to help Felicity with the children, Felicity again began to tap away on her computer, the one source of indulgent satisfaction in her life. Briel comprised an attempt on Brendon's part to provide relief for Felicity – or so he said – and Felicity loved the steady young woman. At first, Felicity had worried about the expense, but Brendon had assured her that they had plenty of money to cover the cost.

A student from Spain, Briel had come to the Miller home a few weeks before. According to Brendon, she had spent the several months previous waiting tables at a restaurant, so Felicity found a sense of satisfaction in providing what she considered a step up for

Briel. Certainly, the nanny reciprocated, offering Felicity some blessed relief from the unrelenting humdrum of her usual routine.

Until Briel had come to work for the Millers, Felicity had felt trapped at home, unwilling to take her two young children anywhere where they might break something, which was everywhere. Unwilling to let Alex play a second mother. Also, Felicity had to entertain, feed, change, direct, and teach the two littles with almost no physical assistance from Brendon and minimal assistance from Alex. Felicity had to be available twenty-four hours every day without a break.

Briel served as a substitute for Brendon, perhaps an attempt to alleviate his guilt for his own unwillingness to help. *No,* Felicity corrected herself. *Brendon has never experienced guilt for anything.* Instead, he tended to feel gratified by his self-proclaimed contributions: he made the money that allowed him to hire somebody to do his part of the grunt work. Thus, no need to show up.

It really is nice, Felicity persuaded herself. Though Felicity occasionally felt a twinge of resentment - she wished he would actually break a sweat himself to help on occasion - she had long ago given over dwelling on her sense of abandonment. If she lived her life angry at Brendon, all her joy would soon abscond, and Felicity refused to live a joyless life.

Felicity did not really believe that Brendon's dedication to work stemmed from a desire to take care of his family, but she let herself think it when it helped her feel better. In reality, success, accolades, rewards, admiration: Brendon craved them. He received enough motivation to work hard just from his work itself. Of course, the money he made proved a nice side effect that Felicity could enjoy. Still, she would have traded all the money he made for the relationship they had enjoyed when they were dating.

Trying to see the bright side, Felicity explained away her unhappiness. Thanks to Briel, Felicity could offer dedicated time to each individual child, uninterrupted by complaining siblings because Briel could handle any arising need. A smart, pretty, and very capable girl, Briel spent hours pushing the younger kids in the swing, all the while teaching them Spanish songs and quizzing them on basic science. Alex thought Briel was incredibly cool so had no problem hanging out with the exotic, experienced college student.

After the strange call and the inexplicable crash, the

predictability of Briel's interest had a calming effect on Felicity. As soon as the young woman walked through the door, the younger children mobbed her, demanding the treat which she often brought. Briel laughed, but she replied only by walking directly to the kitchen and taking over lunch service from Felicity, informing the children that they had to eat their "growing food first."

"How was class last night?" Felicity asked once the kids were seated with their meals.

"It was fine," responded Briel pleasantly, "My advisor says that I only need twelve more hours to graduate."

"That's wonderful!" Felicity exclaimed, though she suppressed an expression of disappointment. "You thought you had at least a year and a half left. That's only one semester!"

"Yeah, but now I have to decide what to do after that."

"Well, you can work here as long as you like!" Felicity offered sheepishly. "I mean until you figure out what to do. I don't know what I will do when you leave!" Felicity could not deceive herself that someone as educated and competent as Briel would want a career as domestic help.

"Thanks," she smiled. "I plan to help out as long as I'm needed."

Falling into their normal easy banter, Felicity soon found her mind wandering to the morning's events. She felt safe sharing them with Briel, and she had been dying to talk about them. "You wouldn't believe the kind of morning I've had," Felicity offered somewhat conspiratorially. "It's been so strange." Felicity handed Noah's empty plate to Briel to clean. "First, we got a call at 6:30 this morning from a French lady."

Felicity reached for Nicholas's plate, but when Briel held it out, it almost slipped. Briel's hand seemed to tremble from the weight. Smiling, Felicity reassured the young woman. "I was about your age when my hands started to weaken. It's just hormones." Briel shot Felicity an appreciative look.

"Anyway," Felicity continued, "then, two cars crashed right beside my house. One driver drove off in his car, and no one was in the other car. I mean, by the time I got there, no one was inside."

Briel gave a slight start, suddenly setting down Alex's plate rather than running it under the faucet. "How unusual!" she replied, her jaw slightly tensed. Felicity watched in confusion as Briel's eyes locked briefly on some unseen object, perhaps visible only in her mind. A terse flexing of muscles in Briel's face resembled a smile before she picked up the conversation in a calm, disinterested tone. "You called the police, of course?"

"Of course," Felicity replied weakly.

What the hell! she wondered. Briel's facial expressions had changed only subtly. In fact, most people wouldn't even have noticed them, but Felicity had always been a good judge of character, and very observant when it came to people. She would not have won any competitions in communication, but she could tell what was happening with the people she was talking to.

Unlike most other of her brain functions, motherhood had sharpened rather than diminished her ability to read people. Telling the difference between a child's mindless but unfortunate accident and his willful destruction of property required a high degree of discernment. And what she discerned from Briel's reaction was odd, not the casual response expected in a casual conversation. It seemed...vested.

Though she tried to laugh off her suspicion, Felicity couldn't quite pull it off. Instead, she felt uneasiness rear its head back over her resolve, her uneasiness from the middle of the night, from the noise and the shadow.

Flustered, Felicity excused herself and walked into the living room, hiding her agitation behind her computer. As she exited the room, Felicity thought she heard an almost silent sigh escape Briel's lips. Something inexplicable had happened with the young Spanish woman. For the rest of the afternoon, Felicity remained home, forgoing her usual errands in favor of staying with her kids. Maybe Briel held no secrets that would affect the children, but Felicity's hackles were up. She didn't care to leave the kids alone with Briel at the moment, not while strange events seemed to converge around the Miller house.

By the time Felicity heard the rumble of Brendon's sports car pull into the garage that afternoon, the several hours of normalcy had returned Briel to her usual, collected self. *Paranoid*, Felicity chided herself again, slapped in the face by the thought of Brendon's levelheadedness.

She had given up all scenarios that could explain Briel's reaction to the car wreck and the phone - nothing made sense. Felicity decided that she must have mistaken Briel's expressions. Maybe it was cultural - maybe the Spanish reacted differently, more dramatically when a friend told a story. Maybe Briel's behavior had merely expressed interest. The thought had eased Felicity's mind to such an extent that by the time Brendon greeted her with a kiss, Felicity had let go of any concerns about Briel's odd behavior.

She definitely didn't want to broach the subject with Brendon unless she had something concrete to tell him; if she brought it up, Brendon would accuse her of being overly dramatic and emotional. Dismissal was his practice.

Dismissal and rejection. Felicity hated them. Only when he and Felicity were alone. and she was the only one around to impress, did he treat her with anything approaching kindness or respect, and that only happened once per week max, and when he had an agenda. She realized that she wished he would stay at work, that he would stay away except when he took her on dates, and the realization made her sad. Yet she did wish him away, even as she missed him.

"Oh, Felicity," Brendon's address interrupted her musings, and Felicity forced a pleasant smile as she turned to him. "I wandered into a shop on Biltmore, because I had to get a gift for Aimée – I think I offended her last year when I told her to order herself whatever she wanted for Administrative Assistant's Day." Brendon paused and grinned at himself before beginning his usual focused stride across the room to stand beside Felicity. "Anyway, I saw this, and I just thought of you. I remember how you like earthy jewelry."

Reaching into his pocket, Brendon casually pulled up a strand of iridescent freshwater pearls, and Felicity felt her breath catch at the shock of the unexpected gift. True, judging by his offhand attitude, he hadn't put much thought into the gift, but Felicity always appreciated the spontaneous acts of kindness even more than the contemplated ones. Not that she particularly cared for flashy gifts like jewelry, but rarely did Brendon think of her when at work, and the feeling almost replaced her usual frustration.

She even managed to suppress the pang of jealousy that pricked at her gut when Brendon mentioned Amy. Not that Brendon had ever given any hint of special attention to the woman, but she always just seemed present in her husband's life. And then all the odd comments from his coworkers. *Just be thankful,* Felicity counseled herself, checking her negative instincts. Brendon had trained her that with him, her instincts were often wrong.

She took the necklace from him, fingering the smooth

shimmer of the beads with appreciation. The various orbs of grey and blue lay on a circle, each bead separated from its neighbor by a delicate silver filigree link. Where the center came together above her breastbone, a silver emblem anchored another link of chain which dropped a couple of inches to a small cluster of the beautiful little pearls at its lowest point. Though delicate and unassuming, Felicity realized that it must have cost a fortune. She reached her hand to his arm in a tender thanks.

"It's beautiful," she smiled, trying to infuse the words with gratitude. "It's exactly what I like."

Brendon wrapped his arm around Felicity's waist and grinned at her with an enthusiasm he usually reserved for others. "Glad I got it right," he smirked before planting a solid kiss on her lips. Of course, even when he seemed affectionate, it was more just affected, but Felicity let herself believe because it helped her keep up her illusion of domestic tranquility. She still believed in the ideal; she just also believed that her husband had been a bit of a wolf in sheep's clothing rather than a true adherent.

When a knock on the front door fractured the moment, Brendon pecked her on the cheek before dropping her to the floor. After regaining her balance, Felicity crossed over and opened the door to the hulking figure of her brother, Nick, his characteristic grin affixed to his mischievous face. All six-foot-four lanky inches of him intruded upon her doorway, and he picked her up in a big, brotherly bear-hug. Felicity felt like a ping-pong ball between hugs. "Hey, sis!" He still grinned as his eyes searched Felicity's living room and fixed themselves on Briel.

"Well, it would be nice if my little brother actually came to my house to see *me*," Felicity murmured. "She has a boyfriend, you know."

"Things can change, Lissie," Nick smirked, again casting an appreciative glance Briel's way. Something in Briel's stance spoke an unusual attentiveness, and Felicity had to wonder if the au pair were attempting to eavesdrop. Just as likely, the young woman was responding to the hulk of a man who was sending out vibes. Years of dealing with her own friends' crushes had taught Felicity that her little brother was unusually attractive. *But I thought Briel a little above that,* Felicity smirked, rolling her eyes.

With Nick's entrance, Felicity purposely set aside her uneasiness and turned her mind back to dinner. It wouldn't fix itself.

Nick always seemed to supply levity to Felicity's intensity, a good combination for companionship. As she considered her present company, the evening seemed to promise an unusual level of enjoyment.

Fortunately, Nick's intelligence and level of expertise supplied gratification for Brendon's tendency to collect valuables, and never complained of the brother-in-law's presence. Wandering toward the middle of the room, Nick took up post on the living room chair which sat nearest to the dinner table. Briel and Brendon had seated themselves at the dining table and had begun a conversation in Spanish.

Feigning casual interest, Nick hovered at the edges of politeness near where Brendon and Briel spoke. He tried, using his two years of high school Spanish, to comprehend what they said but seemed to have limited success.

Brendon could speak fluently. Many Spanish speakers had married into his extended family, so he had heard Spanish spoken since he was a child. Add in several years' study in school, and Brendon could almost pass as a native speaker. Like some doting fangirl, Felicity eavesdropped on the conversation, waiting for a lull so she could insert the only interesting thing that had happened to her in months – the wreck. Of course, her husband would assume Felicity had nothing interesting to say.

After a moment of stewing, Felicity found herself drawn to the conversation between her au pair and her husband. Nick had grown bored and moved to play with his niece and nephews. Although she had a limited vocabulary, Felicity had a patchy understanding of Spanish. As she listened to the exchange, words that Felicity knew floated through the arch from the dining room. She could only extrapolate a few phrases of Briel's request.

"Give Felicity a rest…" Felicity heard, "need a few days off…kids to their grandma's…a month…" A month? Did Felicity understand correctly that she would have to live a month without Briel? The thought horrified her, but Brendon seemed inclined to agree with Briel. Almost as if the pair had already made the decision without consulting her. With Briel's earlier reactions about the car wreck, her request stirred suspicion in Felicity's mind. Surely the nanny would have discussed a vacation request with Felicity first – Felicity ran the house, theoretically. "Parecerá." She had heard that word and could never remember what it meant; she would have to look it up.

"What are you talking about?" she finally demanded, trying to hide her irritation.

"Excuse me?" Brendon demanded, obviously irked by the interruption.

"I thought I heard Briel ask for some time off. I mean," Felicity hedged, suddenly sheepish about interrupting a conversation so obviously intended to exclude her. Still, it did involve her. "I know my Spanish is not great, but I just thought I heard something."

"Can I finish?" he pressed. "We're just discussing possibilities. Once I've decided what we're doing, I'll let you know."

Embarrassed, Felicity mumbled acquiescence. How could he treat her like that in front of her brother and Briel? Felicity didn't even look at Nick because she knew how upset he would be at the rudeness. Instead, she tried to adopt a completely indifferent expression so Nick would think the jab hadn't bothered her. Her earlier gratitude for the necklace evaporated, though she knew that the incidents were completely separate in Brendon's mind.

One reality of life with Brendon? He could be genuinely and intensely attentive and generous. Another reality? The next instant, he could prove totally inconsiderate and almost cruel. On most days, though, he stayed at the office so long that she encountered neither extreme – in all practicality, his jabs affected her little. Brendon seemed to have a great capacity for generosity, and Felicity believed in minimizing the failings of people and focusing on the positives. If the occasional Mr. Hyde appeared from Brendon, Felicity could overlook the offense. Even if she hated him – and herself – for a while afterwards.

When Felicity finally brought dinner to the table, Brendon apparently decided to involve her. He said plainly, "Briel thinks you need some time off."

Is that what she thinks? Felicity deadpanned in silent sarcasm. "Why would you say that?" Felicity asked aloud, turning to Briel.

"Well, I see how hard you work," Briel replied. *At least someone does.* "And I think it would be nice for you to have a break where you didn't have to worry about the kids at all. Plus, I have friends coming unexpectedly into town this week, and it would be the perfect time for me to take some time off."

"Oh," Felicity answered meekly, surprised that the young woman would ask for a vacation after only three weeks of work. Felicity's earlier suspicions resurfaced. "Well, of course, if you need time off. I'm sure we could arrange time off for you. I can handle things here. You don't have to wait until the kids are gone."

"Actually, Felicity," Brendon interrupted, "I've been talking to Briel about doing this since I hired her, but I never nailed anything down. And as it turns out, Bill requested just today that as many people take vacation in the next two months as possible, avoid the typical vacation times of the summer and holidays. Now would be as good a time as any. We can send the kids to your mom's," Brendon offered, though it sounded as if the decision had already been made.

Did she imagine the brief look exchanged between her husband and Briel? Felicity felt her nanny's eyes boring into her as Brendon continued his explanation. "Bill is encouraging management to take any long breaks now so that he doesn't run short during the Christmas season. Considering Briel's request, I decided to take advantage of the timing."

"But," Felicity protested, "I heard you say you wanted to send the kids to my mom and dad for a month." Again, Brendon's eyes darted toward Briel. "Briel said she only needs a week, and your vacations are usually two weeks."

Brendon glanced down nervously at the notepad under his hand, tracing geometric patterns with the pen he had picked up at some point in the conversation. Of course, he had assumed that Felicity wouldn't understand the conversation. *Why would he assume that?* Felicity posed bitterly. *Just because lack of sleep, hormones, and the constant demands of childcare have stripped me of all higher-level thinking skills, and he thinks I'm stupid.*

"I just wanted to keep my options open," Brendon hedged with an uncharacteristic lack of force. "We might take a longer vacation. Or maybe you'll enjoy the time off so much you won't want to come right back. I wanted to plan for contingency."

Felicity couldn't figure out the strange tension that kept flitting across his face, or his repeated silent exchanges with Briel. Everything felt strange and disconcerting. Was there something going on between them? Then, seeming to gather himself, Brendon turned his twinkling smile on Felicity. "Or maybe you won't want to come back at all once I let you out of the house," he teased. When he reached his hand to take hers with his usual solicitousness, when she felt the familiarity of his touch, her stubborn suspicions evaporated.

"Of course, you're right," she allowed. "I guess if we're going to do something this far outside the norm, we should work some flexibility into the plan." She always offered him explanations for his insanity, she realized. She was entirely too easy to suppress.

Brendon used their linked hands to pull her onto his lap, and Felicity pushed her doubts deep into oblivion, wrapping her arm around his neck. "You just keep that idea in mind," he teased, wrapping her in his vice-like arms. The intense gleam in his eye made her face flush. "I'm pretty sure you'll be surprised at what I have planned for the next few weeks. Flexibility is key."

"Um, we're still here," Nick reminded them, and Felicity couldn't help but laugh.

"I can remedy that," Brendon countered and, keeping one arm around Felicity's waist, he rose and headed toward the exit. "We'll see you in a couple of weeks," he deadpanned, reaching to open the door.

Felicity peeled Brendon's hand from her waist and stopped, breathlessly chuckling after the exertion. "Not so fast," she insisted, stepping back into the center of the room. "Nick and I have some things to talk about."

"There are these things called phones," Brendon insisted, but he didn't move to ensnare Felicity again.

"No, really," Nick agreed. "I should go now."

"Children," Felicity accused with feigned superiority, and then headed back to the table where Briel sat smirking at the spectacle before her. Seeing the young woman brought Felicity back to her early disquiet, and she reverted quickly to her previous curiosity. Not that Felicity expected to have time to satisfy herself about the nanny. Not with Brendon and Nick in the room.

"Nick," she changed the subject, "sit down and eat this food I cooked! I worked way too hard to let you leave without even tasting it."

"Well, as long as it doesn't kill me," Nick mocked in a mumble. Five minutes later though, the entire crew had tucked noisily into their dinner, and Felicity smiled. Even with all that happened over the next few days, the normal atmosphere of that dinner would stand an irony against the surreal events that followed.

To her surprise, Brendon had already spoken to Felicity's parents, and before bedtime that night, Briel had packed the kids' bags into the van, and Grandpa was driving them down the road and out of sight. Everything felt so rushed – so Brendon. Spontaneous, insistent, confident. Still, had he really managed all of that since the pre-dinner conversation with Briel? The kids seemed excited, but Felicity worried that such a sudden and dramatic change might cause them emotional trauma. When she last glimpsed the car, Felicity let out a sigh, torn between relief at the removed burden and concern for her children. In the end, however, a sudden thought decided Felicity, making her glad to see the kids go.

Whatever Briel said, the nanny had acted strangely all day. It made Felicity very confused about her young helper. What did she really know about the woman? Had Felicity felt so desperate for assistance that she had let a stranger with strange secrets into her home? With the kids safely in the hands of Grandma and Grandpa, Felicity could relax her concerns for a few days. Maybe in the time before her vacation, Felicity could dig a little deeper into Briel's identity. Maybe the young woman was everything she claimed, but Felicity would know before she let the woman near her children again. Felicity certainly hoped that she wouldn't have to forfeit all the help Briel provided. Whatever the case, though, Felicity needed to know for sure.

Unaware of Felicity's anxiety, Nick convinced Briel to accompany him to a nearby coffee shop, so Felicity saw the two of them to their cars soon after the children had left. *He's asking for trouble,* Felicity mused, though she didn't worry too much for him. Nick was a big boy. Besides, if Briel left the house with him, Felicity would have some time and space to think. *Stay safe, brother,* she silently willed, though the absurdity of Briel's tiny frame affecting the giant Nick seemed laughable. Still, Felicity couldn't shake her unease as she waved them goodbye.

"Thanks, Brendon," she offered upon reentering the house. "This vacation might do me some good."

"It will change your life," he agreed in complete confidence. "I have to go back to the office for a couple of hours to prepare some things before we leave, but I told Bill not to expect me in at all for the next week at least, and then only by FaceTime for a week after that. Prepare yourself for an exotic adventure," he grinned.

Despite her suspicion, Felicity found her own face reflecting his. "Seriously!" Felicity gushed genuinely, her concerns temporarily forgotten. "Where are we going?"

"Don't you worry your pretty little head over it. You're not going to have any say anyway," he teased, grabbing Felicity around the waist and whispering, "…Remember. You will need to be flexible." He placed his lips gently in the indentation below her ear, causing a slight chill to run down her back.

"Now I'm scared," she laughed as he placed her back on the ground.

"You should be," he offered rakishly.

Felicity followed her husband to the front door, laying an apparently complacent kiss on his lips before shoving him out the door. She heard a muffled "Hey!" as she slammed it shut and clicked the lock into place, grinning at the finality of the door's rattling. Even as she did it, though, her instincts shook her. What strange euphoria had inspired her to risk it? Sometimes Brendon could take a joke; sometimes not so much. *It's fine,* she reassured herself. *Nothing you haven't managed a thousand times.* Maybe he would hand out the silent treatment and some derision to accompany her first few days of vacation. Or she might have amused him, bought his interest for a couple of days until he got bored.

As if in answer to her expectation, Felicity felt her cell phone vibrate and looked down to see Brendon's text message.

You'll regret that later, he threatened, and Felicity sighed with relief. Interest, then…

With Brendon gone and no kids to consider, she did something she never did – what she felt like.

Are you still with Briel? she texted Nick.

We just left the coffee shop, he responded. *Get this: I invited her back to my apartment, and she said she would love to.*

Well, congrats, I guess. The development overthrew Felicity's planned spying session.

Don't congratulate me yet, he continued. *She said she would love to some other time. She has some stuff to do.*

Felicity's sensors rose to attention. Maybe the events of the day had spurred her on to some specific activity. *So, did you offer to help?* she prodded.

She has to do some work at home, but she said she couldn't afford any distractions, "even pleasant ones." Her words. Awesome, right?

Actually, it is, Felicity thought but didn't type, invigorated at the thought of what she planned to do. *It's probably a good thing that she turned you down. After seeing your place, she might rethink going out with you – though she might just be putting you off to be with her BOYFRIEND.*

Not everyone is as neurotic about cleanliness as your husband, he jabbed. *And we ARE going out; I just don't know when or where. Boyfriend, shmoyfriend.*

Sounds like a sure thing, Felicity ribbed. *I gotta go.*

Gotcha, Nick agreed. *See you in the morning. I assume I'm feeding the dog while you're out of town?*

And watering the plants, Felicity agreed.

Joy!

G-o-o-d-b-y-e, Nick! Felicity more than hinted. *Talk to you tomorrow, not today.*

Lol. Bye.

Felicity honestly did not understand what had set off her sensors with Briel. Still, finding out about the young woman seemed easier and less threatening than trying to spy on Brendon or figure out the cause of all the strange occurrences from the past 24 hours. All Felicity intended to do was discover whether Briel was who she said she was or not. With the kids gone and Brendon ensconced at work for the rest of the day, there was no real reason for Felicity to refrain. She had hours to find out all she could about Briel Cortes.

Starting with her home address.

Chapter 4

*In his usual manner, Brendon stormed out of the house, completely
unaware of - or uncaring for - the pain he caused me. For the
first time since I married him, I stood still in shock, not
because I feared his disapproval, but because I didn't care.* –
Felicity's Journal, March 10

*Come home, sis. I don't want you to be alone.
*I'm not alone…
– Text exchange between Felicity Miller and her brother Nicholas
Alexander, March 22

Early evening, March 12
    Though she hadn't felt concern about investigating Briel, as
Felicity approached the apartment building, sheepishness collared
her. She knew that, rationally, it made no sense to take such a risk.
As she mounted the stairs to the second level, she had second
thoughts – her slight claustrophobia kicked in at the narrow upward
climb that stretched before her. The external steps ascended a
poorly-lit interior stairwell which turned alternately north then south
with a landing in between. Even though they had eaten an early
dinner, the sun had grown large on the western horizon, and she felt
certain that by the time she left, it would have set into dusk. Felicity
forced herself forward as quietly as possible.
    Removing her shoes, she continued to the third floor in her
stocking feet, increasingly nervous that she might make a noise. Just
before she reached the top, the sound of a voice arrested her. It spoke
in Spanish, and she definitely recognized it. Circumstances had
worked favorably for Felicity, and she had arrived just in time to
hear but not to see Briel. If Felicity had arrived a moment earlier…
Straining her ears to listen, Felicity stilled her breath. The resulting
silence unveiled a one-sided conversation in a whispered tone. *She
has something to hide,* Felicity smirked smugly.
    "Estaba a su casa. El es loco, no?" Briel's voice queried.

"Ayudarle? No, claramente no!"

At his house, Felicity translated silently. *Not going to help him?* The words meant nothing to Felicity, and when Briel pressed through the door out of the stairway, Felicity crept stealthily up to it, pressing her ear against the cold metal. After waiting until the voice faded nearly out of earshot, she cracked the door slightly and peeked through just in time to see Briel turn down a hallway lined with doorways. Felicity tiptoed to the hallway and peered briefly around the corner before pulling herself back. She steeled herself for a moment then rounded the corner in a slow, deliberate pursuit.

A narrow passageway greeted her straining eyes - a very dark pathway, even darker than the stairwell as most of the lights weren't functioning properly. Felicity peered down the inky passage until her eyes grew a little more accustomed, then she began making her way down the hall. She paused frequently, stepping into each doorway niche she passed so she could reassess, make sure she hadn't been detected.

Still, Briel rattled on. Finally, the nanny paused at a door, fumbling with her keys before entering what must be her apartment.

Ugh! Felicity complained. It seemed her mission would end unfruitful; she couldn't very well knock on the door and confront Briel directly. Unfortunately, Felicity had heard just enough to pique her curiosity but even more that told her to avoid confrontation.

"Yo se, yo se," Felicity had heard Briel say. "Trabajo por usted, pero no puedo esperar hasta que haga algo malo. ¡Tengo que impedirlo!"

"I work for you," Briel had said. What the heck did that mean? Did she have another job she hadn't told Felicity or Brendon about? Or had she been talking to Brendon on the phone? Felicity could think of no acceptable reason for such an exchange - especially considering the subject matter.

Someone was at someone's house. *Okay, so what?*

"I can't wait until he does something bad"? The more she thought about it, Briel's words revealed nothing sinister. But "Tengo que impedirle"? Felicity was pretty sure that "impedir" was impede, stop. How could Briel stop anyone from doing anything? 5'2" and barely breaking 100 pounds, Briel didn't look as if she could impede a kitten if it wanted to get past her. Felicity pondered for several minutes, standing unmoving in the hallway, uncertain of how long to wait or whether to give up completely.

Suddenly, a knock shattered Felicity's reverie and sent her heart racing into her throat. She knew that no one had passed her on the way down the hall, but the noise reminded her that she really didn't want to run into anyone in the dark, enclosed hallway. Pressing herself against the side wall of the threshold where she stood, she again held her breath, afraid that the noise of the ragged air whooshing through her tight lungs would betray her presence. She just needed to get out of there.

Briel's hiss pierced through the darkness, riveting Felicity to the spot. She couldn't very well leave until the conversation ended, not without being noticed.

"What are you doing here?" Briel demanded angrily, her slight Spanish lisp deepened by the intensity of her words, almost like a different accent. Felicity held her breath in anticipation of being discovered, but a deep male voice relieved her anxiety when it graveled a laugh.

"I came to see you, of course," it purred. The rich baritone carried easily down the hallway, a faintly foreign accent tinging its tone as well. *French, again?* Felicity wondered to herself with curiosity, though she couldn't be sure.

"It's raining," Briel replied tersely. "Where's your umbrella"

Raining? What the hell was she talking about? It had been sunny for a week.. Felicity could make nothing of it, but Briel's tone might as well have held a threat. It sounded like she expected a fight.

"If you would invite me in, you wouldn't have to worry about that." Though the man spoke casually, Felicity noted a latent urgency in his tone, and her curiosity billowed. Something was happening beyond the veneer of the strange conversation.

"I would as soon stand in the snow," Briel's equally mystifying response.

That deep, velvet laugh. "The snow can't hurt you. That's a false friend."

Felicity heard what sounded like a punch, followed by another deep laugh. Had he hit Briel? Felicity used all her will power to keep from looking. "You would accuse me of that?" Briel hissed. "Which just proves what I tell everyone about you. You may distract everyone else with the charming act, but you tarnished that for me a long time ago. You're at my apartment. You don't want to make me feel threatened. You'll regret it." *A slap,* Felicity realized. But delivered by Briel!

"You really think I'm the one with regret?" replied the man, his voice tense with irritation.

"Considering what you know about me, you can understand why."

"You have misjudged me, Lilianne."

Lilianne?

"I doubt it," came Briel's terse response.

For several seconds after Briel's answer, silence reigned, and Felicity itched to assess the other occupants of the hallway. Had they gone inside? Finally, Felicity could no longer stand the suspense; she carefully peered around the edge of the doorway.

The sight that greeted her eyes could not have shocked her more.

Little, petite Briel stood, hands on her hips, defiantly glaring up at a man, almost a foot taller. Though Felicity could not see his face because of the shadow cast by the corridor light, she could discern the very dark, perhaps black, color of his hair, and his tight-fitting t-shirt revealed defined muscles. Why would this man seem nervous around Briel. Not just nervous, but anxious?

"Lili, I want you to know the truth," he replied, this time his voice hushed, "but you won't be able to do that without all the information."

"Not interested. You're appealing to the wrong person." Without taking her leave, Briel turned immediately to reenter her apartment.

What happened next occurred so quickly that Felicity almost doubted her eyes. The man grabbed Briel's wrist to stop her, and though he did not seem to harbor any overt aggression, Briel spun rapidly upon the man. She adeptly twisted her own arm and her own body in such a way that she, as a result, stood behind the man, her arm free from his grasp. He knelt tensely on one knee, and his arm bent painfully behind his back. He winced in discomfort. No doubt he could have freed himself, but not without unleashing an all-out brawl in the hallway.

"Please, Briel," the man pleaded. "I am sorry. I was upset – I shouldn't have insulted you. This is not about business. I wanted to ask you a personal favor."

Felicity's heart pounded against the inside of her chest.

"Personal?" Briel did not release him, but her tone seemed curious. "You severed any chance of a personal connection years ago. We're all business now."

"Just come have coffee with me so I can explain myself to you. I have information for you. It's regarding your target."

Her target? confusion churned in Felicity's mind.

Briel paused, obviously considering. "Just tell me now," she demanded.

"It is too much," he replied, then glanced furtively back and forth along the hallway. "And too sensitive to share in an unsecured hallway."

Felicity's rapidly beating heart suddenly stopped. Though she felt sure she had ducked out of sight in time, her step had shuffled against the cheap carpet at her feet. Apprehensive, she listened carefully for any indication that one of them had heard her. For a pregnant moment, she heard no sound, and her mind raced with new, more pressing questions than her curiosity about Briel. Most importantly, would she have time to run? And equally as important, could she find her way out through the maze of hallways running full-tilt?

Briel's sudden, whispered reply relieved Felicity's frozen heart and let it beat again. She risked one last peek around the corner.

"Fine," Briel allowed. "Meet me at La Parisienne tomorrow morning." She relaxed her grip on his arm as she spoke, and he rose to face her.

"I can't wait," he replied, a sarcastic twinge replacing his earlier bravado.

The former anxiety returned as the man took his leave of Briel. Again, Felicity froze against the door frame, as motionless as she could possibly stand. Should she make a run for it now? Her indecision decided her, and she did not move until she heard Briel's door shut firmly. She paused a few beats then, fearful lest she encounter the man, Felicity again peered cautiously down the corridor. To her relief, both of its inhabitants had disappeared. After pausing a minute to regain her composure, Felicity glided cautiously through the hallways back to her waiting car.

Her head began to pound. *I'm dreaming,* she postulated. *Things like this don't happen in real life, at least not in mine.*

A moment later, though, her mind wandered to the

conversation she had overheard. What had any of that meant? Whatever it was, Briel had spoken of something much graver than the facade she wore, that of the naive young college student. Most incriminating, why would she and that man speak of a target? Felicity bit her lip. Could Felicity be the target? No way; her life consisted of routine and boredom. *Except for today*, she sighed. But had the day's events really added up to so much drama and intrigue? Felicity could not quite believe it. Maybe her kids?

The thought made Felicity shiver. Maybe Brendon. He was a marginally important person. Or maybe Nick. Nick made the most sense, with his computer clearance. Still, Felicity could not imagine anything so far-fetched. More likely someone completely unrelated.

She slipped her shoes on and made her way back to her parking spot, far from the apartment lest someone discover her. Instead of satisfied, Felicity now felt disappointed and a little bit defeated. In following Briel, Felicity had sought either to convince herself of her own folly or find something with which she could go to Brendon and fire Briel.

Now, though, she had succeeded only in making herself more anxious, and she really couldn't tell Brendon anything. In order to tell Brendon what she had seen, Felicity would also have to tell him that she had followed Briel, and beyond his disgust with what he considered her theatrical tendencies, her recklessness would make him angry. No, she could tell Brendon nothing. Especially because the worst she could tell him was that Briel knew a pretty impressive self-defense move.

Fortunately, Felicity had a month before Briel would be anywhere near her children, and surely Felicity could come up with some plausible reason for letting Briel go by then. Whatever came of the strange conversation, Briel would not last another day in Felicity's house.

If she could have found a way, Felicity would have tried to eavesdrop on the conversation at La Parisienne the next morning, but she had no way to predict Brendon's schedule. Knowing him, he would want to spend all day lounging around the house with her. There was time. A month. Felicity would find a way.

Chapter 5

The problem is, I always saw the anxiety, the pain. What I didn't
notice was what the anxiety produced. It led him to try to
control, and when he couldn't control, he tried to
manipulate, and when he couldn't manipulate, he tried to
coerce, and when he couldn't coerce, he attacked.
I tried so hard to soothe him
But when you try too hard to soothe the savage beast, you don't tame
him. You just appease a savage. – Felicity's journal, April 5

When I look at you, I don't see an evil man. I see a man more
desperate to convince everyone he is good because he knows
he is not. And I see a man who knows he is powerless and
will do whatever he needs to take back power – out of your
fear. I believe people can change, and maybe you are trying,
but the flourish, the façade, the show say otherwise. So,
understand that you will always have my compassion, but
you will not have my complicity. Don't expect me to pretend
with you that you are something you are not. – Felicity's
letter to Brendon, April 5

March 14

On the day of their flight, Felicity tried to bring her world
in order before she left it. She finished and folded all the laundry,
placing it neatly in its proper locations. She made sure the sink was
empty and the counters clean. She even swept and vacuumed the
floors, finally assured that her return home would feel peaceful and
pleasant before the rush of the kids' return.

With Brendon out doing whatever he did when he didn't
work and wasn't home, Felicity pondered the late morning and the
remaining several hours before she and Brendon had to leave. She
didn't want to start a new TV series and have to put it aside for
vacation, she didn't have any current books to read, and she wasn't
the type to call up her friends and gab. So, she did the last thing she

ever thought she would do – she drove to the book club.

Apparently, her instincts to avoid the group had served her well. As she parked on the street a couple of houses over, she glanced up at the too-familiar strawberry hair of Brendon's assistant. *How could she possibly be here?* Felicity fumed. From what Brendon had told Felicity, the assistant lived south of downtown; what would bring her thirty minutes away to Felicity's book club?

Felicity had no reason to avoid the woman specifically, but Felicity had only one reason to go to a book club. It was the one safe place she could give free vent to her opinions. She knew about books and the ideas that flowed out of them. She could speak intelligently on most topics, and book-readers tended to appreciate her insight more than a stranger on the street ever could. But if Brendon's assistant were there to report back what Felicity said? Felicity would never open her mouth. Add that to the fact that the woman had always just grated a little on Felicity's nerves, and the book club could not happen.

Felicity returned to her car, grateful that she had parked half a block away. She gripped the steering wheel and waited for her breath to still. Once it did, she leaned her head back and closed her eyes to think. Everyone in her book club had met at a local mom's playgroup. How would Aimée have found out about Felicity's book club? The only answer was Brendon. *Guess since I wouldn't network, he sent a proxy.* She looked back at the house, her chest clutching with a mix of hurt and guilt.

Why did it bother her so much that a person she held no particular animosity for had attended and event Felicity didn't even really care about? Everything in her wanted to excuse Brendon for it – that was her general habit after all. Another part of her, though, recognized the overstep. For Brendon, there was no Felicity. There was just Felicity's contribution to his agenda. Most of the time, he didn't care what she did – he wasn't controlling in the traditional sense. But apparently, if she didn't step up, Brendon would find someone who would.

This wasn't Felicity's book club. Felicity had no claim to anything, and Brendon felt no impetus to guard Felicity or her interests. Instead, if he wanted something he would take it – regardless of how it affected Felicity. Before the accident, when their interests had aligned better, she had not noticed.

Now time had revealed what Felicity should have seen

before, a mantra that Brendon apparently lived by but had stop verbalizing. When they were young, he had adopted cliches as tools to have something to say in a social group. The habit created a stilted speech pattern, but someone at ProtoComm had finally broken the habit, educating him on the fact that the tendency hid his intelligence. Still, Felicity had known him so long that she recognized the phrases that ran as an undercurrent to his beliefs.

"You snooze, you lose!" was one of his favorites, and though she had not heard the words in probably five years, she knew full well that Brendon still lived by them, cliched or no.

Felicity had accepted his justifications when he had to fire someone at work or had complained to management about a waiter, Was marriage supposed to work the same way? If a spouse failed to live up to levels of competence, was a partner justified in seeking other avenues to meet his or her needs?

Maybe for the peripheral needs, but how was the book club one of Brendon's needs?

The logic did not hold. He could have sent his assistant to a thousand other social group events, but he had chosen Felicity's group, almost as if he wanted to show how ridiculous she was for refusing to do something so simple. Aimée would meet Felicity's friends and make Brendon look good, and Felicity would stay in her hole and be pathetic.

In all their lives together, Felicity had never proven herself overly sensitive, but she felt it now. Not jealousy of Aimée, really – Felicity sensed no real judgment of or dislike for the woman. It was Brendon's transgression into one of the only things that Felicity had claimed for herself. She gave him everything, shared everything, and he took not only that, but anything else that served his agenda.

More than anything, though, Felicity Miller knew how to silence her own complaints, to shove them into an impenetrable little compartment where they endangered nothing but her own contentment. She directed her SUV to the artesian coffee shop that stood halfway between the book club and her fancy new home, and she pulled into the drive through for an extra-large latte. *Who needs sleep?* she reasoned.

The sight that greeted her when she made the turn around the front of the little building sent Felicity's foot to the brakes. Why was her nanny, Briel Cortes, stepping out of the local police station? If Felicity hadn't recognized the diminutive European car, she would have driven right by. Certainly, the slight form of the just-below-average height Briel did not draw too much attention, but her apparent conversation with the chief detective at the neighborhood PD could not escape notice. Was this the Briel who had complained about corruption at all levels of administration, including police?

When Briel reached her hand to squeeze the detective's with familiar affection, Felicity had to wonder. Briel seemed unusually casual with the police in a district she did not reside in. Who was this woman? Felicity watched for a few more minutes, but when the phone buzzed, she realized she needed to head home. No time to obsess over Briel's identity at the moment. As Felicity had celebrated before, the kids would remain far from Briel until Felicity had found time to investigate. In the meantime, she needed to head home so she could beat Brendon and prep his things for travel.

His text informed that she should expect him in twenty minutes, and Felicity needed fifteen for the trek home. Fortunately, by the time she heard the front door open, she had made her way to the primary closet and had pulled out the two large suitcases.

Brendon arrived home from the office in rare form - charming and entertaining, and obviously pleased with himself as a whole. He strode into their spacious bedroom, immediately intent to tease her. She didn't know whether to be hopeful that his mood boded well for their trip or to be concerned that he seemed on some weird high. As usual, she just suppressed everything and followed his lead.

"What should you pack?" Brendon tapped his chin, staring into her closet as if he cared about its contents. Something about the humor in his expression raised Felicity's suspicions. Though he had occasionally sprung into playful moods before Noah's accident, he had rarely done so after. Most of his playing had involved mocking her, and she didn't really trust amusement emanating from him

Then again, he had bought her the beads. He had planned the trip. Maybe he had finally decided to try again. The thought brought her more distress than it should have, largely because his attempts for self-improvement in the past were followed swiftly by relapses into the most intense and erratic moods. Usually with her as the unwitting target, but with the kids easily swept into his bouts of mental cruelty.

Without warning, Brendon turned on her with a grin, stepping directly in front of her and pinning her between the dresser and the wall. He was so charming when he wanted to be, even to her. "Why don't you let me make that decision?"

Rolling her eyes, Felicity feigned boredom to cover her nervous laugh. "I prefer to wear clothing," she snorted. *He obviously expects me to play along,* she reasoned. She lifted on her toes and raised her face with her best impression of a sassy mien. "I think I'll go with comfort. Maybe 14 pairs of sweat pants."

Suddenly, he placed his hands firmly against the wall on either side of her face and kissed her. "So, no tops?" he smirked as he pulled back before leaning in to kiss behind her ear.

"Get off me." She shoved him, smacking him lightly on the arm as she slipped out of his reach.

He burst out in a laugh, obviously amused, and she began to wonder what he intended to demand from her on the trip. When he wanted something, he made it the only option. Usually by charm and persuasion, but occasionally by manipulation and coercion. Felicity had grown highly adept at focusing on the positive, and Brendon painted himself in a positive light as much as possible.

Closing her eyes, she let herself access the visceral part of her that could respond to him – he wouldn't respond well if she let him see her confusion. The crisp, clean smell of Brendon's newly-pressed shirt entwined with the scent of his own musky skin, and she let the scent carry her to past and promise. When he stood above her, the warmth of his body filled the space around her, and she could grab hold of the sensation to connect with him. It was strange, and with her knowledge of his moods, seemed dangerous.

Even with his callousness, everything familiar and alien combined in him, the intimacy of established relationship and the foreignness of the masculine soul. Experiencing the unfamiliar sensations he brought to her world had fascinated her for several years of their relationship, and looking back, she realized that her lack of understanding his velvet maneuverings had rendered her more vulnerable to his barbs. Still, he seemed almost as intent on connecting with her at the moment as he had before they were married. She spun back to him only to find that he had turned to follow her. Now their faces rested inches from each other.

"It really doesn't matter what you pack," he stated nonchalantly. "I imagine you won't care once you get there." He ran a finger down the side of her face, his eyes on fire, and he eradicated the mad buzzing of her thoughts by gripping her arms, using them to pull her to him until his mouth crushed hers, owning her. His intensity burned so aggressively that it startled her, and Felicity floundered, lost and confused for several seconds before Brendon released the kiss.

He moved his mouth only a whisper away to her cheek, his breath stuttering. His grip on her arms squeezed almost uncomfortably tight. Whatever he had played before, he had passed through some veil of intensity in an instant. Felicity tried to find his eyes, but he seemed to stare vapidly at a wisp of hair on her cheek for several seconds, and by the time he finally looked her in the eye, his breathing had calmed and the smirk had returned as if it had never left.

"If you don't get moving, we'll miss the plane," he teased in a low voice. "I don't think you actually want that, though it's hard to tell right now." With a full-out grin, he stepped back, leaving her leaning against the wall that kept her aloft for the moment. He spun on his heels and strode toward the door. "I'll be in the car."

Jerk, she pursed her lips, wishing she could punch him. His tension still ran through her, and she found herself irritated. Leaning across to the nearby chair, Felicity grabbed a pillow and threw it at him. The soft velvet cushion hit him squarely on the back of the head. "I'll be there when I'm ready!" she yelled after him.

Without warning, he had reached her side once again and wrapped his arm entirely around her waist. "You'll be there when I'm ready," he leveled wickedly, then delivered the encore of the previous kiss to devastating effect. She hardly breathed, wishing to prolong the contact as long as possible, and Brendon seemed in no hurry to turn away from her.

As the heat of the kiss faded, the corners of Felicity's mouth turned up in a smirk, finally breaking the moment and softening the intensity of the contact. The second kiss retained the teasing sense even through the heat, and Felicity found herself relaxing from her earlier suspicions. Whatever had bothered Brendon before, he had released it for the moment.

He leaned to his right and reached casually over her shoulder, retrieving his dopp kit from the nightstand beside her before gliding away without ceremony. For a few seconds, she stood examining her nails as if bored by the whole interaction. Her knees had weakened slightly, and she would not risk tripping and looking clumsy in front of him. Once she felt cool enough, she strolled back to her suitcase, grinning. It had been a while since they had played together. It was almost as if he still liked her. For the first time in a while, she was looking forward to a trip with Brendon.

Since she still had no idea what to pack for the trip, Felicity tossed in enough clothes for three weeks. She added a few dresses to a garment bag, making sure to include the backless dress she had bought several years before but had few opportunities to wear. Surely, he would take her to a fancy dinner at some point. A pair of tennis shoes, her snow boots, her lace-up stilettos to match the backless dress, and a couple of less ostentatious pairs of dress shoes to wear if Brendon had less formal plans.

She stared at the backless dress for a second, a wicked grin returning to her face. When Brendon caught sight of her in the blue sheath, he would be the one weak in the knees. After the exchange of the past few minutes, she would relish the thought of dishing out a little torment.

Interrupting her thoughts, Brendon returned to the room, smiling his best salesman's smile. "It's time for you to be done. I'm ready now." She would have rebelled, but when he announced that "the limo" had arrived, a thrill ran through Felicity. *Limo just for me - not to show off at a party. Nice.* His extravagance was always a show, but one he had not bothered to offer her for too many years.

Brendon pulled her luggage to the front door where the limo driver took over and stowed the bags into the storage compartment at the back of the SUV. Felicity had foregone her comfy jeans in favor of a nicer, straight-legged pair. She wore a short-sleeved, melon-colored, cashmere sweater with a low scooping neck, and she had clipped her long brown hair into a sloppy knot on the back of her head.

"Nice sweater," Brendon quipped, expressively glancing at her bare collarbone.

Felicity's skinned flushed. "I think I'll go change," she replied petulantly.

He grabbed her by the waist and held her, "Don't you dare!" he laughed, pecking her cheek.

As Brendon began to drag her to the car, Nick showed up to demand the key to the house.

"Oh, I forgot!" she apologized. "Let go, Brendon," she chastised, unsuccessfully trying to pry his fingers off her waist and squinting at him with an exasperated expression. When Felicity turned to Nick, he rolled his eyes and feigned gagging.

Laughing, Brendon mussed her hair, then released her from his grasp.

"Relax!" Felicity complained to Brendon. "You'll have me to yourself an entire month. Two weeks before you have to go back to work."

Such insignificant words, but her husband reacted to them with a moment of that intensity that had tensed the earlier kiss. His eyes burned, and a muscle in his jaw twitched with an unexpressed stress that he pressed into a plastic smile.

Felicity had spent the last hour convincing herself that she should relegate all of her irrational emotions to the graveyard, burying them and declaring them dead. She had succeeded only moments before. So, what had that expression meant? *Nothing,* she insisted silently. *No, nothing at all.*

She would not let her unfounded worries ruin her vacation. She would prepare herself for a typical journey with Brendon, with all of its glories and all of its pitfalls. As she knew, such a trip would present enough real stresses without her formulating pretend ones. Brendon had never kept secrets from her. If he seemed to now, she had to trust the past decade as evidence that she was wrong.

Turning quickly back to her brother, Felicity pushed the thoughts out of her head. She remembered Nick's little escapade of the day before. "How was coffee?" she pried.

"Well, it wasn't a complete bust." Something like a sheepish grin spread across his face.

"With you, that could mean she didn't slap you!" Another vision from a hallway entered Felicity's mind involuntarily.

"Really, we had fun," Nick returned. "There's something about that girl." He gazed at some nebulous object over Felicity's head.

"I think it's called anatomy," Felicity retorted, trying to keep things light.

"No, I mean it. I like her a lot, Lissie. How serious is this boyfriend of hers?"

Felicity flitted around the kitchen, pulling out the dog food and bowls for food and water, and retrieving a watering can, then handed them to Nick. She pondered his question a moment before answering.

"Well, I honestly don't know. She doesn't talk about him

much, which probably means it's not that serious. Plus, they don't live together or anything, but I don't know if that's a reflection of her commitment level or her morals. Actually, Nick..." Felicity cut off, turning to face him, "I don't think I want you hanging around her too much."

The picture of Briel as she held a man's arm pinned behind him intruded into Felicity's memory.

Nick literally guffawed, unconvinced. "Still looking out for your baby brother?" His shoulders rolled with silent chuckles. "Seriously, Lissie, I'm not worried about getting my heart broken."

"More like your arm," Felicity muttered under her breath as she turned her back on him. "Look," she said aloud, "we don't know her at all. Just do me a favor and proceed with caution."

Still amused, Nick took the house key from Felicity and saluted her. "Ma'am, yes, ma'am," he replied. "I'll make sure that I don't fall prey to all 5' 3" of her. By the way, Lissie, if she wants to have another date, could I cook for her here?"

"Do you seriously think she would go for that?" Felicity asked incredulously, her concern increasing.

"You never know. I can be pretty charming," he smirked.

"Charm is overrated," Felicity muttered. She considered his request, unsure of how much she could protest without eliciting more questions from him. Since she figured the chances of Briel's going along with Nick were slim, Felicity acquiesced to Nick's request. "Just don't do anything I wouldn't do if I were single,"

"That pretty much rules out anything fun," Nick snorted, eliciting an eyeroll from Felicity.

She stuck her tongue out at him - he sure could bring out the three-year-old in her. "Go ahead, but don't say I didn't warn you."

"I would never withhold credit from you for one of your brilliant ideas, dear sister. And just to show my gratitude, I'll fix your computer for you while I'm here."

Grinning, Felicity spun in feigned shock to gaze at her brother. Though Felicity would have described her brother as kind in general, he rarely offered his computer expertise for free. He didn't mind answering the occasional question, but he didn't want to act as anyone's technical support. Coincidentally, Felicity's computer had run very slowly of late despite two firewalls and a daily spyware/antivirus treatment – maybe because of them. For such simple work, Nick had always insisted that "it's below my pay grade." Felicity reached over and grabbed him around the neck, unloading a quick hug on him.

"You're awesome, Nick! Thanks!" Felicity gushed. "I'll have the most competent tech-support on the planet."

"No, prob," he said, and shrugged. "It's the least I could do."

As soon as she released him, Felicity made her way to the door, ready to wave goodbye to her brother and join her husband in the car. Brendon, though, had obviously grown impatient waiting outside. The door swung open and Felicity turned quickly, prepared to answer a reprimand.

Instead of irritation, however, Brendon's eyes sported that same strange expression they had worn several times in the past two days, an ambiguous nervousness which sent a chill down Felicity's spine.

What on earth could make Brendon Miller nervous? Felicity wondered. Brendon feared nothing, at least as far as she had ever seen. Yet, some sort of anxiety had tightened his jaw and hardened his eyes.

Turning to wave at Nick, Felicity said a hurried goodbye before letting Brendon lead her, or more like shove her, into the waiting limo. As Brendon sat down next to her and the door closed, she felt his breathing return. He seemed to have been holding his breath.

"Are you alright?" Felicity finally braved as the limo rolled out of the circle drive.

A look of irritation flitted across Brendon's eyes before he smoothed his expression.

"I'm fine, why do you ask?" His tone was casual, but his muscles remained taut where her hand brushed his arm.

"No reason," she equivocated, beginning to wonder if Brendon really told her everything.

He leaned over to kiss her hair and assured her. "This is going to be great."

"Um, yeah" Felicity stuttered, "great." She hadn't intended her tone to sound so much like a question, but her consternation had escalated.

His head swiveled to look at her, suspicion in his gaze.

"You just look stressed," she explained, returning his stare.

"No, it's fine," he mumbled, shifting his eyes to look out the window. "It's nothing. A situation with work that I'm anxious about."

His explanation seemed plausible enough for a normal person, especially since he intended to leave work for several weeks. And there had been the heated discussion with the CEO. Of course, Brendon wasn't a normal person. He seemed energized by difficulty, as if he lived partially dead until things escalated, at which time he became preternaturally alive.

Still, it was not normal that he avoided her gaze as he spoke.

Watching the Phoenix skyline whir past, she tried hard not to think about Briel's strange behavior recently or the tension in her husband's hand today. The sun rose higher in the east, painting the low hanging clouds on the horizon varying pastel hues which melted from the shimmering gold of morning into the purple shadows of the desert sand.

Only when the glaring lights of the airport appeared over the horizon did the couple stir, and, though she still held doubts, Felicity prayed that she could spend the rest of her vacation in equal tranquility. Something inside her warned Felicity, though, that her misgivings so far were only an omen of things to come.

Chapter 6

Brendon airbrushes the truth, not altering it completely, but transforming it into the image he desires it to wear. – Felicity's Journal, March 10

I am telling you now that there is one reason that the lines of battle have not been drawn so far, and I am that reason. But know this, there will be a moment, if I am pressed, when those lines will become hard-edged and clear. At the moment when your white-washed tyranny promises more destruction then I can soothe with my kindness, you will find out how much of my inaction is due to weakness and how much is due to restraint. I advise you to do whatever you can to avoid that time, because I promise you, you'll not like the outcome of that experiment. – Unsent letter from Felicity to Brendon, April 12

Evening, March 14
"Do you trust me?"

The question came as a complete surprise to Felicity. Certainly, she trusted him for certain things – being a hard worker, being successful, providing for material needs. But trust wasn't something Felicity had felt for Brendon for many years, not trust with her heart. Not trust with her well-being. Not trust to care about her. The question hung in the air for too long, and Felicity grew more anxious as her mind locked up. In the past couple of days, she trusted him even less than she had for the past few years since the accident.

Fortunately, Brendon seemed too caught up in his plan to notice. When Felicity managed a weak laugh, he took it as agreement.

A few minutes later, the brisk air stung Felicity's cheeks as Brendon led her gingerly away from the airplane. Though he held her waist tightly, Felicity couldn't help but feel unsteady as she plodded aimlessly into the emptiness before her. *Fitting,* she laughed mirthlessly. The jacket that Brendon had slipped over Felicity's shoulders hung loosely about her, allowing the gentle but frigid breeze to weave under it and chilling the skin on her arms and neck. The blindfold on her eyes blocked out everything but the tiniest slivers of light above and below her eyes.

"Brendon, how much farther are we walking," Felicity complained. "I'm freezing."

"Relax," he crooned, pulling the jacket a little tighter and securing his arms more closely around her.

"This really is ridiculous," she murmured, hoping Brendon would consider removing her blindfold.

"Just a little farther," he urged. "Be patient." Only about a dozen paces later, his arms arrested her movements. The quiet hum of a car motor greeted her heightened sense of hearing. Relieved, she waited patiently while Brendon left her side. He returned a moment later and led her quickly to the waiting car, carefully lowering her into the seat where the warm air caressed her cold-pinched skin.

"Are you okay?" Brendon queried, his tone reassuring rather than solicitous.

"Better now. Warm," she quipped, snuggling under his arm.

They rode in silence for several minutes until Felicity felt Brendon shift from beside her. The cold left a hollow where his body had warmed her, and he spoke from above her as he spoke in her ear. His heated breath on her neck, he thrummed in a low voice, "I have some news. I lied about our schedule."

"What!" Felicity began to protest, not sure whether to feel relieved or concerned. "Does the company need you back sooner? Did my parents need to send the kids back?" Surprising how being deprived of her vision made her incapable of suppressing her anxiety.

Brendon laughed a loud, wholehearted laugh. "Listen to the words. I wasn't honest about our timeframe. It's not shortened. We're staying the full month here. I told Bill I would be here the whole time."

"A month...?" Felicity trailed off, uncertain of how to feel. "What about your work?"

"I may have to work a little, remotely," he admitted, "but it shouldn't interfere much with the plans."

"And the kids?" Felicity persisted.

"They'll be fine! Your mom and dad have all sorts of stuff lined up for them to do. I paid for a week a Creekhouse, and another at the Grand Resort. They'll be so busy, they'll hardly miss you. And I texted Nick once we landed. This gives me time to solidify some plans, to figure out what to do with you up here."

Though the cost gave Felicity pause, she couldn't but feel relieved at the benefit to her parents and kids. Brendon still sounded so sincere, so honestly excited. Despite her mounting concerns, she began to catch his enthusiasm, or at least to wish it true.

"Wow, Brendon. I really don't know what to say."

For Felicity, a month of uninterrupted free time sounded like a lifetime. Brendon had taken a sweet gesture and turned it into a grandiose plan. *How like him!* Felicity smirked, giving in to amusement. Whenever Brendon planned something, he always went big, turning a struggle into an opportunity, a loss into a gain.

In their home, though, he seemed to run into barriers to his good intentions. He couldn't magically whisk away everyone's problems, as much as he wanted to. His children needed his consistent presence, and Felicity didn't know what she needed; she just didn't want to be alone. Because of the complexity of family issues, Brendon couldn't always find a solution to them.

Why couldn't he solve her? Couldn't he just fix her and move on? When he realized that he couldn't rescue her on his white horse, he turned away, back to more approachable dilemmas. She now stood as a constant testimony to his lone failure. Of course, he no doubt blamed her for his inability. Felicity's "problems" ran too deep for an earthly solution, since they stemmed from her very personality.

He admitted that everyone failed, and actually had patience for most people, but others' failures didn't reflect on Brendon Miller's worth. Felicity's failures did. And Noah and Alex constantly reminded him of her insufficiency. It was obvious in how frequently he informed his daughter of how much like her mother she was. No doubt, that was not a compliment.

Fortunately for Brendon, few knew of his personal struggles, so he remained the hero for his general acquaintance. Thanks largely to him, ProtoComm stock had worked its way into a premier spot on the S&P, its major stockholders now worth more than the GDP of most small nations.

Although Brendon could not initially buy his way into

authority as some had, his competence and risk-taking had paid off in continuous promotions. Now an executive vice-president, one of only five, he held authority over billions of dollars of other people's investments. Felicity tried never to think of the fact – her nerves couldn't take it.

Coming from small town America, Brendon possessed both the advantages and disadvantages of being an outsider. Advantages: outside-the-box thinking, practicality, and a certain mystique. Disadvantages: no connections, no nepotism, and a reputation which painted him as a little simplistic. Granted, Brendon's family had held a sort of aristocracy among the people of his small town, and he had learned the superficial trappings of acting the moneyed man, but he held no actual idea of wealth the way his peers did.

Others like Brendon, smart and ambitious, had tried to force their way into the upper echelon, but only Brendon had succeeded. Instead of accepting his lack of connections as a disadvantage, Brendon had made it his business to create the right connections. As if he had a sixth sense, Brendon had hand-picked several execs to befriend, and by the end of his second year in the business, he was spending two to three nights a week, smoking cigars with the big six at a fancy steakhouse. Within five years, Brendon had climbed a corporate ladder that most scaled over fifteen. No one saw him coming, and some resented him.

Brendon, though, played chess like a pro, somehow navigating the inner mechanisms of the hierarchy with uncanny intuition. Because Felicity wanted to believe in his goodness, she had seen nothing unethical about his behavior. She now realized it was because it wasn't exactly unethical. Just utilitarian to the point that he couldn't care if other people paid for his advancement. Heartless, maybe. But not unethical.

And always enveloped in a miasma of invigorated charm.

Part of her admired his skill, recognized the accomplishment of his achievements, but another part of her saw a less optimal truth: Brendon had evolved, not necessarily to a higher plane, but to a different one.

Felicity wanted to follow him – her intelligence would have allowed her to follow him. To do it, though, she would have needed to leave the kids behind like he had. So to protect the innocent, to guard the vulnerable, she had stayed behind, and he had moved away. Brendon only popped into their world on occasion, an act of benevolence that he expected gratitude for. Like everything about him, he did it for himself and the pleasure he received from the accolades.

"Here we are!" Brendon crowed, obviously enthusiastic about their arrival, though Felicity couldn't see his expression through her blindfold.

Felicity inhaled deeply, bracing herself for another Arctic blast. As she heard the door open, however, warm dry air infused itself through the stale atmosphere of the car, bringing with it the homey scents of pine and cedar. She also smelled something spicy. *Cinnamon?* she mused. After hearing another door open, she felt Brendon raise her up one step and usher her into a place with the most intoxicating mixture of smells. She still sensed cedar and pine, but the cinnamon smelled stronger now, and it blended with cloves, nutmeg, orange, and vanilla. It made her giddy.

"Well, wherever we are, at least it smells good," Felicity mused.

"Wait till you see it," Brendon responded, and she could hear his childlike excitement.

Grabbing her waist from behind, he held her with one arm and with his other reached up to fumble with her blindfold.

"You know," he purred seductively in her ear, "this presents some interesting possibilities." His hand paused at the blindfold, and he traced his fingers down her neck and across the back of her shoulder.

"Cut it out," Felicity tried to complain, and her own hands reached up to untie the blindfold.

Brendon's hand grasped firmly around her upraised wrists as he stopped her. "Careful," he warned with mock severity. "I'm vice-president. You better toe the line," and keeping her wrists firmly manacled, he moved in front of her to kiss her.

"Not vice-president of me!" Felicity retorted sarcastically, but her sudden breathlessness veiled the bite of her tone.

Brendon laughed and kissed her gently, then pulling away, he said, "Fine. Here you go." And with one easy movement, he uncovered her eyes.

Light overwhelmed her vision as the blindfold fell to the floor. It took her several seconds to adjust her eyes to her surroundings, but when they did adjust, she almost didn't believe what she saw.

Wherever they had traveled must have been farther north than she had assumed because the sun had almost set, and Felicity knew it would only be about 7:30 p.m. based on the length of the airplane and car rides. The darkness outside caused the lights in the house to twinkle like streetlamps on a rainy night. Besides the electric lights, candlelight filled the room, explaining the scents which had so pleasantly greeted her senses.

A large, white sofa, plush with pillows, took up the greater portion of a roomy living area into which the garage had emptied. Dark wood floors, cabinets, and a small desk lined the exterior portions of her vision, but everything soft – every rug, every piece of upholstery – wore varying shades of white and tan. A fire blazed in a large hearth beside the sofa, and Felicity could just make out a sizable kitchen beyond the wooden cabinets she had noticed before.

"Brendon," Felicity gasped. "This is amazing!" Her eyes slowly took in as much of her surroundings as they could.

Brendon watched her carefully for a moment and then took her by the hand, leading her past the inviting sofa and delicious smelling candles toward an adjacent room. "I'm glad you like it," he finally responded, kissing the hand he held. "It will probably be a while before you experience something like this again. Now, look at this."

He led Felicity up three or four steps into what appeared to be another living area, this one having an entire wall, at least 30 feet long and 20 feet high, filled with windows. Beyond the windows to the left, steam rose from a lighted pool, obviously heated by some source besides the air.

Straight ahead and to the right, the darkening horizon stretched before her, all below her, because the house Brendon had chosen seemed to rest on the pinnacle of a significantly elevated hill. She did not see the rocky cliffs and craggy peaks that would have signified mountainous terrain, just the green lull of gently rolling hills, though mountains peeked from the far edge of the horizon. Further enhancing the lighting effects of the house itself, twinkling lamps sparsely dotted the swells of the landscape. The beauty stole Felicity's breath.

Unlatching his fingers from hers and placing his arm around her waist, Brendon came to stand directly beside her. They stood in silence for several moments, Brendon apparently enjoying the effect his work had on Felicity, and Felicity simply allowing the sensations to wash over her.

Finally, Felicity crooned, "Thank you, Brendon." She raised her eyes to his, hoping he could read her gratitude in her expression. "This is amazing."

Brendon intertwined his fingers again with hers and led her back to the comfortable sofa, pulling her down to sit beside him. Felicity giggled despite herself. "Come here," he demanded, pulling her next to him and leaning her back into his chest. She could feel the familiar warmth of his chest as they reclined together on the couch. He still seemed oddly euphoric, but maybe it was just because he had managed such an incredible feat.

"This is really amazing. Where exactly are we?"

His voice smooth, expecting to dazzle her, "About halfway between Banff and Canmore, Alberta."

"Like, Alberta, *Canada*?" Felicity's tone was incredulous. "I wasn't aware that was a huge tourist destination."

"Yes," he answered petulantly. "Canada. And Banff is one of the most exclusive ski resorts in North America."

"Denver would have accomplished the same thing." She hadn't meant to contradict him.

"Far too close to people we know." he nibbled on the skin behind her ear.

"Sure," she shivered, shrugging him off. "Wherever we are, it's beautiful. I won't be difficult."

"Good," he teased. "You're never as difficult as you pretend anyway." He seemed to take great pleasure in tormenting her tonight. She squirmed in his arms. "Come on. I'm just messing with you. Relax."

Felicity smiled despite herself and settled back onto his chest.

"Tell me something, Felicity." He began abruptly.

"Okay," his tone made her dubious.

"If I could hire someone else to help around the house, what would that person do?"

This vein of conversation took Felicity completely by surprise, not to mention the abrupt manner in which he introduced it. Such a discussion required deep thought and serious consideration, not a casual chat of a moment's notice.

"Um...I don't know. Does it matter?" Though she regularly spent time in introspection, this type of wishfulness only made her sad. "I mean, I agreed to this job when we had kids. It's expensive to hire someone."

"It doesn't matter – the future isn't set in stone just because of the choices we've made in the past."

"But it's not that easy to do my job. It's not like I can just hand off being a mom."

Brendon wrapped his arms tighter around her. "It's not so hard to hire someone to take over most of your responsibilities."

"Brendon..."

"Wait, I've been thinking about it." His voice grew pensive. "Most of the responsibilities are between housekeeping and childcare – with those taken care of, the kids only need guidance in their character. I hired Briel, and now they have another set of hands to take care of them. If I hired someone else, there would be little left that had to be done by you."

Brendon's uncharacteristic solicitousness confused Felicity. She could remember a similar conversation less than a year before.

Felicity, we can't live like this, he had chastised. *Do you want our kids growing up with so much chaos?*

Felicity had wanted to glare at him, but she rarely defended herself, mostly because she judged herself so harshly. *It's just so hard, Brendon. I am trying to manage a family without going crazy. I mean, it's not like I get to come home at the end of the day and kick my shoes off and leave my work behind me. And you don't really want to pitch in.*

Please, Brendon had complained. *You're not a victim. You don't have to stay home. Get a job if you don't like this one.*

That argument always sent Felicity into a silent rage. Of course, she could get a job, but to what purpose? Some moms could work and still pay enough attention to their kids, but Felicity knew herself. If she went to work and dedicated herself to a job, she would not be able to give her kids her best. At least if she stayed home, they got her strengths as well as her weakness. *If you would just help a little,* she had countered, *everything would work so much better.*

So, you want me to work a full-time job and then come home and do yours, too, he accused.

Again, Felicity wanted to scream. How was raising the kids her job alone? Five years of the same arguments had given her an image of what he thought of her – of what she thought of herself. In his eyes, she loved her kids and treated them well, but she failed at just about everything else about being a mom. And she didn't do too well as a wife, either. Certainly, she wasn't an ornament he could wear on his arm, not the way he wanted her to be. She also couldn't help him manage his belongings or his schedule, she couldn't offer him social or business wisdom. In truth, other than the most basic functions, Brendon saw little value in what Felicity contributed.

In the past year, though, Brendon seemed to have evolved. No, he wouldn't agree to pick up more of the household responsibilities. Nor should he – he didn't possess the consistency kids needed in their day-to-day life – but he would hire someone to take the load off of Felicity. She had to give him credit for what he had done rather than lament what he would not. What had he, Brendon, offered? A chance for Felicity to grow, to develop beyond childcare and housekeeping. Instead of his usual judgmentalism at her weakness, he had seemed to want to help her. Now standing in a beautiful home in beautiful surroundings in a beautiful foreign country, he seemed determined to help her again. Her distrust of him shamed her, and she dug into the depths of her mind to consider. She found nothing.

"Brendon, I…I really don't know. I'll try to think about it." She laughed humorlessly. Felicity feared indulging herself too much in possibilities lest Brendon's unpredictability prove his words a lie. And how could they afford it? He threw money around when it suited him, but he took it back just as easily, claiming that they needed to budget, because he held that power; he made the money. Felicity pressed her frustration back into its safe compartment and silenced its complaint.

Turning sideways, Felicity snuggled herself into his chest and closed her eyes. "Brendon, we've both made sacrifices. You can't rescue me from life."

"No, I figured that out a long time ago." His voice was bitter, and Felicity's heart constricted with her own melancholy. For several minutes, they lay there, Brendon's arms wrapped tightly around her.

Jumping back to his earlier manic state, however, Brendon kissed her lightly on the head and said, "Let's take a swim."

Felicity could have remained with him on the couch forever; it had been years since she had felt so much pleasure in his arms. She would not resist him, however. Reluctantly, Felicity leaned up and placed her feet on the floor, Brendon following her lead.

"It looks so cold," she shivered.

"Don't be a coward," he teased. "Haven't you heard of the

Polar Bear Club?"

"I am not a polar bear," Felicity gazed unhappily at the pool outside.

"Come on," Brendon rose and pulled Felicity to her feet. Meandering over to the suitcases by the door and opening his own, he reached in and held something up. It looked like a napkin. "I brought this for you," he grinned mischievously and handed the lump of material to her.

Holding it before her, Felicity recognized a bikini, not particularly indecent, but certainly not something Felicity would wear in public. She hadn't worn anything like it since high school.

"You're kidding me, right?"

"For me," he pleaded, wrapping his arm around her waist and grinned his most charming smile. "I'm sure you didn't bring a swimsuit. And you don't want your clothes to get ruined if I have to throw you in fully dressed."

Felicity glared at him but sighed her concession. "Fine." And she headed to the guest bathroom to change. Even though she had agreed, she thought about locking herself in the bathroom rather than brave the cold water.

When she left the bathroom, she was glad she hadn't been stubborn. Brendon didn't even ogle her. He just grabbed her hand like a child and led her to the back doors.

"Ready?" he smirked.

Before Felicity could answer, Brendon opened the door and dragged her through the frigid breeze to the edge. He didn't stop. He just pulled her directly into the pool, laughing at her the whole time. As her body broke the surface of the water, she screamed.

Seconds later, they both emerged, Brendon laughing and Felicity gasping for breath.

"Not funny," Felicity spat at him, splashing him as she bounced to her feet. Despite her complaint, the water felt warm against her skin.

"Yes, it was," he chuckled again at her irritated expression.

Contrarily, Felicity swam toward the edge of the pool, daring him to stop her. Before she could clear the steps, he wrapped his arms around her and lugged her back into the water, spinning her to face him.

"You are going to have fun here," he commanded. "You should squeeze every drop of fun out of your life."

Finally conquered, Felicity smiled at Brendon's persistence.

"And *you* are going to be a pest wherever we are," she accused impishly.

Laughing, Brendon hugged her to him. "That's the least of your problems," he murmured, nipping at her ear.

Felicity said nothing, enjoying his attention. After several minutes just melting into his warmth, she leaned back slightly to look at him.

"I am honestly so surprised that you did this for me."

"I have to take care of you. This is the best place to do that."

"Well, it works. Everything. The plane ride, the surprises, this house." Felicity sighed.

Gazing back at her, Brendon leaned his face to hers, forehead to forehead, and pulled her waist as closely to himself as possible. He placed his hand on the back of her head and pulled her even closer until the side of her face rested against his shoulder. Their bare flesh burned where it met, and Brendon began to run his hand up the skin at the small of her back.

The inevitable chills flooded her mind, melding with all the other sensations that assaulted her and causing her mind to cloud. As her head swooned, Felicity caught a glimpse of Brendon's smug expression. Whatever he had intended for the next few weeks, he seemed very pleased with what he had already accomplished.

Why did the chills seem unnatural instead of exciting? Because the solicitous attention rang unfamiliar, unlike anything Brendon had ever felt or done. Depressing how his apparent kindness could create mistrust, the echo of an agenda whispering to her mind. Brendon always had a purpose for his actions, one intended to manufacture his desired end. What was his desired end in regards to her? The husband she wanted to believe in would just want her happiness; the husband she knew would intend his own, regardless of its effect on her.

For months to come, that night and Brendon's passionate abandon would stand as monument in Felicity's mind to his duplicity. She learned that, even knowing what he intended, Brendon Miller could mimic love for his own enjoyment, taking advantage of Felicity's hunger for marital connection to squeeze out a few last moments of self-indulgence before he moved on to his own ambitions. Until the day she died, Felicity would never forget.

Chapter 7

No man can truly feel the lightness of happiness until it is gone. In a happy world, every ebb and flow of circumstance creates its own drama, a nuance of misery or fury. But when the weight of difficulty presses down, perhaps the greatest loss is the recognition of how blessed those moments were. When once there was happiness, even sorrows were levity. – Notes in Felicity's secondhand copy of Dicken's David Copperfield. Undated.

Because I believe in right and wrong, I believe that someone who goes back on his word - without compelling reason - is basically a criminal. He's a thief, and there are no two ways about that. People try to justify it, try to pretend that it's inescapable – as if they were not in control of themselves – but they are not mindless, moved by forces outside themselves to an inevitable conclusion. There is a choice they make, and every choice cascades from that first one. It is and will be the catalyst for all the rapids that follow until the moment the person goes back to the first decision and repudiates it. – Felicity's journal, March 27

<u>March 15</u>

Felicity's first real suspicion that Brendon had lied to her came the next morning.

Brendon had risen early, leaving her mostly asleep and claiming that he would fix her breakfast in bed. Thirty minutes later, Felicity had finally awakened fully and, tired of waiting, she decided to wander out to see if Brendon needed help – he had never proved particularly handy in the kitchen. *Probably painted the kitchen with pancake batter,* she joked to herself, trying not to feel irritated that he had taken so long. Climbing out of bed, she slipped on the plush slippers that came with the cabin, wrapped a blanket around her shoulders, and wandered into the living room.

"Brendon?"

No answer.

"Brendon, where are you?"

Still no answer.

Felicity ambled into the beautiful window room and gazed sleepily at the hamlet village that spread out below. Yawning, she contemplated whether or not to succumb to the inviting warmth of an early morning swim but rejected the thought as the cobwebs swept from her brain to reveal an uneasiness. With all that had happened before she left, she did not like being alone in the cabin. Once she awoke fully, she realized that she should possibly be concerned at Brendon's absence. Turning from the picturesque scenery, Felicity crossed purposefully out into the kitchen, determined to find her husband.

Unfortunately, the kitchen held no more hint of his presence than the other rooms she had explored, no sign that he had opened a cupboard. She continued through the dining room, the garage, and the guest room - nothing. After that search proved fruitless, Felicity retraced her path through the house, taking the time to glance into the closets and bathrooms. Finally, on the mirror of the master bathroom she found a sticky note. It read: *Ran into town for some supplies. Be back in about an hour.*

An hour. She breathed a sigh of relief, laughing at her increasing paranoia. *Well, besides the heart attack he gave me, I guess that makes sense.*

Breakfast in bed obviously couldn't happen anymore, so Felicity decided to indulge in a different luxury – one not dependent on her husband. Gliding to the bathroom, she turned on the water and began to fill the giant tub which housekeeping had stocked with all the amenities: bubble bath, scented soaps, bath salts, and salon quality shampoo and conditioners. One thing Felicity had learned to appreciate as a mom was the power of a long bath for the purpose of rejuvenation.

Though she had no real reason for stress after her good night's sleep, Brendon's disappearance had tensed her more than she would have expected. Maybe lingering doubts from the past few days. *Hot water and aromatherapy,* she counseled, still a little miffed at Brendon, though she guessed that he had left her sleeping. *He'll be back in 30 minutes,* she figured, assuming he had departed a while before she woke. She settled in the hot water and bubbles that began to fill the tub. While the tub filled, she tugged the little tray with her laptop over so she could email her parents about the kids. They hadn't quite managed text messages, and if Felicity wanted to allay her concerns about the kids, it would be email or a phone call. *Not prepared to talk to them while I'm upset with Brendon.*

When she opened the laptop, the name hit her again. "Coping Mechanism."

She had suppressed her resentment when she had seen the words. A couple of weeks before, Brendon had taken the laptop to his best friend for repair. Not that she had noticed anything off about the computer, but Brendon had insisted it needed an update, and his friend was an expert. When she had gotten her laptop back, he had changed the name. He claimed it was a joke, but it was a complaint. His favorite and only complaint against her was that she used the laptop as a replacement for a life. *Maybe,* she realized, though she hadn't known how to connect with people when it was so hard for her to leave the house. She quickly clicked past the offending words, responded to the email from her mom, and shut the device, realizing that for once, it wasn't helping.

Breathing deeply, Felicity settled into the water, and she practiced relaxing so effectively that she soon realized she had dozed off. The bath pillow under her head had kept her in place, and she now sat up abruptly, sensing something alien that she couldn't pinpoint.

"Brendon?" she called, hoping to chase her heart down from her throat to its proper place. Probably a dream, she realized.

Felicity glanced at the clock. 9:15 a.m. Brendon had left at least an hour and a half before, and that assumed that she had found the note only a few minutes after he left. Reaching over her head, she grabbed the plush, hotel-quality towel from the bar and carefully stood while she wrapped herself with it. As soon as she stepped out of the bath, she pulled a robe from its hook and traded the vulnerability of the towel for the security of the robe's extra wrap and ties. Felicity dried her feet on the rug, then cautiously shuffled to look out into her room. No sign of anyone.

Really, she chastised herself. *You're being ridiculous.*

The demons of the misgivings she had felt in Phoenix had followed her to this cold, foreign place. Even with so many strange occurrences, she still couldn't justify her fear. Except...

Her thoughts trailed off as her skin began to crawled at the memory.

On the plane, Felicity had dozed on one of the sofas. Brendon's phone had sounded, and he had begun a conversation in Spanish. Felicity had not really been awake enough to process the words, but she remembered a fuzzy, sleepy thought that had passed through her mind. "...no tengo miedo de ti," Brendon had said, "Es de mi mujer." Felicity's mind asked, "'De'? Does that mean of or from?" The thought had melted into dreams, but she felt certain she had actually heard them.

The words recalled themselves now that adrenaline had intensified the clarity of Felicity's thoughts. Was he afraid of her or afraid for her? Brendon had no reason to be afraid of her. But why would he be afraid for her? To be honest, Felicity had been afraid for herself, but she felt largely confident that she was imagining things, that all of the little occurrences over the past few days were incidental. If she kept up the paranoia, she would need to go to counseling – something wasn't right. Absolutely nothing exciting or dangerous ever happened to Felicity, so why would she be so jumpy lately? Why did she suddenly not know how to read Brendon after so many years?

Of course, if Brendon fears for me, Felicity couldn't help but think, *maybe I'm right to be afraid.* Despite herself, her courage fled, and both her forward motion and her heart froze for a moment as indecision strangled her.

After a moment, though, the blood that had left her extremities rushed back into them as she decided she needed to move somewhere less exposed than the middle of the room. Though her feet felt heavy, she dragged them toward the closet where her jeans and sweater awaited her.

Bursting through the closet door, she threw her clothes on and searched frantically for her cell phone. She came to the realization that she didn't even know if she was in the city or the country, so she had no assurance of cell phone service. As futile as it seemed, she searched the closet for something she could use as a weapon. A wire hanger served better than anything else she could find. *I'm just overreacting,* she assured herself, though she felt no conviction in her words. How had someone so usually steady become as skittish as she now felt?

Glancing through the crack in the closet door, she peered as thoroughly as she could around her room to ensure that she remained alone, or to put down the coat hanger if she saw Brendon. No one visible, Felicity carefully opened the closet and crept cat-like toward the bedroom door, still peering around to make sure no one surprised her.

Had her imagination become overactive, or had she just seen a shadow by the front door? Glancing around the edge of the bedroom's threshold, she noticed that the trees that lined the front drive cast their shadows into the entryway, and the wind had sent them dancing wildly. Finally, feeling completely exposed, Felicity sprinted toward the kitchen. All she needed...

A door slammed. Felicity dropped behind the kitchen counter trying to conceal herself from the sound's source. Her back against the wall, she slumped to the ground trying very hard not to breathe.

"Felicity?" came Brendon's voice.

Her breath returned with a rush almost making her head spin. Though she wanted to burst out laughing, embarrassment restrained her. How could she possibly explain to Brendon why she sat on the floor? There was something wrong with her. She fumbled for an excuse as she tried to calm herself, feeling both utterly ridiculous and infinitely relieved.

"Hey, Brendon," Felicity finally responded, trying to infuse her voice with its usual casualness. She hoped he didn't notice the slight break in her tone. "You surprised me," she continued, standing to her feet and covertly pulling her phone from her pocket, as if she had picked it up off the floor. "Made me drop my phone."

She glanced his way with what she hoped was a sheepish look and placed the phone on the counter in front of her.

"I was worried you had – " he admitted before breaking off the sentence. "You should really be more careful." Had she heard him correctly? Never had Brendon betrayed any worry for her personal safety; only for her property or her image, usually in reference to his own. For him to show, once again, such solicitousness for her seemed out of character. It didn't help her peace of mind that, as Brendon spoke, he furtively averted his eyes from hers.

"So, where's my breakfast?" she complained in a light tone, not prepared to address her concerns. "I've been out of bed for about an hour," and she glance at Brendon to see his reaction.

He leveled her a skeptical look. "You've been out of bed for any hour. I only left forty-five minutes ago."

Felicity's face fell in confusion. Had she misread the clock?

Maybe she hadn't actually fallen asleep in the bathtub, but had just started to, But, no. The clock had said 8:00. It was after 9:15, now, and she had actually minimized his time gone. Hadn't she?

"I admit," he offered, "that it took me longer than I expected. The store didn't have much selection, and I made the mistake of going north toward Banff, which it turns out is quite a bit farther than Canmore." Then, in a lighter tone, "But if you give me five minutes, I'll deliver an outstanding omelet."

"Is that five minutes real time or Brendon time?" she mumbled. *All is forgiven, all better be forgotten,* she mimicked Brendon's expectations. Well, he had placed enough doubt in her mind that she wouldn't confront him.

"Watch yourself..." he threatened, though he couched the comment in teasing. He seemed to think he had sufficiently distracted Felicity from their unspoken conversation.

Though Felicity tried to laugh, the sound was forced, unnatural. Brendon's continued lack of forthcoming had begun to rile her, and although she loathed arguments, she felt one brewing in her mind. After fifteen years learning passivity, Felicity found herself suddenly less than willing to let an argument go.

Had Brendon lied about where he had gone, or had he really spent two hours unsuccessfully shopping for waffles? Some internal sense in her kept peeling layers off of Brendon's façade, but rather than reveal the source underneath, there were never-ending layers. If something didn't change soon, she thought she would lose her mind. *Maybe I already have.*

Chapter 8

*It was almost a familiar sensation, the stopping of time. The hollow
vacuum opening in the pit of my stomach. That sense that I
floated in some horrid, unforgiving void of emptiness. One
vertex of focus. Only one convergence available to the
senses, sucking in everything else in my world like a black
hole. Once, the lone vision had been the blond curls of my
son disappearing beneath the water. My terror for my child.
Now the terror was all for myself.* – Felicity's Journal, March
26.*

*And thus I clothe my naked villainy
    With odd old ends stol'n out of holy writ;
    And seem a saint, when most I play the devil.* – William
Shakespeare, Richard III

March 19

Her first clue had been the familiar face. Not really a clue,
she guessed, because she hadn't exactly recognized the person. More
an impression that she was having déjà vu, or that maybe she'd
inadvertently passed some character actor she had seen in several
movies but who had never played a starring role. Very disconcerting.

First thing in the morning of day four, Brendon had informed
Felicity that he had to go into town to utilize an online meeting
room, one with whiteboards and other collaborative, interactive
tools. *Typical,* she rolled her eyes. "How long, do you think?" she
wondered aloud.

"Maybe two hours," he shrugged. At least he hadn't snapped
at Felicity for being so inconsiderate as to ask the question. He
didn't like to be micromanaged.

Two hours Brendon time meant anywhere from two to eight
hours, perfectly justified by some reason or other. It had already
happened three times since their arrival, at random hours that made
no sense to Felicity. She tried to suppress her simmering bitterness.

Well, it was Felicity's vacation, and she would not sit around waiting for Brendon like she did at home, where she at least had her children to distract her, and like she had the previous two days. She pulled out her phone and checked for a signal. It was weak but functional. Opening a map, she found her location and search the area around her. Pretty much nothing but nature in the immediate area, but Canmore lay a couple of miles south, and Banff lay twenty minutes north.

After searching each location, she decided that she would rather walk around and window shop, or find a bookstore or coffee shop. Canmore was nice enough, but she thought Banff seemed farther in the mountains with better hikes, and since it was more for tourists, the options seemed more consolidated and easier to access without too much planning. Plus, Brendon no doubt had found his technology in the closer, larger city, and Felicity didn't really want to run the risk of running in to him in her current state of mind.

She had noticed two envelopes on the dresser, one labeled "Canmore" and the other labeled "Banff." She grabbed Banff and headed to the garage. She wasn't even sure she had a vehicle, but when she opened the garage door, a grey sedan sat inside. Felicity walked over to it and saw the keys in the cupholder.

No need to hide them inside the garage, she imagined. Seated behind the wheel, she opened the envelope and considered all the flyers. In typical fashion, she didn't find anything exciting about the tourist traps. A hike would be nice. Followed by coffee. After perusing several options, she decided to make her way through the town and to a nice hike of about an hour.

With the drive and the walk, she would be home in three hours, probably in time to meet back up with Brendon. *And if he comes home earlier, he can just wait for once.* Her nonchalance made her wonder at herself; did she only keep the peace at home to protect the kids?

Rather than waste time analyzing herself, she set to work. In the envelope, she had found several day passes into Banff, and she pulled one out and put it in her cupholder. Pushing the button, she opened the garage door and pulled out into the beautiful mountain lane, surrounded by aspen and fir trees, with a mountain view peeking from between the trunks and through the leaves.

Once she reached the main highway, the view broadened into an amazing expanse, snowcapped mountains on every side, but a clear straight path ahead. The whole vision exhilarated her, erasing any nerves she felt at not consulting Brendon with her plans.

Heading north, she made it to the city of Banff in under twenty minutes, and then through to the far side where she had seen the trail she wanted to hike. Her excitement built as she got closer. In the town lay rows of quaint buildings and shops, picturesque as a fairy tale. A little too picturesque for Felicity, but she could see the clear, natural view that lay at the far end of the town – her destination.

Her destination was a very interesting, self-contained area with several attractions that appealed to Felicity. Even better that every walk between buildings came with a breathtaking view of nature. First, she would pass through the little art gallery on the way to the hiking trail. Then her twenty-minute jaunt out to see the "castle" across the river, which was really just a hotel but gave an epic view and a good option for pictures. After that, she would grab a quick lunch at the bistro before heading back to the cabin.

Until the familiar profile of Jenna Whitfield entered the large glass and wood building thirty feet in front of Felicity, she had grown increasingly enthusiastic about the day. The unexpected sighting sucked away all of Felicity's strength. It was surreal, like the Twilight Zone, something known but out of place. Then suddenly, the past few days made so much more sense.

The two-hour wait for a nonexistent breakfast.

The many trips into town without her, insisting that she stay and enjoy the beautiful cabin. For hours at a time. Since they had arrived, Felicity had spent more time alone than with Brendon. *Kind of like at home*, she simmered.

And then Jenna. It was like a slap in the face with a branding iron.

The truth will out, Felicity mused bitterly as she covered the distance to the glass building in less than a minute. Of course, not just Jenna. Peering through the huge glass panels, Felicity saw what she had suspected as soon as she had seen the woman, a veritable ProtoComm convention. An actual convention, she realized. A few higher-level employees she had encountered at parties or corporate events each stood in the middle of several circles of filled chairs, holding miniature conferences. Everything in Felicity boiled.

Why had he not just told her? Honestly. Was he afraid she would refuse to come to Canada with him?

Well, maybe she would have. Maybe she wouldn't have. But

the utter disrespect of not giving her the choice! *I mean, should I be surprised he doesn't respect me?* she recognized with a sick pit of resentment in her stomach. The lie, the pretense of giving her something special, when he had actually just let her be a tagalong. The presumption!

Felicity wasn't the type to make a scene – she had no intention of confronting anyone, but she wanted to find Brendon. Would he try to convince, as she always let him, that she had misunderstood That he had told her about the conference? *That the conference is a figment of my imagination?* Cluster after cluster of ProtoComm employees and admin dotted the large atrium, and Felicity found herself growing more furious. Even with her distaste for spectacle, she found herself wanting to make one. Badly enough that she fled. She ran out a side door and sought a safer location, one she knew would offer her comfort – the library she had seen on the map.

Once among the books, Felicity let herself breathe. Breathe the familiar scent of books, soak up the artistic and colorful spines, search out her favorite authors. Her heart finally calmed, settling into a normal rhythm and ceasing to hammer the inside of her chest. Across the large room, she noticed a collection of art books. She hadn't made it to the gallery, so she decided she would peruse the impressionists and Fauvists. Usually she let music rage away her anger, but she actually didn't trust herself to drive just yet, and her phone was a poor stereo.

As she crossed the expanse toward the wall of art books, her mind tacitly processed the
row of computer cubbies that lined the windowed wall at the edge of the room. She reached for a book on Renoir but was arrested by a sound – a laugh. It was a low sound, almost undetectable, but it was like breathing for Felicity. As familiar as herself. It was Brendon.

Brendon, his lower legs just visible under the cubby wall. Shoes off. Crossed casually with the bare feet of a woman. A woman who followed his laugh with her own feminine giggle. Drawn like a moth toward a flame, Felicity drifted across the space as if pulled by a current, to the convergence of the temporary walls and the crack where they joined the neighboring cubby. The red hair of the woman obscured Brendon's face as she leaned toward him in an intimate whisper. Within a moment, though, the veil slid away to reveal Brendon's profile.

For the past half hour, rage had oscillated inside of Felicity, ebbing and flowing as her mind flipped through the images of all the ProtoComm employees she had just seen.

All of the rage evaporated in an instant.

One could not feel rage when the immaculately crafted human mind cut itself off from all feeling in order to protect itself.

Brendon sat in a very sensual position with his assistant, Amy. Her red hair lay against his cheek. His hand rubbed down one of her thighs. No, they weren't about to throw down in the library. But the entire scene was the comfortable intimacy of lovers.

Momentarily, Felicity realized that she could feel the spinning of the earth through space and time. She couldn't breathe, though. Glancing around, she looked for the cameras, the friends or acquaintances who would approach her and explain the joke, that it had been a setup, a game. She imagined all sorts of ridiculous possibilities, like that her husband was a spy on a mission, and he had to pretend to be a couple with the young woman. Or that ProtoComm was shooting a commercial, and they had chosen to use Brendon as the face. Brendon hadn't told her because he thought it would upset her. The woman was blackmailing Brendon to get ahead in the company.

And then her mind stopped.

She stopped it.

None of those was true.

He had lied.

Lying was his native language.

Anything he said to her from this point forward would be a lie until proven otherwise.

He lied to her.

She would not lie to herself.

Not stupid, delusional lies. Not practical, realistic lies.

Brendon was having an affair.

In fact, Brendon had taken steps to replace Felicity in his own life. He had hired a nanny, he had made a list of tasks that Felicity did for the kids, and he had even sent Aimée to the book club that Felicity always shunned. Because she didn't compress herself into his vision of his narrative, he replaced her. *He is well paid to notice nothing and forget everything.* Felicity had to wonder what Brendon had spoken of, what he had paid the driver to forget.

When she finally processed the blackness in her vision, she

realized that she had held her breath so long she was close to fainting. To breathe, though, she had to look away. To look away, she had to run away.

So, she ran. She ran down the stairs because standing still in an elevator would have given her time to think. Something she could not do. She ran toward the lot where she had parked her car, unsure if she planned to drive away or sit inside and cry or blast music to drown her thoughts. Before she made it past the next building, though, her body rebelled. If she did not pause, she would collapse. She would not collapse. She refused. Instead, she ran up to a long unbroken wall of stone and leaned against it, her face in her arms, just breathing.

Maybe she should have cried, but tears weren't available yet. She didn't feel sadness. She didn't feel anything. She felt the opposite of anything, stronger than feeling nothing. Only the weakness and disconnect in her body gave her any sense of the effect the discovery had on her.

"Felicity?" the familiar voice intoned gently.

"No, no, no," she managed, willing the voice away.

"Felicity, you don't look well."

Against her will, her shock-addled mind twisted toward the voice, robotically compelling her, beyond her cognitive function.

Inexplicably, Jase stepped across the few feet between them and pressed his hand against her cheek, staring deeply into her eyes. Somehow not an intimate or presumptive gesture; just concerned. Besides, her mind told her, he hadn't been touching her face at all. He had touched someone else's face, the person on the outside of her. Felicity herself had felt nothing.

"You're in shock," he announced.

The pronouncement meant nothing to Felicity. He could have said, "the mountains are purple dinosaurs" and it would have made the same amount of sense to her brain.

Jase reached gingerly for her elbow, grasping it firmly and speaking to her as if to a child. "I think maybe you need a hospital. Are you hurt?"

"No hospital," she managed. "Not hurt." *Not that way.*

Still, he moved her, leading her away from the wall. She didn't resist. If she did, she might scream. She might devolve into a rabid, screeching monster that would bring the whole city to the commotion. So, she let him lead her to wherever he led.

Until she smelled the coffee, her mind processed nothing. Strange, she thought, that a smell could make it all the way past the person outside her and into her brain. Of course, the distance seemed shorter now. Glancing around for the first time, Outer-Felicity's eyes sent the message to Inner-Felicity that she was in a coffee shop, that there were delicious looking pastries in the display, and that the lights were warm and pleasant. Inner-Felicity understood but didn't feel any of it.

"Breathe, Liss," the Jase voice spoke again, and Felicity finally felt herself pulled back to her surroundings as she looked up into his eyes with confusion.

"Where are we?" she queried, disoriented but impassive.

Placing his hand on hers, he peered back into her eyes. His hand was warm.

"In a coffee shop," he explained as a grey-haired woman walked over with a tray. Felicity vaguely processed that the woman placed a cup of coffee in front of her and a small croissant beside the coffee. "Merci, Claudine," Jase smiled. "Vous avez les meilleures pâtisseries au Canada."

Felicity heard the language, and some primitive part of her reacted with a smile of pleasure.

"You speak French," she murmured. She remembered when she had met him. *C'est impossible,* he had said, after he had laughed at her comment in French. *Interesting,* her automaton mind processed even as her sensations felt nothing.

"Eat, Liss," Jase insisted, not bothering to reply. "And drink some coffee."

Obediently, she took a sip of the black, bitter liquid. *Amazing,* her mouth purred to her brain, and she found Inner-Felicity slowly creeping through to the surface of herself to tap into the rush. Back to where the pain resided. Panting breaths cut off the subtle groans of misery as she resurfaced from the black water with herself in tow.

"Shhh," Jase soothed.

"It doesn't work," she gasped.

"It doesn't?" he wondered.

Squeezing her breath into a tone, she whispered. "I read somewhere that a person couldn't feel pleasure and pain at the same time, so if someone is hurting, you just need to give them a backrub or hold them in a hug, and they won't feel the pain as much."

"But it doesn't work?"

"Your hand," she glanced at the table. "It feels nice, but there is still enough pain that it doesn't really matter."

Jase smiled sadly. "Maybe it dulls it a little."

"Then don't stop," she whispered, "because I don't think I would survive anything worse than this."

"You already have."

She processed his words slowly. "No," she disagreed. "I ran away. I hibernated. The pain was too much. Now it's back."

Jase just brushed his hand over hers, saying nothing.

"Drink some more coffee," he finally commanded.

Once she seemed firmly nestled into her coffee, he finally removed his hand from hers.

"Eat the croissant now," he urged, and she dutifully grasped the flaky little pastry, bringing it to her lips. As she slowly chewed and swallowed the bread, a very small crumb of her strength made its way back into her body.

"Do you want to tell me what happened?" he prodded, but she was shaking her head before he finished the question.

"No, it's not right to talk about it with you."

Felicity saw something flash in Jase's eyes. Anger maybe? But she didn't think at her.

"Besides," she continued. "I think everyone at the company knows. It explains some of the comments I heard and the looks I got at the party the other night." Wrapping her arms around herself, she tried physically to hold the breaths steady that were gasping out of her. Not in a restaurant. She would not fall to pieces. Not in front of this person. Not in front of anyone.

Nodding, Jase breathed deliberately and said nothing.

After a few minutes of silence, Jase put his hand back on hers.

"Do you want to go somewhere else? Do you want to walk?"

In the back of her mind, as the pain evened from jagged shards into a steady burn, Felicity's thoughts took more comprehensible form. Hadn't she prepared for this? She had known, a thousand years ago when she had married the husband, that people were human. That people were fallible. That people had affairs.

And right-now-Felicity knew that she had three children with the husband.

She knew that, regardless of the pain to her, if it would serve her children best, she would stay with him. She had read stories of recovery and reconciliation and healing. Beautiful stories. That's what would happen, she suddenly realized. She would make it happen.

Brendon had fallen to his humanity.

Now that it was out in the open, he would have no choice but to acknowledge what had happened and, since Felicity was willing, to fix the marriage. It was the smart thing to do, and everyone knew Brendon was very smart.

Maybe the marriage could even be better for paying attention to and fixing the problems that had plagued it for years.

Felicity even knew that she was mostly not just lying to herself, engaging in wishful thinking. She believed that it could happen.

Fortunately, the barrage of thoughts infused breath into her. Not lungfuls of air, but a thin stream of breath. And with returning breath came returning steadiness. She was up to fix this.

Still, she cringed when she remembered that she would have to tell him she knew.

Glancing out the window to the street, Felicity sighed. "I guess I have to go find him now, and talk to him."

Jase seemed surprised.

"You're going to go talk to him?" he repeated.

"Jase," she ventured eye contact, determined that if she could speak convincingly to Jase Hamilton, she would convince herself. "We have children. We have to figure out what we're going to do."

Pursing his lips, Jase looked irritated. "I imagine that is exactly what you would do. Go talk to him." His mouth curved up sardonically on one side.

Suddenly coming to herself, she cringed lightly at Jase. Of all the people to come to her rescue! True, he had just treated her with more respect than she would have imagined he ever would, but she hadn't forgotten the party. His very blatant attempts to lure her to him. That was a minefield that tattered and broken Felicity would not go anywhere near.

"How…how far away from my car are we?" she queried with a grimace. "I don't remember much about the walk."

"Are you parked here or in town?"

"Here," she nodded firmly.

"Then you're probably right over there," he pointed to a

nearby lot, only about twenty feet from the coffee shop. "I'll walk you over."

A full smile graced Jase's pretty face, and Felicity made a point to glance over at the pastries until she could speak.

"Okay," she agreed.

With the sun just past noon, it had moved over the buildings until it shone in her eyes. She smiled at the nearness of her escape, a strange sensation that threatened the gasping breaths again. *You're not allowed any feeling but pain right now,* Inner-Felicity hissed, and Felicity grunted as she realized she hadn't become quite as coherent as she had hoped. She could drive, though, she knew.

Standing carefully to her feet, Felicity reached into her jacket pocket for her car keys.

Jase stood to his feet, reaching to steady her when she wobbled. "You're sure you're okay."

Nodding, Felicity stepped back, transferring her support to the chair back. "I don't really know how to thank you, but now is not the time I would expect kindness. Kind of seems like a fairytale at this point in my life."

"Not a fairytale," he assured her. "I'll be there when you need me."

Felicity blew out a fast breath. "You know why that's a really bad idea.," she corrected.

"Not bad for me," Jase grinned.

"But you're not the only one to consider here," Felicity chastised.

"Not bad for you either," he insisted.

"You don't know that. And I don't believe that," she challenged. "And there's more to consider than either of us."

"Surely you don't mean Bren -"

She cut Jase off. "Don't say his name. And, no, not him. My kids. I have to do what's best for them."

"And if that's not your husband?"

She stopped walking and stared at him, not processing how to be offended at the suggestion – not through her trauma – but knowing he shouldn't have said it. "Then I'll have to spend some serious time in thought," she drawled, picking up her foot stiffly of the ground and forcing it forward. She peered at her car with intention, as if it were the other side of a bridge. She had to make it there before the bridge collapsed under her. "I have to make a plan for the kids and me to go forward, "she mumbled, not wanting to use too much energy to speak." You can't help me with that either."

Successfully rebuffed, Jase smiled flatly, stepping back and opening the car door as she reached it. "Take care of yourself then," he urged as she collapsed inside. "And be careful."

"You know," Felicity turned back, her thoughts flowing freer once she didn't have to support her body. "I've been a little uneasy around him lately. Like I wasn't sure whether or not to be scared of him. But this explains everything." She shouldn't share with this man, but she needed to get the words out. "This is an awful situation, but it's a different kind of fear than I had imagined. On one level, it's harder to deal with. But on another level, it's more tangible and so it's more solvable."

"But you'll be careful?" Jase pressed, as if he didn't agree with her.

"I'll be careful," she smiled at him from the far side of her mind. "Thank you." Without looking back, she put the car in drive. Steeling herself, she headed back to confront her husband.

Chapter 9

Suddenly, it all felt like a dream, as if I had built up some kind of fairytale that had never really existed. I had imagined my world, and Brendon has taken a sledgehammer to the fantasy, rendering it a shattered heap of worthless images that mean nothing. – Felicity's Journal, March 27

A casual stroll through the lunatic asylum shows that faith does not prove anything. – Friedrich Nietzsche

Evening, March 19

To her relief, Felicity returned to an empty cabin. She had to suppress a pang of nausea as she considered whether Brendon remained away to indulge in his mistress, but she needed not to think about it. She needed to distract. Distract in whatever way she could manage. Distract with something that filled her mind with thoughts, not demanding enough to require actual attention, but active enough to grab and keep her mind occupied. *A bath and a laptop,* her instincts supplied, and she strolled into her room, digging in her duffle for her computer. Then she continued into the bathroom and began to fill the huge bathtub, pouring in some fragrant bubbles supplied by whatever housekeeping service managed the cabin.

Felicity clicked past the offending login information, now rife with new meaning, and opened an app, scrolling through a list of possible shows recommended by her preferences to click on one that looked interesting. Soon, she lay surrounded by warmth and comfort and thoroughly distracted by the clever banter between the scifi captain and his female co-captain. *So cliché,* she scoffed, unsure of whether she spoke of the show or of her own life. Suddenly she had become a cliché, she sighed. Unbelievable.

Her mind wandered for a while, but she found herself very alert in an instant.

"Felicity?" an anxious voice called, and Felicity settled deeper into the water. How would she face him?

Rather than answer, she lay back into the sultry sting of the water, allowing its heat to draw the burn from the depth of her chest. After far too few moments of grim peace, Brendon stumbled into the room, seemingly unaware of her presence. As usual, his countenance spoke some kind of determined consternation, a deep puzzle of thoughts twisting in his mind that only he could solve. Felicity watched him, her entire body submerged beneath the water save her face. Maybe it was just her imagination, but she thought she sensed a flowery aroma emanating from his as he neared the bathtub. No, she definitely did not want to talk to him.

She hoped by remaining still, she might escape his notice until he had passed through into the closet. For half the distance across the space, he seemed destined to answer her wishes, but then his eye caught hers in the mirror. She did not move, a burn rising in her throat that wanted to spit out some fiery accusation. Before she could, though, his expression arrested her, an expression she would never have expected: fear.

"How long have you been in here?" he spoke in a hushed tone, almost intimate. "You didn't answer me."

In her newly unapologetic candor, she did not appease him – did not even explain. "I didn't," she leveled coolly.

The fear seemed to grow as he took in the deadness in her voice. Somehow, he still expected her to respond to him. *Because he doesn't know you know,* her brain supplied.

"It's just," he paused, "you look almost poised for something there, your whole body under the water like that."

Felicity laughed, understanding the expression. In the past, such emotion on his part might have moved her, but now it just brought a barrier of ice to the surface of her skin, despite the heat of the water. "You're afraid I'm going to go Ophelia!" she snickered. Was he actually anxious for her? Or just anxious that he was caught? "I just might," Felicity simpered, her voice rising to a near-hysterical wisp as if she held sanity by a weak thread. "I always thought Ophelia so weak, you know. Now I have a lot more compassion for her."

With a momentary pang of nerves, she watched ice freeze his own expression, the look of an injured dog backed into a corner. If he hadn't suspected before, he did now.

"That's right," Felicity continued, not caring to hear his thoughts. "It's my problem. My mental deficiency. I will do what I do, irrespective of your choices and decisions. Irrespective of the fact that you smell like betrayal. Don't worry about it."

She plunged under the water, literally holding her breath with the hope that he would walk away. When her lungs finally burned too much to resist, she surfaced and found him gone. Apparently, he wasn't too worried that she would off herself. The dull ache of his absence seemed less intense a pain than watching the rejection she feared she might otherwise encounter. Sitting up, she pulled the plug. She would find no more pleasure in anything for a while. For once, maybe Brendon wanted to avoid conflict. *That's because there's no way to explain his way out of this one.*

Still, neither of them had actually spoken the words, so Felicity had no confirmation that he knew. As she slid on her robe and moved toward the armchair in the bedroom, she considered how she could test his patience with her, see if she could stress him into revealing something.

"Are we going to the party tonight?" she spat.

"The party...?" he replied, insecurity distorting his normally assured expression, "How do you know about the party?"

"A friend told me," she offered coyly, relishing the doubt in his eyes.

"But you never want to go to a party."

"Oh, I don't!" Her reserve fled. "But since your entire company is here, why not? You've dragged me to these miserable parties for years! And the fact that I don't like them has given you plenty of reason – " She cut herself off, but Brendon seemed not to notice. When she escalated things, he tended to get so defensive that her words didn't matter,

"Are you seriously doing this?" he accused. "I have important business to do here - "

"Important?" Felicity mocked, barely hiding the rage in her voice. "That's right. What's happening between us is just a little thing. I'm sure you would never hide anything really important from me."

To her surprise, Brendon looked as if she had punched him in the gut. The color fled his face, and his words almost panted in the weakness of his breath.

"Really important," Brendon whimpered. "Not the lie about this trip."

Felicity chewed her lip. Though she had hoped he would tell

her the truth, now that she felt the imminence of the confession, she wasn't sure she wanted to hear it. Had he really expected to hide it forever? "That's right," she made herself press. "I'm sure there's no dark, dirty little secret that you would want to keep from me at all costs."

"Is this about ProtoComm?" Brendon stammered, and Felicity had to press her lips together not to burst out in derision.

Still, her words exploded, harsh and intense. "ProtoComm? I mean, peripherally. From what I've figured, there was a time when your conduct at ProtoComm would have really set off my sensors, but you cleaned up your act there. You're too smart in business to let petty indiscretions risk your position in the company. Instead, you committed huge personal indiscretions that no one in the company would mind."

To her surprise, Brendon took a step toward her, his face crumbling in what resembled panic. "How did you find out?" he strained out, and he seemed actually to have trouble standing.

"Find out what?" she pressed mercilessly. "I'm sure you wouldn't do anything really reprehensible."

"I'm surprised you see it that way," he hemmed, as if he believed she were serious. "It was just Aimée..."

Time stretched, dark and undefined, as Felicity experienced the difference between suspicion and certainty. For her, suspicion had felt frantic, hectic and unsettled. Though she hated it, she had known some form of it her entire life – that anxiety of the unknown.

But certainty? Certainty resounded like a huge churchbell, echoing and sending reverberations, erasing all surroundings, the past and the future, reason and thought, base emotional sensations. Certainty stood eternal in a moment, a standard and monument of deep, resonant, dark, hollow pain.

"Felicity," he began, stepping toward her. She held up her hand, arresting his forward motion lest he place himself in reach of her claws. "Felicity, you're my wife. This doesn't change that. It has nothing to do with you."

Jumping to her feet, Felicity strode to the other side of the bed, beginning a frenetic pacing that seemed the only way for her to control herself. "You have got to be," she leveled through clenched teeth, "the most delusional man who has ever lived. Nothing to do with me? Who, exactly, does it have to do with?"

She watched his countenance with utter disbelief as he spoke the words without the slightest compunction or guile. If she believed his expression, he meant what he said. "It has to do with me. With me and Aimée."

Incredulous, Felicity's eyes flitted around the room, almost as if looking for confirmation from a nonexistent judge or for someone to share her incredulity. "You can't honestly believe that," she accused, despite her reading of his body language. "You're a smart man. Brilliant, even. There is no way you believe that."

"Of course, I do, Felicity. You aren't seeing this clearly. Don't you love me?"

Somehow, she did not rush at him and punch him in the face. She had put up with his manipulations for so long, let him tug on her guilt to distract her from his transgressions. No more. "You obviously have no idea what that means!" Felicity scoffed. The word "love" emitting from his mouth at such a moment felt like a desecration, a testament to his depravity.

For years, Felicity had argued with herself over the faults in her husband, the insensitivity he had shown their children and her parents, his tendency to press friendly arguments until people ceased being his friend. Felicity had always laid at least part of the blame on the other party: they took offense too easily, they didn't think clearly, they got emotional. Now, for the first time, the veil stripped off of the illusion she had let herself build up and share with her husband. She had played accomplice to an asshole.

A brilliant man, a skilled politician, a generous contributor; but in his personal relationships, when he had to spend any extended effort on a relationship, he pissed people off, and they left him. Only she had stayed by him for all these years, buttressed in part by the children who depended on his attachment and by her hope that he would prove himself a good man. Apparently, a misplaced hope, and the possible ramifications began to wash over her.

If he would do this, what else would he do? Would he leave her destitute? Would he abandon his children? Would he sacrifice her, her children, his reputation, anything else to the idolatry of his self-indulgence and egotism?

As he stepped toward her, she recoiled physically, though she kept her expression in check. Where was his remorse? His compassion? Absent. Still, the image of her children flashed before her eyes and restrained her. Alex, Nicholas, Noah: maybe Brendon had treated her like trash, but would he so easily dismiss his children? If there was a chance in hell that he would father his children, she couldn't kick him to the curb. Not Brendon.

One thing Felicity knew, if she pushed him too far, he would blast them all to hell. No one really beat Brendon. Just because his ego needed approval, his actions tended toward the generous and benevolent. If he believed that she thought well of him, he would continue to find some manner of acting well. If she revealed the full depth of her disdain at the moment, he might act in a consistent manner with her belief – heartless.

Felicity wanted to scream; she wanted to throw things if not *at him* at least *of his*, shattering them into a million pieces. Yet she restrained herself.

When the ringing of Felicity's cell phone shattered the tension, she jumped at the chance of an interruption. She reached for the phone, turning from Brendon.

"Are you serious?" she heard him complain. "You're taking a call right now?"

She pretended she hadn't heard him, her pulse pounding in her temples as she swiped to answer. "Hello?" she barked, not even bothering to look at the caller ID.

"Felicity?" the unsteadiness of the voice on the other end took her aback.

"Nick?" she asked incredulously. "Is something wrong?" Using the drama of the question, Felicity left Brendon standing in the room while she headed to the closet. She could think of three reasons Nick might be calling, and the significance of those options sent Brendon to the background. Either Nick had called about her kids, her parents, or Briel. None of those options felt insignificant.

Nick turned Felicity's question around. "Are you okay?" he begged, and Felicity thought she caught a manic hint in his tone.

"Yeah," she threw the word out haphazardly, "why wouldn't I be?"

"Well," Nick paused, and Felicity heard a deep breath on the other end of the phone. "For one thing, you sounded awful when you answered the phone."

"Ha!" she laughed humorlessly. "Sorry. I'm fine." She offered no explanation. "What's the other reason?"

"Well..." Nick hesitated.

"Well?"

"I noticed something weird on your computer."

"Something weird on my computer..." Felicity quizzed. How typically obscure.

"Uh, yeah. Well, not so much *your* computer. Really, Brendon's."

A stab of stress pierced her between the eyes. As if she didn't have enough suspicions about Brendon! "What the hell, Nick? What are you doing on his computer?"

"Look, I'll answer your questions," Nick insisted, "But before I do, is Brendon there with you?"

"Well, he's here at the cabin," she offered, peeking out into the bedroom and noticing his absence, "but I don't know where exactly. I'm in the closet."

"Just keep your voice down, then."

With building anxiety, Felicity felt her stomach clutching. "Nick," she insisted, exasperated, "Just tell me what's wrong." She didn't think she could handle anything else at the moment.

"Does Brendon have any dealings with..." Nick paused as if unsure of his next words.

"With what?"

"Foreign trade?"

"Are you kidding?" Felicity snickered. "Brendon works for an international communications company. Of course, he does, though I don't know the specifics."

"Well, I found something a little more *provocative* than 'communications.' And there are some things Briel has said."

"Provocative?"

"Lissie, I found a couple of files on Brendon's hard drive, hidden and password protected, that seemed to contain something odd. And I found some offshore bank accounts – I doubt you knew about those."

"You hacked his stuff?" Part of her wanted to punch Nick; another wanted to give him a high five.

"You're missing the point. Are you going to let me tell you what I found?"

Why should she be surprised? She obviously didn't know her husband, having lived for who knew how long with a belief in his character. Now, how could she know whom she had married? No qualms about an affair, something she had heard him speak against a million times when they had first gotten married.

If he could justify an affair, what else could he justify? She had considered that he might abandon the children, cut off their financial support. It didn't seem such a stretch to think he would do something illegal, that he would figure out a way that the legal restrictions were small-minded and overly simplistic. Breathing deeply, Felicity braced herself for another asteroid.

"Let me guess. Something salacious and scary." She spoke the words deadpan, but the sarcastic tone revealed more irony than skepticism.

"Look, Lissie. Just because I found this doesn't mean I'm saying anything against Brendon. It may just be something his company is doing," he explained. "I found malware on your computer, a kernal-based keylogger. If you had been infected, then he might have been as well. I was trying to do him a favor!"

"Just tell me the dirt, Nick. It's not going to shock me as much as you imagine."

Nick hesitated, "I don't have anything concrete yet..." He seemed to be stalling, and Felicity's anxiety made her impatient. How bad was this? "I can't make out *all* the details, but I made it through the first level of security and accessed the file names. According to Briel, some of the terms inside sound like Darknet pseudonyms."

"The nanny knows Darknet pseudonyms?" Felicity snorted. "Doesn't seem a particularly good qualification for child-watching." *Though it seems perfectly in character for the woman I saw at her apartment.*

"Well, Felicity, apparently, Briel has been working for Brendon in some capacity other than as your nanny."

For Brendon? Felicity grew more distraught, her breath speeding again. She had thought she was beyond any more shock. Though it explained some of the conversation in Briel's hallway.

"I mean," Nick continued, "we've been spending some time together. And some of the things she said about Brendon when she saw the files – it just sounded like she knew something."

"Like what?" Felicity carped. "Like how to navigate the criminal Internet?"

"It's not the criminal Internet, Felicity," Nick chastised. "It just happens to be used by a lot of criminals – drugs, arms, trafficking, etc. And Briel is not the problem. It's Brendon and his company. There is something going on there."

His company? As if Brendon's personal issues weren't bad

enough – now his business was suspect? "You're just looking for trouble because you could never resist a conspiracy theory. I mean, Nick, we've both known Brendon for years, and the last thing he would do is something like you're talking about." *Of course, until yesterday, I swore up and down that he would never cheat on me, and now that seems pretty foolish.* Since she didn't know anything about the business, she was afraid Nick would drag the affair out of her, and she was not ready to share that misery with anyone else yet. "There are a couple of shady characters at his office, but at a company that size, that's not surprising. But that doesn't have anything to do with me. What could cause me trouble right now? I'm in another country on vacation with my husband." *And a good portion of his apparently corrupt company.*

"Just be careful, sis."

"Honestly, Nick. I'm just a boring mom with a boring life. There is nothing to be concerned about except that my brother is far too nosy."

Nick laughed, offering tacit agreement. A moment later, the gravity had returned. "But you'll be careful," he repeated. *He sounds just like Jase.*

Shaking her head, Felicity breathed herself calm. "I'll do my best," she conceded. "But you stay off Brendon's computer! I'm sure it's nothing." *Lie.*

"I'll do my best," Nick retorted, and Felicity would have reprimanded him had Brendon not entered the bedroom at that moment.

"Bye, Nick, love you." She adopted a light tone. "And don't let Briel push you around," she said, only half joking.

"Love you, too, sis," Nick responded, still serious. "And be careful."

"Right." Click. She did not want Brendon to ask her any questions about Nick's call.

Rounding out of the doorframe, Brendon reared up in front of her. "Are you ready?" he barked, eyeing her disheveled appearance.

I confront the man about his affair, and he still pushes me around? Unbelievable.

"Do I look ready?" she sassed. "I still have an hour."

"I just wanted to know if I was going to have to carry you."

Felicity glared at him. He wore an impish look which would normally have softened her, but in this case, it only galled her.

"Don't even," she leveled, and his expression transformed into base anger. True, she had agreed to go with him, but it stemmed more from her desire not to be alone with him than her love for social events. Still, she subdued her tone before continuing. "I'm coming, but. I have to change. I'll hurry."

Brendon crossed tentatively to her, reaching a hand to take hers. She wanted to draw back, but she held her breath and let him grasp her fingers, though she continued to scowl at him. *Don't do anything rash,* she admonished herself. *Make it through tonight for the kids.*

"Let's not fight," he pleaded, his eyes falling to their joined fingers. Did he honestly expect to erase the distance between them with a touch? *Delusional,* she reiterated.

A moment later, Brendon had wrapped his other arm around her and pulled her to him, his lips meeting her upturned mouth with an urgency Felicity couldn't explain. She let him kiss her. Self-loathing enveloped her as she didn't move. If she meant what she had said to Jase, that she would try to work it out for the kids, she had to look forward to his touch for at least another fifteen years until little Nicholas was grown. She swallowed her nausea and tested her endurance. *Another fifteen years…*

After several moments, Brendon stepped back, leaning in for a last kiss on Felicity's forehead and releasing her. "You get ready," he commanded. "I'll get everything else set."

As she closed the closet door behind her, Felicity leaned against the wall, allowing her head to fall back and breathing deeply. One thing she had always prided herself in was her ability to read people, to know things about them that they didn't know themselves. With Brendon, though, Felicity found her instincts constantly confused.

Because he seemed completely justified in his own mind, he never wore the guilty aura of a deceiver. Personal conviction, though, did not equate to the moral high ground. Still, his actions usually seemed noble. How else could she have stayed with him for more than a decade? Brendon sometimes championed the weak. Maybe out of personal contempt for those in power, maybe to look like a hero, but he had helped them.

Unfortunately, though, something about Brendon seemed to have changed recently. ProtoComm had gotten to him – maybe corrupted him – and he seemed much more possessed by the money and prestide. About one thing Felicity was certain now, and with a certainty she rarely had: Brendon had lied, about too many things. And hearing Nick's suspicions, Felicity realized that she could count on nothing in regard to Brendon. If she couldn't trust him, she couldn't trust him. Infidelity or criminality? The fact that she had to ponder either option made her sick to her stomach, and she stood still to breathe for a few seconds.

The numbers on her watch suddenly leaped out at her: 6:25 p.m. No more time for emotions and confusion, not if she intended to follow through with her plans. Grabbing her backless dress, the only appropriate dress she had brought, she gathered her other necessities and ran to the closet. Coming through the door, Brendon smirked appreciatively at the dress. *I'm not wearing this for you,* Felicity retorted in her mind, glowering.

She threw on everything but the dress, then she proceeded to brush her teeth, straighten her hair, and managed cosmetics in a matter of minutes. Lastly, she drew on the dress, requiring a more-than-willing hand from Brendon to fasten the halter strap behind her neck. Kissing her bare shoulder, he crooned, "You should wear the necklace I bought you."

Shrugging, her body responding to his touch even while she hated him, Felicity reached over to a bag that sat on the bathroom counter. She drew out the strand of freshwater pearls, in greys and blues, and reached to place it on her neck. It dangled deep into the V-neck of the dress, and she sighed at the obvious sensuousness of the effect.

Before she could manage the hook, Brendon grasped her hands, gently extracting the necklace from her grip. He stepped behind her, brushing his fingers along her collarbone and up her neck as he brought the two ends of the chain to meet, lingering with his hands on her shoulders before finishing his task and closing the clasp. As he drew his hands away, she felt his lips warm the skin beneath her right ear, and a shiver ran up her spine. "I wish I didn't have to let you out like this."

As the cold air replaced the heat of his skin, Felicity split into two, half of her infuriated at his gall, and the other half almost stirred by his touch. Hurt had rendered her desperate for connection, and even his damaged, destructive touch promised to soothe the ache. Fortunately, her mind was clear. That promise was like every other promise he had made her – a tantalizing lie.

"Too bad," she leveled, spinning away from him.

"Maybe we don't have to go," he answered quietly. At first, Felicity thought that Brendon was teasing, but his face conveyed heated sincerity when she looked at him. She recognized that look. Not tonight. Eventually, she realized, if she were really planning to stay with him. Her head spun before she righted herself.

"I want to go," she responded coldly. When she looked back at that moment, she would wonder if Brendon had held second thoughts, and if she had reacted differently, would he have altered his course. When she looked back, though, she wasn't sure she would have wanted him to. His character would not have evolved for the better, and more of the same would have led down an even darker road.

Her expressed desire to attend the party ran so counter to Felicity's established manner that Brendon peered suspiciously into her eyes. After a second, though, he stepped back and let her pass in front of him. Felicity sighed in relief. He waited patiently, his expression gone cold, while she threw on a few last-minute touches and laced the ribbons of her stilettos. Then taking her by the hand he led her to the waiting car. As he pulled her down into the running vehicle, she couldn't escape the impression that he was dragging her into her tomb.

Chapter 10

Of course, I have told myself that I gave up my dreams because I found a worthy cause, but what I now find is that the underlying truth, some portion of my motivation, I drew from Brendon. I have done so much of it for Brendon, for the shared vision we began more than a decade ago. I have sacrificed almost everything about myself for what I had thought an ideal, a higher calling, and now I have found out that I have sacrificed myself for a lie. Is there anything left of me to salvage now? – Felicity's Journal, March 28

You seem to misunderstand a lot of things, but I want to make myself very clear because I don't want to blindside you like you did me. You seem to interpret setting boundaries as an attempt to manipulate, but I am setting boundaries nonetheless. So here is mine. You will not have us both. If you insist on keeping her around, the best you can hope for from me is our living apart while you live however you want. Then if you come to your senses, maybe I'll still be available, maybe I won't. Otherwise, you will have to cut her off. Get her transferred to a different department, a different city, never see her again. If you want me, that is what it will cost you. – Unsent email from Felicity to Brendon, March 19.

Late evening, March 19
Felicity managed a laugh. How she even knew the song she couldn't conceive, but the vague remembrance painted her brain with an image from her childhood. She had thought it strange for a rock song to have numbers in it; she didn't know why now. And at the time she hadn't known what a .45 was or what 5'9" meant. Now the song lulled, sultry in the dim lighting of a small dining hall. *With just one look I was a bad mess,* it lamented, and Felicity smirked at the unlikely grunge of the music. She liked it, but it didn't seem particularly "Bill Henry." A sort of shimmering mist enshrouded the

air, and a scent clung to the fog, something Felicity didn't recognize – spicy, earthy, intoxicating.

Someone knew how to throw a party. Finally. The music, the aroma, the haze all worked synergistically to invoke a sort of hypnotic pulse in the room. The obscurity suited Felicity because she didn't know how she would function throughout an entire night with the ProtoComm people. A cocktail party had been torture enough, but a night like this? While she played the dutiful wife to a philanderer? At least at Saturday's party, the numbers of people let her disappear into the wallpaper. Here, each person would scrutinize her every movement, and she had no desire to encounter Jase in her current state, not after their last meeting.

Now she thought she might understand why people chose to drink at company parties. *At least if I make a fool of myself, maybe I won't remember,* she groaned, determining to drink at least two glasses of wine for a nice, tipsy buzz. A little liquid courage. Especially if Amy showed up.

As soon as they entered, Brendon began the round of introductions. Felicity had expected the other VPs: Edward Pope from Oakland; David Farnham, Houston; and Anna Waters, Chicago. Felicity's blood chilled slightly as she shook Jack Buckley's hand. She had never been able to expunge from her thoughts the hunch that Jack Buckley had a hand in the disappearance of John Mitchell a few years back. Even though Brendon reassured her, Felicity remained suspicious. *His reassurances are worthless anyway,* she realized.

Of course, Jenna Whitfield imposed herself glowingly on the arm of Jase Hamilton, her face sporting a sparkling smile and his, a stiff resignation. When assured that Brendon's eyes focused elsewhere, Jase dispatched a knowing, somber smirk in Felicity's direction, and she glared impudently in return. Still, her stomach clutched.

Why did his smile appear to hide anxiety? He had definitely not forgotten her upset at their last meeting. She tried to feel irritated at his presumption, but just couldn't make herself. Still, she could let anyone know how badly she wanted to unload her own worries on him – the only friendly face in the room. Instead, she relaxed her tension into her best approximation of a flirtatious smile. What could it hurt to indulge herself a little? *Too soon to tell,* she realized as her eyes dropped. She wished she could have seen Jase's reaction, but her soul still ached too profoundly to engage in games.

Breathing deeply, she turned back to take the lushly upholstered seat offered by her husband. Unlike at the other dinner parties she had attended, everyone ate at this small gathering, because the food made the centerpiece for the discussion. Twenty people lined a dark solid wood table with Bill Henry, CEO, at the head.

No Amy. *Thank God,* Felicity sighed. She glanced covertly at the other diners, first at Bill, then around the table. Through the haze, David Farnham seemed less sinister than she remembered him, though at the moment she didn't trust anyone from ProtoComm. Jack always made her think of the smarmy car salesman, and Felicity could never imagine how a man like that had become vice president of such a powerful company.

When Felicity looked at Bill Henry, though, he oozed power. Something about the man exuded utter assurance, a confidence that everyone around him thought of things exactly as he intended. For the most part, he smiled and simpered, offered noblesse oblige to his employees and charmed their wives or significant others.

Not Felicity, of course. She would have needed to catch his eye, something she would avoid at all cost of civility. Because beneath the veneer of his courtesy, she sensed a shadow of duplicity or artifice. *Like Brendon,* she realized. Everyone wore masks, she knew, but she could see past most of them to their cause – insecurity, judgment, manipulation. Felicity could not decipher Bill's mask, and she therefore wanted nothing to do with him.

Since he spoke to Ed Pope for the duration of the meal, it didn't seem to be an issue, but she noticed Bill's eyes on Brendon several times during the conversation. Bill also shot several covert glances toward Jase and toward Jack Buckley. Breathing deeply, Felicity reined in her errant imagination and forced herself to focus on what lay in front of her. The man was sending messages, but Felicity had no hope of figuring out what they were.

The meal came course by course, seven in all, and Felicity concentrated on the etiquette that she usually ignored. On one side of Felicity sat a small swarthy man, someone she had never met.

He had some kind of Italian name, or so Felicity thought. *Pietro?* she searched her memory for the recent introduction. Though she couldn't remember the particulars, she knew that every time she saw him, he wore varying shades of forgettable tan, and she could only describe his hair and eyes as generic brown. Her mind immediately dubbed him the "tan man."

Brendon held her other side, while across from her sat the vanilla Anna Waters. Fortunately, Jase sat several chairs to her left on the opposite side. She had absolutely no occasion to glance his way. That did not, however, keep her from feeling his eyes on her much more than could be considered proper, and she struggled to restrain herself from peeking toward him. If his initial expression indicated the rest of the night, she knew that if she looked at him again, fire would erupt in her veins.

If at any point the party had no dish before them, Brendon entwined his fingers firmly in hers, interlocking them in almost vise-like fashion. It felt less like a connection and more like shackles. Under normal circumstances, his possessiveness would have annoyed her, but tonight his powerful presence provided a buttressing effect against her insecurity. Even though he had betrayed her, he was also the only one who knew her secret pain – or at least a small portion of it.

Well, and Jase. But Jase was off limits. She wondered if the other people in the room could feel it, the rift between Brendon and her. It seemed tangible, and Felicity found it hard to believe that others could miss it. She felt more exposed than she could ever desire, the ostentation of her apparel adding to her unease. At least Brendon's familiarity offered her a small measure of comfort.

The slight breeze from the ceiling fan overhead caressed her bare back and found gaps where the cloth of her dress didn't cling. At some point, the drape of the fabric teased loosely down the sides of her torso, and Felicity began to severely question her sanity in choosing to make herself so vulnerable. Her puerile desire for vengeance on Brendon back in Phoenix had backfired. If she'd known about the party any earlier, she would have gone shopping.

Sweeping her eyes around the table, Felicity appraised the other women near her. No one else had chosen to attire themselves in quite so dramatic a fashion. Anna Waters had definitely traded her femininity for power, dressing herself accordingly in a slightly tailored tuxedo. From what Felicity could see, the only hints that it had been intended for a woman showed in a tapered waist and a flared leg.

Jenna sported a tight-fitting, very short sequined dress, colored with the cascading effect of mother-of-pearl. She honestly looked lovely, but the outside didn't reflect the inside, Felicity knew. All of the corporate wives dressed in suitably classy attire, but nothing particularly daring. Felicity mused gratefully that as long as they sat, she could hide herself beneath table linens since most of her height came from her long, statuesque legs.

Unfortunately, dinner ended before she finished her first glass of wine. In desperation, she crudely swigged the last of the glass, afraid the alcohol wouldn't hit in time to deaden her to the anxiety she felt. Just before she would be forced to stand, the server intruded between Felicity and the tan man with another glass of malbec.

All of the chairs followed that of Bill Henry in scraping backwards and evicting their occupants. To Felicity's surprise, Brendon never let go of her hand. He did not chase after conversation with the most interesting or powerful or helpless people in the room. No, he stood staunchly by her chair, awaiting her movement. As she unfurled her feline length, she felt more than one pair of eyes assessing her. Unused to the spotlight, Felicity kept her eyes played on the carpet unwilling to see who watched her. *Stupid dress,* she fumed, *this was supposed to torment Brendon, not me.*

Brendon instinctively drew her closer to him as if he, too, noticed the stares from around the room. Felicity was grateful that the wine had started to work. Still, even through her increasing stupor, Felicity sensed the urgency in Brendon's grasp. She laced her arm through his, not feeling entirely stationary on her own. Though when sober she reviled Brendon, in her near-sodden state she reverted to her usual child-like attachment to him.

Why did I take that second glass of wine, she bemoaned, too late. Even though she had drunk less than half the second glass, she found her attention wandering, unable to fix on anything in particular. Unfortunately, she did manage to catch the unexpected entrance of a lovely female form, a vision in blushing pink, where she glided into the room. *Amy,* Felicity huffed, and a hollow, heavy emptiness opened inside her gut, a million pinpricks of pain radiating from its depths and sapping the strength from her limbs.

She felt her frantically rapid breaths begin to race out of control. To his credit, Brendon froze, glancing first with horror at Amy and then with increasing concern at Felicity's sudden panic. He rubbed his hand comfortingly up and down Felicity's arm, and she found the pain temporarily anesthetized when she leaned into him. A moment later, though, she felt herself being deposited onto a stuffed, oversized armchair, and the disorientation of drunkenness added to the return of the ache.

The increasing effects of the alcohol began to slow her breathing even as Brendon's action raised her ire, and Felicity stared in sodden disbelief as Brendon made his way cautiously to Amy's side. Within moments, Brendon stood in intimate conversation with his lover – *his lover,* Felicity sobbed silently, the alcohol deadening what would no doubt otherwise have burst from anguished lips. Infuriatingly, Felicity's head swam so out of control that, even with the obvious importance of keeping an eye on her husband, Felicity could not.

Instead, from the corner of her eye, she suddenly became aware of Jase Hamilton as he deposited a drunken Jenna Whitfield onto the arm of someone Felicity remembered as maybe Gregory? Almost immediately, Bill Henry motioned to Brendon that he wanted to talk. Glaring, Felicity leaned back in the chair, stabbing Brendon a thousand times with her eyes as he maneuvered his way from Amy to Bill.

In leaning back and crossing her lanky legs, Felicity suddenly realized that the slit along the front of her dress exposed her from ankle to mid-thigh. It was a full thirty seconds before Felicity's sodden senses responded by uncrossing her legs and using her hands to make the two sides of material meet.

Felicity had not been able to finish her second glass of wine, but she had drunk it quickly enough that its effects seemed to have hit with intensity. Now that she sat still, the deadening of her senses left her feeling not just exposed, but isolated. Her dress exacerbated the sensation. *What an idiot!* she laughed at herself. At least the alcohol kept her from taking the situation too seriously.

Once again, it was the spicy scent that washed over her first, and her mind quickly flew to the anticipation of the touch – a flashback to the first night when Jase Hamilton had come to her rescue. Jase did not disappoint, and the thrill when his fingers scorched the tender skin above her knee eradicated the memory of the heat on her back those weeks before. The burn traveled up the skin of her leg, and she closed her eyes to wrestle control from the alcohol that threatened to render her impotent against the feeling.

"*Ta tenue est sensationnel,*" Jase's deep voice rumbled, and a slow pulse of air stream from Felicity's lungs, a soundless whistle releasing the steam from the sensation. Her dress was stunning? Instead of sitting in any of the adjacent chairs, as any proper gentleman would, Jase placed himself on the edge of the solid wood coffee table, his knees just inches from Felicity's.

"Bonsoir, Jase," she giggled, and the sound rumbled deep and velvet.

"You're drunk," he asserted, amusement lighting his features.

Felicity barked a sardonic laugh. "I am not!" she retorted. "I have only had one and a half glasses of wine." She certainly felt more drunk than she should have.

Jase looked suspicious, lifting her glass to his lips and breathing in the bouquet. "When is the last time you drank?"

"*Samedi*," Felicity pouted. "So, there." *Did I just say that last part out loud?* she scoffed to herself, even as the ache worked to suck her down into a deep well.

Jase smiled, somehow a somber expression. "I watched you Saturday. You never even finished a glass. Tonight, you chugged the first one, and I only see a few sips left in the second one." He pointed to the nearly empty glass he had placed back on the table.

"Not drunk," she insisted. Biting her lip, Felicity frowned. She felt drunk. *I guess I did finish that second glass,* she mused.

Her dander ascended languidly, and she leaned back again in her chair and crossed her legs, so as to increase the distance between Jase and herself. She didn't remember the dress until his fingers stirred on her knee, and her breath hitched. For an instant, the ache receded, the weight retreating under an ecstatic warmth that muted her misery. Still, a voice thrummed coolly from inside her mind that she could not give in to the pleasure, that it was a false friend.

"Stop it, Jase!" she complained, frowning sullenly.

"Why?" he insisted, not removing his hand, but reaching toward the fabric with his fingers. Was he sliding his hand up her leg? Or was he pulling the material shut? She couldn't tell – all she felt was the heat of his fingers on her skin, the electric pull of his touch.

"I don't know," she pouted, her heart thrumming with excitement. "It's not proper. And there are people everywhere." Despite retaining a remnant of her usual principled mind, Felicity's breath sped excitedly. She licked her lips, reaching her hand to arrest his, though she paused, their hands entwined on the flesh of her leg, before she finally pushed him away.

As if he read her hesitance, he leaned closer, his other hand pressing the satin fabric of the dress onto her thigh. "No one will see," he smirked, his expression inviting. His eyes, though. They seemed...nervous? Concerned? They flitted around the room as if in search of something. "Brendon is occupied elsewhere," he explained, reaching for the dress again. As if Brendon's absence excused the liberty! Still, she didn't stop him, sighing with the sensation of his hands on her. Jase's eyes scoured the room. "I'm pretty sure Bill has swept him off for a conference."

"Evil conferences," Felicity whined, her fuddled memory flitting to an argument with Brendon that she couldn't exactly remember.

Some subverted vestige of her rational mind wondered that two glasses of wine could have quite so dramatic an effect on her, but she couldn't form the thought adequately enough to examine it. Jase had said something, though, that Felicity needed to process. She closed her eyes to block out the room around her – to block out her drunken craving for Jase.

"You said Brendon!" she brightened. "Brendon, that's why. I'm married to Brendon!" Still she didn't move.

"What?" Jase feigned confusion, leaning in as if to hear better. His fingers brushed the tender skin inside her thigh as he leaned toward her, and Felicity shuddered with pleasure.

"That's why, your hand...Brendon..." her thoughts grew more confused as a muddled sense of unease suddenly gripped her.

"*Brendon est un bâtard égoïste, et tu mérites mieux*," Jase whispered, and Felicity wondered how his lips had traversed the distance to speak so closely to her ear. She moaned lowly at the brush of his hand across her cheek. Jase had spoken the truth: Brandon was a selfish bastard, and she did deserve better. Unexpectedly, heat eased into the chair with her, and Jase threaded one arm behind her back. A fire spread inside her as he pulled her against his muscled chest, and she let her head fall back as she opened herself to him. *Brendon wouldn't mind,* Felicity assured herself. *He wants someone else anyway.*

Felicity couldn't think; she couldn't talk, but a battle raged inside her. She felt herself lean away from Jase, a last rush of resistance stirring her strength, yet even in her attempted rejection, she turned her face to him, her lips parted as if in invitation. She felt her eyes close. From far away she heard Jenna's voice.

"She doesn't look well," Felicity heard as confusion muddled the foreseen kiss. Where had Jase gone?

"...can't hold her liquor..." Jase's voice, his arms somehow distant even as they held her "...don't bother Brendon...I'll take her."

From somewhere inside her head, Felicity screamed in protest, but no sound escaped her lips. Jase spoke to others as if she were walking by herself, his arm merely supporting her, but Felicity knew her legs couldn't possibly be moving. She couldn't feel them. Where was he taking her? Had he slipped something in her drink? Had she completely misread him?

Brendon! her mind screamed, but all that escaped her lips was a mumbled, "Mmm..."

"Sssh..." Jase soothed, but the clattering of her heart screamed, "No! Brendon, help me!"

No sound would escape. Even if it had, Felicity knew Brendon wouldn't help. He didn't care. Jase could do whatever he wanted with her, and Brendon would probably be relieved. She felt herself being laid down on something soft, and she panicked. When her mind processed the sensation, though, it arrested her fear. A gentle rumble sounded in her ears. *A car?* she wondered. Then Jase, leaning over her, whispered, "*Pas de panique.* You'll be okay. I'll come and find you. I won't let them hurt you. I'm sorry for the show back there. *Les yeux sont rivés sur moi.*"

Eyes are on him? All sentiment of seduction had left him, replaced by a grave intensity. Then, too far gone to feel any reaction, Felicity felt him brush his thumb lightly across her forehead, the spicy scent trailing from him as he caressed her cheek reassuringly before standing and shutting the door between them.

As the darkness fell, she looked through the car window. For an instant, Brendon's face, hard and severe, stared at her through the glass. *I swear, I didn't want him to,* she pleaded silently to Brendon's furious gaze. Then he turned away, a flash of Amy's nervous face appearing as Brendon placed his hand on the small of his lover's back, and Felicity remembered nothing else.

Chapter 11

Pain does strange things to people, makes things that used to look bad or immoral seem logical or right. Anything to stop the pain. It cuts off portions of the conscience, sending your heart into a panic to avoid the pain it predicts. It makes me feel a little sorry for him. But not sorry enough to give him what he wants. – Felicity's text to her brother, Nick. March 21.

Take care of this girl. There's something about her. I like her. You like me, and I like her. So be nice to her, and I will count it as a favor. – Text from Esmeralda to Carlos, March 21

<u>March 20</u>
Tiny missiles pelleted her cheeks and sought to penetrate her eyelids; Felicity's sensations returned before full awareness. She could feel the grating of the wind rasp harshly across her face. Sitting up, she turned her back to the pounding wind so she could protect her eyes long enough to open them.

When she did so, she tried to brush the grit away from her lashes. Blinking her eyes clear, she glanced around her; what little she could see seemed unfamiliar. Felicity could just make out the outlines of a road - an intersection, actually – beside which she lay. In front of her, the horizon stretched flat and unchanging. She could barely discern the silhouette of several dilapidated edifices scattered on either side of the road, but she could not see them clearly.

The light filtered down through a golden haze of dust, as if the party's smoke-filled room had expanded to the external world. From the way the sun bled around her, she couldn't tell the time of day, whether midday or dusk or dawn, but not nighttime. Overshadowing all her senses, Felicity felt as much as saw the thick cloud of sand that had engulfed her world, grains much larger than she would have expected; it obscured anything more than a few feet in front of her.

Since Felicity had no idea where she was or where she

should go, she dragged herself slowly to her feet and began plodding in the direction the wind was blowing. The movement allowed her a few inches of clear air in front of her, enough to keep her eyes open and enough to breathe without inhaling sand.

Every muscle in her body ached, but no bones seemed broken, and no pain overshadowed the minor irritation of her sore muscles save a slight pang in her right ankle. *I must have twisted it falling from the truck bed,* she thought.

The truck bed, she repeated incredulously. She, Felicity Miller, had jumped from the truck bed of a moving vehicle. *Unbelievable.* Felicity huffed the deepest breath she dared among the thick haze.

Knowing that someone would eventually notice her disappearance from the truck, Felicity forced herself forward, deciding that she would risk trying to ask for help. She approached the buildings on the left-hand side of the road, mostly abandoned ruins - cheaply-made, fallen-down shells in the adobe style typical of the southwest U.S.

How long had I been held in that truck? she worried. She was pretty sure that they had started out near the Canadian border which meant that they had been traveling at least 10 hours to reach even the northernmost part of the Southwest. She didn't remember being transferred from the softness of what had obviously been a car into the cold hard back of a pickup truck, and she doubted that her captors had ridden with her over 1,500 miles exposed in the back of a truck.

The erasure of an indefinite time period in her life unnerved Felicity, and she had not even a faint memory of the elapsed span. She did, however, remember waking up in the back of the truck. With the disorientation of her awareness mingled fuzzy remembrances of the time before her abduction: a fog descending on her as she sat in a comfortable chair talking with Jase; feeling a caress on her face as Jase laid her into the backseat of the car; and Brendon's cold expression as he stared at her through the glass of the window, his lover at his side.

The expectation of concern from the one man; the expression of concern by the other. A stabbing pain in her heart robbed her of breath for a moment as she remembered, and she paused to gather herself.

When she had realized that she lay in the back of a speeding truck, Felicity had forced herself to pushed down her confusion and think rationally. Whoever had placed her in the back of the truck had either assumed that she would stay asleep or hadn't clearly communicated that she be restrained.

Why else would she remain unfettered in an open-bed truck? Relief had mingled with her misery as she had watched small town lights blur past her. She was alive and unharmed, but someone had kidnapped her. A positive to go with the negative. As the truck had slowed at an intersection, she climbed carefully over some trash bags that had, with a thick blanket, prevented her from rolling around the back of the truck.

She then used them to shield her movements from view of the driver. From her new vantage point, she could peer occasionally at the rearview mirror and watch the driver's eyes. After watching for at least 20 minutes, she felt the truck slow at what appeared to be an intersection.

Holding her breath, she locked her eyes on the mirror and waited until the dark-eyed driver glanced behind him and then gassed the truck forward. Knowing he would return his eyes to the road, Felicity used the opportunity to climb as discreetly as she could over the back right side of the truck. A sudden lurch sent her crashing over the back end and onto the pavement, her head cracking into the blacktop. Above her, the world swam, and the lights danced as her consciousness waned yet again. She struggled against the blackness of her brain, though, forcing herself to crawl off of the hard road and out of the path of any oncoming vehicle. When she felt the soft sand at the side of the road, she finally gave up, succumbing to her exhaustion and the pain in her head.

Felicity could not estimate how long she had lain in the dirt, unseen and undisturbed. Though she could not currently determine the time of day, she knew that she had jumped from the pickup sometime in the night. She was safe, though – she had to focus on staying that way.

Most likely, the dusty haze had obscured her from any passersby, because a woman wearing a dark blue cocktail dress and lying in a gutter would surely have otherwise attracted attention. She considered seeking help.

What would she do if she found someone? Whom could she call? Felicity wouldn't want to contact any of her family or friends, not until she knew what was after her. In the past she would have called Brendon. He would have hired someone to come retrieve her and then spent the few weeks making fun of her or berating her for being stupid enough to drink that much wine.

Was Brendon her enemy? A few days ago, she would not have thought it possible. Even after, did it mean a man was a criminal just because he had a mistress? Then half the men or more and a quarter of women through all of history would be criminals. Problem was not the mistress. Problem was the deception. If a man would take the systematic and intentional steps to conceal something like he did, then he was the sort of man who would take the systematic and intentional steps to conceal something. And almost worse, a man who pretended to be a good, upstanding citizen, the pinnacle of moral virtue, while engaging in the practices that are the bedrock of all criminal behaviors. She just had no idea who he was anymore.

His tone for the past few days had held such a sense of urgency, his eyes an anxiety and panic since before they boarded the airplane, and those expressions seemed to betray a desire for her well-being. Might it rather have been anxiety that she, that someone, would mess up his plan? She wanted to believe he meant her no real harm, but she had found out in the past 24 hours just how far she would go to believe whatever made her feel better. *But just because it makes me feel better doesn't mean it's true,* she reminded herself.

Two strong images rose up in her mind, and she had trouble dismissing either one. Perhaps because, in her rage at Brendon, she wanted them to be significant, but she couldn't ignore them. Two images: Brendon's glare, Amy on his arm, and Jase's concerned eyes as he said the words. *I'll come and find you,* Jase had said. *I won't let them hurt you.*

Did she trust Jase? She couldn't trust anyone. But outside of finding her attractive, what self-serving agenda could Jase possibly have? If he only wanted a woman, his options were numerous. Felicity had seen a dozen beautiful women flirt with Jase. Why would Jase reject those other women for Felicity if, in order to have her, he had to brave kidnappers and ProtoComm and who knew what other hurdles to "come and find" her? It seemed motivated by at least some noble intentions inside him.

Felicity felt faint again, not from the pain in her head, but from the intensity of her emotions and the disorientation they wrought. Her knees gave way beneath her, and she sank to the ground.

What could she have done that would deserve this? Surely Brendon could just have divorced her if he wanted Amy. Not like Felicity had money of her own to fight him in court. Kidnapping seemed an inconceivable overreaction, especially for the ever-controlled Brendon. Unless kidnapping was the easy solution...

With a dawning thought that her mind fought against, she remembered Nick's words to her on the phone. "I found something a little more *provocative* than 'communications," he had insisted. He had also claimed, "It may just be something his company is doing." For a normal person, a divorce was the easy option. For someone with a multinational powerhouse, hundreds of millions of dollars to play with, maybe kidnapping was the easier solution. It just didn't seem real. Brendon's fight with Bill at the party became significant in Felicity's mind. *I'm not going to let this blow up in my face,* Bill had complained. *This is far outside our SOP.*

Looking physically around her as if for answers, Felicity slumped her shoulders in pain. She couldn't breathe. Of course, she had always heard about broken hearts and had thought that she understood. Now, though?

A tight constriction, just off center in her chest kept her physically held down in the earth. It wasn't so much the heartbreak of Brendon's affair. It was the heartbreak of the betrayal of all that was good and beautiful. If Brendon had managed her kidnapping, then the world was a lot darker than she had let herself believe. The loss of that kind of innocence was devastating.

Though she tried to filter through the violent black haze that had just choked her mind into uselessness, she could not find a ray of light; she could see no silver lining. *Just stand up,* she commanded herself. Past the squeezing of her heart and lungs, she sucked in a breath as far as it would go and lunged to her feet. It felt like she had just ripped herself out of molted skin, and she stood raw and exhausted for several seconds.

Maybe she should have just crawled out into the road and waited for some passing traffic, blinded by the dust, to end her misery. Without warning, Noah's smile flashed before Felicity's mind, and a sob heaved inside her. How could she even consider leaving them, her children? How was any of it their fault? Would she punish them, make them lose their father and mother on the same day? Or worse, leave them with Brendon and Amy as the only adults in their lives? Felicity took one step and fought to stay upright. Still, she wondered how exactly she would make it across the road and endure the inescapable search for a way to go forward.

As if in reply to her thought, Felicity swallowed and nearly flew into a coughing fit. The lack of saliva in her mouth induced a searing pain in her throat, dry from hours or days without liquid. While death might sound appealing in theory, Felicity's body apparently wanted to stay alive, and adrenaline kicked in with the discomfort. Her immediate physical needs superseded the mental anguish which she wanted to nurse. *You want water,* it told her. *Quit crying and go find some.*

Felicity stood to her feet and plodded purposefully toward a row of houses, though she saw no signs of life. Perhaps she could find a working garden hose. After several fails, she finally found an occupied house. Before that, she had only encountered falling down commercial establishments or vacant mobile homes.

Finally, better than a garden hose, she spotted a lone horse standing statue-like but very much alive about 30 yards off of the main road – a live horse meant that a live person who took care of the horse lived nearby. Felicity could just make out the outline of the wire fence that corralled the horse and, behind it about 20 feet, several edifices in varying stages of decay. On one of those buildings, she could also see a rectangular light shining through the dirty fog. Indeed, Felicity had encountered some form of humanity. As Felicity approached the house, she could see that the other buildings were just utilitarian additions to the poor rustic dwelling: a lean-to chicken coop; a small, broken-down, barn-like building; and a generic shed.

Reaching her hand toward the door, Felicity knocked at first timidly, then more demandingly on the ramshackle wood. Felicity wondered if she had been wrong about its occupancy when no one responded for several minutes. How long could it take to walk from the back of that shack to the front? Then, out of the corner of her eye, Felicity saw a shadow of motion behind the lone lit window. A flutter of the curtains? Someone looking out? Glancing down at herself, Felicity's heart dropped. Though she had left Banff a stunning lady, she stood outside this door dirt-encrusted and disheveled. Who knew how many hours in the bed of a truck, a leap onto a dirt shoulder, and a dust storm had all done their worst, and Felicity showed the battle scars.

For some reason, however, the soul inside the house chose to have pity on her. Felicity heard a faint scraping and the slow turning of a doorknob. Then a crack of light joined the nearby rectangle as the person inside opened the door into a semblance of civilization. A very small form caught Felicity's eye, so small in fact, that Felicity thought the form a child. As Felicity stepped in out of the storm, however, she realized that the form was in fact a tiny woman. The woman had a slightly rounded, motherly figure and the dark hair, skin, and eyes of those with Spanish and Native American descent. Her first words confirmed Felicity's thoughts.

"Que quiere?" the woman demanded suspiciously. Her gaze swept up and down Felicity's disheveled figure.

I can do this, Felicity encouraged herself.

"No hablo español," Felicity grasped at her limited knowledge. "Solo un poquito."

"Okay, okay," was all the woman said.

"Agua?" Felicity pleaded, touching her throat.

The woman just nodded and trod off into the back of the house. *Shouldn't take too long in a house this small,* Felicity thought tacitly. Almost carelessly, the woman had left her door open and now beckoned Felicity into the tiny room - some sort of kitchen and living space combined. Felicity glanced around the room; cozy would have been a generous description of the space. On one wall stood a baker's rack, and a round, wooden table took up the center of the room. A sofa bench rested against another wall. Though tired, Felicity didn't dare invite herself in to sit at the table – not without the woman's permission.

As she waited, Felicity felt safe to spend a few moments thinking. She literally had nowhere to go and no one to call. *Move forward,* her psyche told her, and her emotions spit back, *which way would that be?* She could hardly stay long with the poor woman whose house she now invaded. At most, Felicity could hope for some sustenance, maybe a... *A phone.* Despite her hesitance to involve anyone else, the idea of a lifeline opened for Felicity a sliver of hope. Her last conversation with Nick convinced her that he knew something that could give her direction. Plus, although Nick would definitely lose his cool, Felicity thought she could count on him to let her make her own decisions. Most importantly, if the revelation brought danger with it, Nick could take care of himself.

At this point in Felicity's deliberations, the little woman

returned with a mug of something that Felicity didn't recognize. Not "agua." Maybe some sort of tea? Placing it on the diminutive table, the woman gestured for Felicity to have a seat. The concoction didn't smell too bad, so Felicity surmised that it would be safe to drink. *And if not,* she mused ironically, *I have nothing to steal. She can drug me, but she can't rob me. And I'm already kidnapped.*

The liquid in the mug did cause Felicity to calm down, but not the befuddled calm of the alcohol the night before. *Was it the night before?*

"Qué día es hoy?"

"Hoy es miércoles," the woman replied.

Wednesday - so Felicity had traveled from Banff less than twenty-four hours before. From the increased darkness outside, Felicity surmised that Wednesday had passed on into evening. The feel of the app night took Felicity back to the previous night, how it had begun in hurt and anger and had ended in devastation. Brendon's glaring face rose before her, and she quickly forced the picture from her mind before she could lose her cool again.

"Como se llama Usted?" Felicity begged, searching for a topic to divert her.

"Me llamo Angela."

"Angela," Felicity weighed the name. "Usted es como un angel para mi." *Like an angel to me,* Felicity managed a smile.

The woman smiled in return and ducked her head. "No problema," she shrugged. The compliment seemed to ease something in Angela's mind. "Necesita Usted algo de mi? ¿Como puedo ayudarle?"

How can she help? That's the question of the decade, Felicity groused, hoping her discomfiture wouldn't appear on her face.

"Teléfono," Felicity mumbled. "Teléfono, por favor," Felicity pleaded again, a little confidence returning to her voice. The woman dug in her apron and handed over a small, inexpensive cell phone, which Felicity immediately put to use.

When Felicity heard the voice on the other end of the call, she almost burst into tears. Nick sounded worried, almost panicked, and Felicity knew he needed reassuring. "Is that you? I can hardly hear you. Where are you calling from?"

Turning to Angela, Felicity begged, "Donde estamos?"

"Quido."

"Quido? Donde?"

"Quido, New Mexico."

Felicity almost dropped the phone she held, and for a moment, thought failed her.

"La frontera?" she asked Angela, not knowing exactly how to ask if she were near the border.

"Treinta minutos al sur."

Good Lord, Felicity exclaimed. *Thirty minutes from the border with Mexico.*

Suddenly, the pickup truck made sense. At some point, someone had transferred Felicity from the hands of swanky ProtoComm. What had Nick said he found out about ProtoComm? The Dark web? The playground of traffickers. Her sudden fear retreated instantly to its safe place inside her mind so she could think about a very real danger. Someone was taking Felicity, dressed in a slinky blue dress and stilettos, across the border into the wild western waste of Mexico. If she hadn't awakened; if she had been tied up; if the truck hadn't come to a stop light...Panic crept into her throat, choking her until her brother's anguish wrenched her back to reality.

"Lissie...Lissie, are you there?"

"Oh, Nick..." The tears came, uncontrolled spasms of terror and pain gripped her, rendering her unable to speak or move for several seconds. Why she reacted this way now she didn't know. Maybe the adrenaline that had kept her moving when she was in danger had finally waned, releasing the flood of emotions that she had needed to suppress before. Still, she had to get a grip.

Angela looked a little frightened but just sat staring uncomfortably at Felicity. The realization that she might scare off her refuge finally made Felicity check her crying and enabled her to answer the anxious calling of her name through the phone.

Her voice still breathless, Felicity finally answered Nick's inquiries.

"I'm okay. I haven't been hurt. I don't know where Brendon is, probably still in Canada. I'm in New Mexico, near the border with Mexico. I'm really okay except I twisted my ankle jumping from the back of a truck."

At the mention of jumping from a truck, Nick unleashed a tirade of curses. "You could have been killed!" he finally finished. "What has Brendon gotten you into?"

Felicity flinched when Nick mentioned Brendon. Whatever

Nick had found, he assumed Brendon's guilt. She couldn't yet broach that subject, so raw from recent injury. *One thing at a time,* she decided.

"Listen, Nick. I need you to do something for me."

"I'm coming to get you is what I'm doing for you."

"No, not yet. Just wait. I can't go home. I don't know what I might bring with me. What I need from you is to send me some money."

"Sis, you are insane! You need me to come get you. I can find some place to hide you."

If she let herself think, she knew Nick was right. Alone and without resources, Felicity stood little chance of survival. Still, going home seemed counter-intuitive. Home would obviously be the first place anyone would look for her, and she didn't want Nick used as leverage. Plus, she didn't really want to share the news of Brendon's infidelity with anyone yet. Anyone who heard the two stories together would conflate the two, and Felicity knew that she had to separate them. Just because Brendon had proved unfaithful didn't make him a criminal. No, Felicity needed to figure out the kidnapping before she delved into her more personal betrayal.

"I'll let you come get me soon," she appeased him, "but I need money now. Once I figure out what I'm doing, I'll tell you where to come. But first send me money. Just a minute," Felicity turned to look at Angela.

"Angela, tiene esta ciudad un..." she fumbled for the word, but decided to just go with the English, "un Western Union?"

"Si, si. Va a abrir mañana a las ocho por la mañana."

Felicity spoke into the phone, "Western Union, Nick. Quido, New Mexico." She could have used apps on her phone to pay for most things, but apps came from bank accounts or credit cards, and those could be tracked or canceled. She wanted cash.

"Necesito pedir dos cosas," Felicity turned back to Angela. "Podría mi hermano mandar un poquito de dinero en su nombre para mi. Podemos pagarle algo a Usted. Y podría dormirme aquí solo por una noche."

Could Felicity have the money sent to Angela's name? Less chance of tracing Felicity through the money. And could she stay the night with Angela? Angela seemed to seriously consider the requests.

"El dinerito, si. Esta bien. Pero, mi esposo va a regresar..."

Angela trailed off uncertainly.

Angela's husband. Felicity hadn't thought of that. And if Angela didn't want Felicity there with her husband, then Felicity didn't want to be there. Undaunted, Felicity instructed Nick on what to do. Felicity felt a hint of confidence return to her as she ordered around her baby brother. "Okay, listen, Nick. The bank opens at 8:00 tomorrow morning. Please go as early as possible and send me as much money as you can spare. Any idea what that will be?"

"I have a couple K in my savings. That would be no problem."

Felicity sighed in relief, certain that such a sum would support her for more than enough time to make a decision. After working out the details with Angela of the how, when, and where, Felicity communicated the details to Nick.

"That's perfect. Thanks, little bro," she smiled, letting herself accept the relief that welled gently in her chest. She had no overarching solutions, but for the next few hours, she had a plan.

"You're not-so-little bro. Big enough to beat the hell out of anyone who wants to hurt my big sis," he promised dangerously. Even so, Felicity grinned widely at his protectiveness.

"Of course, you are," she agreed. "Nick?" Felicity grew serious again. "Don't hang out at my house anymore. Take the dog to your apartment and forget the plants. It's just not safe for you to be there." Then, ignoring his protests, she ended the conversation.

She turned to Angela to beg for some sort of resolution about the sleeping arrangements.

"Yo puedo dormirme en uno de las casitas a fuera. O si tiene usted un poquito de dinero, puedo ir a un hotel."

Though Felicity didn't really relish the thought of sleeping in one of the barns outside, it beat the alternative of sleeping on the ground in a ditch, in a slinky dress and stilettos. Angela crossed over to a cabinet that hung on one of the walls. Opening it, she pulled out a can, rusted with age, its label long faded, and she took from it a small wad of bills.

"Es todo que tengo."

All she has? Felicity balked, realizing that the small number of bills were also small denominations. When she had finished counting, Felicity had eight $5 bills. Forty dollars for a very cheap hotel. *It'll do,* she thought. Unfortunately, the idea of going back into the black night, which had been obscured further by the furious sandstorm that raged, caused Felicity to quiver with fear.

Timidly, she looked up at Angela, the insecurity apparent on Felicity's face.

"Si es possible," Felicity began haltingly, "No quiero salir sola."

Felicity didn't think she could make herself go back out into the dark, alone and unprotected. Her ridiculous clothes made her feel all the more vulnerable – as if she didn't feel exposed enough – and Felicity held no confidence in her ability to find her way around town in the dark. Angela nodded, sighed, and surprised Felicity by calling out to someone in a loud voice.

"Eulogio!" the woman called. "Eulogio, ven acá!"

A child, not young but maybe barely in his teens, appeared from nowhere out of the door through which Angela had gotten the drink.

"I couldn't..." Felicity began to protest.

"Eulogio, venga con esta mujer al hotel a la esquina de Main y Calle Tercer."

"Señora," Angela now addressed Felicity, "Eulogio va a ir con Usted al hotel. Por la mañana, el y yo vamos a regresar a su cuarto así podemos ir al banco."

Felicity really didn't know what to say. This woman had paid for her hotel room, sent her adolescent son out into the night with a stranger, and agreed to help that stranger get some much-needed money. Although Felicity's faith in all Mankind had been shaken in the past few days, she couldn't yet dismiss any possibility of good. Angela would receive no reward for her kind deeds, save what Providence gifted her. Even so small a glimpse of hopefulness helped Felicity smother her ever smoldering fears and, as Eulogio closed the hotel room door behind him, Felicity felt herself succumbing to sleepiness. When her head reached the pillow, darkness once again engulfed her mind, but this time, the darkness of respite.

Chapter 12

I've started to see that God doesn't necessarily give answers; he gives strength. – Felicity's Journal, March 31

Esa es una mujer poderosa. Nunca confundas amabilidad con debilidad. – Esmeralda's conversation with Carlos after they helped Felicity Miller

Early morning, March 21

A light streaming in through the flimsy white shade roused Felicity from her fitful slumber. Dreams had riddled her sleep, causing her to wake feeling only slightly more rested than when she had fallen into the uncomfortable bed. Though the sun had not risen, its glow offered her a shrouded view of the room around her – the outline of the curtained window, the night stand, the bedside lamp, the television across the room.

For several seconds, she strained her eyes to acclimate them to the sparse light. After a moment, forms grew a little more distinct, and she started to push down the covers to get out of bed. She froze the motion almost instantly and smothered a cry of terror. Just inside the room, his silhouette barely visible against the crack of light from the door, stood a man. Felicity's mind whirled with options. Should she pretend to be still asleep? Should she grab the lamp and wield it as a weapon against the uninvited guest? Should she speak and find out the visitor's identity?

When she heard his voice, it awakened both hope and terror in her chest, and Felicity held her breath as she remembered the words. *I told you I would find you,* came her last memory of Jase. Once she had pulled the blanket back up to her neck, she found that she couldn't move.

For the next few minutes, she had to force herself to remain aware of her surroundings as she pressed her leaden limbs to respond. The blue tint of moonlight filtered through the thin, gauzy curtains and filled the room. Not yet day, she realized. She stopped her struggle against her paralysis, confused by the loss of time.

Hadn't the sun shone in a moment before? In the moonlight, Felicity could just see a reflective sheen across Jase's eyes, and she tried to read their expression. Certainly, he did not seem malicious. As he crossed the room and bent over her reclining body, her mind screamed for her to be afraid, but her body still did not react – not even when Jase leaned down to her, placing his cheek against hers and caressing her hair with his hand. It could have been strange, invasive, but instead it was familiar and right. Though she could see him and hear him, she could not feel any warmth when his lips touched her skin.

When Jase rose, Felicity heard a sound from behind him, and she became vaguely aware of Brendon's cold expression glaring at her over Jase's shoulder; of Brendon's frigid, angry face peering down just as it had that night.

Jase placed himself defensively between Felicity and Brendon, an action which infuriated Brendon further. With murder in his eye, Brendon cleared the distance from the door in two steps, quickly sliding between Jase and Felicity. Her confusion overtook her momentarily, and the images dancing before her eyes blurred into meaninglessness.

When she again became aware, Jase lay unconscious on the floor at Brendon's feet. Brendon stalked to the bed, lifting Felicity's still immobile body up into his arms. *Just leave me alone!* she screamed silently. *Why can't you just let me be! Why do you hate me so much!*

'*It has nothing to do with you,*" Brendon insisted.

When he stepped through the doorway of the small room, Felicity found herself inexplicably in their cabin near Canmore, and she realized that the fight, Jase's kiss, Brendon's interference, all of it – Felicity dreamed. *Thank God,* she panted, though she still fought against the paralysis. She couldn't wake.

She watched Brendon with new eyes, a spectator in hope of finding out what her mind really had determined about the situation. After laying her on their bed, Brendon bent down to her, and mimicked Jase's affection, cheek to cheek, the caress, the kiss. With Brendon, though, Felicity felt the distinct burn of his lips on her skin. The pulsing light in Brendon's eyes sent a terrified shiver through Felicity, finally freeing her limbs and wrenching her awake.

Felicity glanced out the real window, realizing that the night hovered somewhere between its depth and its end. Her heart raced and her mind whirred with the questions that she had repressed but that her mind had revisited through slumber. Was Brendon as evil as he seemed? Certainly, her dream had denied it. Was Jase? The dream offered no answer, only a suspicion of what Brendon thought. Of what Felicity felt. If Jase really came to help her, would she accept what he offered? She knew Jase's complicity in the kidnapping. She only suspected Brendon's. Of course, she had very credible reasons to doubt everything about Brendon, so she had no qualms about distrusting him.

Her eyes flitted nervously around the room, irrationally expecting Brendon or Jase to show up, or even the tan man from the party. When she became fully conscious, Felicity remembered that she was in the middle of nowhere, and no one knew her location. Felicity lay back in the bed, staring at the ceiling.

Though she wanted to lie around and ponder the meaning of the dreams, she knew how thoroughly she needed her sleep. She couldn't put it down, though. Why had the dream Brendon taken her to their cabin? Why had she felt Brendon's lips and not Jase's? Awake, Felicity had no trouble remembering the feel of Jase's fingers on her skin, and the memory brought chills to her spine. Maybe because Brendon was a very concrete danger, and Jase was an image of rescue with little substance.

It wasn't the memories that disturbed her if she thought about it. It wasn't even the gaps in her memory. If she analyzed the situation, she would have said the gaps were no different than how her memory always worked – patchwork pieces of life's timeline and tapestry.

Instead, what really disturbed her was that her mind told her she should remember the gaps, that somehow every instant of her experience had significance, and if she couldn't remember something, it would hurt her. And how each vivid memory wore a jagged lambent outline, a shard that had so obviously been ripped from a whole – a whole that, if she could piece it together, would explain why her life had ended so suddenly and without explanation.

Felicity abruptly stopped the thoughts. She did not have time to wander down useless paths of fancy. Brendon wasn't hers anymore, not unless she misunderstood the situation, and even then, not unless he completely altered his life. Jase was irrelevant, an imagined fancy, either of hers or of his. Either way, not terra firma. For now, Felicity was terra firma. She would just have to do. Having no idea what the morning would hold, Felicity forced herself to close her eyes, and surprisingly, she fell into a dreamless slumber.

Though she should have expected it, the knock on her door sent Felicity scurrying across the room and into the tiny bathroom in fear. Pausing, she breathed deeply and forced herself to be reasonable. *It's Angela and her son,* she reasoned. Still, she crept cautiously toward the door, unable to suppress a shudder. Peering through the peephole, Felicity prepared to see Angela and Eulogio. When she saw a familiar male face instead, she froze. *Peter, Patrick, something with a "P,"* Felicity tried to recall. So much from that night seemed lost in a mist, completely swallowed in fog. Her strange distrust of the tan man had definitely deepened to terror, though, and she felt her knees weaken for a moment.

Without prelude, the man turned and hurried away. Almost on his heels, Angela and Eulogio arrived. Felicity closed her eyes, able to breathe again. Before they could knock, Felicity opened the door and pulled them inside. Angela could see the anxiety on Felicity's face.

"Que pasó?" she queried, looking around the room nervously.

Felicity's stomach clutched. Was she putting Angela and Eulogio at risk just by asking them for help? Perhaps, she realized, but unfortunately, Felicity couldn't allow herself to worry too much about some nebulous threat to Angela. Surely the woman was no threat to ProtoComm or to Brendon. Felicity would soon leave Angela and her son behind, and Felicity did not imagine that anyone would look twice at the poor, Hispanic woman afterwards. When Felicity left, so did the danger. Felicity, on the other hand, would carry danger with her, and she wanted to hash out a way back to see her own children and leave the danger behind.

"Nada," she finally answered Angela. "Estoy bien.," Felicity breathed deeply, "Al banco, por favor." Felicity calmed her mind and, glancing both ways down the hotel balcony to assure herself the man had gone, she steadied herself to walk calmly out ahead of Angela.

The bank building lay two blocks south of her hotel, and the hurried walk proved uneventful. As soon as Felicity had the money, she took a bank envelope and, turning away from Angela, stuck two fifties into it. She then sealed it and gave it to the woman, instructing her to open only when she arrived home - Felicity didn't want

Angela to refuse the money out of some unnecessary sense of nobility. Felicity could never really repay the debt she owed to the poor woman and her son. With the thought of the little, tan man in her mind, Felicity took her leave from her rescuers. She reached timidly toward Angela and bestowed on her a gentle hug. Then, she mussed Eulogio's hair before she walked away. She didn't allow herself to look back to her refuge. Instead, she stalked on with intention.

The money bought her independence, and that independence bought her some relief. Felicity sauntered more confidently, despite her disheveled appearance, to a teller at the bank and asked where she could find the nearest clothing store.

"Well," the woman responded, a slight Mexican accent softening her words, "we really don't have much in Quido. We usually go to Las Cruces for that." Then eyeing Felicity ruefully, the teller acceded, "You could try Juanita's. It's two blocks down by the coffee shop."

Even now, Felicity's heart leaped at the word coffee. Not that all of her problems would be solved, but to have a pair of jeans and a cup of coffee would feel fairly close to heaven at that moment. She abruptly remembered one more thing. "Anywhere I can get a cell phone?"

"Sure. We got One Stop Cell Shop over a block south of Juanita's." Felicity guessed that everything extant lay within a few blocks in a town this small.

"Thanks," Felicity beamed, and going barefoot rather than wear stilettos, she stumbled out of the bank into the baking Southwestern sun, glad she had found herself there in March before the summer heat had hit. Recalling herself, she glanced nervously around her, searching for some sign of the tan man. She saw none so turned in the direction indicated by the bank teller and strolled as casually as she could in a blue evening gown down the two blocks to Juanita's.

Juanita's was not Felicity's cup of tea, but she guessed it fit well with lying as close to the border as it lay. Stereotypically, the store held racks of bright, colorful dresses with full skirts. Probably intended for tourists. All were made from a frilly crepe-type material which made sense for the oppressive heat. Juanita's seemed almost more of a costume shop than a clothing store.

Thankfully, she did find jeans, though her unusually tall

frame required her to buy a size too small – they didn't carry a long size. She settled on a white shirt with billowy sleeves, the least costumey she could find. Stepping into the dressing room, she quickly slid the impractical dress from her shoulders with relief, stepping into the jeans and slipping the shirt over her head. Her hand brushed against the beads that still framed her neck. *Betrayal beads,* she snickered, covering her sickness with an attempt at humor. Remembering the moment he gave them to her, she simmered. He had bought them for her as an afterthought when he was shopping for Amy.

Unlatching the necklace, she compressed it into her palm, sliding from the dressing room and over to the register to pay for her purchase. She did not notice any visible trash can within the store, and she would not ask the woman to dispose of such an obviously expensive item. Instead, she stepped from the small shop, determined to trash the memorial to Brendon as soon as she could.

Again glancing cautiously up and down the street, Felicity began to head next door to the coffee shop. After only a few steps, a voice arrested her movement. She hurriedly shoved the beads into her jeans pocket and concentrated on what she was hearing. The voice held nothing familiar, but its words held a very personal meaning to her.

"She has contacted someone. They know where she is," the tenor voice stated. "The blond? No, but we have contacts on her team, and they've proven very helpful. Don't tell him. No, Bill doesn't trust him completely, but I am to finish this job for him."

Felicity peered around the corner of Juanita's and spied the characteristic beige shirt, khaki pants, and brown shoes of the tan man as he stood, his back to her, still speaking into the phone. Though Felicity could not discern all of his meaning, she felt certain that he referred to her recent call. If so, how did he know she had called Nick?

"So, he still doesn't know what happened to her? Will he find out? I don't want to get crucified for this." Standing in indecision, Felicity considered. She would have loved to be back at Angela's little respite instead of anywhere near the tan man. Had he followed her from Canmore? Had he been the passenger in the truck that had brought her to Quido? Unwilling to stand exposed any longer, Felicity retreated back into Juanita's, apologizing to the salesperson for forgetting to buy shoes.

"Oh, you poor thing. I can see you didn't bring the right shoes for walking," the woman smiled sympathetically.

Petrified, Felicity couldn't force her tongue to function again. Keeping her eyes on the front store window, she sidled to the small rack of shoes. She realized that she had only a slim chance of finding her size, and she realized that she really didn't care. If she could avoid the man outside until she got a cell phone and a rental car, she would drive shoeless wherever she needed to.

The saleslady, Esmeralda, noticed the direction of Felicity's gaze. She must also have noticed the fear on Felicity's countenance. "Um, what size do you need?" Esmeralda asked, still watching the trajectory of Felicity's eyes.

"A nine," Felicity stuttered. She heard the sound of her words as if from a far distance, and she felt certain that she looked stoned.

"Oh, I don't think we have nines right now," Esmeralda offered placidly. "Um, maybe an eight and a half sandal?"

"Sure, that'll be fine," Felicity muttered.

Just then, Felicity met Esmeralda's gaze for a moment as the woman finally turned away from the window. Felicity watched through a crack in the shoe rack as Esmeralda returned her eyes to the storefront where Felicity's pursuer strolled slowly in front of the store. Rushing to the front door, Esmeralda pulled out her keys and began to lock the door. The man hurried to her, looking a bit irritated, and Felicity's heart thudded heavily against her ribs.

"Que paso?" the man demanded angrily through the glass.

"Estamos cerrados," Esmeralda retorted through the door in the rich, beautiful accent from the deep south of Mexico.

"¿Cerrados? ¿Porque?" The man pointed to the sign denoting the store hours.

Closed, Felicity sighed in relief.

"No tengo ayuda. Necesito almorzar cuando puedo," she shrugged.

The man looked as if he wanted to resort to violence, but then he seemed to relent, wandering slowly toward the coffee shop. He glanced covertly back toward Esmeralda several times, but she didn't unlock the door.

"I don't know what happened to you," Esmeralda declared returning to Felicity, "but that man looked dangerous. I can see it in his eyes. We have a few men like that who come through here sometimes. I let you out the back, and you go straight to the police."

As soon as the man had walked away, Felicity's breath had calmed, and the world had returned to its proper perspective. It seemed that she had grown somewhat accustomed to the fear, and her heart slowed more rapidly than she would have predicted.

The police? Felicity considered. Strangely, she hadn't considered the possibility. Her mind was reeling from the revelation of the affair. Once she awoke on the side of the road, she hadn't taken the time to do anything but run from danger. She had only once in her life called the police, to report the crash near her house, and that had not been when she was in danger. Somehow, strangely, it wasn't her first instinct.

Once she went to the police, there would be no turning back. She didn't know exactly what she would tell them that would make them believe her. She had passed out with one set of people. She had woken in a truck. She had no evidence of that fact. Did she think Brendon, or Bill if he was involved, couldn't make up a believable enough story? *She drank a lot. I lost sight of her when I was called to a meeting, and I've been looking for her ever since! It's just now been 24 hours, and I knew I couldn't report her until she had been missing a while.*

Brendon Miller was certainly a liar. Brendon would do whatever served his purposes. Brendon may or may not have engineered a plot to have her kidnapped and sold into human slavery. And Bill Henry, arguably as intelligent and definitely as unscrupulous as Brendon, was involved. They would have no problem covering their tracks.

When the vision flashed before Felicity's eyes, chills erupted on her skin. Briel gripping the hand of the detective in Phoenix. *The extremely wealthy are beholden to no one, except those who hold their secrets.* If Briel helped guard the secrets of men like Bill Henry and Brendon, maybe going to the police was opposite to Felicity's interests.

Of all the people she considered appealing to, the police were probably the least concerning – less power therefore less necessity for corruption – but even so, if she went to the police and she was wrong, there would be horrible ramifications. For her and for the kids, especially in a divorce. No police. Not just yet. Maybe if she could find out more.

What she really wanted was to get her giant of a brother on

the phone and have him come act as bodyguard, and if Brendon had been the only consideration, she certainly would have. ProtoComm, though, brought a much more monumental element to the mix. Nicholas Alexander, colossal or not, was not as colossal as ProtoComm.

"Thanks," she finally offered noncommittally. "I'll look up their number at the phone company."

"You're sure?" the woman questioned skeptically.

"I'm sure," Felicity dismissed. "The cell phone shop?"

Without further discussion, Esmeralda turned and paced to the back of her store. Luckily, Juanita's backed on a small docking yard that it shared with the cell phone store, so Felicity wouldn't have to venture to the street. Esmeralda knew the owners of the cell phone store well, so she left her front door locked and accompanied Felicity to the back door of the phone shop.

"Soy Esmeralda," she responded to the inquiry when she knocked. After the salesman answered, Esmeralda began a soliloquy most of which Felicity didn't understand. At the end Esmeralda told him, "Este hombre aparece peligroso. Ella está sola. Comprendes?"

"Si, si. Entiendo. Hasta luego. A las seis?" the man asked with a smile.

"Si, a las seis." Esmeralda smirked. "Hasta luego."

Turning to Felicity, the cell phone salesman - his nametag read "Carlos" - declared, "Esme said you need a phone. Your's been stolen or something?"

"Something like that."

"Okay, well, what do you want?"

Felicity started to say she wanted the cheapest thing he had, but then she realized that she didn't know where she intended to go, and she needed maps and data to help her find her way.

"Um, could I get the cheapest thing you have with maps?"

"You don't want a plan? It's pretty expensive if you don't buy a plan."

"Oh," she lamented, and her expression became so glum that the man seemed to take pity on her.

"Look," he said, "I give you my employee discount. That's like forty or thirty percent off."

"I can't let you..."

He interrupted, "Hey, look, missus. I like Esme a lot. She likes you. You let me do this for you, then she likes me. We all win, okay? So, just say yes."

"Okay, yes," Felicity chuckled. Once again, the generosity of a few seemed in such stark contrast to the treachery of others. "May I use a phone to call my phone company? They'll need to switch my service."

"No problem."

Carlos remained in the back with Felicity through the duration of their conversation, keeping her hidden in the stock room. Obviously, something Esmeralda had told him communicated that he should keep their business low key. Felicity began to relax. Ironically, she had almost foregone asking for help; how differently her day would have unfolded had she tried to go it alone! Taking a deep breath, Felicity forced herself to relish the moment of calm. Who knew how few such moments she would have in the near future?

Steeling herself, she dialed the customer service for her phone company and began the security procedures for replacing her lost phone. After keying in her number, Felicity heard a pleasant female voice. "Hello, welcome to Janus Cellular," it crooned. "May I have your name please?"

"Yes, thanks. It's Felicity Miller."

"Could I please have the account holder's name and phone number?"

Felicity relayed Brendon's number and identifying information.

"Um, I'm sorry. That doesn't match our records."

Felicity felt the blood flush her cheeks, irritated at the bureaucracy ubiquitous in large corporations. Why would Brendon have changed the phone setup? *Oh,* she realized. She wracked her brain for some idea of how Brendon might have listed the account, but she could come up with nothing. She didn't want to sign up for a new plan and lose her number.. "I am on the account, right?" Felicity reasoned with the woman. "It's my phone. I can give you any information you might need about it, even phone calls I've made. Isn't there some other way I could pass through security?"

Felicity heard a long pause, and she prayed that the service rep would have pity.

"Well, let's see if you can answer a few questions for me. Maybe there's something I can figure in the process." The woman bombarded Felicity with several account-specific questions, which

Felicity answered correctly, and the interview finished with, "Well, I can't change the phone for you unless you know the main account holder," she paused again. "But I can give you a hint."

"Thanks so much," Felicity gushed, relief apparent in her tone.

"This is a corporate account, right?"

"No..." Felicity began, but trailed off. A flurry of thoughts rose like yesterday's dust storm. Brendon had changed the account. Why leave her name and number functional, though? Probably he wanted to track her number as a precaution. Felicity felt sick. Should she forgo the phone completely? Though she had no determined destination, she knew with certainty that she must leave Quido and the tan man behind her as soon as possible.

"Ma'am?" the voice on the phone repeated for Felicity didn't know how many times. "Ma'am, are you there?"

"I'm here," Felicity admitted. She wiped her palms on the legs of her jeans.

"Do you know the company's name?"

Resignedly, Felicity drew a breath to answer. She had no choice; she needed to get out of Quido fast. She would figure out how to change the phone later. "ProtoComm," Felicity almost whispered, her fear and fury stifling the strength of her voice.

"Um, that's right. And the contact name for the account?" the woman urged.

Felicity wavered. The woman had said Brendon didn't hold title on the account, so who did? She cleared her throat, trying to speak confidently.

"Bill Henry," she declared, suddenly certain of the answer.

"Right, and the password?"

Well, at least now she felt certain. The inconspicuous CEO, the mild-mannered politician with the veneer of civility, had signed off on her kidnapping. Signed off and, if she interpreted Nick's words correctly, probably spearheaded.

For the first time, the scope of the forces coming against her hit Felicity, and she felt a hysterical laugh bubbling to her lips. Who would ever have thought that Felicity Miller could be on the wrong end of a plot involving so many people willing to commit crimes against her? It seemed so unlikely as to be near an impossibility. *This isn't really happening,* her mind tried to deny. Before she started imagining spies and blackmail again, she shrugged out of her dissociation. No such luck that she lay hallucinating in some sickness-induced delirium that had manufactured the entire situation.

Felicity shook her head and refocused on the current conversation. She tried thinking through logical options for a password that would pertain to ProtoComm. She tried simple words first: communications, fortune500, BillHenry. The possibilities were endless. Maybe something specific to Brendon.

When she had the idea, the hysterical laugh she had before repressed finally escaped her lips. She couldn't help but see the irony - if she were right.

"Calvario," Felicity finally exclaimed. The representation of Brendon's philanthropic heart. And now Felicity realized, the possible source of his least philanthropic endeavor. Calvary. Of course, she could be wrong. Bill could have made the password and used some company standard. If Brendon had chosen, though...

Though the woman had no doubt felt shocked to hear the manic laugh on the other end of the phone, she replied with total composure. "That's right."

Relief mingle with anxiety when Felicity heard, "We can transfer your phone. It will take about 15 minutes to update the software."

"Thank you so much," Felicity offered sincerely.

"My pleasure."

Hanging up the phone, Felicity turned back to the storeroom door. She would unpack her epiphany later. Now, she had to make at least a short-term plan. She probably had a while before anyone noticed she had reactivated her phone. As long as she could avoid the tan man, she might get a couple of hours ahead of them and reach a large city before ProtoComm started searching for her. Maybe the guys from the truck hadn't yet reported that they had lost her.

Carlos returned from the front of the store where he had been helping someone else purchase a phone.

"So, did you get that all worked out? I can't comp you a service plan *and* a phone."

"Yeah, thanks. I got it. Now where do I get a rental car?" Suddenly she looked chagrined. "Oh...I don't have any ID." The realization also meant that she couldn't get another phone plan even if she wanted to.

After a moment's thought, Carlos smirked casually at

Felicity. "I actually think I can help you with that," he began, startling Felicity. She squinted at him quizzically. I got friends. A buddy who works rental cars. I'll have him deliver a car to you here, in my name, and you can just take it wherever you need to go and drop it off there."

"I can't let you do that," Felicity protested. "What if I can't turn it in? It'll cost you a fortune. And if I get pulled over driving a rental car in your name..."

"I'll take out the insurance. And my friend will cover for me," he responded, a knowing smile gracing his features.

"But what if the men who are looking for me..."

"Look, I've sold cell phones to a hundred drug dealers, not because I want to, but because they come to me. I have friends enough to stay safe. No one is going to come to my barrio and mess with me, I promise. Just let me get you a car," he insisted. "I won't let you say no."

"Okay," she finally agreed. His insistence melted her resolve.

As she waited for word from Carlos that she had a car, she considered her next step. Her first course of action would be to call Nick again; he must be going crazy. She glanced at the employee clock – 1:45 p.m. She had promised she would call in the morning, but the appearance of the tan man had pushed her commitment to the extremities of her consciousness. Now, she realized that her brother would be busting a gut.

After what seemed an eternity, Felicity exhaled as Carlos reentered the back room, smiling and extending his hand.

"Come on," he grinned.

His reason for mirth escaped her until she saw the shiny black convertible in front of his store. *That's inconspicuous,* she sighed resignedly, and determined to trade the eye-catching vehicle for a more modest one if she could find a way. Still, she thanked Carlos sincerely, promising to return the car to a rental shop as soon as she could. She could not predict where the car would take her, but she had little hope that she would enjoy the ride, despite its superficial appeal.

Chapter 13

An identity is bigger than a single action. Everyone lies, but you are
*   defined by your lies. That is what makes you a liar. –*
Felicity's unsent letter to Brendon, March 30

Now is the dramatic moment of fate, Watson, when you hear a step
*   upon the stair which is walking into your life, and you know*
*   not whether for good or ill.* – Sir Arthur Conan Doyle

Midday, March 22
        Glancing in her rearview mirror, Felicity sighed in relief as she left the bucolic border town and the strange tan man behind. At least, she hoped she had left the man. The terrain did not allow for much concealment, so Felicity began to breathe a little easier when, after ten minutes, she still saw no sign of him.
        After the allotted 15 minutes, she picked up her new phone and dialed Nick, preparing herself for both his fear and his fury.
        "Felicity?" the panicked voice bellowed into the phone.
        "Nick, I am so sorry!"
        "You better be! Where in the world have you been?" anguish tempered the irritation in Nick's tone.
        "Nick, I'm okay. I just ran into a...." she paused, not wanted to cause Nick more anxiety, "a complication."
        "Don't play with me, Lissie. I've been going out of my mind."
        "Look, a guy followed me. Someone from ProtoComm. It just took me some time to ditch him."
        "But you did?" he quizzed, relief obvious in his tone.
        "I've been looking over my shoulder for about 20

miles now, and I haven't seen any sign of him."

"How can you be sure? This is really important."

"Nick, it's pretty flat here. All I see are fields, grass, and yucca plants for miles."

Nick hadn't asked why she would want to avoid someone from ProtoComm. Either he had put two and two together, or he knew some new information. Felicity waited for her brother's response, but he didn't speak for several minutes. When his voice came, he sounded imploring. "Lissie, come home. I know I can't do much, but...." he paused again, "You know I'm pretty competent to take care of you. I don't want you to be alone right now."

"So, what, Nick? I come home and put you in danger?"

"Lissie, I wouldn't be in the same danger you are." He sounded sure.

"What are you talking about, Nick. You think ProtoComm will develop a conscience when it comes to hurting you?"

Nick hesitated, and when he spoke his tone was sardonic, "Well, for one thing, if they do anything to me, a nasty virus will spread in their computer systems within the week. It's going to happen eventually either way, but I'll use it as a bargaining chip until I have you back."

She scrunched her face in exasperation. "Nick, why would you do that? You don't want to go up against these people."

Felicity heard Nick let out a deep sigh. "Yes, Felicity, I do."

She didn't know what to say, so she waited.

"Remember how I told you about the password protected files on Brendon's computer?"

"Yes."

"Lissie, ProtoComm is into some pretty bad stuff. Um, really bad."

"You told me that before, but I didn't want to listen to you," she admitted. "I'm pretty sure I get it now. Tell me what you found."

"Well, for one, they're involved in human trafficking."

Though she had suspected, the confirmation made Felicity feel physically sick. She pulled to the shoulder and waited for her heart to start again. Opening the door, Felicity leaned over the side of the car, her empty stomach clutching for something to expel.

Now she knew for sure. Someone had sent her to Mexico to become a slave.

All of her life, Felicity had feared death, not because she worried about her eternal soul, just because it would prove so difficult and inconvenient for those around her. She had children to take care of, her parents relied on her, her husband counted on her steadiness, or so she had thought. For the first time, Felicity pictured a fate that felt much worse than the death she had feared – a fear much more personal. She knew what happened to women who ended up in the modern-day slave trade.

"Lissie? Lissie?" she heard distantly, and she recognized that the note of panic had returned to Nick's voice. "Please, answer me!".

"I'm okay!" Her voice choked on the lie.

"Is it ProtoComm? Did the man find you?"

"No, Nick, no," Felicity assured him. "I'm just really upset. That was just really hard to hear." She paused, not quite able to continue. "That's why I'm here," she finally whispered. "I had my suspicions, but you confirmed it for me. I was being taken to the slave trade." A fresh wave of nausea followed the words from her mouth.

"Lissie," he comforted, but she couldn't respond.

She made no reply for several minutes, finally causing Nick to call her name again.

"Lissie?"

"Yeah, Nick. Um, I need to think. I'm gonna have to call you back."

"Wait, Lissie? You need to know..." he seemed reluctant. "ProtoComm seems to have a lot of side businesses. And don't get mad at me, Felicity – I'm just the messenger - but Brendon has his hands in at least several of them. I can't get to all the information yet, the material is behind serious security, but what I've already found is shocking. He has been monitoring a lot of activity, maybe managing it."

"Why would I be mad at you, Nick? There are several things I'll be telling you about Brendon when I'm ready. Not much you tell me could shock me. Just keep talking." Might as well get all the trauma over with at once.

"Well...it looks like drug smuggling, slave trade, and illegal weapons trade to name a few. I'm not sure what all the technical terms mean, but I think ProtoComm is kind of a middle man. Buyers approach someone named Jack Buckley, and Jack or his people find a supplier. ProtoComm never actually touches any contraband; they just make phone calls, push paper – communications."

Of course. Jack Buckley. And Brendon possibly managing it all.

Every imaginary bulwark which had surrounded Felicity's pretend mundane world had washed away with an ocean of reality, all in the past couple of days. The corruption, to an extent she had never imagined, explained Brendon's deception. She felt something splinter in her heart. How much more could it suffer before it stopped beating altogether? *Maybe that would be the best option,* said a voice in her head. Still, her practiced optimism had scoured her mind for some rationalization, some excuse that would offer an explanation for Brendon and the events of the past few days. Maybe Brendon had started out a better person, or maybe she had never really known her husband.

"Nick, I'm okay. Really." She considered for a moment, drawing a fortifying breath. It wasn't true, exactly, but she had shoved the darker thoughts far enough down that she could ignore them for a while. "Honestly, I'm not sure what I'm going to do. I just know I need to get moving in case the man from before is coming after me. I took the main highway north out of Quido. It won't be hard for him to follow me."

"Then come home, and I'll take care of you."

"Nick, no…I love you. You're the best baby brother ever. For now, I'm safe. Going home is what they'll expect me to do. I'll call you next time I stop for gas or something." Felicity paused. "Don't tell mom and dad. I don't want to bring them or my kids into this until I figure out how to get some help."

"At least call the police."

"I will, just not yet. I have to think. Once I call the police, if they bring ProtoComm into this, there will be no hiding for me. There will be statements and checks for evidence. And who do you think is going to control the evidence? All I have is the two people in Quido, and all they know is that I showed up and asked for help. Brendon has Bill Henry, a powerful company, a slew of witnesses whose livelihoods depend on the company. I haven't really told you what happened exactly, and once I do, you'll understand. But I need to think right now."

Felicity understood the value of the police, but she also understood a lot of other things. She had seen it too many times. Usually, the police did their job. They tried to protect people. Then they sent their evidence to the courts, and all hell broke loose. The liar – whether the accuser or the accused perpetrator – would do what he or she did best: lie.

Lawyers would do their best to get the evidence they wanted in and the evidence of the other guy kept out or misconstrued. The truth wasn't totally irrelevant, just largely. With the right kind of evidence, though, even the best lawyers were stuck facing the truth.

Just fighting the odds to get there was something Felicity could not endure at the moment. She was not ready to be put on the stands and forced to defend her accusations. Suddenly, her stomach turned sour. The thought of being laid bare – in her current state of vulnerability – felt a whole lot like the worst possible violation she could imagine. *Except, of course, slavery,* she corrected.

"I don't like it," Nick admitted, "but I know better than to believe I can change your mind. If I don't hear from you by tomorrow morning, though, I'm coming to look for you."

"Of course," she placated him. "Bye."

Turning back onto the highway, Felicity looked at the clock. 2:25 p.m. The afternoon sun streamed onto her unprotected skin, exposed because of the convertible. Though the wind felt good and the music on the radio soothed her mind, her heart alternated between hollow ice and raging fire. Like a response to her wavering emotions, the terrain began to heave up and down, the foothills to the Rockies starting their gentle undulations. Felicity stopped once in Colorado for gas and something to eat, but her appetite had not yet returned. The never-ending road and the rising moon began to lull her anxiety and cast a trance-inducing hue over the mountains.

Hey you, standing in the road, always doing what you're told, can you help me? the radio requested.

I can't even help myself! she lamented to the unhearing radio.

Hey, you...don't tell me there's no hope at all, it answered.

I'm all alone, betrayed by those who should love me best, in danger, afraid. What hope can I have?

As if in answer to her unspoken demand, Felicity's phone rang. 10:27 p.m.

"Thank God," a familiar deep voice sighed when Felicity answered. "You're alive."

Felicity's hands began to shake making it difficult to maintain control of the wheel. A dozen emotions flitted through her mind, but she suppressed them.

"Jase?" Felicity queried shakily. Her voice failed her as several memories intruded upon her at once. His hands on her when she lay drunk in the chair, his apology, his gentle touch, his reassurances. She couldn't decide if the hollow pit in her stomach drew from the excitement in hearing his voice or her suspicions. He had knowingly laid her in the car that would take her to slavery.

"What do you want?" she barked, her voice cracking on uncertainty.

"Are you kidding?" he scoffed. "I've been sick, waiting to call you, afraid that when I did, you wouldn't answer."

"How did you get my number?" she asked, furious at his feigned concern.

"It's in company records. Not the public level, of course, but insiders can get to it. I have a few privileges at ProtoComm because of my job title."

"Privileges like groping me before you hand me into slavery? I remember, Jase." The heat of her anger mixed with a different fire that rose in Felicity's cheeks as she remembered his hand on her thigh. *What is wrong with me?*

"Liss," his voice was appeasing, "Please let me explain myself."

What made him think he could use an endearment for her name? She considered hanging up on him, but something restrained her.

"I had to do that!" he insisted, urgent persuasion in his tone. "Bill and Brendon were keeping tabs on me. They were literally standing over me." Felicity hissed involuntarily when she heard Brendon's name. "I had to do what I did, but I told you I would come get you."

You had to touch me? she scoffed disbelievingly. "And where are you now?" she accused aloud.

"I couldn't get away, but I paid Perry to stay with you and stop the truck before the men crossed over the border. I figured the further south you were, the harder it would be for Brendon to track you when Perry got you out."

"Got me out?" she interrupted, confused.

"Of course, Liss. Did you think…?" He paused, swallowing obvious incredulity before continuing in a more measured tone. "I couldn't let them sell you into slavery."

Felicity scoffed, "Why would I 'think' anything about you? I don't even know you? You're saying the tan man was trying to help me?"

"The tan man..." Jase chuckled. "I guess that's an apt description. Well, Perry was helping *me*."

Felicity hesitated. Why would she dare believe Jase? "You knew I didn't have my phone. Why would you expect me to answer it?"

Jase paused, "Look, you're on ProtoComm's phone account now, not your own. All I had to do was monitor your number through the website records. I'm the only one who would have expected your phone to show up. They think it's being pirated to some street dealer. As far as they know, you've already been delivered to the buyers."

Felicity swallowed hard. She had to hope he was right about no one else monitoring her.

"Since Perry told me that he had lost you, I've been watching - hoping really - that you might think to buy a new phone. I wasn't sure you would get past the security, but..." he trailed off.

As if to pressure her into accepting him, the sound of his voice awakened the loneliness she had suppressed since she had awakened on the side of the road. Jase's words seemed to line up with circumstance, but Felicity could not justify trusting him.

Still, he had said he would come get her, and though he hadn't come himself, he had ostensibly sent someone. Felicity had even seen that someone. Too, Jase had promised he wouldn't let them hurt her, and somehow, her kidnapping had been so bungled that she was able to escape. How often did that happen? It wasn't proof, but it was circumstantial. He had called her within a few minutes of her cell phone coming online. He could be her monitor, or he could be her savior.

Finally, she realized he had been calling her name. "Yes?" she queried as his voice reached her mind.

"*Permet-moi de venir tu chercher,*" he pleaded.

Could she possibly let him come get her? The clear night sky over Wyoming contrasted with the foggy memory in which she felt Jase's arms lay her gently down into the car. She really didn't want to involve Nick in the danger she would encounter in the near future. From what she could discern, Jase knew enough about dealing with her situation. And she couldn't escape the fact that, if he was as independent as he claimed, he had no self-serving reason to help her. Until a week ago, he hadn't even known her.

You'll be okay. I'll come and get you. I won't let them hurt you. Her memory told her he had spoken in earnest, and her senses told her the same now.

A sudden opposing memory surfaced, and it drew a start contrast in Felicity's mind: Brendon's cold stare as he watched her captors place her into the car. For many years, she had not sensed that much concern from her own husband. As she now knew, people could prove very convincing in a lie. But her mind had new data she could process and hold up against Jase's words. Brendon's waxen words had for many years left her insecure, standing on air when she needed solid ground. The contrast between whatever her instincts were taking in could not have been starker.

When the words left her mouth, though, they did not reflect her growing conviction of his good intentions. Instead, she stuttered, "I…I want to Jase, but I can't." Without waiting for an answer, she ended the call, blowing out a breath that left her flat and bereft.

If she had decided to refuse him, why had she said the words? Why had she acknowledged that she wanted to accept his help? Since she had rejected him, though, her words would matter little. Placing both hands on the wheel, she pressed the pedal to the floor and sped incomprehensibly back toward the scene of her demise.

Chapter 14

I feel like I'm holding on more to a wish than to a hope. - Felicity's
   Journal, April 1

Pre-dawn, March 23
Felicity had made the ten-hour trip into the middle of the
Wyoming wilderness by the time Jase finally called her again. After
her impromptu decision to reject his help, she had continued through
the flat and empty Wyoming prairie, driving into the early morning.
The monotony lulled her senses – she needed sleep.

When she actually answered his call, Jase's voice rang with
surprise, but recovering quickly, he pressed her for a place where he
could meet her. Fortunately for her determination, she really hadn't
even known where she was. "I told you I couldn't accept your help."

"Yet you took my call…"

He was right, of course. "Look, all I know is that I'm on I-25
somewhere in Wyoming. I don't know when the next major town
will show up, so I couldn't even tell you if I wanted to. I'll just crash
for the night in the first town I hit, and maybe I'll answer you again
tomorrow."

He tried to argue with her into stopping somewhere and
waiting for him, but Felicity had several reasons to refuse – not the
least important being that she was exhausted, and falling asleep at
the wheel in the unpopulated flatlands of Wyoming would be
disastrous. She had already seen enough disaster; she wouldn't push
herself. So, she pulled sleepily into the Lakeside Hotel in Glendo,
grateful that it remained open late enough for her to check in.

As Felicity undressed to shower, she wished she'd had the
presence of mind to buy an extra set of clothes in Quido. She didn't
relish the idea of putting her already-worn clothes back on, but
Lakeside hotel was not the kind of establishment that provided a
robe and slippers. It was nice enough that she didn't fear having
prostitutes or drug dealers for neighbors, but it was very rustic and
simple, albeit clean.

They *did* provide cheap shampoo and soap, and Felicity spent several minutes letting the hot water stream evenly over her sore muscles, washing her hair thoroughly several times to remove all the sand and grit from the sandstorm two days before. She almost hated to leave the warm massage of the shower, but she abruptly felt exhausted. If she didn't lie down soon, she would collapse.

Reluctantly, she turned off the spigot and stepped out onto the bath mat, grabbing a scratchy towel from the nearby rack. She folded her jeans and left them sitting on the nightstand near her bed.

She thought about switching on the TV to lull her to sleep with mindless drivel but decided that she would rather have total quiet so she could hear if Perry came back. Though Jase had assured her that Perry worked for him, she remembered Perry's angry look from the store and decided that she didn't trust Jase's recommendation enough to let Perry near her when she was by herself.

Of course, the silence grew eerie before sleep overtook her. As a result, Felicity's mind exaggerated every noise, filling them with meaning they did not possess. The subsequent adrenaline rushes prevented her falling into a peaceful slumber despite the physical exhaustion that overwhelmed her. Once or twice during the night, someone strode loudly past her room causing her to jerk awake with sudden fear. She sat up, covers pulled up around her, watching the handle to her door to see if it moved, watching the window for someone's prying eyes. Nothing materialized into real problems. Finally, about an hour before dawn, Felicity reached a state of fatigue that pulled her unwillingly into dreamless repose.

When she awoke several hours later, the sun streamed in at a steep angle. Looking at the clock, she realized that she had wasted almost half of the day making up for her sleepless night. 11 a.m. *Nick,* she remembered with chagrin. Nick would probably want to kill her if he found out she was still alive and hadn't called him yet. Scrounging on the bedside table, Felicity found the phone and swiped it open. Six missed calls! She hoped Nick hadn't yet called the police or FBI or something.

Scrolling to his number, she hit send. He answered on the first ring.

"What in the world have you been doing that you couldn't pick up the phone when I called?" he yelled into the phone not even waiting for her greeting.

"Hi, Nick."

"Hi?" he continued his rant. "Do you know how close I came to calling the police? If Briel hadn't dissuaded me, I would have already filed a missing person's report!"

"Nick, I am so, so sorry. I really don't have any excuse except that I have been sleeping all day. It was a rough night." *Why is he still seeing Briel?*

His anger turned to concern, "Did something else happen?"

"No," she answered quickly. "No, I just couldn't sleep! Every noise sounded like a footstep. Every creak was a hand on my door. My brain couldn't rest until 5 or 6 this morning." Felicity sighed.

Nick didn't respond immediately. Felicity knew him well enough to know that he either wanted to gather his ire before the attack or collect himself before letting her off the hook.

He chose the latter. "Lissie, I'm so sorry I freaked. You know I've been panicked."

"I know. That's why I called you as soon as I woke up. I've only been awake for about two minutes."

"I'm sure you needed sleep. I mean, you've been through hell."

"Why did Briel talk you out of calling the police?"

Nick said nothing.

"Nick?"

"Lissie, I am trying to cling to reality in all of this, but really, things are beginning to get more and more unreal."

Breathing deeply, Felicity readied herself for some equivocation. Still, she had to ask. "What are you talking about? What does this have to do with Briel?"

"Brendon hired Briel, ostensibly to protect you."

Now it was Felicity's turn to be silent. She didn't have energy to drag things out of her brother. As far as Falicity was concerned, Briel's purpose had been to prepare and manage the "target." Keeping her around, whether she posed an immediate threat to Nick or not, seemed like a horrible idea. Still, without going through every detail, she didn't know how to convince her brother.

"I don't know why Brendon really hired her, but Lissie, Briel wants to help you. She mostly did intelligence gathering for him, but she's amazing at physical protection, too. You just need to tell her where you are."

"Um, Nick?" Felicity contemplated how she could make him back off. "I don't want Briel to come help me. Why would I ever trust someone who had worked for Brendon?"

"Listen, I've seen her credentials, I've been on the company intranet. Briel is legitimate; she's freelance. Whatever Brendon hired her for, she wouldn't have involved herself in the crime aspect of his business. And she's not convinced Brendon is involved in thise."
Company intranet? Not ProtoComm?

Felicity wasn't persuaded, but she redirected her little brother. "All the same, Nick, I haven't decided what I'm going to do, so I can't give you an answer yet. Let me think about it and get back to you."

"Just don't think too long. I can't shake the feeling that the closer you get to Canada, the closer you are to peril. I think you're being stupid."

Felicity was grateful that her brother didn't possess her husband's domineering characteristics because, as tired as she still felt, she didn't know how long she could have resisted his entreaties. Despite her exhaustion and fear, however, Felicity couldn't bring herself to return home. Her fearful journey north had become a kind of foolish quest for truth.

Not knowing whom she could trust, not having any evidence to support her story, Felicity decided that she had to just trust herself and her own resourcefulness. If she had gone to the police that first day to have her blood tested for the drug, she would have some evidence, but she had been so overwhelmed, probably in shock. She could barely remember most of that day once she awoke in the back of the truck. Now it was up to her. She would find a solution if she didn't die first.

"I'm not going to Canada. I'm just driving, trying to keep moving while I come up with a plan. I have no doubt I will need your help before this is all over, okay? I love you. I promise I'll call you." Felicity hung up the phone before Nick could protest. If she knew him, he would give her time before he called her back.

Still seated on the bed, Felicity let her head fall into her hands and tried to moderate her breath in a slow, easy rhythm. She actually had no plan at all. Jase hadn't called, and Felicity didn't know if she wanted him to. Certainly, Felicity couldn't trust him – even toying with the idea of accepting his help now seemed foolish. He had at least been complicit in some of ProtoComm's crime, if she had interpreted his words correctly. Jase had sent Perry after her. Was that a good thing or a bad thing? Was that to save her or to catch her? Felicity honestly had no idea.

A thunderous knock on the door sent Felicity's heart into spasms of fear. Glued to her bed, she didn't respond in any way. She heard at least two voices outside her window, discussing something in elevated tones.

"Mrs. Miller?" one of them called. "Mrs. Miller, this is Elliot from the front desk."

Could she believe even him?

"Mrs. Miller, we've been trying to call you."

Felicity glanced over at her phone. When she had arrived, Felicity remembered unplugging the hotel phone. Irrationally, she had been trying to ensure that no one called and woke her up.

Rather than answer the door immediately, Felicity tiptoed to the window and looked out. She recognized the teenager from the "Employee of the Month" photo. With him stood a man who appeared to be a janitor or facilities manager. The man had a ring of keys in his hand. She turned her back to the curtain, nervously biting her cuticles while she debated with herself.

"Mrs. Miller, if you don't answer the door, we're going to have to let ourselves in. We've been alerted that you might be in danger, and we want to make sure you're okay."

Felicity turned back to the window and peeled away the corner of the curtain, revealing only her face.

"Give me just a minute!" Even if she had wanted to hide in her room with the door locked, she knew that Elliot could enter without her permission. She didn't really think baby-faced Elliot had any ulterior motive for his intrusion.

Leaning across the bed, she grabbed her jeans and rapidly pulled them on. Then, she raced quickly to the door to speak to the anxious Elliot.

"I'm sorry," Felicity apologized as she cracked the door. "I was sleeping. I unplugged my phone."

As Elliot took in the room, a sheepish look crossed his features.

He stared at the floor, "Oh, I'm sorry. It's just that the man on the phone said..."

Felicity rubbed her eyes and placed her hands on her temples as if trying to hold her head together. "A man called about me?" Felicity had no idea what to think. "Did he have an accent?" the picture of Perry intruded into her mind.

"Well, he kind of sounded like he was from the south."

Jase? she wondered silently.

"He said he was a friend of yours and that he had been trying to reach you all morning. He said you were in danger."

Felicity flipped open the phone she still held in her hand. She had assumed that the six missed calls had all come from Nick. Felicity pushed the call button and a list of all calls displayed on her screen. It showed one completed call from Nick, two missed calls from Nick, and four missed calls from a number she did not know.

"You can see I'm fine. Thanks for your concern."

"If the man comes by? He said he was nearby and wanted to come check on you himself, but I thought I should probably check on you first. Should I tell him where you are?"

"No!" Felicity almost shouted. "No, please," she stated, more subdued, pleading. "Um, I have his number. I'll just call him."

"Okay, are you checking out today?" Elliot sounded hopeful.

"If I didn't miss the deadline..."

"No, I think it's okay considering..." his eyes avoided hers.

Felicity got the feeling that Elliot wanted her to leave, perhaps because small-town Wyoming didn't have a high tolerance for "danger."

"I'll be out within the hour," she assured him.

As he shut the door, Felicity looked down at her phone again. She had received only two calls yesterday: one from her brother and one from Jase. So, if the number that had called four times today matched the unknown number from yesterday, she could assume that Jase had called her cell phone and the hotel today. The only other option was that someone from ProtoComm had called her – Felicity shuddered at the thought.

She scrolled down the list and compared the number from the morning with the morning from the previous day. They matched. Felicity sighed in relief.

A gentle knock sent Felicity's pulse racing, but she forced herself to calm down. *The manager,* she assured herself. Strolling to the window, she glanced out as a precaution. Elliot *did* stand outside her door again with the janitor, but now Jase, as if materialized from her dream, stood facing the younger man and chiding him angrily.

"Did you even look inside her room?" he upbraided the poor clerk. "If something were wrong, she may not have been able to tell you."

"She said she had been sleeping."

"She said - someone could have been in her room threatening to hurt her if she asked for help."

Jase's tone sounded dangerous, and Elliot's cowering posture stirred Felicity's compassion. Too many times, she had been on the receiving end of an irritated lecturer, and she could not stomach it at the moment.

Drawing a deep breath, Felicity opened the door to the startled faces of the three men.

"Jase, give it a rest!" she insisted, screwing up her face in consternation. "He's just a kid."

"*Tu vive!*" Jase gushed, rushing through the door. Though Felicity had prepared herself to confront Jase, he allayed any plans she had made by throwing his arms around her. He laid his cheek on the top of her head, and her surprise froze her in place and rendered her speechless.

"Felicity, what's wrong?"

She stiffened and blinked and could do no more. Then her brain kicked in, and she began squirming to escape his grip.

"What the hell!!" she spewed at him. "Keep your hands off me!"

When she had extricated herself from Jase's arms, she looked beyond him. Elliot stood blinking, his mouth open, obviously completely at a loss as to what his role as manager required of him under these circumstances. Felicity took pity on him once again.

"I'm fine," she insisted. "He's fine. You can go back to work now.

A grateful and relieved look softened the young man's face, and Felicity thought she heard him start to breathe again.

Thanking him, Felicity stood at the door, obviously waiting for Elliot to take her advice and return to his desk, which he did. She then turned her back to the open door, wheeling to face Jase. Did she run? Her keys were on the nightstand. How far could she get if he decided to chase her? The she took in his amused expression.

"Typical," he smirked, and something about the familiarity made her want to slap him.

"What exactly is that supposed to mean?" she gawked.

"Here you are, running for your life, and you're worried that I'm being too rough on the manager." His voice softened, and he looked at his hands. "I'm sorry." He glanced back at her, "When you didn't answer this morning, I was afraid someone else had tracked your phone and found you. As soon as we talked, I looked up Glendo and caught a flight to Cheyenne. I've been traveling all night, but I was afraid I was too late."

Felicity stared at him, confounded. What was his game? He had to know she didn't trust him; at four inches taller and with muscles that belied obvious physical prowess, he also had to know it would take little for him to overpower her. He obviously wasn't above drugging her if it served his purposes. So, why was he standing in her room staring at her like some forlorn puppy.

It has to be an act, her reason told her, but the instincts that Brendon had suppressed for all those years were tapping politely at her subconscious. *When is the last time someone showed that much concern for you?* it asked her. *Besides, do you really think you could get away if you tried? He has already found you once.*

When his expression changed, her subconscious gloated, because it would have been hard to interpret his attitude as dangerous to her, though he certainly looked dangerous. His head jerked up, his eyes alert and searching the space behind her – the empty balcony. The look reminded her of the last time she had seen him, that night when someone had drugged her, and Jase had facilitated her kidnapping.

Something that night hadn't made sense: when he had sat with her in that chair, he had seemed…desperate. His senses on edge, he had peered around the room with preternatural vigilance – as he had fought her drunken and drugged self to protect her dignity. His hands had worked to hold her dress together when she would have left her decency on display for anyone who happened to glance her way. Why would he protect her dignity if he intended to ship her off into slavery? The man made no sense.

The uncertainty restrained her. She was alone, which of course made her vulnerable to him, but oddly, he looked as if he were ready to leap out of the door in an instant, assault any threat to her. She guessed he could have just wanted to protect his prey, but he didn't seem ready to leap at her – that had to mean something.

"I appreciate your concern," she finally hedged. "I do. But…why should I believe you? You come barging in here, looking like you want to protect me, which makes no sense. I don't know what you expected from me. It's not like I'm going to just trust someone because he speaks pretty words, no matter what language.

The last man I trusted pretty much destroyed my life."

A flash of some strong emotion flitted through his eyes as he brought them back to hers, something at the mention of her husband's betrayal, but Jase only said, "Of course – you're smarter than that. I just had to take the risk. I couldn't believe that you would be st – would decide to drive alone through a no-man's land. It was so dangerous. I was afraid you weren't thinking clearly. How could you? You don't have any experience with this kind of thing, and you've been through an extreme trauma." His voice lowered to almost a whisper, and he dropped his chin. "I just wanted to make sure you were safe." Then he laughed as if at himself. "That you were okay."

Part of her wanted to laugh back at him – had he been about to call her stupid? Well, the whole thing was kind of stupid, and she had acted accordingly. For Jase to call her out on it would hardly endear himself to her though. She kind of appreciated the candor of the near-slip.

When a small jolt of pleasure ran through her at the intensity of his tone, she sucked back in her amusement. She couldn't afford to appreciate him. When he followed his words with a gentle squeeze of her hand before pulling her farther into the room, she turned to ice, stiffening in response to her fight, flight, or freeze instincts. He reached above her head to close the door, and her mind splintered between the fear at recognizing she was now trapped and the strange sensual pleasure at his proximity and touch.

She spun slowly away from him, unable to meet his eyes with equanimity. "I'm sorry I reacted so strongly," she apologized, steeling her voice despite the turmoil in her chest. Finally, she forced steady eyes to his. "I just...I have to be honest with you, Jase." *It's worth a shot.*

When he raised his eyes to hers, she gulped. He was beautiful, and he gazed at her with so much concern. Still, she spoke as coolly as she could manage under the circumstances.

"I don't trust you."

Jase smiled a sad smile, "I don't blame you," he acknowledged, and Felicity scolded herself for letting his ostensible emotion raise her guilt.

Then she offered him an explanation in case she owed him one. "I don't trust anyone right now," she explained. *Except for Nick,* she qualified to herself. "I don't have a plan, I don't know where to go, and I don't know what to do."

"You can trust me." His eyes spoke earnestness.

At the words, though, a laugh burst past her lips. Perhaps not the smartest reaction while under the power of a trained agent, but since she had done it, she might as well use the lapse to test his goodwill. *The truth it is, then.* "Jase, do you realize how ridiculous what you're saying sounds? A man who basically carried me to the car where I was abducted. You expect me to trust you just because you say I can?"

"No, no! You're smarter than that. But I will prove that you can trust me. If nothing else, maybe you can see that I risked a lot to stop you before the border."

"So you say, though I guess I can never know, can I? Because I stopped myself. And if you were going to stop me, you sure were cutting it close."

"I told you I be there when you need me."

"Then you laid me in the car that carried me to slavery."

"No, Liss!" He turned back to her, his fervor apparent. "I laid you into the car that took you away from Brendon, away from ProtoComm and its machine of terror. Brendon had convinced Bill to get rid of you, and Bill Henry would have seen things through. The only way I could have stopped them was to insert myself into the process and manage your deliverance."

Felicity didn't know that everything he said made sense, but it was certainly persuasive. "Okay, Jase," she sighed. "Say that I temporarily work under the assumption that you are trying to help me; you have to know that you can't trust me either, that I am going to be looking for every opportunity to get away from you."

Jase crossed gingerly to face her. He started to reach for her hand again, but obviously thought better of it, because he dropped both of his hands by his side. "Felicity…" He sought her eyes. "First of all, I'm not going to hurt you, Whatever you may think, I fully intend to help you. But secondly, there is no need to 'get away' from me. I'm not going to hold you hostage. You can walk out that door right now if you need to. Leave your phone on the bed so I can't track you, and walk away." Glancing around, his eyes locked on the keys at her bedside, and he stepped over to retrieve them, pushing them into her palm.

Gently, he gripped her hand before releasing both her and the keys and dropping his hands again. Then, to her utter shock he backed away from her until his legs hit the bed and he lowered himself to a sitting position. His eyes seemed to study something behind her as he thought. "I understand why you can't trust me yet. It's not as if I can really tell you everything I know."

"Okay…" *Certainly seems sincere.*

"But if you leave, then I can't protect you. And that is all I want. It's not right what has been done to you, and for once, I feel like I can do something about it. *Pour une fois, vouloir.*"

"Why do you do that? Are you trying to impress me?"

Jase's expression when he peered up at her wore surprise. "What did I do?"

"You throw in French phrases or words, whenever you want me to pay closer attention."

Jase laughed, running his fingers through his hair. "It's because I'm not sure exactly how to do what I'm trying – this whole 'rescue' idea is fairly new to me, at least with someone I'm not being paid to save. Someone I care to save."

Even through her suspicion, his words threatened to reach her. "How does that explain the French?"

Smiling, Jase fixed his gaze on the cheap print above the bed. "I only do that when I feel extreme stress, fall back into the language of my childhood. When I'm on a job, there's a shell I wear, and it doesn't crumble. But this is not a job – I'm not really sure what this is."

"So, you're saying this isn't a job? You haven't come for ProtoComm, to take me back to them? To test him, she eased toward the door, reaching for the handle. His shoulders drooped, and he cast disappointed eyes to the carpet at his feet. He really meant it. Jase would let her go.

Her freedom was within her grasp, but what, exactly, did that freedom look like? She was already heading back to the hornet's nest. What did she think she was going to do there, by herself and with no knowledge of how to find answers? She turned the knob and pulled the door open, her eyes fixed on Jase as the click of the door sounded and light flooded the room – he didn't move, just stared at a spot on the floor, though his shoulders slumped imperceptibly. If he was manipulating her, he held a skill beyond anything she had ever encountered. He had literally handed all the power to her.

Even when she paused too long in the doorway, he just stared at his feet, and hope swelled in Felicity's chest. Not hope that she would get away, but hope that maybe she didn't need to. Was she being a complete idiot? *Only one way to know.*

"I assume you can tell me what we do now?" she leveled, her heart thudding against her ribcage as she fought her mind's battering rage at her stupidity.

At the word "we," Jase raised his face with an alluring grin. *Stop it!* she ordered the butterflies that danced in her stomach. Staring into the ebony depths of his eyes, the sensations returned from that first night she had met him, when his gaze had focused past the dancing throng of partiers and found her where she leaned against the cold skyscraper glass. Even as he had tried his hardest to portray cool sophistication at that party, to play the heroic rescuer, he couldn't quite mask the ageless animal that lurked behind his placid exterior. Jase was attracted to her, for whatever reason. Certainly, he had a wide array of options, but somewhere in that panoply of women, he had noticed her.

He was probably just an incredibly virile man, alert to attraction and to women's attraction to him. Of course, there was nothing special about her, but in her current state, she worried that she might respond to that kind of energy. The reality scared her, especially since she had not paid attention to such things in over a decade. She had no idea if men had looked at her that way before, because she had intentionally shut off that portion of her mind once she married Brendon – it was the right play for a married woman. Now that her marriage was over, though, why did the attention scare her? Because she was in a shambles, and she had no ability at the moment to use proper judgment. Certainly, she hadn't noticed Jase's level of fixation toward her since – *since Brendon.*

At least Brendon had initially intended to fix his attention on her, not just on the nearest woman. A man like Jase Hamilton? If Jenna Whitfield's attitude meant anything, Jase likely played the lothario on a regular basis. His attention to Felicity was likely nothing personal.

In fact, his attention to Felicity did not make any sense unless he had been sent to rectify a botched job. Which would mean she was in incredible danger at the moment. Jase Hamilton had been sent to retrieve her, and as a libertine, he would use the time before he delivered her to toy with his prey.

Of course, that was one interpretation of circumstances. The other interpretation almost raised her anxiety even higher than her potential incarceration and intended seduction. What if Jase was what he claimed? A man determined to protect a woman in danger? Someone whose very intention to help placed him crossways with his boss and placed him in a position of insecurity? If Jase were telling the truth, then he might prove incredibly useful for her purposes. And both the idea of callously utilizing his mind and her own sense of loneliness terrified her in regards to Jase if he were sincere.

Not that he could serve any purpose in her life beyond using him as aid against ProtoComm, but if he really wanted to help her, she was in better shape than she had been when she awoke in her hotel room alone.

"Okay, then," he broke into her thoughts with a return to his usual cocky attitude, and his words upended any sense of reason she had tried to establish in her mind. "We go back to Banff."

Chapter 15

*More in number than the hairs of my head are those who hate
    me without cause; mighty are those who would destroy me,
    those who attack me with lies.* – David, King of Israel

*Every other minute, I doubt my sanity. Have I fallen into a coma and
    lie in a hospital bed and all of these occurrences are the
    dreams of a damaged mind? Am I under the influence of
    mind-altering drugs, sitting catatonic in an asylum? These
    things don't happen in real life. Unless, of course, the life I
    led before was the delusion. If that were true, I guess I would
    finally be waking up.* – Felicity, March 25

Felicity knew her mouth had dropped open, but she couldn't
help herself. Where else would he have taken her? Considering that
she had, somewhere in the back of her mind, always planned to go
back to Canmore, she really shouldn't have reacted so negatively.
Still, she had known that her plan was insane which was why she
hadn't ever voiced it; therefore, she had assumed that Jase would
prove more logical than she.

She had some vague idea about watching the goings on of all
the ProtoComm people, looking for evidence as they went about
their convention. Knowing that if anyone saw her, she would end up
somewhere worse than in the bed of a truck. While hiding out and
not letting anyone see her…it was a pipe dream. It required that she
be some superspy with the power of invisibility and the ability to
walk through unlocked doors and break into filing systems. Yeah,
Canmore had been insanity.

Of course, Jase wanted to go there. Because it was also
insane for her to trust Jase.

"Nice plan to gain my trust, taking me back to my
kidnappers."

A look of surprise spread across Jase's face. "Well, I had kind
of assumed that you were going there anyway."

"But..." she stuttered. "I wasn't actually going back to Banff, just kind of aimlessly wandering towards it. I didn't know what I was doing; I'm irrational right now. Traumatized."

Jase laughed. "Actually, I'm surprised at how rationally you've acted, considering what has happened to you in the past two days."

Felicity bit her lip. *Quit trying to soften me up with compliments,* she commanded silently.

On seeing her expression, Jase's mouth donned a conspiratorial smile. "So, since you don't 'rationally' want to go to Banff, and you agreed to let me come to you, where will we go? I can think of a lot of places more fun than Canmore or Banff. Tahiti? Bali? Just name it. I'm in."

Felicity started. True, she had agreed to stay with him, but if they didn't go to Banff, where else would make sense? "No, I..." Embarrassment overwhelmed her, and she grasped for some escape. "I have to get back to my children. And I just thought you might know some other course we could take besides direct confrontation. I mean, I don't really want to be under Bill's eye at the moment." She covered her blush with an irate glare. "Assuming you're not working for him."

Jase didn't deny it fast enough, and Felicity felt her pulse racing, both from embarrassment and nervousness.

"My relationship with Bill is... complicated."

Once again, his honesty disarmed her. A smooth response would have cemented her suspicion, but his uncertainty oddly recommended him to her.

"What the heck does 'complicated' mean?" Felicity couldn't keep the sarcasm out of her tone, and Jase smirked at her in response.

"Look, as far as Bill is concerned, you're in Mexico." Jase paused to let his words sink in. "I have enough pull with the guys who were taking you across the border that I convinced them to tell their bosses they had delivered you to the trade."

"'Delivered me to the trade'," Felicity harumphed. "Nice way of putting it.*"

"Yes," he continued undaunted. "I convinced them to keep your disappearance a secret. I told them that Bill would be particularly disturbed if he found out that you had escaped, and that he might consider terminating our business relationship with them.

And a relationship with Bill Henry is a very lucrative relationship."

"Is it?" Felicity leveled resentfully. "How lucrative is it for you? Yet you expect me to believe that you're putting it in jeopardy for me?"

The words seemed to reach deep within Jase, and the look he leveled at her gripped her heart with its sincerity. "Felicity, *j'ai assez d'argent*, all of it gained legally and most of it gained ethically – I'm working on that. The work I do for Bill is aboveboard; I can't say I was completely unaware of his ties to the black market, but I didn't know the extent. I just act as liaison on some deals. I manage communication pathways, streamline flowthroughs, carry messages from one party to the other."

"From one party to the other. I'm sure the results were a 'party' for your victims."

"My victims?"

"The ones you helped Bill enslave? What would you call them? Contractors?"

Jase balked, his shock genuine. "Felicity, I didn't understand exactly what Bill was into. I admit: I didn't dig for the truth, and I had my suspicions, but I've never involved myself in something like this before you. I've made sure to work only on non-criminal contracts – I'm not a mercenary, though I don't broadcast that fact to Bill. I'm extremely intentional about looking like an insider, but I carefully avoid actual participation in crimes."

"How noble of you!" Felicity laughed. Did he really think his conscientiousness exculpated him? Hardly. He was still in bed with criminals.

"Most of Bill's business is legitimate, and even what isn't stays far away from corporate headquarters. He likes to keep his hands clean, remove himself from the ugly side of ProtoComm's operations. Your abduction was a rare exception because he allowed himself to be personally involved. And it's an absolute exception for me. Once Bill finds out what I've done, my relationship with him will be over, which is fine except that I need to stay inside until I figure out how to help you. Bill was counting on your abduction to keep Brendon stable, and I screwed that up. I guess you did, more accurately. Not even I expected you to escape abduction by professionals."

"Yes, my abduction." The words effaced all of her questions about Jase's guilt, bringing her own plight back to the forefront.

"And this was all just because Brendon wanted to leave me?"

"Well," Jase looked at his hands. "It's probably better for you if you don't ask that question right now. You won't like the answer, and *tu en as assez vécu.*"

"You're right, Jase. I have been through hell the past couple of days. I've been kidnapped and sent into slavery. I've been through so much, in fact, that I don't think what you could say could hurt me much more."

Jase pondered for several seconds, as if searching for words. "Well, Brendon…" Jase offered hesitantly. He seemed to collect himself, though Felicity couldn't tell for what purpose. Because he didn't want to hurt her? Or to prepare himself for a lie? "If I had to guess, I would say he wanted to protect two things: his image and his money."

"His money?" Felicity wavered between fury and devastation. "Is he really that shallow"

"Are your parents married?" Jase asked inexplicably.

"My parents?"

"Are they married?"

"Yes…"

"Then you probably don't have a lot of exposure to divorce, but there are a lot of ugly things that happen in divorces. Brendon has no high ground for this. You're a great person. He can't claim any abuse or neglect or mistreatment from you."

"But I can't prove any mistreatment either. No one cares that he screwed his assistant. It's literally the most cliched affair on the planet."

"But usually the guy can claim something. I imagine that's why he put in the cameras – to get something on you. But there was nothing. You didn't yell at your kids. You didn't have a secret drinking or drug problem. You didn't have a guy on the side – nothing."

"Okay, I call BS. Most women don't do those things. That's like a myth."

"Try proving that in court; there's a preconception that makes sense that there's always more to a story, some justification for an affair. If he could have proven that you had a weakness or that you were a neglectful mom, it would have saved him lots of time and money. He works in a high-profile job, and a good chunk of his wealth is posted on SEC reports. If his money had been less public, he could just hide it. Strip you of financial support so you are forced to negotiate with him or live in poverty and desperation. Render you powerless to fight him in court because you couldn't afford the lawyers. But with so much of his portfolio in public view, though, you could devastate him financially. If he can't prove you're crazy and he goes through a public divorce, not only does he look like an absolute loser; you get a huge chunk of his wealth."

"He knows I don't care about the money." Felicity shook her head.

"No way," he countered. "He can't know that, because he could never believe it."

Felicity peered at Jase with a skeptical squint. "He's known me almost his whole life."

"Did you ever attribute your own motives to him?" Jase challenged.

"I mean, I guess. I always assumed he wanted to be honest, and a good person. I assumed that he would fight against his demons so he could be a good husband and father."

"Did you ever have any evidence of that?"

Caught by her own words, Felicity smiled sardonically. "I made up evidence where there was very little."

Jase returned her smile, though much kinder in manner. "He does the same thing. He ignores the signs that you don't care about money, and he imagines that you are as greedy as he is."

"He's an idiot, then," she murmured. "Because I don't care about his money."

"You're going to have to learn to care," Jase insisted.

"Please, I don't want to be anything like him!"

"But if it's not for you, if it's for your kids…"

"How could it do my kids any good for me to be greedy?"

Jase shook his head again. "Not greedy. Just omitted to justice. You stayed home and gave up your career and earnings potential to take care of his kids. If you hadn't done that, he would have needed to pay someone to care for them."

"I didn't expect to be paid – they're my kids."

"Of course you didn't. But you also didn't expect to be kicked out without any resources because your husband broke his word, because he holds all the power. Do you have some big stockpile of personal savings you can tap into to take care of your kids? Because if not, and if he figures out how to hide what he has, you will be going from that nice upper-middle-class neighborhood in Phoenix to government housing. Even if you got a fulltime job – have you worked since your kids were born? What kind of job do you think you could get and still have time to take care of the kids? So then maybe his high-dollar lawyers will get him custody of the kids since you can't afford them. And those would be your problems under normal circumstances. You, though, were attacked and kidnapped. You won't be safe until you have leverage on these people, and if you're not safe, your kids aren't safe."

Felicity shivered. "You sound like you've been through something like this. You know so much about it."

Jase shrugged. "Not the kidnapping part, and not me personally. My best childhood friend. She ended up an alcoholic, in and out of rehab. Injustice sucks. Watching her ex screw up the kids was worse. I mean, you could always just let him be in charge and do whatever he wants. That's the alternate if you can't take care of yourself and the kids."

With a surge of disgust, Felicity's face contorted in horror. A man like that? What would subjection to him look like? Her kids needed her to be strong, needed her to fight.

She couldn't ignore her gratitude to Jase for educating her in the possibilities. Somehow, she had never considered what would happen if she tried to negotiate with a criminal with power over her kids.

All the talk about a potential divorce and the politics of it made Felicity's head spin, but the offhand comment about needing leverage to keep herself and her kids safe crowded out the other concerns. "That does sound horrible, but most of that is a battle for another day. Maybe Brendon wanted to avoid court and risking his money. But kidnapping? Lots of people go through awful divorces; they don't send their spouses into slavery. That's not realistic."

"Most people are not favored VPs in a multinational corporation with access to several Central American trafficking centers…"

Felicity closed her eyes, slowing her breath. Of course. She had already speculated the possibility that sending her into slavery was easier than fighting her. Was she just in a really stubborn state of denial?

"Do you have any idea what he does at work all day?" Jase prompted. "I can see that you don't. Well, I can tell you that he is intimately involved in all aspects of Bill's business. Specifically, Jenna Whitfield's division in Central America."

Felicity felt a fist punch into her gut. Jenna Whitfield?

"Jenna and Jack have been managing Bill's Mexico division, which is a clearinghouse for all of ProtoComm's criminal activities. In the past year, Brendon has taken over thirty percent of that division.

"Calvario…" Felicity realized.

After a sympathetic pause, Jase confirmed her suspicions. "Calvario. Haven't you noticed how much money Brendon has spent lately?"

Thinking about the necklace, she considered the other expenses that had seemed unusual. The new sports car, Briel's salary, even the expense of the trip to Canmore. A private jet? Had he really gotten the use from a friend, or had he paid for it with his newfound wealth? And he had probably spent a similar amount or more on Amy.

"That asshole!" Felicity hissed, her voice breaking from pain. "Painting his worst offense as a virtue! I knew he was feigning something about that place, but I thought it was just an exaggeration of his accomplishments; he's always done that, Lapping up the offered attention. He was actually committing horrible crimes there – or at least overseeing them."

"To his credit, he balked at the idea of killing you-"

"To his – oh, of course," she cut him off. "He couldn't have that. It wouldn't give him plausible deniability. Though it would have effected the same thing since I'm sure I would live to a ripe old age in the slave trade."

"Sorry. Your sarcasm radar is probably not at its best right now."

She managed a weak smile, then sat up straighter. "But wait, what if Brendon had nothing to do with the kidnapping? I mean, I know he had an affair, but that doesn't make him a monster – just a weak man. He has a history of taking up cause against unethical management, so I know he has some sense of nobility. There was that whole thing with the guy from the office…John?"

Jase paused, unsure. "Who?"

"A little number cruncher in Jack's division who found discrepancies in the bookkeeping. Brendon helped him."

"John Mitchell, yeah. I remember him. You think Brendon

helped him?"

"He did!" Felicity insisted. "That's his name, John Mitchell. Brendon took John's information and cleared up some pretty serious ongoing embezzlement by upper-level employees."

"How do you know that?" Jase deadpanned.

Felicity bit her lip. "Well, Brendon told me, but – "

"Did he mention where John Mitchell is now?"

Nervous, Felicity said nothing.

"I came on right after John Mitchell disappeared, over a year ago. The only reason I knew who he was is because my job partly entails monitoring the computers for suspicious activity – the ones for the legitimate part of the company. I saw what he saw, saw his name on the documents. I asked around – discreetly. I've actually been keeping his work going, keeping it in a private database in case I need it. Either John Mitchell took off under the cover of darkness, or someone disappeared him."

"Poor guy," Felicity worried. "And you found this because you monitor suspicious activities at ProtoComm? At least you're not bored."

"Ah, there's your sarcasm," Jase smirked. "I monitor suspicious activity, meaning dangerous to ProtoComm's commercial interest. If what I have gathered is correct, John Mitchell had flagged too many of the key entries that had hidden the criminal activity."

Felicity stood up from the little wooden chair that served for a cheap hotel's living space. "So, they did to him what they wanted to do to me." She shivered. "Except I doubt they sent him into slavery, and I doubt anyone rescued him." Her voice broke, and she couldn't speak for a minute. Finally, she turned back to Jase. "Maybe this is a little premature, but thank you," she offered awkwardly. "For coming to help me."

Surprise flashed briefly across his face, but he suppressed any real reaction. "I saw the order, Felicity. When I sniffed out the inexplicable way they were monitoring you, I went in search of an explanation. I pressed my way in to Bill's apparatus, offered my services. Since he only knew me by reputation – and that of extreme competence – he had no reason to suspect I had another motive to insert myself. Point is, I heard the communications between your husband and Bill. You can't talk about trusting Brendon. I'm sure not all wayward men are monsters, but your husband is."

"So, what you're saying is that Brendon planned and

executed this with Bill's help? You're saying that even a year ago, before he started all this insanity, he was already an unethical boor? So he helped catch John Mitchell..." She almost couldn't believe it, even with everything that had happened to her. "...and then came home and lied to me to impress me? Does that make sense?"

"I don't know," Jase shrugged. "People are complicated. I mean, it was probably before he decided to send you away. He knew that you would be impressed with him helping the little guy."

Moving to the window, Felicity peered out through the slit in the curtain. The sun stood over halfway to its zenith above the vast, flat expanse outside of the minuscule town. She wished she could at least have seen the mountains that she knew lay beyond the horizon, but those were blocked by the never-ending plain. She was hemmed in and hindered by a lack of boundaries. *A good analogy for my life right now,* she scoffed bitterly. She could go anywhere, do anything, but she needed to know why, and she needed to know what would work. Apparently, Brendon knew how to make his decisions.

"That was before Brendon decided his money was more important than I am," she pressed in a small voice.

"I mean, for one thing, he needed his money to impress other people after he wrote you off, and you might take that away from him. But I think probably more compelling to him, he knew how strong you are, and how principled you are. If you ever figured out the source of his money, you would have no qualms about turning him in to the police – even if it left you broke. You couldn't be reasoned with." He finished sardonically.

"Damn right I couldn't!" Felicity actually would not have made such a black and white statement, but she needed to vent some of her anger. "Cause by 'reasoned with' you mean 'bought out'!"

"Exactly. Bill had the mechanism in place to get rid of you; he only needed Brendon's help to get you to Banff and to that party. I was surprised that Bill would agree personally to sully his hands, but you have no idea how valuable Brendon is to the company's dealings."

"I understand Bill, but Brendon? I'm his wife. We were kids together..." Felicity choked.

At her pain, Jase seemed to war with himself. Whatever won him over, his decision didn't ease the ache in Felicity's gut. "And you're a constant reminder of how far he's fallen, a constant prick on his conscience. Having you around meant that he would lose the money, lose Aimée, lose his ability to live with himself."

Felicity had been wrong. Jase's words *could* hurt her. A wave of nausea swept through her again as she was reminded of the other betrayal. Brendon and Amy. Why did it hurt more to her that Brendon had cheated on her than that he had sold her into slavery? Maybe because Brendon's crimes only reflected on his own lack of character. His rejection of her reflected her value. In the end, his criminality was a statement about himself. His affair felt like a statement about her.

Collecting herself, Felicity looked back at Jase, her voice strained. "What does he plan to do with my children?"

Jase tapped his finger on the blue formica tabletop. "The same thing he has always done, I imagine. However he treated them before, he'll treat them the same now. Maybe a little better because he will have to make sure no one suspects him." The words seemed trapped by his reticence.

"A man who could send you into the slave trade? He justifies that behavior somehow. No one can live with the belief in their own evil. They maintain vestiges of good behavior so they can justify their existence. Brendon can send you into slavery and still raise his kids like a 'good' dad. He'll hire out childcare and housekeeping, go to ball games and parent socials."

Felicity shivered, remembering Brendon's words. *It's not so hard to hire someone to take over most of your responsibilities.* He had made it sound like he wanted to help her. Instead, he wanted to replace her.

"And I'm sure he'll question himself at times. But when his plans work out, he'll put it behind him. You would disappear, he would wait the requisite period for the appearance of respectable mourning, then he would "fall into" the comforting arms of Aimée. If your kids are lucky, he won't spiral down and turn into a Bill. And he won't grow increasingly more callous, focused on power and money to the exclusion of all else. I think he has let himself pretend like this wasn't so bad by handing the responsibility off to Bill. In his mind, it's like he didn't really do it. He can wash his hands. So maybe he hasn't given in to full-on depravity, just delusion. I mean, not to cause you more pain, but Aimée is actually kind of nice. She's certainly doesn't seem involved in ProtoComm's dark dealings. I would guess Brendon pictures some sort of domestic future with her."

Wave after wave of disgust and pain rolled through Felicity. She doubted his words, but not enough to fully dismiss them. She started to associate stories she had read, betrayals she had seen from afar as merely interesting, in a much more personal and painful light. How could a pastor minister to the sick with one hand while stealing money from his church with the other? How could a philanthropist donate millions of dollars to charity then go home and beat his wife for a minor offense?

How could a doctor dedicate her life to protecting the health and well-being of people and yet make extra money by writing prescriptions to feed the illegal habits of her patients? Only a fool would deny the possibility that Brendon could feign benevolence but act unscrupulously, and no one had ever accused Felicity of being a fool. She could believe it, even if she wanted to deny it.

The situation went so far above and beyond her own betrayal.

Of course, that hurt her the most, but if what Jase suspected were true, Brendon was responsible for hurting so many more people than Felicity. And what had she fought against her entire life? Bullies. People who took advantage of others. Callous jerks who ignored the pain they caused to gain for themselves. In an instant, her misery transformed into fury. Brendon planned to escape with her children to raise them as his legacy.

What kind of legacy was that? A man so unscrupulous could only pass on infamy to his children, and when Felicity thought of Noah or Nicholas or Alex? She had envisioned such ambitious futures for them. Part of her wanted to give up and walk away because the battle was too difficult, but how could she abandon her children to the future Jase had described?

"I get it," she huffed. "I really think I do. So, what is our plan?" she demanded, her voice surprisingly steady. She would have to lose him at some point, but for now, she couldn't escape the comfort of having another mind to bounce things off of, to give her direction. He certainly understood these people better than she did.

With a subtle smile, Jase peered up into Felicity's eyes, and she immediately questioned her wisdom at the idea of accepting his help. He had finally reached to take Felicity's hand, and she realized that her mind had said "yes" to the concept of another person's thoughts to buttress her own. She had discounted the vulnerability of her battered soul, and she realized that she would need to tread with caution.

In a time when her feelings vacillated between agony and deadness, Jase Hamilton's touch sizzled, warm and alive on her skin, and she remembered that she was not just comprised of thoughts. She was also feelings and sensations, and he, specifically, held the ability to overwhelm her from that perspective.

Pulling in a breath, she fortified her thoughts. It was fine. She could manage it. Would it hurt if, for the time being, she let herself believe him sincere – as long as she used caution? She could just frame his gestures an offer of kindness. Dropping a veil between her internal workings and the onyx eyes that now peered at her with such compassion, she didn't draw back. Jase seemed hesitant enough, and with the sheer euphoria of his skin on her skin, she let the contact stand. Even managed a smile for him as she wrapped her hand around his.

"Really, Felicity…" His own countenance reflected much more sobriety than she would have expected at her allowance. "I don't like the idea of taking you back to Banff either, but if you want to go back to some semblance of life, I have to find something on Brendon that will convince him to leave you alone. It's the kind of thing Bill keeps close to the vest, but he has things on everyone he needs it on. There's some on-premise storage at a couple of his non-corporate locations. Private servers, no internet connection. There's one in Banff."

"So, where would we find those? Wouldn't he keep that at his corporate headquarters or something?"

Jase shook his head. "Isn't that the first place you would look?"

"Fair point," Felicity smiled.

"Plus, it's hard to limit the number of visitors to corporate. Out in the middle of nowhere? Anyone who shows up is suspect. He has blackout locations in Banff, a small town in France, and in southeast Asia. Probably he won't have all the information at each location, but all I need is one or two things to get Brendon off your back. Unless you're really up for travel -"

"Which is irrelevant because I'm not dragging my children all over the world.

"…which is actually irrelevant because of your kids; Banff is our best bet."

"So…that means that he'll have even more reason to kill me?"

"If you're the one threatening him, maybe. But you won't be. It will be me and your brother."

"Not my brother!" Felicity insisted.

"You're far too worried about your brother – he can take care of himself - but I didn't actually mean that Brendon would know about your brother. I just mean we can use Nick's computer knowledge to make my threat have legs."

Nodding slowly, Felicity began to see the plan. Leverage over Brendon and the ProtoComm machine. "And you can only access the information from this 'blackout' location?"

"Exactly," Jase agreed. "So we go back to my place near Banff and figure out how to find what we need."

Felicity acquiesced weakly, pulling her hand back as she crossed her arms across her chest. Her two minds warred, the one that wanted relief with the one that wanted solutions. Rubbing her palms up and down to warm herself, she tried to breathe normally. Brendon had taken her to a cabin in the woods – she didn't really want to return to similar circumstances.

"Are they monitoring my phone?" she changed the subject.

"They weren't when I left. They expect that your phone was sold to someone in Mexico, and with the account transferred to ProtoComm's name, they assume you wouldn't be able to gain access." He smiled. "Of course, you're smarter than they think."

"Thanks," she offered reluctantly.

A boyish smile of pleasure lit up Jase's face, and Felicity remembered how thoroughly attractive she had found him. "Glad I could help. Really. So, if I go back to Bill," he picked up the conversation, "it will accomplish two things. First, I can watch him and see what he knows. Secondly, I can divert suspicion from myself while I move around some resources. Once I have things in place, you and I can settle somewhere more secure."

You and I? she wondered, but she chose to question a word just as unlikely. "Settle?" Even the thoughts of "settling" and "Jase" in the same sentence sent Felicity's stomach into flips.

"I mean, figure out how to get you into a more permanent situation, somewhere you can move your kids. It will need to be out of the country, I imagine, but first, I would like to convince Bill that you are really gone. Then we can get you settled and supported so you can handle children. I guess you were thinking if I did this, you would just stay in your house and live in Phoenix?"

"I hadn't really gotten that far…" Not that she wanted to create any kind of permanent situation with Jase, but she couldn't deny the appeal of having his resourcefulness close by. She certainly couldn't figure it out alone. And once she had reminded him, he had quickly accounted for her kids. Tears sprang to her eyes, though she quickly suppressed them. *Use him, don't feel grateful to him,* she reminded herself. Glancing around her empty hotel room, she assessed her own resources. Nothing. Absolutely nothing. She didn't even have anything to pack.

"I agree with you in principle," she acceded, "but I am not really willing to make commitments that far down the road. I do think that for the time being, you're my best option." She forced her hands to her sides, striding to the bedside to pick up her phone. She wiped the moisture off her cheeks. Whatever she decided, she did not want to waste time hanging out in a hotel room with Jase. "Let's get out of here," she commanded, striding to the door, "and you can tell me the rest of your plan while we're on the road."

"Wait," he reached his hand out to restrain her. "Just hold on a sec. I brought you a change of clothes. Do you want to clean up and get more comfortable for the long drive?"

Felicity's eyes widened in surprise, and the tears threatened again.

Jase seemed to reach his hand toward her in comfort but thought better of it, shrugging into nonchalance. "Size 6 long, right?" He grinned at her shock, apparently attributing it to his unexpected knowledge. "Credit card records. Online shopping. One of my specialties is security exploitation."

"So, you're a computer hacker?" she asked incredulously; he hardly seemed the type.

"Just small time," he shrugged, though he seemed to take her question as an invitation to explain himself to her. "Nothing compared to your brother. I serve in most aspects of security: surveillance, computers, security systems. My specialty, though, is communications, all aspects, which is why I fit with ProtoComm. I deal with formulating correspondences in the way most advantageous for my employers; I liaise in person to broker strategic agreements…"

He stopped short, turning to meet Felicity's eyes. "You don't care about all that," he asserted, and Felicity got the distinct feeling that he had forgotten himself, that he might not be casting himself in the most favorable light. Suddenly, his eyes appraised the tight fit jeans. "I can see you couldn't find the right size wherever you bought those." Though his words held no insinuations and his tone had spoken disinterested observation, Felicity got the distinct impression that he approved of what he saw. Her cheeks glowed red.

"Uh, right," Felicity responded, dazed. Everything about him confused her! Did he really want to help her, or did he just plan to exploit her in some way? "You do realize that you come across just a tad like a creeper…"

Jase's mouth burst out in a laugh. "That is the first time anyone has ever accused me of that. Usually, I'm the one being stalked."

"Humble, aren't we?"

"I think the problem is this situation. I have literally had to spy on you, and I'm never sure how much to tell you, so there's the whole 'he's lurking' vibe. I don't know…" He paused for several seconds. "I honestly don't know how to make sure I don't deceive you while I protect you from all the stuff I know, and how I can make sure you know I'm on your side without stepping over boundaries."

Felicity blew out a breath. "Wow," she acknowledged. "That was a lot of ambiguous candor." At his puzzled expression, she explained. "You want to tell me stuff, but not too much, and you want to make a connection, but since you know me so much better than I know you, it's like there's a weird discrepancy between us that shouldn't be there."

As she spoke, Jase started shaking his head. "I know everybody thinks Brendon is really smart – "

"Because he is…"

"Because he is, but I think you give him a run for his money."

Felicity smirked. "You know, Brendon couldn't buy me with money, and you can't buy me with compliments."

"Just being honest," he shrugged, and Felicity rolled her eyes. "Let me go get your stuff," he offered casually. "It's in the car. Be right back."

Her stuff? As Jase left the room, Felicity seated herself, statue still, on the edge of the bed, gnawing nervously at her cuticles again. Should she lock the door and call the police? All her earlier reasons for refraining still applied, and she honestly believed she had found a middle ground with Jase. She dared not allow herself to think beyond that. After about a minute, Jase returned with a small duffel bag and handed it to her. He then seated himself in the chair by the front door. "I got these for you."

Suspicious, Felicity tentatively reached for the bag, pulling open the zipper and glancing inside at a pair of jeans and a T-shirt.

"Thank you." She looked up at him gratefully.

"Don't give me too much credit. One nice act doesn't make a nice person. Get changed and we'll get out of here."

"I think I'd feel more comfortable if you went outside," she hedged, trying not to sound too prudish.

To his credit, he seemed to judge his own lack of consideration. "Oh, of course. Sorry," he grinned sheepishly. He stood back up and walked toward the door. "I'll be waiting right outside."

Despite the thick privacy curtain over the window, Felicity would change in the bathroom even with its the cramped size. Would she describe the way he looked at her as leering? No, she knew, that sounded too creepy, but there was some definite "checking her out" behind his eyes. After many years of being purposely oblivious to any male attention, her new sensitivity disoriented her.

In the bathroom, she seated herself on the edge of the tub and began sifting through the contents of the bag. Jase had included everything she could need: shirt, jeans, jacket, toiletries, personal effects. And she could just catch the gentle scent of some fabric softener, so he had even washed the clothes before he had brought them for her. He had thought of everything.

After quickly trading outfits, Felicity placed her clothes from Quido in the bag, and stepping out of the bathroom, she crossed the room to open the door.

Though Jase appraised her casually, she sensed heat behind his eyes. *Oh, God. Please don't look at me that way,* she pleaded on several levels. "Okay," she offered aloud, hoping to distance herself from him by her indifference. "Let's go."

Chapter 16

*I'm through mistaking need for love. Someone who loves you may
    need you, but need does not signify love. Love looks like
    sacrifice. It looks like awareness and intentionality and
    sensitivity. If I love you and see that you are sad, I feel sad,
    too. If I love you, and I see that you are happy, I am maybe
    even happier than you. When I hurt you, it doesn't take very
    long before it hurts me even more. Then I will go to you and
    beg your forgiveness and spend some serious time self-
    searching to figure out how never to do it again. How to
    change because I love you.* – Felicity's Journal, April 18*

*Ta copine est très charmante, mais elle ne va pas durer longtemps,
    je pense.* – Amélie in conversation with Jase.

The gentle swells and expanses of the Wyoming terrain
melded into the grandiose waves of the Montana landscape. Felicity
had asked if they could fly into Banff, hoping to shorten her time
spent alone with Jase, but Jase refused. "Airports require too much
security and documentation" he had informed her. "You are going to
have to learn to roll under the radar if you're going to survive the
next few weeks."

When they had reached Cheyenne, they dropped off Felicity's
convertible, but even so, Felicity's sense of exposure returned as they
neared Canada. What if Jase was wrong, and ProtoComm had
monitored her phone? Would Bill's men be watching for her? How
powerful were they? Would they have surveillance on the roads? Did
the ProtoComm CEO monitor his employees closer than Jase knew?
Was Jase driving her into a trap?

"Should we be on the major roads?"

Jase laughed, a seemingly nervous gesture. "Huh, I wish I
could say we didn't need to worry about that, but I can't guarantee
that Bill isn't somehow tapped into traffic cameras, at least once we
get to Calgary. But I have some alarms in place. If he starts
monitoring me too closely, I'll know."

Jase's nervousness rubbed off on her. Not that she felt totally safe with Jase anyway, but she trusted him more than ProtoComm or Brendon. She did not want them to find her.

With that thought, her insecurity bubbled over into words. "Why are you doing this?" she demanded gently.

"What?" he replied, guileless.

"Why are you saving me? Going against your boss. Risking your job." Her eyes darted surreptitiously to his face. "It's not like you have too much of a conscience to abduct someone."

"We already went over this." He seemed hurt. "I've never abducted anyone or participated in an abduction in any way."

"No, just benefited a company that did."

For a moment, Felicity noted the distinct flare of Jase's nostrils as he appeared to hold in an angry retort. Felicity expected his anger; Brendon had always disliked her black and white principles. To her surprise, Jase did not reply. Instead, his eyes stared straight ahead at the road. From Felicity's perspective, he appeared to deliberate over what he wanted to say.

Finally, he spoke with surprising contrition, "You're right, of course. I've done a lot of things you would find reprehensible, and I've justified them. Lately, I've started to wonder about my lack of conscience. You don't know me, though," he offered soberly.

"There are many things I won't do, places that are too dark for even me. I had a…troubled childhood, and I saw things that exposed me to the cruelest version of humanity. It predisposed me to see darkness in everyone, but I didn't want the world to be like that. It just meant that I didn't expect any differently for most of my life. I ran into a few people who made me doubt my belief, but I couldn't figure out how they made any difference. I tried, but I got tired of seeing how much corruption still filtered into even the most noble attempts to battle it. Part of the reason I got out of government work was because I needed to be able to question my bosses when something felt off."

"Government work?"

"Federal law enforcement stuff. A lot of security people come from that background. And I thought for a long time that I didn't have a choice. Even after I moved to ProtoComm, I was stuck in that pattern. But you were my first…" he trailed off.

"That sounds very salacious, Jase."

Jase laughed out loud. "I guess it does," he grinned, glancing at her. "Sorry."

"So, explain yourself," she smiled back.

"I did turn a blind eye to what Bill was doing. Like I said; I didn't participate, but I could easily have found out. I was in this weird position. In government work, I had to keep an eye out for any illegal activity, but if I saw my bosses doing something, I had to keep my mouth shut in most cases. They really did have legitimate reasons a lot of the time. When I noticed some discrepancies at ProtoComm, my old job would have compelled me to notice and ignore. For once, I wanted to ignore in ignorance, if that makes sense."

"I mean, sort of…" Felicity allowed.

"But about two weeks ago – just before that first party where I met you – Bill asked me to oversee the installation of a surveillance system. He'd had me do it at all of his residences – palaces, more like – so I didn't think much of it. Your house, though, is pretty small compared to his."

"My house?" she demanded, anger bubbling in her throat.

Jase sighed. "I didn't know that at the time. I had no idea what Bill had brought me in on. Maybe he figured I knew how to follow orders and keep my mouth shut because of my previous occupation, because I kept my head down, but I only realized what was happening after I had finished and was testing the cameras."

"Oh my gosh; cameras in my house." Felicity's stomach churned furiously at the violation.

"Only in the common spaces, not that that makes it okay, just maybe not quite as horrific. But, yeah, cameras. And when I switched on the first test, there were you and Brendon. To be honest, I sat and watched the camera for a few minutes because Brendon was such a plastic person, I wondered what he was like when the mask came off. I'd never seen you before. And there Brendon was yelling at you like an asshole."

Felicity scoffed sourly. "Don't let Brendon hear you say that. He claims he never yells – just speaks intensely."

"Brendon can go f – " Jase cut himself off and glanced sideways at Felicity, who puffed an unexpected laugh from her lips. "I had to do this video check once a day," he continued when she didn't say anything, "and I would watch everything at super high speed just to make sure there were no video anomalies or outages, and he was just never there. He would wander in at two or three in the morning a lot of the time, and that just didn't match the image he put out in the company. Or to the public, for that matter. The 'family man.'"

Felicity had to agree.

"I was kind of fascinated by someone who could so effectively pull off the Jekyll and Hyde routine. I mean, he didn't beat you or the kids, but everyone talks like he is a saint, and even before I knew about this, I realized he was kind of a jerk to anyone worth caring about. It's like he had no idea what was valuable in life, how rare it is to find someone who would fight for what was right but still care enough to show kindness." His expression turned inward, and she had to wonder what story he had seen or lived that stirred up the longing she read in his face. Still, she would not let herself care – not while she had to get back to her children.

"I'm sorry, Jase. I can't listen to you talk about this anymore." She huffed. "I don't really need that kind of validation right now. I need the kind that will keep me focused – not wallowing in self-pity about how I've been wronged."

Jase nodded. "Okay, so what finally moved me off of my 'don't ask questions' mindset was you. I mean, when I first set the system up and saw whose house it was, I just kind of assumed it was a test or something for Brendon. Keeping an eye on him because Bill didn't trust him. But it bothered me because, as far as I could tell, there was nothing else in the system like that. I mean, was he going to spy on me if he didn't trust me? Who else was he doing this to?"

"But I could only find the one house. Yours. Once I started poking around Brendon's files, there were a couple of files specifically about you. About your habits. Your tendencies. Your family. ProtoComm didn't have files like that on any of the other company spouses. I admit I slowed down the tapes a couple of times, trying to figure out what was so interesting about you to Bill."

"You realize this whole 'watching me' thing doesn't help your status as creeper."

"Nature of the trade, I'm afraid. Surveillance people watch. It's stalkerish. But we don't usually meet the people we watch, so it's kept separate and professional. I just didn't see a way to stay separated from you and get you away from Brendon. And I didn't expect to actually care what happened to you. But then you were…you. Brendon was such an awful person at home, but even when you fought with him, you were never cruel or rude. It was almost…kind."

The words hung in the air. If she were to be honest with herself, she could see his dilemma. It didn't make her feel less weird about the fact that he had actually watched her before she had known him.

"You make me sound like a saint. I'm not a saint."

Shrugging, Jase looked out his window. "Not a saint," he agreed. "Just unusually kind, and self-controlled, and sensitive. Look," he scoffed. "I'm trying to lose the creeper label. Let me just keep going with my explanation."

"Fine," Felicity smirked. "Go ahead."

"On one of the quick runs, I saw Brendon there alone. He was on the phone. I was curious, so I slowed the system down and eavesdropped."

"And…"

"And he just laid it all out. I mean, I had to fill in some of the blanks. Like, for instance, he didn't say his mistress was Aimée; he just mentioned his 'girlfriend.' I didn't know he was bringing you to Canmore. He just said he had to displace you."

"Displace me?"

"Get you to a remote location. No one of your acquaintance knows anything about Canmore or Banff or the thousands of acres of wilderness that surround them. Brendon could easily fabricate your disappearance. You wandered too far from a hiking trail, there was a bear, there are cliffs, there is a lot of unsettled land. Plus, he could get rid of you and not tell anyone for a month. By the time the police or your family started looking, the trail would be ice cold."

Felicity shivered in spite of herself.

"So, I came to Banff. I wanted just to tell you everything that first day, but you knew almost nothing about me. We had flirted at a party-"

"I did not flirt with you!" Felicity insisted, aghast.

She saw him grin, and one eyebrow shot up. "Okay," he leveled skeptically. "If that's what you think. But I knew you wouldn't believe me, anyway, and you had just found out about Aimée."

"Her name," Felicity interrupted. "You say it so strangely. Not 'Ay-mee' but 'Ay-may.'"

"Aimée. She's French."

"Aimée…I wonder if she's the one who called my home the

188

other day, just before the party in Phoenix. If she did, it's hard to believe she had the nerve."

"She has the nerve to cheat unapologetically with a man who has three children and a wife. She's probably not particularly demure."

Felicity shrugged irritably. "So, Brendon laid out his plan…"

"Brendon laid out his plan, and I waited for a chance to get you away. I set up a couple of cameras outside the cabin to watch for anything suspicious, but Brendon barely went there, and I didn't see anyone else but you go in or out. I was a nervous wreck at the party because they could have slipped you out at a thousand points in the night, and I didn't think I would be able to keep you in my sights as much as I needed to. But then you conveniently wore that dress, and half the guys at the party spent the whole night with their eyes on you."

Felicity hid her face in her hand. "That was such a big mistake," she sighed.

"Well, it worked strategically for me, though I had my eye on you mostly for different reasons than the other guys." He grinned, and Felicity slapped him on the arm, which only made him grin wider. "When they told me to drug your drink…"

"That was you?" She felt her first stab of hurt by something he had done.

"You're lucky it was me. It took a lot of maneuvering to work my way into that responsibility. I know that sounds crazy, but it could've been Jack. I wouldn't have done it if it hadn't been the best way to get you out of there. I measured the dose to make sure you woke up before Mexico. It was a failsafe in case Perry couldn't get to you in time."

"You sure cut it close."

"I'm not a pharmacist. I was kind of playing a guessing game. But if I hadn't managed it, someone else would have, and Bill would have made sure you were delivered where he intended. I would have lost track of you completely. I had hoped – when I ran into you outside that coffee shop – I had hoped I could persuade you to leave with me then. Of all the opportunities…but you, of course, had to be ridiculously principled, talk about working it out. Without telling you what I knew, you would not have caved. And even if I had told you, you had no reason to trust me. I don't really know why you trust me now – at least enough to agree to this insane plan."

She tried to come up with reasons why he was wrong. Drugging her was so dangerous! He did unconscionable things. But she realized that Jase hadn't made the danger. Brendon had. Bill had. If she believed him, Jase had made the danger less dangerous. In a perfect world, she could have blamed Jase for not returning her immediately to her children and bringing her captors to justice, but she knew he had made something decent out of impossible odds.

"Thank you again," Felicity offered meekly. "I get it; I understand what you were up against. If I second-guessed you, I'd be playing armchair quarterback. You managed a pretty amazing feat."

"As did you," he contended. "Waking up to a couple of human traffickers, and having the presence of mind to escape? That was remarkable. You don't have any training."

"Ha!" Felicity shook her head. "You'd be surprised how much of being a mom requires keeping a level head in really terrifying situations."

Jase smiled at her, and her awkward reference to her "regular," pedestrian life scraped a raw sensation over her thoughts that she couldn't figure out how to follow with words. She glanced at Jase, but he just offered a kind – maybe even pleased – smile and allowed the aftermath to settle into silence. Could he possibly feign the level of simplicity that would appreciate her banal world? Play boy Jase Hamilton. Sighing, she turned from him and lay her head against the window, fixing her eyes on the whimpering hills that failed to fulfill their promise of mountains. If he didn't feel the need to press her for conversation, she certainly wouldn't force herself into any more.

After a time she couldn't measure, Felicity blinked at the change in the sunlight as she peered out the window at the unvarying grasslands. She gradually realize that her head rested against her bag as a pillow, and Jase had laid his jacket over her at some point.

How had she slept? Sitting up, she peered around her in an attempt to gain her bearings. She noticed in her peripheral vision that Jase was glancing her way. "You seem like you needed a rest," he offered, and Felicity huffed her irritation at how comfortably she had slumbered.

Lowering his jacket off of her shoulders, she rested her hands on top of it on her lap. *It's not kindness,* she reminded herself. *It's a manipulation.* She would make her mind stay sober, keep telling herself to maintain vigilance, even if her heart mocked her for her stubbornness and silliness. "How long have I been asleep? Where are we?"

"We are still in Montana, believe it or not."

"Is there anything in this state besides open fields?" she complained lightly, and Jase chuckled.

"We just turned west, so we'll get into the Rockies soon enough. You were pretty out of it, but I think it woke you up when I slowed down. I wanted to refuel before Billings. We should be able to make it into Canada on one more tank of gas. Would you like to drive for a while?"

It's a manipulation. He wouldn't really give you control. Unfortunately, she didn't really want control at the moment. One thing that uncovered Brendon's ire as much as anything else was bad drivers, and he easily considered her one of the worst – despite her stellar driving record.

"I…I'm not much of a driver," she hedged. Even if she believed herself more than capable, she didn't particularly want to risk that Jase would have a reaction similar to Brendon's.

"He really did a number on you, didn't he?" Jase leveled, and she could read suppressed anger in his tone.

"No, I…I don't want to drive. It's not Brendon, " Felicity lied. "I mean, you're right – he can be harsh, but I'm not traumatized or anything. I joked about his yelling, but yelling wasn't really his biggest issue. Before the kidnapping – he wasn't exactly mean, not in the traditional sense. In fact, that's why I have so much trouble believing he did all this. He wasn't always like this."

Shaking his head, Jase countered, "No, he was smart enough that he could be cruel and intimidating with veiled threats and insults. Don't make excuses for him, Felicity. Brendon Miller is a self-important, arrogant ass. He was always like this. He wasn't always this brave."

"I really don't think so," continued Felicity. "It was like his heart died after Noah's accident,
and he had to build himself a false one to keep from disappearing. He made a false mind, a false life, a false heart."

"You need to stop giving him so much credit. He behaved until he didn't have to."

"So you're saying this has been going on for a long time? I've had to wonder, how long has he been playing me the fool?"

"This is not on you, Felicity. Lots of people hide their infamy until they gain enough power so that there are no repercussions when they don't. And the smarter the person, the better they hide."

"Are you hiding?" she wondered, and when she turned to the stark profile, his jaw had tightened.

"I don't hide…" he offered tersely. "I wear a strong armor, but I always show my face." Staring at that face, it seemed to reflect his claim. The near-black hair met a deep shadow of stubble that had sprung up overnight, and she found the image terribly striking. He was hiding something, but if she read him right, he was no pretender. Then again, her record of accurately reading men was currently zero to one.

"You don't hide, either, Liss." He threw her a glance. "And your armor is much more flexible than mine because it has to be. You inhabit a different world. But I see how this whole experience might force you to harden. I intend to keep that from happening if I'm able."

"But how long did I deceive myself? How did I miss this? Maybe I need to be harder…" she wondered, peering out at the stony canyon that had sprung up outside her window.

"No, no!" Jase reached for her hand. "You have children, Liss. You need to grow strong under the armor. You are just the right amount of toughness and tenderness. You fought for your kids but you were kind to your husband. If my mother had held half your strength, maybe Meg…"

He cut off the sentence, and the pain in his face restrained Felicity's curiosity. "Jase…" She squeezed his hand. "You don't owe me anything. I'm not your responsibility. Helping me won't undo what you have been through."

Turning fully toward her for a moment, he flashed her a brilliant smile. "Don't psychologize me, Felicity Miller. You do not want to go there. Why does anyone do what he or she does as an adult? There are always reasons. Even your shyster husband has reasons why he feels he has to screw the world to benefit himself."

"But the accident – "

"This is not about what happened with your son. If anything, Brendon has just used that as an excuse to be the person he already wanted to be. You faced the same struggles, and you didn't create a pretend self to fake your way through life after. You're real," Jase insisted, his voice rising. "That's why he hates you. You were a reminder every day that he was a pretender, something without substance or significance. And in a mind that worships significance, that made you the enemy."

"But I'm not! Doesn't he understand that? I am the only person who can understand his pain and offer him the compassion that would help him – not blind worship or excuses."

"He doesn't deserve that from you!" Jase's hands gripped the steering wheel so tightly his knuckles whitened. "What did you do with the pain you were handed? You are still overflowing with kindness and optimism. You give him everything while he tries to destroy you. I know that because you are you, you cannot write him off, but he is beyond your help. Maybe someday, after his artificial world crumbles under its own lack of substance, he will be ready for compassion. But right now, compassion is just another tool to buttress his house of cards. Maybe the best thing you could do for him is just step away and stop giving him that sense of reality in the middle of his illusion. Let the cards fall!"

"But how could I know? I mean, I just don't believe the way the world works now…if you 'fall out of love' you just drop a nuclear bomb on the stability of little kids, you throw a man under the bus because you realize he's human. We're all human – we all fail and make mistakes. When should I have walked away?"

"I mean, maybe it's less about dropping a bomb and more about peace talks. If you had insisted on counseling or something early on, maybe you would have realized his issues long before they had such intense consequences."

Felicity huffed a breath. "But I wouldn't have Noah or Nicholas if I had figured out Brendon's issues early on. I can't say I wish that, no matter what."

"And I guess that's where we have to resign life to the hand of Fate or Providence or whatever. I mean, I'm starting to think that really good things can come out of bad situations. It doesn't excuse the perpetrator, but it can give hope to the victim."

"Don't call me a victim," Felicity commanded.

Shrugging, Jase clarified. "Not a victim in essence; just a victim in position. You didn't choose this; you didn't participate in the affair or the crime. Brendon did – this was all him. This suffering – for you and your kids – was all brought on by him and his choices."

When Jase finally pulled into a station, Felicity just stared out the window again. His words had mostly rung true, at least the ones about Brendon. Jase had vastly exaggerated her own virtues, but he seemed to hold a pulse on Brendon. Felicity even wondered if Jase spoke from experience – either as a man whose cards had fallen or as a man who had needed to separate himself from someone else's choices.

Both of them seemed drained by the emotion of the exchange as the night wore on, and Felicity's melancholy returned. She eventually spied the border ahead, and leaving her country, even for as benign a neighbor as Canada, stole Felicity's confidence. Jase somehow provided her with a measure of courage, though. She had no idea what demons haunted him as he stared at the blue and silver metal that served as a gateway to a foreign land. Maybe one day he could explain.

One day? She knew better. She intended to be done with him as soon as she figured out her own plan. There would be no "one day." Once they had passed the border, Felicity grew impatient.

"I have to call my brother," she insisted. She knew that much about her plan – it included Nick's input, his knowing as much of her day-to-day situation as she could manage and the insight he could offer..

"Not a good idea," Jase answered too coolly, and Felicity gritted her teeth. "They have your home phone lines monitored."

"Who says my brother is at my house?" she challenged, and another smile curved Jase's lips.

"I heard you telling him to feed your dog and take care of your plants. He wanted to invite Briel over for dinner."

Damn! "Yes," she admitted, irritated, "but I told him to leave. And take the dog. And I'd use his cell anyway."

"He hasn't left your house," Jase countered with complete confidence. "Before I left Banff, Bill asked me what Nick might find on your home computers. Nick uses ProtoComm for cell service. Apparently, your brother's been trying to hack them, so Bill has an alert on Nick."

Jase's tone held both censure and admiration for Felicity's brother. *The jerk*, Felicity silently chastised her brother. For her part, she couldn't see past the fact that Bill had suspicions of Nick. Even without going home, she might bring calamity on her family. She needed to get Nick off of ProtoComm's cell service.

"Will Bill go after Nick?"

Jase shook his head. "Bill doesn't have time for this to turn into a web of cover-ups. Considering who set those files up, I doubt there's a man on the planet who can unlock them, and even if they do, I'm betting the files all relate to Brendon more than to ProtoComm. Bill will monitor the computers and not act unless he sees something dangerous to the company. So far, all Bill has seen is a few errant clicks. As long as you don't call him, Bill won't have any further reason to notice Nick.

How convenient, Felicity realized bitterly, that I can't call the only person besides Jase who I can count on! She considered finding a public phone if they still existed and contacting her brother anyway. She could instruct him not to reveal her identity over the phone. For the moment, though, she accepted Jase's imperative.

"What is this place?" Felicity changed the subject as Jase consulted his GPS.

"Nanton. Just an unremarkable, small town. Nice enough, as those things go. You won't see much of it, though, since you'll have to stay with me in the room."

The words brought butterflies to her stomach once again. *This keeps getting better and better*, she cringed. How often would she have to sleep with him before he started asking her to "sleep with him"? Not that she would – she had been thoroughly off-market for fifteen years, and she felt no desire to jump back into the game when the corpse of her marriage wasn't even cold.

Once in the city limits, Jase turned off the main road, passing through an apparent industrial area and into a neighborhood.

"Why are we here?"

"ProtoComm is more likely to have eyes on bigger towns, like Lethbridge. We can blend in here. Plus, there's an alternate route out of town just south of where we're staying. It could go through any of several towns, or to the foothills, where we could go on foot if we needed to."

So now Felicity might add to her experiences living off the land while hiking through the foothills. On the bright side, if she decided she was ready to lose him on the hike, she thought she probably could – assuming she wouldn't lose herself in the process. "Why not drive through the night?" she wondered.

"I don't know about you," Jase laughed, "but I'm a little tired. Plus, we want to be alert and clear-minded as we near Banff. I should have access to all the information I need to safely navigate around Bill's security there, but not all surveillance is electronic. I need to be acutely alert if I'm going to avoid dragging you into a trap." He narrowed his eyes in thought and his voice lowered in concern, "I have the feeling that if they found you now, you would be in worse straights than you were to begin with. This may be the last night of good rest you can have for a while."

I don't see how anything could be worse than being a slave, she mused. But then qualified, *Except leaving my children to be raised by a sadistic criminal*. She would just be grateful she was free for multiple reasons.

Jase pulled off of the road, into the driveway of a charming house with a "Bed and Breakfast" sign out front. She cringed when Jase signed them in under the names of Mr. and Mrs. Green, but she guessed that the owners would had learned not to ask questions of guests.

Obviously attuned to the expression on her face, Jase tried to reassure her by his own demeanor. As soon as they were far enough away from the desk not to be heard, he explained, "Even in this day and age, nothing is as inconspicuous as a married couple traveling together. I'm just trying to hide our tracks – well, really just your tracks – as well as possible."

Typical of a bed and breakfast, the room bloomed with flowers, real and tapestry, covering every possible square inch. Still, the sheets and the floor were clean, and a comfortable chaise looked out the window toward the foothills. The room wasn't large, however, and Felicity couldn't quite relax with Jase's proximity.

He took the chaise, a position he said he preferred anyway as it was closer to the door.

Though Felicity wished she had someone between herself and Jase, she couldn't help but feel grateful that he would get between her and an unknown assailant. He obviously didn't concern himself too much about the possibility because, within minutes, Felicity heard the steady, even breath of sleep emitting from the couch to her right. *I could be insulted*, she snickered, but she in fact appreciated his obviously innocuous intentions. Bolstered by his confidence, she settled herself into a fairly undisturbed slumber.

Chapter 17

- Nick, I'm going to Banff, Alberta. Come and get me.
- Hey, Nick. I'm going to hop on a plane in the morning. Pick me up
    at the Phoenix airport at 2 PM.
- Have you figured out Briel yet? Is she a good guy or a bad guy,
    cause I could use as many friends as I can find?
  – Unsent texts to Nicholas Alexander from Felicity on her last night
    on the road with Jase.

Two souls, alas, are housed within my breast, And each will wrestle
    for the mastery there. – Goethe

Early morning, March 24

Felicity's uninterrupted repose lasted five blessed hours
before she found herself dragged unwillingly to wakefulness.
Struggling to shake off her sleep, Felicity gradually became aware of
a form reclining behind her in the bed, pouring heat over her in
waves. Only a thin sheet and her clothes protected her from skin
contact. Instantly, her senses went on full alert, a scream building in
her throat.

"Shhh..." A voice told her, and a hand clamped itself over her
mouth.

Completely defenseless, Felicity complied. She could smell
the slight hint of Jase's cologne, and she almost began to thrash out
of his arms....*innocuous intentions,* her mind reminded her
ironically. Had he interpreted some nonexistent signal from her as an
invitation to her bed? Something in the tension of his body stilled
her, though. She realized he wasn't lying down – he was leaning as
if to whisper in her ear, and his terse breath spoke vigilance, not
arousal. Heart pounding, her unseeing eyes froze wide with fear.

As her eyes adjusted to the scant light that filtered into the
room around the edges of the drapes, her initial irritation returned.
She saw no immediate peril that would justify her current need to
ignore the muscled ridges pressed against her back or the heat of

Jase's breath on her neck. Her suspicion converted her reaction to him into anger, though she knew her impulses wanted her to turn toward him and run her hands up under his shirt. Instead, she forced her eyes to strain against the darkness.

For what seemed like several minutes, the form behind her lay motionless, breathing shallowly, and pinned her so that she did the same. After the protracted moment, a hand pressed itself gently on her raised shoulder, vacating the space behind her. As a result, she found herself lying on her back, Jase's face inches above hers. She licked her lips. Jase's shirt brushed her chest and the heat of his body cocooned her. She swallowed – her "impulses" were liars. The thought that he might intend to seduce her – that she might want him to – terrified her. He lowered his lips to her ear, and she closed her eyes, trying to focus beyond his proximity. Then in a whisper so low she had to freeze to hear it, Jase tore her out of her irrational illusions.

"Don't move," he breathed. "Someone was here, trying to get in. I think the person has left, but I have to check."

Felicity came back to her senses, and her eyes popped open. She lay frozen as Jase raised himself gingerly from the bed and glided to the curtained window. Without moving her head, she watched Jase creep around the room – the air around her chilled with his absence, and the breath she had held slowly filled her lungs. Had she wanted him to kiss her?

Watching him where he slid through the shadows, she convinced herself to the negative. There was some hollow inside of her that ached for a connection, where her commitment to Brendon had died and lay moldering. Any hint of connection infused her with relief, but she knew it was just a drug – not a cure. Forcing her mind back to the moment, Felicity considered what she should do.

Jase hadn't looked back at her. If he truly expected danger, why didn't he produce some sort of weapon. He merely slipped along the edge of the room toward the window, empty-handed. After checking every hidden corner of the room, bathroom, and closet and carefully peeking through the curtains, he rushed quietly back to Felicity's side.

"Sit up," he commanded.

She complied, and he placed two pillows behind her back as if she were an invalid, ordering her to remain where she now sat. Reaching into his pocket, he produced a cell phone which he held out to her.

"This is my cell phone. I have to leave the room to check the rest of the house. If it's possible for us to get out of here, we need to do it now." As he spoke, his usual slight drawl transformed into a new, unfamiliar accent that transfixed her thoughts. Some portion of Felicity's brain registered the fact and recognized the accent, but she didn't have the capacity to both process novel suspicions and listen to Jase's instructions.

"You're leaving me?" she whispered harshly, trying not to sound desperate.

"Just for a few minutes," he smiled tersely, brushing his hand down her hair. "Do not open the door to anyone but me, not even the owners. I'll knock five times. If someone else shows up and tries to get in, open my phone and hold down the six key. This will call a friend, initiate a protocol. A trace on our location. I set this up years ago as a fail-safe in case I'm ever in more trouble than I can handle."

His hand paused, cupping her face, and he gazed heatedly into her eyes. "If you do what I ask, you'll be safe. I intend to take care of you." Then he leaned in to her and gently placed a kiss on her forehead. Not waiting to see her reaction, he hurried to the door and crept carefully into the hallway.

Felicity sat frozen where he left her. What was he trying to do to her? Her emotions churned with conflicting pains. Unlike the last time Jase had touched her uninvited, Felicity did not feel the righteous anger and violation she should feel. Even fear fled as the longing for connection warmed her from the core. Unfortunately for her tough-minded intentions, Felicity responded far to instinctively to Jase Hamilton – scoundrel or no.

If Brendon had honestly sent her into slavery, where lay her reasons to reject Jase? Just the ghost of her dead marriage refusing to rest in peace. *you would have said no to someone like Jase before you were married. You would have said no if you had never married. Because you can't trust him.* She wouldn't put her faith in Stockholm Syndrome to direct her into good choices.

Taking the opportunity to cool off, Felicity closed her eyes and fought back the tears. Yearning stripped away the carefully packed earth under which she had buried her emotions. They were still entirely too fresh to dig up, but part of her craved what Jase offered. It was like the rush of pleasure buried the dull ache. *Like a drug,* she realized. Maybe she overestimated her own strength, her ability to resist an offer of connection when she stood so alone.

Ironic, she realized. The isolation of her previous life mocked her now. She had only thought she was alone then! She needed to get away from Jase, but where would she go if she did. Usually, she would call her parents, and as a last resort, she would call her brother.

If Felicity's husband had just cheated on her, maybe her dad could have called Brendon in, given him a stern talking to, paid for a lawyer. What exactly could Harry Alexander do against Bill Henry and ProtoComm, though. A retired post office logistics manager versus a Fortune 500 company that held secrets on some of the most powerful men on earth? She couldn't ask her dad to help, and the fact that her parents now had the kids gave further reason to avoid involving them.

Eventually she would involve Nick, but not until she had a better idea of what she faced. Not only did she worry that he would run in guns blazing, he also was currently being courted by Brendon's henchwoman. He seemed thoroughly convinced of Briel's benevolence, and Felicity didn't hold the position at the moment to contradict whatever evidence Briel would manufacture to prove her objectivity.

So, for the time being, Jase was her best option. She just had to make sure she ignored all semblance of her humanity long enough to get away from him. Surely she could suppress whatever alien urge had overcome a decade of adulthood and turned her into a hormonal teenager. Fortunately, her suspicion of his intentions gave her just enough resistance to tell her juvenile self to go sit in time-out.

She could in no way trust Jase. How did she even know if he had heard an intruder? What if he just manufactured an excuse to leave her so he could contact ProtoComm? What if he had joined her in the bed to confuse her, leave her flustered so that she didn't follow him. With that thought in mind, she swung her legs over the side of the bed, determined to find him and figure out what he was up to. She could not afford to be afraid.

The banging at the door proved her thoughts liars as her heart leapt, panicked, into her throat. Afraid.

"Felicity, let me in! I'm here to help you!" an unknown male voice hissed through the door.

She couldn't move. Her mind willed her muscles to respond to her command, but terror had rendered them immobile. The pounding in her chest and the increased speed of her breath were the only evidence of her being human rather than a statue.

A new sound propelled her from her frozen state and sent her flying to the door.

"Felicity," Jase's voice called frantically from outside.

"Jase!" she gasped. Felicity did not open the door, but dashed to it and looked through the peephole to see what was happening. She could see a white-haired man, very muscular and athletic looking, hands raised defensively, facing to her left, but she could not see what he was seeing. Fortunately for Jase, the owners lived offsite, or they definitely would have called the police.

"Jase!" she cried again and, despite Jase's warning, she cracked the door, wedging her foot behind it to slow it down if someone tried to push it open. Before the stranger could react, Jase angled himself so that he cut off any option to bust into the room.

Jase, in a mirror pose to the man, was a little taller but, now that Felicity saw him in this perspective she realized, almost the same build. The fact that Jase looked like he could match the unknown intruder calmed some of her anxiety. She would have no chance against either – not without a weapon. And even more encouraging, the fact that a stranger had actually shown up to claim Felicity proved the truth of Jase's concern. Maybe if she stayed with him long enough, he could actually convince her that he intended her no harm.

"Stay where you are, Liss. I have him."

Of course Felicity would stay where she was. Maybe she should have closed the door, but if the men moved far enough away, she fully intended to escape to the car. She prayed that Jase had the same idea.

"Leave now," Felicity heard Jase say, though with an infinitely more dangerous tone than any he had ever used with her. Could he fake the danger that emanated from him toward the other man?

"We're going to get her sooner or later. You may as well give her to me now, and no one needs to get hurt."

"I think not," Jase retorted.

Felicity didn't see who threw a punch at whom, but the next thing she knew, Jase and the man had begun a steady exchange of blows, hands and even occasionally feet barraging each other's forms. She cringed as a firm blow from the man's fist connected to

Jase's cheek. Though she wanted to close her eyes, Felicity forced herself to watch, knowing that the outcome would determine her fate. She had no idea what she would do if Jase lost. Still, she could hardly follow the blur of blows exchanged by the men.

Suddenly, Jase had the man on the ground under his knee, his hand to the man's throat.

"*Fuis*, Felicity!" she heard Jase command. "Get the keys and get to the car!"

Run...Shaking uncontrollably, she tore herself from the spectacle outside her door and roamed the room with her eyes until she saw the keys on the nightstand beside her bed. She dashed across the room, grabbed the keys and the phone, and then darted back to the door. Was she an idiot to put herself in the power of a man who could fight like that?

Peering out, she saw that though Jase still held the higher position, the stranger fought fiercely to free himself from under Jase's knee. She threw the door open and narrowly dodged the man's outstretched legs which he appeared to thrust toward her in an attempt to trip her up. With all her might, she sprinted down the stairs and out the door. She didn't want to be alone again. She didn't know where to go. But she knew that if she didn't get away quickly, she might find herself a prisoner again, and isolation seemed the better option. So, she dashed toward the car, leaving the sounds of Jase's struggles behind her.

Though the sun had begun to lighten the eastern horizon, the shimmer of the dawn's transition actually made it harder for her to see. Or, she wondered, was it her utter horror blocking her vision? Felicity finally made it to Jase's car in the little lot behind the house, and she made a beeline to the driver's side door, throwing herself into the seat and locking the door. She knew she should hurry, but she hated to leave Jase without resources, without help. Not that she could provide much. Suddenly, she remembered the phone. Which number had he said to push?

Her hands quaking, Felicity tried to unlock the phone so she could call for help. Unfortunately, the nervous tremors of her fingers made pushing the right combination of characters almost impossible. She nearly screamed in frustration the fourth time the phone refused her entry.

The sudden banging on her window released the scream she had stifled before, and she dropped the phone. Cringing away from the glass in terror, Felicity upbraided herself for not placing the keys in the ignition as soon as she got in the car. Now, she had to fumble to find the right position to shove them in the ignition. When she registered the face in the window, her heart restarted, and she floundered to unlock the door.

Relief washed over her. Before she could reach the handle, Jase had opened her door and reached in to pull her out of the car. She nearly jumped into his arms, throwing her arms around him in her pleasure at being safe. The relief didn't last long.

For one brief moment, Jase placed his lips softly against her cheek, and his hand caressed her hair. She felt herself relax, and her breathing returned to normal. He pulled away almost immediately, though, and ordered her to get in the passenger side.

"We have to hurry. I didn't kill him, and I couldn't knock him out," Jase informed her when she was seated safely in her seat. "He's hidden somewhere in the house, but he probably heard me go out the front door. It will only be a matter of seconds before he's out here."

As he spoke, Jase threw the car into reverse and then peeled out of the parking lot, whipping onto the grass as they approached a car that blocked the drive – probably the intruder. Glancing behind, she recognized the man's blonde head where it veered into her view from around the red brick corner of the house. Felicity threw on her seat belt and leaned her seat back slightly so that she could calm down. Her opportunity to escape had passed, but she couldn't really regret it. Wise or not, she seemed to have committed to her course. She prayed she wouldn't regret it.

"Who was that?" she panted. "Someone from ProtoComm? Have they found out you're helping me?"

"No, actually. I didn't recognize him, and he didn't know the passphrase the ProtoComm operatives use. I'm not sure, but he may be from the traffickers I stole you from. They need to find you before Bill finds out they lost his material."

Great! Now I'm Bill's material. "What do we do now?" Felicity wondered, half angry, half anxious.

"We stick to the original plan. I can still work best out of ProtoComm. And the traffickers headquarter in the south. Going north is our best option."

"But don't you think that man can guess where we're going?" Felicity didn't like the idea of doing anything predictable.

"No. I think they traced your phone. I need it."

Surprised, Felicity handed him her phone. He pulled the car over and began to dig through the center console. A moment later, he pulled out a safety pin and pressed it into the side of the phone. A small rectangle popped out revealing a piece of plastic which he promptly snapped in two. Then, he placed her phone on the ground outside his door and drove away. Felicity could hear the crunch of the tire as it ran over her phone – her lifeline. Though she trusted his rationale, she felt a kick in the gut once she realized that all her ability to contact the outside world had been crushed with her phone.

Jase had taken good care of her so far, but she had relished that one link to her independence. Now she had none.

Chapter 18

Sarah stared out the window into the night.
She wondered if the darkness would ever warm her again, invite her
to amble pleasantly in its somber beauty. All she saw now
was the sinister shadows that held unspoken threats.
I miss you, she smirked joylessly at her once-friend. No, she did not
see any near reunion with the dark.
– Excerpt from the popular novel Felicity read her first night at the
cabin.

"Please ensure that all common areas are covered. Include as many
entrances into and egresses out of each room as possible.
The feed will need audio as well. Please take special note of
any unexpected visitors, preferably male, who enter the
house and into which rooms they pass." – Internal
ProtoComm memo, offering instructions for the installation
of the surveillance system at the home of Brendon and
Felicity Miller.

"I have to contact Nick," Felicity insisted as they passed
through the last town before Canmore.

"Absolutely not," Jase snapped at her.

"Excuse me?" Seemed a little early for him to play a
controlling hand – Felicity was still far enough from Banff that if she
could manage to get away, she thought she could find a path home
before someone could ferret her out. "I need to contact my brother.
Last time I delayed calling him, he was about to go to the FBI. If he
does that, you may wind up in trouble with ProtoComm and the law.
And neither of us wants that."

Jase smirked, apparently unconcerned. "Would that be bad
for you. Maybe you're afraid they'll think you're in league with me."

Scoffing, Felicity glared at the side of his face. "Hardly. If I
contact the FBI, I'll just tell them you kidnapped me," she corrected.

The smirk turned into a grin. "That will never work. I have

friends at the FBI. I'll tell them you kidnapped me."

Despite herself, Felicity laughed. "Saint Felicity?" she offered tongue-in-cheek. "How would anyone believe it?"

Jase laughed, too, but his expression quickly fell somber as he peered out at the passing landscape and the mountains visible in the near distance. For some reason, he oozed sentimentality. "I'm sorry," he explained. "This whole thing is just so wrong. That someone like you would have to go through this..."

Though pain lanced through her chest with his sympathy, Felicity managed to restrain herself to murmured agreement. "Because apparently I married the wrong man," she intoned. She glanced over at Jase, afraid he would use her expression of vulnerability as an inroad. Fortunately, though, he didn't react, and Felicity managed to relax into her own melancholy. She turned out her own window, irritated at herself for her ambivalence. Every time she thought of Brendon, her heart ripped in half, half wanting to wipe him off the planet and the other half wanting to go back to him and pretend that nothing had happened. What would he do if she just showed up at the house when he returned?

Without preface, Jase reached over and placed his hand on hers where it rested on her knee. She should draw back, but his touch radiated a strange, soothing heat that seemed to numb the pain. *I can use him,* she assured herself. *I can indulge in a few moments of pleasure as long as I don't go too far. As long as I leave him in the end.* Jase could just act as a painkiller - Vicotin for the heart.

Glancing down to where he had laced their fingers together, Felicity worried that he might prove too powerful a drug. The relief was so great that she felt herself in danger of becoming addicted. At a point in her life where death crept over her, Jase promised a spark of life, and desperation tempted her to give in to anything that kept her alive. She forced her eyes back to the scenery, keenly aware of the heat of his skin against hers.

"I can't do this," she breathed, pulling her hand back as she leaned against the window.

Whatever vibe radiated from Jase told her that he had heard her, and he read some significance into her words. She didn't even know the significance of her words. She just hoped he would read less than she felt. What havoc might he reap on her spirit if he tried to pursue the connection they both obviously felt? She was in no condition to manage that kind of vulnerability.

After several tense moments of silence, Jase finally addressed her. "You can't call Nick," Jase insisted, "but if you write him a message, I'll email it to him. I can hide my tracks pretty well as long as I don't use my own equipment."

Likely story. Nick was the only contact with what her life had been, and giving up contact with him would leave her with no recourse besides Jase. He might think he had cut her off from Nick, but she would find a way. In the meantime, she would fly under the radar. She just didn't really want to argue with her only chance of a companion. *Story of my life.* Grabbing Jase's phone, she typed out a quick note on his notepad. If he really meant it, Jase could send it when he believed it safe; Felicity made sure to use Nick's public email so as not to disclose any important information.

As if they didn't have a care in the world, Jase wound his way slowly down a maze of bucolic roads, some seeming to lead nowhere until they curved deceptively onto another country lane. Unlike Felicity's makeshift map application on her cell phone, Jase's satellite GPS had no reception problems out in the middle of nowhere.

Even knowing they weren't lost, though, the hills made her dizzy. Not naturally a weak woman, Felicity found herself exceptionally disoriented because the sense of helplessness seemed so new to her. *Maybe if I were one of those mewling, fainting women, I could handle this better. It would be familiar territory.* Or, she thought, maybe motherhood really had made her soft, like Jenna believed.

"You're going to stay at my place near Banff." Jase broke into her reverie.

"You have a place in Banff?" she interrupted.

Jase laughed. "Not exactly. Bill owns extensive land up here, and he regularly conducts ProtoComm business from his residence here. So, coming up here is convenient for Bill – the guy who has a private jet so he doesn't have to worry about airfare. When I went to work for Bill, he called me up here often enough – security issues for all of his high-dollar guests that got a place. I don't like staying where Bill is and always being under his eye. So I set up a cabin outside of town."

"You like to be the one with eyes everywhere," Felicity leveled.

Jase shrugged. Pausing, he glanced at her with concern. "I

will need to be gone a lot during the day. As far as Bill is concerned, I just made a two-day trip to purchase equipment, and I need to make a show of installing that equipment."

For a moment, Felicity's heart dropped. What would she do alone with her thoughts? The first couple of days had proven so brutal. Then Jase had shown up, and Felicity had found her mind filled with enough upheaval that she didn't have room to worry about anything. Not that she wanted him around, exactly, but he was better company than her damaged memories.

Her face must have shown her emotion because Jase again reached his hand to hers. "Let me get you something to distract you. I mean, I obviously have a television, and you can stream content, but I also have access to a large book collection. What do you like?"

What are you trying to pull? The look on his face, though…he meant it. He intended to entertain her. She snickered internally at the idea, as if he would break into song and dance to keep her from boredom. "Um, thank you," she smiled, almost in danger of gratitude as he placed his hand back on the wheel.. "I do love books," she allowed. "Anything classic. Jane Eyre, anything Dickens or Austen. Les Mis, Tolstoy. I'm not difficult to please. Just stay away from modern trashy romances."

"Nothing with bare-chested male models on the cover?" he chuckled.

When Felicity laughed, too, the feeling opened something in her chest, and the ache released into a threat of levity. Brendon's betrayal had smothered Felicity's usual serene tendencies for the past several days, but Jase just kept such a steady flow of consideration and energy, it was near impossible to hold onto suspicion while carrying on a conversation with him. He started in on Dicken's inspiration for Scrooge, and Felicity had to draw on some esoteric memories from college English class to keep up with him. It had been a while since someone had threatened to tax her knowledge of books, and she quickly lost herself in the energy of the conversation.

For the first time since her abduction, Felicity relaxed. She and Jase spent the next half-hour in such a nerdy, mind-bending, philosophical conversation that Felicity completely lost herself in pleasure. Occasionally, during a lull in the conversation, Felicity heard her fear tapping on the underside of her mind.

Felicity sighed silently as Jase expounded on the moral value of the transformation of Jean Valjean from criminal to saint. *Ironic,* she mused silently. *Or perhaps strategic,* she corrected. But even the thought just made her laugh at the contrast. Everything superficial had spoken to the fact that Brendon would be the perfect match for her. She built her life on it. Instead, this person who came from a background so thoroughly different from her own; he managed to connect with her in a way her husband never had.

A marriage of convenience, she thought wryly to herself. Maybe it would feel good to pretend for a while. Maybe it wouldn't hurt anything.

As they approached Banff, Jase seemed to notice her abstraction. Instead of trying to pry her out of it, he satisfied himself with one glance toward her. Then he stared, mirroring her silence, over the steering wheel and toward the horizon that rose to greet them.

They continued in silence until Jase turned onto a steep dirt drive that jagged immediately into a copse of thick trees and brush, obscuring its course from anyone driving by on the road. Littered with rustic, battered signs which read "No Trespassing," the barbed-wire fence evinced comparisons with the forsaken rural drives she had passed when in transit across the Arizona desert - the kind she wouldn't dare transgress for fear of ricocheting bullets. Rather than nullifying the forbidding comparison, the obscurity of the trees and brush increased the sinister feel of the landscape. Add to that the hovering darkness of the woodland hills, and Felicity couldn't escape the sensation that she had been dropped into a suspenseful movie where ghosts lurked behind every tree.

Despite her usual bravado, Felicity gulped.

Jase glanced at Felicity and grinned. "Do you think this will keep curious people away?"

"Yes," she agreed reluctantly. "But will it keep the *right* people away." She could see the ease with which a malevolent person could escape detection as he flitted through the thick underbrush that surrounded and invaded the rough gravel path to the dwelling.

"As always, an excellent and insightful concern," he smirked. "Don't worry. No one knows about this place."

Somehow, that knowledge didn't bring her any peace of mind, and she glanced nervously at Jase. Visions of crazy ax murderers and other generically evil characters flashed through her mind. She rather felt more vulnerable for the isolation. Adding to her discomfort, she realized that not only was she stuck in the middle of nowhere with Jase, she was glad she was stuck with Jase. *Stupid, stupid, stupid,* her fear shook its head at her, as if it had been nagging her and she stubbornly wouldn't listen. *Now do you believe me?* it chastised. No, she actually didn't. Instead, she wanted to hole up and cuddle in front of the fireplace with Jase. She bit her lip and glanced at him, but she quickly forced her eyes forward. *Not going there,* she insisted.

Shaking the vision from her head, she kicked herself back to reality. "Where do Bill and Brendon think you're staying?" she demanded. "What if they come to look for you and can't find you?"

"That's why I have to be gone during the days. I'll spend my time trading back and forth between ProtoComm's headquarters and my normal in-town residence. I need to seem the same as usual. I won't come here until after sunset; I know how to get around in the dark."

Somehow, the fact didn't surprise Felicity at all. Didn't everything macabre prefer the dark? *You keep telling yourself he's dark until you believe it,* she upbraided herself. Sure, she intellectually knew that Jase had problems, but she had begun to feel completely safe with him. The only unsafe thing about him was how much she enjoyed him.

After about half a mile of rough terrain, the brush began to clear a little. A few seconds later, the trees and bushes ceased entirely, revealing a small clearing, about a quarter of an acre in size. Toward the back of the small clearing, a very small house, more like a large shed or a small cabin, sat perched on a raised foundation. The wood siding had once been painted white, but the darkness and moisture of the forest seemed to have invaded the porous texture of the wood and inserted its green variations into the paint's surface. A small overhang covered the door, just enough to protect oneself from rain while placing a key into the lock.

Felicity shivered.

"Are you cold?" Jase queried solicitously. "It's pretty damp out here."

"No," she replied quickly. "No, um...I just have these flashes." She hugged herself.

"Come on," he responded, his tone reassuring. "You'll be safe out here for a while. And I'll figure something out. I promise."

As he spoke, Jase opened his door and moved around to hers, and before she realized it, he had opened her door and had her hand in his. Without asking permission, he pulled her to her feet and caught her around the waist to steady her. Despite her intended disinterest, she found herself breathless at the intimacy of the gesture. She stepped back a step, uncomfortable with his proximity, and turned abruptly toward the door, extricating herself from his still firm grasp around her waist.

She would have preferred to hold his hand as she traipsed across the gloomy span, but she wouldn't let herself. Felicity needed space to think now that an extended time alone with him loomed ahead. Did she intend to let the flirtation he had begun in Phoenix continue? After all she had been through, how could she even consider it?

Undoubtedly, Jase had helped her. He had not harmed her, he had saved her from the man at the hotel, he hadn't turned her in to Bill. All of those factors spoke in his favor, as did her growing knowledge of his intellectual prowess. Not just gritty practical intelligence, but refined philosophical sophistication – without pretense. If she had found him in different circumstances, she held no doubt that she would have admired him.

Interrupting her thoughts, Jase caught up with her then and grabbed her hand despite her reluctance. He led her up the steps and to the door.

"It's not as scary as it looks," he grinned impishly at her and opened the door.

At first, Felicity could tell little about the shrouded house because all the interior lights remained unlit. When Jase did turn on the lights, though, her paradigm of Jase shifted.

From the first moment that Felicity had met Jase, he had carried himself as suave, sophisticated, with only an occasional lapse into humanity after he had come to "rescue" her from Quito. The cabin, though, did not ooze sophistication. Instead, it glowed with charm. Cozy, homey charm.

An old-fashioned braided rug curled warmly in front of a cast-iron stove. In the same room across the space of the living area, an antique recliner reposed next to a camel-back sofa whose tapestry spoke age. To her left, she could see a shallow hallway, but could not see to where it led. Despite the age of the furnishings, no thick layer of dust blanketed the visible surfaces, as Felicity would have expected in a rarely-used cabin. Instead, everything looked neat - and even somehow smelled clean, a quality that old homes and furniture rarely possessed. Examining the details, Felicity realized that the living area doubled as a kitchen, the stove both for heat and cooking.

"How old is this house?" she wondered.

"The house itself is about a hundred years old, but most of the furniture is much older." The grin again, "Not the recliner. It's an original Barcalounger."

Felicity barely reined in a laugh at the unexpectedly enthusiastic declaration. Was Jase Hamilton a closet nerd? What was a Barcalounger, and why did Jase even hold that kind of knowledge? Her lips twisted in an attempt not to smirk at his eagerness.

Even with her amusement, though, Felicity lost sight of Jase and his unexpected humanity as soon as she sat down on the little couch. Jase had made his way to the kitchen area and was describing some hidden luxury that she couldn't quite grasp, and fatigue suddenly lay a blanket across her normal astuteness. Though the day had only reached noon, a sudden lethargy overwhelmed her, almost as compelling as the night that, drugged, she had felt herself laid into an abductor's car.

She couldn't ignore the fact that Jase admitted to drugging her that day, and suspicion washed over her mind at her sudden exhaustion. If he had intended to take her back to Brendon, wouldn't he have delivered her directly to ProtoComm? What if he had something else in mind? Something almost as sinister? What if he had nabbed her from her flight just so he could drug her again, but then trap her for himself rather than hand her over?

Felicity shivered. Despite her anxiety, her exhaustion dragged her down, tugging her toward slumber as if in confirmation of her fear. She clearly remembered, though, eating nothing but restaurant food in the past 24 hours, and she never left her food alone with Jase. Common sense flashed for a moment, and she abruptly realized that she had not felt safe in many days. Maybe the drug that now pressed at her consciousness was not a narcotic; maybe it was safety. She finally felt safe, and her body grasped at the opportunity for much-needed rest.

She strained to listen to Jase's initiation into the amenities of the house. One bathroom, a small cupboard beside the stove, an antique refrigerator, a table and chairs for two: all charming and, under the present circumstances, soporific. Felicity began to doze as visions of by-gone eras floated across her mind. She woke from a dream in which villains with Colt 45s wearing black suits and Fedoras chased her in black Model-T Fords, and she found herself upon waking surrounded by their furniture contemporaries, including an ancient quilt that Jase had obviously covered her with at some point. She almost felt like she had run into one of the homes that lined the streets in her dream.

She had been dead to the world from the moment she nodded off on the couch until she awoke to full alertness, who knew how long later. Unsure whether or not Jase had left her, Felicity sat up quietly from her repose, peering around her and trying to shake off her sleepiness. Jase had left her alone? Why would he risk it if he wanted to keep her in his grip? *Because he thinks he has convinced you to stay?* she answered her own question. The sun glared at her through the large living room window. She wondered that no curtains filtered its brilliance, but a slight tint minimized the visual discomfort.

Rising, Felicity crossed to the tiny cupboard and refrigerator that comprised the kitchen. Inside the cupboard, she found various cans and boxes, all fresh, but uninteresting. The refrigerator held similar various nondescript staples, nothing particularly exciting except for several variations of French cheese. Perhaps Jase not only spoke French but enjoyed French culture. Felicity shivered with a moment of pleasure at the thought.

More than anything, the cabin created a contrast in Felicity's mind. Jase seemed poised and polished, but his private sanctuary wore an earthiness, an organic cool so different than polished ProtoComm. From Brendon to Bill to Jenna, and even the oily Jack Buckley – a superficial sheen flashed and shivered across their personalities, their appearances. Even with his chiseled physique and his careful portrayals, Jase stood apart, a vigilant creature inside the armor he claimed he wore. The concept both attracted and terrified Felicity.

If he intended her benefit, she doubted that any other person could manage it quite as successfully. If he did not though, or if his other motives interfered with his better angels, then Felicity could not imagine with what ease he could manipulate someone like her – a woman, alone, damage, betrayed, and fearing for her life. *I would be a fool to hand him control.*

Well, she just wouldn't. She would force her mind away from him and keep her eyes on the practical world before her. Turning from the kitchen, she made her way to the front door. It was locked with a keyed lock, but after a quick glance around, she spied a small entry table, and the tiny drawer held a key that, upon placing it in the lock, turned to allow her egress. Hardly a nefarious attempt to restrain her.

She stepped outside, pausing on the porch for several seconds to see if an alarm sounded, but when nothing happened, she made her way into the clearing. On her right stood a small, green-roofed wooden shed, covered in moss and vines. She popped open the door to the sight of a shiny, blue ATV. On a low shelf rested a gas can which turned out to be full, and Felicity shook her head. He had literally provided her the means of her escape if she chose to do so. What was he about?

When she glanced over the top of the little shelter, the shadows of the forest seemed to reach their dark claws toward her, and she realized that even if she might leave, she would wait until she could do so under the full exposure of the sun.

Felicity rushed back across the clearing and in through the front door, pressing it shut behind her before clicking the lock shut. After taking a moment to calm her breath, she replaced the key in the drawer and focused on a safer environment to explore the house.

She crossed to the little hallway she had seen on the other side of the living room. Directly in front of the doorway into the hall perched a small bathroom, unremarkable in any way except for the quaint claw-foot tub and hand-held shower. It reminded her of the Victorian romances with dramatic heroines. She wondered whether those women had struggled with hopelessness before their hero returned and saved the day.

Jase's hero credentials were sketchy at best, and Brendon had relinquished the role. No. No unlikely hero presented himself to remedy Felicity's bleak situation, though Jase brought some really good looks to the secondary character category. Felicity smirked. So, she needed to focus on how she, herself, would salvage the unglamorous reality that remained available to her.

Turning to her right, Felicity entered a small bedroom, complete with a painted wrought-iron bed and small wicker dresser. The bed wore a patchwork quilt in red and white, matching red curtains decorating the small window which overlooked dense trees. Pleasant, but not particularly noteworthy. The other bedroom proved comparable, but opposite. Instead of painted wrought-iron, the bed's frame was dark, sturdy wood. The diminutive dresser matched. She plunked her bag down onto the bed. Opening the top drawer, she noted several neatly-folded men's shirts, obviously Jase's.

His and hers, she mused wryly. At least he didn't sleep with every woman he brought to the cabin.

Returning to the living/kitchen area, she noticed for the first time a small faded wooden cabinet to the right of the couch, unobtrusive because it fit so perfectly with the other furniture. Its contents, however, shocked Felicity with their modernity. An understated stereo sat on the top shelf, a remote control and several CDs on the lower. A cable sat next to the disc player, ready for MP3s, but she had no access to that technology at the moment – Jase had crushed her phone. Felicity picked up the remote and pressed play. Somehow, inexplicably, the room behind her filled with the sudden sound of rich, warm music. The abrupt appearance of the velvet sound literally made her jump.

Turning to face the room, Felicity searched futilely for the source of the music in the walls. Fascinated, she took one moment to search out the name of the CD which played.

Mahler's Fifth Symphony, she mused as she placed the case back on top of the stereo.

She then stood and wandered, somewhat bemused, into the other rooms to see if she could find more hidden treasures. The music followed her first into the bedroom on the right, and then into the bathroom. Shutting the bathroom door, she found that though the music played at a subtle level, she could still hear the tune clearly. She saw no place to hide speakers.

Running her fingers along the tiny chest that held the sink, she noticed that the faucet had no handles. She moved her hands from the rough grain of the aged wood to the polished copper of the faucet and nearly screamed when the water began to flow at her touch. *Deceptive,* she reflected, completely taken aback by the advanced state of technology in such an archaic dwelling. Amused, she wondered to herself if the stovepipe stove would turn into a convection oven. She turned off the water.

At that moment, a slightly panicked cry sounded from the

living room.

"Felicity!"

"I'm right here," she responded, somewhat embarrassed at his urgency. "I'm fine. I was just exploring, trying to find out the other luxuries you have hidden here," she ended wryly.

"Surely you didn't expect me to exile you to sparse misery," he greeted her as she opened the bathroom door.

How could I know you well enough to expect anything from you?

"You fell asleep before I could fill you in on all the good stuff," he continued, grinning.

"Where are the speakers?" Felicity asked, probing the walls with her eyes.

"Heating vents. Did you really think that a room this small needed so many vents?" he explained as she turned toward the living room.

"I guess not."

"Did you see the rooms?" he wondered, and he reached to open his bedroom door.

Felicity lurched past him, shock blossoming on his face. "I did," she fumbled, grabbing her bag off of his bed. "I was just…" she couldn't really formulate an answer to why she had put her stuff in the room so obviously his. She stepped the few steps to her room and threw the bag inside the room.

Other than a smirk at her obvious discomfort, Jase did not acknowledge her awkward display. Instead, he took a breath and peered at her with curiosity. "Did you go outside?" he probed.

What did she say? Did she admit it? She decided he might have cameras, and if he did, the question would prove a test. She had better answer truthfully, though she might see if she could hide the fact that she had discovered the vehicle.

"I did," she hedged. "This area is so beautiful, and I've been on the run or hiding in a hotel room for too long…"

His eyes narrowed, but the expression came across more as concern than suspicion. "I know this has been tough, but you might let me take you on any extended tours. If you survived all the insanity of the past week only to get lost in the woods? That would round out a week of injustices."

"How did you know I went outside?" She refused to acknowledge his apparent care.

"I didn't, exactly. I knew someone had been in the clearing. Mostly, I was concerned that somehow, someone had already found you. The chances are highly unlikely, but I don't want to take your safety for granted."

Gritting her teeth, Felicity felled an even tone. "Just me, as far as I know. And you don't have to worry about my venturing out on my own. The shadows are as deep as caves out in the trees." Not only had he provided a completely plausible excuse for knowing she was outside, he had framed it as solicitousness for her concern. How many times did she have to add the qualifier "if"? If he meant what he said. If he intended her benefit. If he was protecting her. How many times did she have to have confirmation from his actions before she believed his words?

Jase portrayed, in many ways, the mirror image of Brendon – a man who would say whatever he needed to mask his intentions. Conversely, Jase performed and behaved like a tortured, principled man – while bearing nonchalance as a mantle. Felicity couldn't quite buy it. "Well," she pressed, unwilling to dwell on his character, "I have been safe enough. Just exploring. This place is surprisingly well-appointed for a rustic cabin."

"I've done my best," he shrugged, though she could tell he was pleased. "…and wait till you see this." He darted across the living room to the paneled window frame and, to her surprise, one side of it opened on a covert hinge. He reached into the hole and pulled out another remote.

"Push this button," Jase commanded.

Stepping behind her, he reached around and placed the remote into her hand, his arm supporting hers as he raised it toward the huge window. With his chest pressed against her back, his warmth served the dual purpose of stirring a visceral pleasure within her and taking the chill out of the air.

Though her instincts tried to suppress her reaction, the sensation of his heat behind her, his arm brushing across hers, his fingers playing gently around hers – it stunned her..

Since her engagement to Brendon more than a decade before, Felicity had not experienced the feel of another man's arms, and she had not felt the need. Still, her current circumstances had altered the nature of her thoughts. She was no innocent, not pristine and untouched, but the last time anyone but Brendon had touched her, she had been a youth, and her partner had also been a youth.

Innocent, curious – not like Jase.

Jase was no innocent, and neither was Felicity. For more reasons than she could enumerate, Felicity no longer considered herself bound to her legal husband; it wasn't guilt that withheld her desire to lean back into the heat of Jase's chest, to use their joined hands to pull his arm around her. The idea was neither morally nor sensually offensive to her.

Strategically, though? What held her back was the rational understanding that she could not afford to make herself vulnerable to someone she did not trust. Turning to him, welcoming his kisses, indulging her appetites – the actions that followed would strip Felicity of her objectivity, and she could not risk muddled thinking at the moment.

So, she tried to pretend that she felt nothing. Jase pointed to the proper button and, using his arm to direct Felicity in the right trajectory, he waited unmoving while she pushed it. Unfortunately for her resolve, a glow seemed to burn through her at the sensation of his closeness and his skin on hers.

Unexpectedly, the window transformed into an opaque television screen, the glass itself inexplicably forming pixels and colors. The perfect view from a position on the couch. The wonder of it erased her discomfort at Jase's nearness for a moment – a very dangerous moment.

"Qu'en penses-tu?" he hummed, his lips so close to her ear that the warmth of his whisper caressed her neck. Apparently, he had sensed her vulnerability. *And there's the lothario,* her brain tried to warn her.

What did she think? Her breath caught for a moment, and she closed her eyes in pleasure. Then desperate to stop her thoughts, she whirled quickly to face him, realizing too late that he had stepped closer to her as she turned. Now his face rested inches from hers, and his eyes raked longingly across her lips. He licked his own and raised his hand to cup her face.

No! her reason reverberated in her mind, but when she met his ebony gaze, her determination faltered. Everything about him pulled her to him, from the lash-rimmed warmth of his eyes to the physical heat that emanated from the etched ridges of his chest. He was beautiful and considerate, and most importantly, he stared at her now with a hunger that stirred a long-dormant craving in the depths of her chest.

Fortunately, though, Felicity had never been slave to her impulses – she had to heed her rational mind. If Brendon, who had known her and shared a history with her, could betray her so completely, how could she trust someone she barely knew? The answer seemed obvious – she couldn't. "Stop," Felicity whispered, suddenly unable to find her voice. She looked down to break the intensity of the moment. Her feeble communication revealed more weakness than she would have liked, but she had to get the word out of her mouth. She stood tenuously in the compromised determination of a betrayed woman, and she feared herself as much as she did him. How she longed to reach for him, to brush her hands across his face and test the heat of his lips!

When she imagined the feel of his embrace, though, her battered soul buttressed her mind's determination. She was afraid to take the risk, to go to the place where she lay herself open to him ,and she wasn't the kind of woman who could just indulge herself in physical pleasure without connection. The desire in her threatened to break open a cavern of pain that had lain hidden beneath the hardened shell she had erected as soon as she awoke on the side of the road in Quido.

Quido. The word rose unexpectedly, and the room around her wavered as if in a dream. The memory of that day, the hopelessness and emptiness, rose substantial before her, as a wave to swallow her vision, and even Jase's presence couldn't dam the swell of desolation that engulfed her. What had just happened? Why could she not breathe? Suddenly, she realized that her chest had tightened, squeezing strength from her, and she gripped her arms tightly across her belly. Her breath came in gasps, and Jase stepped back, shock and concern apparent in his eyes.

"Jase, I..." She couldn't exactly explain what had overcome her at the moment. The complexity of it overwhelmed her, and words failed her. Instead, she resorted to the least important excuse. "I'm still married," she gasped.

Skeptical, his eyes squinted in irritation. "It's Brendon?" Jase scoffed. "*Le bâtard qui t'a vendue en esclavage*? I don't believe you. You're too smart to buy into some twisted morality that holds you to a broken commitment."

"Please," Felicity gasped, turning from him with tears brimming in her eyes – she couldn't let him dig in for a deeper explanation. The surface was the only one she could manage.

"Please don't push me. You have no idea how badly this hurts."

"Of course it hurts," he asserted callously. "Because Brendon Miller hurt you."

The overt words stung, more than all of the tempered exchanges they had engaged in before. Felicity stumbled her way to one of the chairs by the table and fell into it, doubling over in pain. How did she travel long stretches of peace without thinking about it? She had no idea.

An instant later, Jase fell to his knees in front of her. "I'm sorry," he pleaded. "God, to think that it was okay…To think I could expect you… *Je suis vraiment désolé.*"

Felicity couldn't move. All of the hollow ache that had plagued her through her entire ordeal coalesced into an acute stabbing in her gut, a reaction to the violence of Brendon's duplicity and Jase's words. Gasping for breath, she held herself tightly as if her arms could squeeze away the misery.

Brendon had rejected her. She shouldn't care – she should know that his betrayal reflected his own character and not her failure, and she had forced the belief onto her battered heart for almost a week. But once the dam broke, she realized that she had not eradicated the doubts stirred by his betrayal – she had only buried them. Some dark, forsaken part of her heart still pulsed the message that he had known her and deemed her unworthy of love. Jase's overtures had awakened the insecurity that she had until then suppressed.

For several minutes, she just let herself feel the self-loathing that had lived inside of her for a decade at least – if not for all of her married life. Tears streamed from her eyes, and she couldn't even care when Jase seated himself next to her and wrapped his arms around her. Her mind compressed to a hot black coal of despair, and she could form no coherent thought for several minutes as she sobbed out the fury inside her.

Fortunately for her, however, a heart could not deem itself worthless for long and keep beating with a desire for life. She knew she had to live, so she cried out her self-hatred and then sat up and began to breathe deeply to quell the flow.

Jase waited patiently, anxiously, helplessly.

Finally, her breathing calmed, and she was able to straighten up in the chair, her eyes closed against the heat of spent tears.

"I'm sorry," Jase whispered again as he eased back in front of her and grasped her hands.

Felicity raised her chin and opened her eyes. Breathing deeply through her nose, she looked past Jase to the faceless window before her, too emotional to meet his gaze. "For what? Being honest?" she acceded. "It's not right for me to hold on to him after what he's done to me."

Jase dropped his eyes. "You've been through a lot, Felicity. It's right for you to do whatever you need. I'm sorry I pushed you. I got lost in the moment. It won't happen again."

The earnestness in his voice threatened to drive all suspicion from Felicity's mind. If all else proved false, she heard in his tone that at that moment that Jase had hated to cause her pain.

She closed her eyes again, smiling wanly and squeezing their joined hands. "Hopefully you don't get tired of hearing me say this. Thank you," she whispered, lifting her gaze and locking it on his.

He returned the squeeze of her hand and reiterated his promise. "I won't do that again. You have my word." He lifted her chin so she could read his sincerity. "You owe me nothing, and I will remember that you are not a mission. No more pressure."

With melted eyes, she poured her gratitude out to him. Whether or not he should have initiated a physical connection, circumstances had offered him the chance. For him to restrain himself showed consideration, no matter the impropriety of his impulse.

Over the next few days, Jase's actions proved the veracity of his words. He did not step into any level of intimacy, instead allowing her days to fall into a routine. Not that she considered staying where she was indefinitely, but with Jase so intent on providing her a refuge, she thought she might allow herself a respite, a healing moment to recuperate.

Having ascertained from their conversation the type of books Felicity preferred, Jase returned to the cabin the first day of her confinement with a veritable library of books, along with a bundle of comfortable and utilitarian clothes. Felicity wondered tacitly where in small-town Banff he had secured quite so many books without arousing suspicion. Maybe he'd split the purchases with Canmore. Of course, he had included a few of his own favorites hoping, he admitted, to sway her to the value of modern authors. His attempt at persuasion evoked a much-needed laugh.

Every morning, Felicity arose to the smell of breakfast and

coffee wafting through the intimate doorways of the cabin. The constant sickness in her gut subsided into more of a dull unease. Upon entering the living room, she would hear Jase's invariable greeting, accompanied by a smile and some sarcastic comment about sleeping all day. The familiarity of the situation both soothed and irritated Felicity. Soothed her because it distracted her from her heartbreak; irritated her because she didn't *want* to be quite so comfortable with Jase.

By 7:30 each morning, Jase had to be out of the house, off to play his role at ProtoComm and hopefully secure escape for Felicity. She held her breath each afternoon as she anticipated some news that he might find a way to get her home. Part of her wondered whether Jase really intended to work toward her freedom - he seemed rather to enjoy the illusory oasis he had established with her.

On her third day in the little cabin, Felicity woke feeling more rested than she remembered in years. Sniffing the air, she closed her eyes again and smiled when the scent of fresh coffee greeted her sense. Once she sat up, the chill air brushed over her tank top and sent a shiver across her skin. She threw on her robe and reached into the drawer for a pair of socks. When her hand brushed the beads, she sucked in a breath.

How could she take the risk again? After what Brendon had done to her, how could she let herself forget to be careful?

Of course, she hadn't actually forgotten why she was confined to a cabin in the middle of nowhere. She had just let current comfort smother her concerns and press them to the back of her mind. Had Jase done it intentionally? Or was he, out of kindness, just trying to help her deal with a miserable situation?

Either way, she could not let herself forget. For the time being, forgetting Brendon and his betrayal would require forgetting her children – something she would not do. Eventually, she would be able to separate the two, but not until her kids were protected.

With that in mind, Felicity slipped on her socks and began to plan, even as she followed the routine that Jase had no doubt grown to expect. Her first step would come in confronting him about his inaction. If she didn't receive a satisfactory answer, she would take some initiative behind his back. Felicity dug around in her bag, intending to set out on a short trek into the forest to assess the area around the cabin.

Once Jase left, she returned to her room, pulling some of her clothing from a bag to make space for supplies. If Jase found her, she could claim she was unpacking. He'd like that. After pulling out a thick jacket, a pair of convertible hiking pants, a thin turtleneck, and a warm sweater. She folded them, placing them into the bottom drawer.

Again, the beads.

If he despised her so much, why had he bought her the pearls? Why did it matter? All that mattered was that she not forget again. She didn't know if it made sense, but she needed a reminder. Reaching behind her neck, she put the beads on, recognizing that they now meant something entirely different than when Brendon had first placed them around her neck on that day before the trip. Her last day of ignorance.

Now her desperate mind lay in danger of establishing another delusion, this time with Jase? Never. – Felicity would not be a fool. She still hoped she could return from her trip to Banff in time to pick up her children from their grandparents' house, her future plans fully formed and actualized. Of course, she hadn't figured out how she would explain to them why their daddy would never see them again. Or that they couldn't return to their home. She also didn't know what she would do if Jase found out, how he might react.

She couldn't care. Jase claimed that he intended, in a little more than a week, to come up with a solution, execute it, and get her back to her kids. Well, maybe he would or maybe he wouldn't, but Felicity was not prepared to sit idly by and wait for someone else to determine her future – or more accurately, her kids' future. Jase had said she needed leverage, and if he didn't provide it, she would find it.

Now that the wounds of Brendon's betrayal had lost some of their raw edge, Felicity realized that she could not place her entire destiny in the hands of someone else. She had made that mistake for fifteen years – placing her trust in a questionable source. Instead, she had to utilize whatever resources she could scrounge up.

Her greatest resource for leverage, if she could access, would be her brother.

According to Jase, Nick had not responded to the email Jase had sent. Didn't seem likely. More likely, Jase hadn't even sent the email. Unless the unexpected contact had set off Nick's conspiracy theory tendencies.

Though no public computer could really be secure, Felicity

thought that Nick's personal website would probably be very secure. If she could send a message from an unknown email to Nick on his private email server, she felt fairly certain that he would trust it; plus, it would prove untraceable.

She originally thought to walk into town and knock on the first door she saw, but then she remembered Jase's assertion that ProtoComm could monitor the roads. Unless as a last resort, Felicity would not go anywhere near Banff.

Her next thought took her into a more practically, if not actually, hazardous situation. After donning her prepared clothes, she stepped from the filtered light of the cabin into the sliced shadows of the forest. Taking care to mark her trail on the trunks of the trees she passed, Felicity made her way behind the house, heading what she assumed was south into the forest, along a river. She trudged cautiously toward her undefined goal, praying that she had headed toward someone's house, anyone's house. Praying that she didn't head into a basically endless wilderness. Not having a phone with maps made a huge deficit in her capabilities.

Since Jase would return at approximately 7 p.m., Felicity would have to pay attention to the time in order to ensure that she arrived back with enough margin to shower, change, and hide the evidence of her excursion. About four hours into her journey, Felicity realized she hadn't prepared anything to eat. Her stomach growled angrily. Irritated at herself for such an obvious gaffe, she turned and started back toward the cabin. She did not enjoy the idea of waiting four hours before her hunger could be addressed.

After an equal time in trying to find her way back, Felicity gratefully acknowledged, that her stomach had done her a favor. Had she not turned when she did, she would never have made it to the cabin in time. Although she could easily find her markings on the trees, the process of searching for them took longer than she had expected. The return journey took her until 6 p.m. With relief, she broke through the last of the trees into the clearing and ran, panting, in through the front door. Her heart beat in her throat as she realized the significance of what she had done.

Was she an idiot for trekking through a never-ending wilderness, counting on questionable tactics to reach a questionable result? Even beyond the general danger of her day-long hike, what about the danger she returned to? She had left herself with no margin for error.

If Jase had arrived a little early for some reason, he would have found her missing. Even if he didn't harbor any violence toward her for her infraction, he would definitely be angry. When she processed the thought, it sent a shiver down her spine – she had seen him fight.

What did his anger look like? Was it violent? Was it strategically vindictive like Brendon's? When she had observed Jase's anger before, they had been on the road, and he had needed to keep his cool so that she would stay with him. Now that he had her isolated, what did she need to fear? Was she a prisoner? Would Jase let her leave if she insisted? She didn't want to leave yet, though. The cabin was a refuge, wasn't it?

Steeling herself, Felicity pressed down her fear and assessed her situation. She had survived the day with little ill-effect. She had returned with time to obscure her days activities. Rather than discourage her, if she actually analyzed what she had done, she felt more pride than fear. For twelve years, she had accomplished little. Suddenly, she had managed a pretty amazing feat alone.

When she rushed into her room, grabbing the soft terrycloth sweats that Jase had bought her, she headed into the bath with a smile on her face. She regretted that the cabin did not have a real shower. *So much quicker.* Slipping off her tennis shoes, she began cleaning them with a washcloth and water.

That will have to do, she conceded as she wrapped them in a towel and placed them to dry next to the sink. Stripping off her clothes, she threw herself into the bath, frustrated at how slowly it filled, and frantically worked, using the handheld showerhead, to remove any twigs or leaves from her hair. Finally satisfied, Felicity pulled the plug to let the water drain and stood to her feet, ready to step out of the bath.

The sound of Jase's voice froze her in her place. *So much for not being afraid…* Her heart battered against her ribs as it wildly sought to clarify her thinking by increasing the bloodflow to her brain. With his presence, new worries battered her mind. Mainly, had she successfully hidden her tracks? She prayed wildly.

"Felicity?" the voice came again, closer this time. He searched for her, apparently concerned because she hadn't answered him.

She responded tenuously, "I'm in here."

Clutching the towel tightly around her, she stepped hurriedly but gingerly onto the bathmat and began to dress herself.

"Are you okay?" he wondered, his voice at the door now.

"I'm fine," her voice was high, her tone more strident than normal.

Removing the towel from the shoes, she tossed it messily on the bathmat. She used the towel she had on her body to wrap her hair. She carefully folded the other towel inward as she saw a streak of dirt left from the shoes she had cleaned not quite successfully. Wrapping her shoes in her clothes, she reached for the handle.

Opening the door, she blocked the opening with her body.

"I'm fine," she asserted more calmly.

Jase stepped back to let her out, and Felicity sucked in a nervous breath as she saw a confused look pass over his features. Somehow, she had missed something.

"This is hardly your normal routine," he accused as she carried her things into her room.

"I have routine after a few days?" she sassed. "I was just reading a book and lost track of the time," she called to him from her room.

Something in his eyes as she turned back warned Felicity that she lay poised on a dangerous precipice, one in which Jase did not trust her instead of the other way around.

Rather than wait for Jase to extract information she didn't wish to share, Felicity went on the offensive. "Did Nick answer you today?" She tried to wear an ingenuous expression as she crossed to the table. If he had been lying to her about contacting Nick, as she had begun to suspect, then her interrogation might throw him off her trail.

Felicity watched Jase, his eyes avoiding hers as he sat across from her. "I finally had a chance to send it. It took me some time to get to a computer that wasn't monitored by ProtoComm." Though he apparently hoped this would please her, she still sought to distract him from her own deception, so she gave vent to her genuine shock and frustration.

"You just sent that to him today? I thought you sent it days ago! It will be a miracle if Nick hasn't done something reckless."

"Felicity, don't be upset." He reached a hand for her arm. "I'm sorry, I really have tried. But Bill has me under close wraps. Since your abduction and my absence, Bill has kept me on a tight leash. I can't be sure, but I think word of your escape may have reached him."

Sudden fear gripped her. Had Jase done something to expose her, placed her in more danger? *Just as likely placed himself in danger,* her conscience upbraided her. "What makes you think Bill knows?"

"He seems to have enacted some kind of damage control. I've heard rumors around the office. He has put in place factors that will allow him plausible deniability if word leaks of your abduction. I mean, maybe it's just a failsafe, but I can't be sure."

"Or I'm right about Nick and he did something that put Bill on guard."

"Maybe, but it doesn't seem to be about Nick – more about me. I've noticed that Bill has shut me out of several important meetings, things I would usually know about. Of course, being the security programmer, I have my methods of finding out information people want to hide. I mean, that's how I found out about you."

The man was brilliant. If there was a chance that he meant to help her, she would be a fool to refuse his help. *You just have to keep your other options open.* The idea didn't preclude accepting any genuine aid from him. "Jase," Felicity begged, her excursion forgotten. "I need you to get me home to my kids."

For a moment, something like guilt passed behind Jase's eyes, and Felicity's suspicion returned. She had no way of confirming anything that Jase said, and she felt entirely helpless to verify any of it. Maybe he didn't want to send her back.

"I will, Felicity," he promised, his expression almost resigned. "Just give me time, and I will."

"Time is one thing I have in short supply," she countered.

"I know. And if my suspicions about Bill are right, your time may be even more limited."

Felicity could not know what he meant, but she prayed that he would have enough opportunity to get her out if Bill suddenly showed up at the door.

As if he read her thoughts, Jase placed his hand on top of hers. "I will make sure that I have time to take care of you," he promised tenderly. "Redeeming you and getting you back to your kids are the reasons that I can still go face Bill every day. Otherwise, I would have packed up and left a month ago, when I first realized the nature and extent of Bill's operation. I will take care of you, *peu importe le coût pour moi.*"

The cost for him? Somehow, amid all her suspicions, Felicity hadn't considered the cost to Jase. Part of her believed that he might have said the words to elicit her guilt, to stop her from pressing him to move. Still, once he had her, had he really needed to manufacture such a complicated scheme to get her back to Brendon – to ProtoComm? Not at all.

If it had been a professional move, he just would have handed her over to traffickers again. If he intended some twisted kidnapping scheme, why head back to Banff? Better to keep her as far away from anyone who knew her as possible. Since he had brought her back to Banff, didn't it mean that he meant what he said? Who was this man?

Huffing a sigh, Felicity crossed her arms over her chest. "You don't make sense, Jase. All this stuff about me, about why you intervened for me. Do you expect me to believe that a man who has purposely closed his eyes to the misdeeds of his coworkers – who had callously enriched himself inhabiting the periphery of the criminal world – would suddenly turn hero, put himself in danger and risk his career to interfere on my behalf?"

Jase peered at the ground, rubbing the back of his neck with his hand. He blew out a breath. "Liss, I –" For a minute, it seemed like he wouldn't answer her, but he steeled himself and turned to face her. "You're right, of course. I have turned a blind eye, and there's no excuse for that, but the way my job works, the situation had never been laid out so clearly before me. In a way, I'm grateful that the first time I got to see things up close and personal was to see you."

He met her eyes with a pained expression. "I decided that people like you didn't exist, and so I wasn't really crossing any major boundaries. My family wasn't like you; certainly, my mother wasn't like you. On the few times I observed your fights with Brendon – back when I justified actually watching the videos because I wanted to ferret out Bill's plan – I was amazed at how you redirected Brendon's rage away from your kids. It was like you could sense the storm and stepped in to shield them. My mother would never have done that. She guarded her own comfort – supported my father – at the expense of her children. It was…"

He blew out a breath, still staring at the ground, and pain etched his voice into jagged shards. With the ensuing silence, Felicity found herself reaching to take his hand. "Jase, I don't need you to go into all this. I've seen your actions so far. That's how I'm going to make my decisions about you."

"*Mais je veux que tu comprenais.*" Jase covered the hand she held with his other hand. "I – you made me doubt everything, my whole life paradigm. How many people like you existed, had been taken out of play by these people I've engaged with, because they didn't have any idea that the world could be so dark. I don't mean the stupidly naïve ones, the ones who should have known and made stupid decisions that led them into danger. I mean the ones who acted in good faith, who trusted someone they shouldn't have trusted and paid the price. But it was even worse when I saw you, because you were strong, and you fought back. You stood up for your kids, but you were still respectful of your asshole of a husband. I just can't –"

"I appreciate everything you're saying. I'm not sure there's anything so remarkable about how I've lived my life. Obviously, I've lied to myself about a lot of my existence – lived in denial. So don't put me on some pedestal."

"I'm not." He gripped her hand tighter, and he met her eyes with a childish fervor. "I don't think you're some mythic figure, Liss. I just hadn't – I was going to say I hadn't had the chance to see, but that's not right. I hadn't believed in good people, so I hadn't looked. I interpreted information from the perspective that everyone would serve themselves, so I didn't have any reason to look for anything else. Now I'm doubting myself, Felicity. My whole life. And if people like you exist, and I have these skills and abilities that could protect them, isn't it my responsibility to do it?"

Staring into his zealous expression, Felicity had trouble doubting his sincerity. Had he really lived his life believing that everyone was greedy and self-serving? What an existence! If it were true – if it weren't a ploy to play on her sympathies – how could she judge him, especially now that he seemed to have changed his course with the new information?

"Okay, Jase. Okay." She placed her free hand onto their joined ones. "If what you're telling me is true, then we can go forward with this for now…" Felicity suddenly realized what he was offering her, what he was risking. "Do what you can to take care of me. But let's see if we can figure out how to manage it without getting you killed."

He turned to her with melted eyes, and for a moment, she

thought he might try to kiss her again. That small, irrepressible part of herself was moved to respond, but Jase seemed to read her ambivalence and thought better of it. Instead, he lifted their hands to his lips.

Without a word, he unlatched their hands and stood up, and she laughed as he stepped to the little stove and began to fix their dinner. How was she going to remain separated if he continued as he had begun? She had never cared about someone she simultaneously considered a threat, and the nagging doubt wouldn't let her respond with the connection the prior few minutes wanted to create in her. Her mind had learned to be cautious, and it knew her children had to be her top priority. Unfortunately, the human and vulnerable portion of Felicity wouldn't subject itself entirely to reason, and cracks began to form in her otherwise stalwart defenses.

Chapter 19

– *Stay alive*
– *Find evidence as insurance to make sure I can go on living*
– *Figure out what to tell the kids about their father*
– *Get away from Jase*
– *Get back to my kids*
– List of priorities from Felicity's journal, April 3

Will you be my wife? – Jase's text to Amélie, April 1

March 28
The following day - Friday, Felicity realized - she prepared
herself more effectively for her day-long trek. She would have little
opportunity to explore during the weekend – *an uninterrupted
weekend with Jase* - so she needed to do it immediately. Digging
through the shallow pantry, she found a box of granola bars and
another of trail mix. She grabbed two packets of each, and refilled
the water bottle she had taken with her the previous day. Unlike that
day, Felicity allotted extra time for the return trip. No more than
three hours hiking northwest, then begin the return trip before lunch.

At first, the day began almost identically to the previous
day's journey, but heading west instead of south. The dense forest
surrounding the cabin clutched menacingly at her hair and clothes,
snagging them and decreasing her ability to focus on the path of her
feet. As a result, Felicity stumbled several times, once scraping her
arm against an aged oak and leaving a hole in her sleeve.

Damn, she worried. *How will I hide this from Jase?*

Proceeding more carefully, Felicity continued until she began
to notice, with relief, a slight thinning of the trees around her. Could
the diminishing density signal the presence of a clearing, maybe
another house? Unfortunately, she found herself on a public trail. As
soon as she could, she would step off the path, but it did offer a
measure of comfort, the assurance that she wouldn't be lost in the
woods. Still, when the path met with the highway, Felicity knew that

she had to strike off the path even if it took her nowhere.

Cutting south, she soon found a rustic route that seemed to lead somewhere – which could prove good or bad. She had stopped marking trees once she hit the public trail, but she picked the practice back up once the way grew narrower and more irregular. She only had a few minutes before she would need to turn around, but she couldn't admit defeat too soon. She didn't think she could try again if she failed this time. Finally, a beautiful cabin rose before her.

Felicity wanted to feel cheered by the sight, but doubts assailed her as she approached the edge of the woods. How could she know that it was safe to approach the house? Jase had said that Bill owned extensive property near Banff, but most of the area was public land. What if the place she found was some kind of outpost or science center? What if there was not a computer in the building?

To her relief, as Felicity approached the house, she could see an elderly lady sitting in a rocking chair watching as her aged husband putted golf balls into a makeshift hole. *Not Bill Henry.*

"Hello," Felicity greeted them loudly, hoping that the shock of her sudden appearance would not send them running. Plastering on her most warm-hearted smile, she advanced a couple of steps into the clearing.

The couple eyed her warily. "Hello," the man returned, hesitant.

Hands in her pockets, Felicity adopted her most sheepish grin, "I know it's probably a shock to see me way out here."

"You could say that. We don't get many visitors - by choice."

"I'm so sorry. If I had any other way, I wouldn't dream of bothering you."

The man continued to stare dubiously at her.

"Um," Felicity stuttered nervously, "my husband and I are staying at a cabin just southeast of your home."

"Oh," the man relaxed a little. "You must be Mrs. Green."

Surprised, Felicity stared wide-eyed at the man before she was able to answer, "Why, yes. How did you know?"

"Well, you're staying on our property. You're quite the hiker to make it out here."

For a moment, confusion paralyzed her as she processed the new information. She had assumed that Jase owned the land. "I didn't realize that," she finally managed.

"Yeah, Mr. Green comes up here from Calgary sometimes to get away, but he's never brought his bride. Congratulations, by the way."

Felicity tried to appear cheerful, "Thanks." She glanced at the ring on her left hand, for the first time realizing that she still wore it. *I'll have to take that off as soon as I leave here.*

Obviously, the owner of the home had relaxed his concern, and Felicity watched anxiously as the minute hand inched toward noon. She decided she had to broach the reason for her visit as quickly as possible.

"I feel kind of foolish asking this," she smiled shyly at them, "but, do you have a computer with internet? I promised my brother that I would email him when we reached our retreat, but I didn't realize we wouldn't have a computer. My cell phone won't work up here, and he won't answer a number he doesn't recognize. Mr. Green went into town early this morning before I realized that I was so isolated up here."

The man laughed. "Yes, one of the many hazards of escaping civilization. The difficulty of staying connected to it."

"George, don't tease the poor girl. Let her use the pool-house computer."

"Thank you so much, Mrs...." Felicity suddenly realized she hadn't asked their names.

"Mrs. Henry," the woman replied with a smile.

Felicity's just recovered heart restarted its manic rhythm at the name. Surely there were numerous Henrys at any location in North America. They didn't have to be related to Bill. She almost changed her mind about emailing Nick, but desperation made her brave. *Or stupid,* she quipped to herself.

Following the slightly-hunched form of the man, Felicity glided across the close-cropped grass to a glass-enclosed structure on her right. "We had a computer installed out here so that Ann can surf the net while I swim," he grinned.

"I can't tell you how much I appreciate this. It should just take a few minutes."

"Take your time. I'm not swimming any time soon. Just make sure you shut it down when you leave. That dinosaur of a computer overheats and erases stuff all the time."

Felicity started to thank him, but stopped herself as a thought occurred to her.

"Would you do me a favor, Mr. Henry?"

"Call me George. Probably, what is it?"

"Okay, George. Would you mind *not* telling Mr. Green that I came over here? He would be livid if he found out I trekked by myself through the woods just to find a computer. As far as he's concerned, my brother can just wait till we get back like everyone else. In-laws, you know," she tried for an exasperated smile.

"I guess I can do that. But take my advice: don't spend too much time avoiding a fight, or that new wedding ring will outlast its usefulness."

"Don't I know that," she murmured under her breath morosely, thankful that she hadn't yet taken off her wedding ring. "Thanks, George. I'll try to remember that."

With that, George Henry took his leave and returned to his Astroturf putting green.

As Felicity entered the pool-house, she couldn't escape the sensation that she had stepped into her crypt. Not that the largely glass edifice hemmed her in, but if she had really stumbled on the home of Bill Henry's parents, the CEO had most likely installed software to monitor the activity. She found herself furtively peering over her shoulder lest George Henry appear at the door with a key to lock her in.

So, the quicker she could get Nick, the quicker she could escape. Her next move would be more complicated than just sending an email. Felicity felt sure of that, but she had to press on. *Leverage.* If she knew her brother, the solution was likely almost within her grasp.

First, she created a new email address, one which referenced a misspelled nickname he had given her from her favorite childhood book. If she emailed from her own address, she thought that someone might trace it, but surely Nick would recognize the word from their history.

She would also have to download a shredder file to cover her tracks in case anyone came looking for her transactions on the computer. More than any other time, she wished now that she had paid attention when her little brother had begun his tireless discourses on computer security. *What was the program that masks your location?* She wracked her brain to remember, but gave up when she realized that her phone said 12:25, twenty-five minutes after she wanted to be on her way.

The shredder would have to be sufficient.

nightengale@mailman.com: Hey, it's me. Please, please, please have on your email alerts! Can you start a secure chat with me?

Felicity bit her cuticles nervously as she watched the unmoving screen for what seemed an eternity. Finally, the very irate response came in all caps.

root@kernalNick.net: WHERE IN THE HELL HAVE YOU BEEN?!!!

Felicity sighed in relief that Nick so obviously recognized who the email belonged to. But would that mean others would recognize it, too? Nick's site was very secure, she knew, so she didn't allow herself to worry.

nightengale: I'm near Banff, Alberta, the place my spouse took me. I'm with a guy who's trying to find a way out of this situation for me. I'm fine. Were you able to pull anything else up off of that file?

root: Not yet. I'm having to bruteforce it. What are you doing so close to your husband? Aren't you afraid he'll find you?

nightengale: Not likely. I'm in the middle of nowhere. I had to hike three hours to find a computer. Look, can you send me those files somehow? When you've finished?

root: Not unsecured.

nightengale: Of course not. Encrypt them. Another question. I found out about some private servers. Is there some way I can get you access to those? They wouldn't be connected to the internet.

root: I have to get access to the system. Can you get a phone?

nightengale: I have no idea.

root: I need that to get in. You have to broadcast the signal somehow. And a flash drive for software, if you can find one.

nightengale: I'll have to see. Not like I can jog into town for supplies.

root: Yeah, please don't. And you better get out of there, wherever you are. You've been on long enough for people to notice. Check back tomorrow if you can. I'll send you those files as soon as they're ready. And I'll take care of your trail. Love you. Be careful.

nightengale: You, too. And you, too. And, hey. Change cell companies!

root: Haha. Okay.

Felicity quickly erased and shredded her history, praying that would suffice to stymie any pursuer savvy enough to pinpoint the computer she used. Then she uninstalled the shredder and emptied the recycle bin. *I really wish I'd paid more attention to my brother when he talked about computers*, she lamented again. *Too late for regrets.*

Shutting down the computer, Felicity turned quickly to the door. Surely no one had time to trace her whereabouts in the scant few minutes she had chatted with Nick. She crept out the door and glanced to where the elderly couple sat blissfully, sipping something hot out of mugs while they held hands across a petite wicker table.

Felicity paused there, watching the idyllic picture that the two presented. *Of all the times to feel sentimental*, she sighed. What she wouldn't give to sit at Brendon's side, the past two weeks erased from existence, and do something as mundane as sip tea or drink coffee! Then she remembered how messed up Brendon really was, and Felicity could feel nothing but gratitude that she would never have to endure that sickness again. She hadn't lost all faith in the ideal; she just recognized that she didn't have it.

Turning toward her makeshift domicile, Felicity trudged unwillingly back to the waiting grey peace of the cabin, an ephemeral disillusionment all that she could hope to find. After getting back in touch with the other anchor in her life, Nick, Jase's nascent affection felt too illusory. Yet, it was also necessary for now. Maybe the relationship was based on a fiasco, but she needed help to escape the fiasco, and for now, that help came from Jase.

Once she reached the cabin, Felicity stretched herself as fully as she could on the short couch. Because of her stature, she draped her legs over one of the sofa arms, her own arms stretching over her head in an attempt to relax her breathing. She refused to indulge her nerves, instead letting herself dwell in a sense of accomplishment. She had tackled a tough task that may pay off in a big way.

When she finally heard Jase enter the house, Felicity tracked the sound of his footsteps as he approached her and found her in the same pose, Mahler's masterpiece playing for the third time.

"Felicity?" he whispered, his habitual greeting subdued by her lack of response.

All evidence of her morning's expedition removed, Felicity really preferred not to break the spell Mahler had woven over her, but she knew she would have to open her eyes eventually. She didn't particularly want the drama of Jase's solicitous concern at the moment, so as not to worry him, she smiled without yet opening her eyes.

"Hi," she hummed.

"Hi," he echoed, obviously closer. He sounded amused, or maybe pleased. Felicity did not open her eyes to see which.

"You seem to like this piece," he commented on Mahler.

"Hmmm..."

"Shall I leave you two alone?"

"Ha," Felicity laughed a short laugh, but still did not open her eyes. She wished she had Brendon's blindfold. How nice to shut out all the things she didn't want to see!

"Would you like some wine?" Jase suggested.

"Mmm, no thank you," she murmured. Though the idea sounded pleasant, she didn't want to move enough to drink the wine.

She suddenly felt the warmth of Jase's body edge into proximity in front of the sofa, but she didn't move, praying he wouldn't touch her again without her permission, as he had promised.

The music swelled and grew, battled and resolved repeatedly, evoking again the tempest and alleviation of tension within Felicity. Even with Jase inches away from her, she buried herself in the rhythms and melodies, unwilling to shatter her absorption.

Finally, the music raced to its climatic ending, and Felicity reached reluctantly to push the button on the remote. For a moment she lay still, breathing in the dizzying conclusion.

"What are you doing?" she eventually mused with a smile, though her eyes remained fettered.

"I'm trying to figure you out," he professed. Definitely amused.

Though she knew her present vulnerability, she didn't want to confront the reality that would face her if she opened her eyes. At last, however, Jase sighed an exasperated sigh, and Felicity forced her lids to open.

"Would you like dinner?" he pressed gently, reaching for her upraised hands, asking permission by his hesitance.

"Sure," she conceded grudgingly, opening her hand and taking his.

He raised her to her feet, and pulled her lazily to one of the seats at the table.

"You know, I'm growing rather spoiled with your cooking all

the time."

"That's the idea," he teased, peering longingly at her in a sideways glance. His skill in the kitchen soon revealed itself with the delicious aroma of ginger chicken.

Despite her earlier languor, Felicity's mouth began to water. She inhaled the succulent scent, "That smells amazing." She closed her eyes again.

Whether her success of the afternoon or her subsequent relaxation, something rendered her bold and confident. She confronted Jase gently.

"What is it you hope to accomplish here?" she demanded, opening her eyes and peering up at him.

Jase paused, placing the lid over the pan to steam the vegetables. "Ginger chicken," he responded wryly.

Felicity grimaced at him. "No," she rolled her eyes at his bad joke. "With me. What do you hope to gain?"

He pulled the other chair backwards toward her, straddling his chair and resting his chin on the back. His eyes gazed evenly at hers.

"Your safety, of course!" he insisted. "I'm going to fix this, to get you home to your kids, to make sure you can live the life you were meant to live – free from the insanity that evil men intended for you."

"But that's not all that this is, Jase. That doesn't require you to cook me dinner, to buy me books. Don't tell me you are doing that because you are the most considerate person on earth who hates for anyone to be uncomfortable. You're not that kind of helpful."

With a sigh, Jase ran his fingers through his hair. "I mean, I would hate for anyone to sit, bored, under my protection, but you're right. That's not my kind of kindness. No, Liss. I just – I'm not trying to accomplish anything, exactly. But I can't say I don't hope."

"Hope?"

"That you will be open to possibilities."

"What in the world does that mean?" Felicity couldn't fathom what he thought would come out of their situation.

He dropped his eyes to her hands, reaching for them and entwining her fingers in his own. She didn't pull away, waiting to hear his explanation.

"Someday, this whole ordeal will end." He sounded like he was promising her. "When that happens, you will want someone to..."

He waited so long, she prodded him. "To what?"

"Well, I was going to say to take his place," he grimaced. "But that's not really what you need. You need someone to be what he wasn't. You need someone who recognizes your value." His steady inspection of her face unsettled her a little.

Felicity sighed, exasperated. "Jase, how am I supposed to even think about that right now? Even if you manage to work everything out, even if I'm safe and Brendon is behind bars, I still have to take care of my children. I have responsibilities."

"It'll work out," he offered confidently.

She peered profoundly into his eyes, searching for his intent, willing her words to have clarity. "Jase, I'm sorry. Since we're being so honest, I have to tell you that my life will eventually settle down. I'll have my children to think about."

"And you'll need help."

"And you're going to be that help? That's a risk I don't know if I can take."

Frustrated, Jase shook his head. "When will you figure out that you can trust me?"

"I'm beginning to hope I can," Felicity mumbled, staring at a spot on the floor. "And it scares me." She had grown to count on him so much, but even as she realized the fact, she recognized that she had gone behind his back to contact Nick. That she would continue to deceive him about her attempts. She reined in her expression to reflect her sincere gratitude. "I know how much I owe you."

"No, Felicity," he pressed. "No. You owe me nothing. It's fine for you to feel grateful – you have that kind of heart. But you have no obligation to me. Do you think I would want you to stay with me because you felt bound by some bought loyalty? I know that it will be hard to filter through all of the insanity of our time together, but when you are safe, I want you to remember that you can trust me, and that you actually like me."

"Who wouldn't like you?" she found herself grinning, and rational Felicity could have slapped herself for the allowance. "Okay. I got it – no obligation. No loyalty. My choice, in this as you have offered in everything."

Jase seemed satisfied with her admission, smiling and pressing her hands to his lips, so she extricated herself gently from his grasp. She *did* owe him, and as he wished, she would not let that obligation pressure her into making a bad decision.

Having served Felicity dinner, Jase seated himself facing her. His melancholy grew with each moment of her pensive silence. After an obligatory bite or two of food, Felicity excused herself to bed. Her hunger had evaporated. In reality, the two solid days of hiking had greatly tired her, and her muscles ached with the unusual exertion.

"Thanks," she smiled and rose to leave.

"Goodnight," Jase mumbled dejectedly.

Remorse gripped lightly at her mind, but not enough to turn her around for conversation. She stumbled leisurely to bed, plunging herself into the plush feather-top mattress and conforming pillows. Before sleep could overtake her completely, her mind wandered. The state of her expectations had reached somewhat of a standoff; she neither hoped for nor feared much in her immediate future because she just couldn't make out the possibilities.

Apparently, Jase held some illusion that when her situation resolved, she would stay with him. True, she appreciated his obvious attraction to her, and she certainly felt something in return, but the kind of commitment that would make her stay with him, bring her children to him? She couldn't quite reconcile herself to the idea. She cared about him in a way, she felt immense gratitude, his admiration of her made her heady. *How shallow,* she chided herself.

If she could completely remove every thought of concern for others, would she let him have his way? She didn't know. Unbidden, the image of her first night in the cabin rose to her mind, as he stood behind her displaying the window television. Her imagination altered the memory, edited reality so she could consider her desires. When she looked down, insecure and confused, Jase had stepped closer, lifting her chin.

Staring into his eyes, she read his desire, and her lips parted in anticipation. *I will take care of you,* he reassured her. *I love you.* She cringed at the words in the imagined memory, not yet comfortable at hearing them from anyone, much less Jase, whom she didn't quite trust. Still, she couldn't deny the appeal of the image.

The pain of not seeing her children, though, the affliction she felt when she thought of their being raised by Brendon wouldn't let her dwell on the pleasure. In fact, thinking of them at all brought on a wave a nausea. If she indulged her image of Jase, her children had to fade into insignificance. She could not do that. But what if Jase couldn't find a way; what if she couldn't make it back to her children and stay alive?

If she could not go back to her previous life, maybe Jase could provide the closest thing she would find to peace. He, of all people, would not mind the transitory life she would be sentenced to if she had to stay on the run. Certainly, his resourcefulness and experience would help protect her since she herself knew so little about self-preservation.

Because she had always consigned her protection to Brendon. *Obviously, a bad decision.*

Another sigh of sadness pushed past her lips.

Felicity could come to no real conclusion. Instead, she determined to make no definite plans at the moment, not when she hadn't exhausted all of her own resourcefulness. In fact, she had a plan already at work. Only if Nick could offer her no help would she revisit the possibility of life with Jase. Until then, she would focus on staying alive.

Despite her conscious resolution, her subconscious mind struggled with ambivalence as she tumbled roughly into dreams. Her mind warred between longing for her illusion of the past with Brendon and anticipation of the future with Jase, unable to determine which desire pulled more strongly on her heart. Veiled by dreams, her desires battled throughout the night.

Chapter 20

...every time she met him there surged up in her heart that same feeling of quickened life that had come upon her that day in the railway carriage when she saw him for the first time. – Line from *Anna Karenina*, read by Felicity in Jase's cabin

I think romantic love is the most powerful of all the vices because it most closely resembles real love. For both romantic and real love, people surpass their own abilities to serve the beloved. For both, people try to better themselves. For both, they deny themselves. But for one, the service is all for oneself. For the other, the self is not the point. – Felicity's Journal, April 4

March 29, After midnight

Felicity did not panic this time as she shook off the shroud of slumber and became aware of the presence sitting behind her in the bed. The echoes of an incubus reverberated through her momentarily, and she melted subconsciously into the warmth of his body, brushing her lips across the hand across her mouth. For several seconds, she did not register reality, but when she did, she nearly lurched out of his arms. Unmoving, his grip held her in place, as if he had anticipated her reaction. Thankfully the darkness concealed the burn in her cheeks.

"Felicity," he breathed, any reaction to her proximity well masked if present.

Felicity did not reply immediately, waiting until she could control her breath. "What is it?" she finally whispered.

"Someone is here. Not in the house, outside." He leaned down slowly onto one arm to look in her eyes. "I need you to come with me."

Inaudibly, he scooted backwards off the bed, holding Felicity closely in his arms as he pulled her with him. Whatever fear gripped her held a tenuous grip compared to the iron vice of his body heat.

Probably still half asleep, Felicity couldn't keep her priorities straight.

Keeping his arm around her waist, Jase led Felicity silently out of her bedroom and into the hallway. He led her to the small coat closet which mirrored the laundry closet.

"You want me to hide in the closet?" she asked incredulously, nervously eyeing the door. The possibility finally shook her from her drugged infatuation with Jase and back to the glaring starkness of reality.

"Not exactly. Stay back a minute."

Opening the door, Jase reached above the high shelf over the hanging rack. Without seeing exactly what he had done, Felicity gradually became aware of a crack of murky light that appeared between the side of the closet and the back. All at once, the back of the closet disappeared, to be replaced by a narrow descending stairwell. Felicity shivered.

"Come on," he commanded.

The flight of steps was, thankfully, very short. Four steps straight down, then an acute left-hand turn, followed by four more steps down. The confining staircase opened abruptly into a low, sparsely furnished room. A wooden chair sat next to a small side-table, and a narrow cot lined one wall. From somewhere overhead, light crept murkily into the meager dwelling adding to its unearthly sense. It reminded her of a hidden cellar in a horror movie.

"Safe room," Jase explained. "Don't turn on the light. It will give away your location."

Jase's eyes smoldered with some latent anger, but he spoke with more than usual softness. He raised his hand to cup her face. "Please don't do anything. Don't try to solve this yourself." He sighed, exasperated. "I told you I would take care of you." His thumb brushed gently down her cheek, and her eyes closed at the sensation. Then he turned abruptly and retreated up the stairs, his expression frightening her almost as much as the gloomy accommodations.

What had she done? What had he found out? If someone had seen her trekking through the woods, what else had she revealed? Felicity tried not to walk down the paths of the thought, instead turning her attention to the room around her. The decrepit chair looked as if it would buckle under her weight, so she sidled to the bed and perched herself, cross-legged, on it, her back against the wall. The room felt cold, and she pulled the thin wool blanket off the bed to wrap it around her shoulders. At least the blanket smelled clean and freshly washed. Perhaps Jase had freshened the room after her arrival in case he needed to hide her even more deeply than his cabin in the woods. She didn't know if the idea made her feel safer or more anxious.

Though she strained against the stillness, no noise made its way down to her from above.

The silence began to weigh on her, and her mind wandered into nervous thoughts. If something happened to Jase, what would she do? Honestly, she thought she would still most likely manage an escape from her circumstances. Her personal peril didn't worry her quite as much as she would have expected. Instead, she found herself actually concerned for Jase's safety. Her trip to the Henrys' seemed incredibly foolhardy. What if something she had done got Jase injured? Or even killed? Her stomach knotted with the errant images that her mind stirred, images of Jase with a broken limb or beaten and battered. She found herself so convinced that her actions had brought him danger that she jumped at every creak of the walls against the wind, hearing in it the beginning of a gunshot.

Before long, she couldn't stand the tension, and she stood to her feet to pace the little room. Forcing her mind away from what she couldn't see or hear outside, she turned to what she could control. If something happened to Jase, could she get out of the basement? If Jase had locked her in, she would need a lot of resourcefulness to escape without him. She tried the door, but could not open it.

Scouring the walls with her eyes, Felicity searched for the source of the dim light that offered the room's only scant illumination. It could not be artificial. The moon, perhaps? The sun had not yet lightened the horizon, though her eyes could perceive more than when she first awoke. Despite the gloominess, Felicity easily found the source of the glow. Four evenly-spaced windows dotted the ceiling, their dusky glimmer seeping in unexpectedly green. Felicity could not tell if the glass was green or if the moss and grass above obscured the clarity of the moon's rays.

Surprised, Felicity noticed that the ceiling surrounding the lights had a strange texture. She grabbed the chair and tested it, gingerly standing on it until it supported her entire weight. It held steady. Dragging it directly below one of the windows, she stood carefully, stretching as high as she could to see if she could reach the ceiling. Her hands easily touched the surface, and she began purposefully probing it with her fingertips. A gentle smattering of earth tumbled onto her face. Shaking her head to clear her eyes, Felicity peered carefully back up at the window.

She thought the entire window sat framed into the soil, but she could not be sure. And even if it were, she felt no certainty that she could work around the window to open an escape. Surely the pane needed some structural support sturdier than the dirt. She needed a light.

Stepping down from the chair, she scanned the room again. From the little table against the wall, she notice what looked like a cord protruding out the back. As she got close, she saw that it was plugged into the wall. She tested the wood on the underside of the table, searching for the cord's source. Bending down, she glanced under the table and could see that the cord disappeared into a little paneled compartment under the table.

She poked and prodded and pushed, and a small drawer finally popped open. Inside she found a phone, a small electronic tablet, and a wound up ethernet cord. Jase seemed ready to survive down here a while. Felicity would have bet that, if she spent enough time in the room, she would find some stockpile of supplies.

If her brother had not suffered from the same tendencies – he insisted hackers had to prepare because they knew just how bad it could get – she might have decided that Jase was some kind of crazed survivalist. She rubbed her face to brush away the thought then pulled the phone out of the drawer and stepped back to the chair.

The dim light of the phone revealed the soil that surrounded the window, and Felicity began digging cautiously with her index finger to reveal the edge of the pane. Though she dug through three inches of dirt, she encountered no firm structure. Finally, her fingertips brushed a thin line of metal, likely a frame. She wasn't as strong as she once had been, and she decided she would have to drag the table under the skylight, stack the chair on top, and do her best to balance to pull herself out.

Her fear of being trapped just muted the questions her mind tried to use to slow her down as she carefully scaled the structure. When the vice grip of arms yanked her from the chair, the shock tore her breath from her lungs almost as much as the force of the fall.

Though she still felt arms tight around her, the speed of her descent felt like uncontrolled plummeting toward the ground, and for a moment, she wasn't sure if anyone would catch her. Then a powerful grip snatched her from the air, preventing an actual fall to the floor. Though grateful, the force also restricted her desired freedom to spin and face her assailant. A weak scream escaped her lips as the arms grasped her against an iron chest.

"Were you trying to get out?" Jase's voice demanded huskily. The anger that he had masked before issued clearly in his tone now.

She couldn't speak. Although she felt a modicum of relief when she realized who held her, she couldn't swallow the terror that had overcome her when he had grabbed her. She stood, panting heavily for several minutes, not fighting to extricate herself.

Finally, Felicity squirmed in Jase's arms, struggling to turn herself toward him. He relaxed his arms just enough to allow her to revolve in his grasp.

"Oh, Jase," Felicity moaned, burying her face into his shirt. "I'm so glad it's you." Fighting off a sob, Felicity remained there until her breath calmed and her heart slowed.

As her own unease quieted, she became aware that Jase's breathing had sped. His hand caressed gently down her hair, and he moved his lips down to rest lightly beside her temple. When he spoke again, some stronger emotion subdued his anger.

"What were you doing?" He did not relax his grip.

She couldn't look at him – he held her too tightly – so she turned her face to the side so he could understand her.

"I wanted to find a way out. In case you didn't come back.

His anxiety leaked through his tone as exasperation, "I told you not to do anything!"

"I wasn't, really. I was just planning. I wouldn't have done anything for a long time."

He pushed her a few inches from him so he could look her in the face. He gave her a skeptical look, ironically brushing debris from one of her cheeks before placing a hand on either side of her face and pinning her eyes to his.

"Your planning would have gotten you killed!"

"What?"

Jase sighed again pointing to the window and releasing her face.

"The man saw the light you held up to the window. He would

eventually have found a way down to you if I hadn't seen him in time."

Felicity furrowed her brow, concern melting her usual calm. "Where is he? Was it the same man from the hotel?"

"I took care of him," he stated matter-of-factly. Felicity shivered. "He was definitely ProtoComm; one of Bill's favorite operatives – merciless. I knew him."

Jase knew him. Past tense. Felicity shuttered again. Someone had died because of her. And Jase had killed him. Though she had intellectually accepted Jase's help in whatever form, she had never considered that it would require killing.

As if he had read her thoughts, his tone softened. "I'm sorry, Felicity. You're not used to this world." He lifted her chin until their eyes met. *Your world,* she accused. Though she sensed his concern, she had to force herself not to glare. "This guy was going to kill you this time, Felicity, not kidnap you," Jase urged insistently. "I made sure before I killed him. He tried to kill me to get to you. If I had left him alive, you and I would both be dead."

Despite herself, Felicity peered at Jase with a new respect, for the sheer physical ability of a man who could not just stop a trained assailant, but overpower him and even kill him. She bit her lip. What chance would she have against him when time came for her to leave him? What chance would she have against Brendon without him if she did?

"I need to know what you've done," he took her face in his hands again so she couldn't escape his gaze.

"What do you mean?" she asked innocently.

"Something led that man to this place. I've had this house for over a year, and never once has anyone happened onto it. You're here for four days, and suddenly I have an intruder. What did you do? Did you contact someone?"

Felicity fumbled for some excuse, some reasoning that she could feed Jase in order to explain the man's presence. Nothing came. She wasn't quite ready to abandon her plan that did *not* include Jase.

She had no guarantee that he actually would try to secure her freedom, and his character, while seeming noble, could not yet be trusted. She could, however, think of no convincing evasion that would appease him. She settled for a half-truth. "I contacted Nick," she hedged in a small voice.

"You..." Felicity watched him control his anger. "How?"

"Um," she debated whether or not to tell him about her hikes. "I called him," she lied.

"With this phone?" he finally released her face and wrestled the device from her clenched fingers.

Felicity shook her head furiously. "The one you gave me in Nanton," she hedged. "It's upstairs in my room."

A look of understanding flashed across his face, then fell into deep consternation. Felicity didn't see the danger until it was too late.

"I need to see the phone."

Breathing deeply, Felicity turned and headed up the stairs. Jase followed behind, and Felicity's stomach practiced a few flips. She had no idea where the phone was – probably buried somewhere under a seat in the car. Cornered, she turned back to him. She had lied to him. For a good reason, she had told herself, but the idea of convincing him seemed unlikely.

When they reached the top of the steps, she turned to face him, stopping him with a hand to the chest when his eyes stood level with hers.

"I lied," she admitted, her insides churning. She guessed that now she would find out just how much of her belief in Jase's goodness was based on wishful thinking.

Rather than react, Jase closed his eyes. He placed his hands over hers on his chest and breathed deeply for several seconds. "I understand," he finally crooned, thoroughly calm if a little sad. "I just need you to tell me what you really did."

His patience melted her resolve, and she bit her lip. "I emailed him."

"How?" he inquired coolly.

She really didn't want to explain to him about her hikes knowing that they, over every other concern, would upset him most. Still, his composure gave her a little more confidence. She needed to conceal the substance of her communication, but she hated to lie as blatantly as she would need to if she were to protect the nature of her exchange with Nick. Impressed or not with Jase's placid response, Felicity could not hand him all the cards. She settled for a partial revelation.

"I found a house - it belongs to a nice elderly couple - and they let me use their computer," she explained, avoiding his eyes nervously. "I made sure no one could follow my trail, though," she insisted more brightly, meeting his gaze.

Jase controlled himself. *"Found a house…"* he wondered cynically. *"Maybe that would have worked,"* he sounded exasperated, "if the couple hadn't been Bill's parents. Theirs is the only house you could have reached in less than a day of hiking. They don't know anything about his business, but I happen to know that he monitors their internet activity. You didn't leave a physical trail – just a virtual one."

Felicity chewed her lip. Yes, the cabin belonged to Bill Henry's parents. And so did Jase's cabin. Even though Felicity had intellectually withheld her trust from Jase, she found that the idea of confronting him about it distressed her, and not for the reason it should. She ought to fear for her safety, to worry about upsetting an unscrupulous man who was obviously in league with Bill Henry. Instead, though, Felicity found herself not wanting to break the emotional connections she had made with him, to threaten such a fragile bond. She shouldn't want to preserve those, but they preserved her in a way her thoughts and reason could not.

"What did you tell Nick?" Jase continued, and Felicity grasped at the direction for her topic.

Now the lies needed to stick. "I just told him that I'm okay. I said I would contact him when I had a better idea what I was doing, but that I was safe for now. "I started to think you had lied to me, that you had no intention of contacting him!"

At least she felt certain that, monitored or not, no one could decrypt Nick's security to read the messages. She risked a surreptitious glance at Jase, hoping her accusation would distract him from her equivocation. "I told you he would panic if he didn't hear from me. I mean, he was desperate. Briel told him not to go to the police, and maybe she told Bill. Maybe that is how the man found us."

Without answering, Jase stared pensively at the wall over Felicity's head, one hand still cupping the side of her face. He stroked her skin absentmindedly with his thumb while he thought, and she licked her lips, unwilling to move away from the heat that trailed down her cheek.

"I'm…I'm trying not to lie to you, Felicity," he began with low supplication. His obvious struggle weighed his eyes to the ground, and he dropped his hands to his side. Felicity couldn't quite suppress her guilt – she actually understood why he didn't try to explain everything to her. Of course, she also understood that the fact meant she had to keep her own agenda and not just trust his.

"There is a strategy here to keep you safe," he continued. "I'm taking risks, but, Liss…" He raised his eyes and searched hers imploringly. "I'm trying to take most of the risk on myself. There is no reason you should believe me, and I know that. But everything I am doing is to keep you safe until I can get you back to your children. Our end goal is largely the same, though I recognize that you have reservations about my intentions. If you will just tell me what you did, I can know if I need to adjust my strategy."

The pressure ignited her natural rebellion, but she forced herself to tap into her reason. What did he need to know. "Okay, then. When you left on Thursday, I put on my tennis shoes and started walking due south."

"But there's nothing due south for about 50 miles."

"Right," she continued. "I didn't find anything on Thursday. That's why I was in the bath when you came back." She grimaced at him. "Then, Friday, I turned southwest and hiked all morning. I found the Henrys' house about noon."

"How did you find your way back?" he questioned, genuinely curious.

"Part way I followed a public path, and where I had to hike through the woods, I marked on the trees as I went with a piece of chalky rock that I found."

"Huh, Impressive," he murmured. But then his tone changed to calculating. "That's what I needed to know. Will you show me?"

"Um, sure."

Of all the things he could have wanted to know, this seemed the most benign. Maybe he genuinely was concerned that Bill's man could find her again. Jase led the way out of the house, pulling her by the hand. Once outside, she took her hand away and strode to the clearing's edge in the direction she thought she had taken the previous day. If she let herself touch him anymore, she might lose her resolve to resist him. And since she was still lying to him, it didn't seem like a safe time to be vulnerable.

"It should be here somewhere," she mumbled as she searched. After a couple of minutes, she found the first mark. It had faded with the morning mist. "Ha! Here it is."

Jase examined the mark and nodded, seeming satisfied.

"What is it?" Felicity asked.

"I had hoped that maybe that man had followed the trail you left, but it's too faded for that. Maybe the guy just stumbled upon the place. If so, that's good, because ProtoComm still wouldn't know exactly where my cabin is. Even Bill's parents don't know its actual location since they own thousands of acres and never asked for plans or visited the site during renovation. Let's get back to the house so I can figure out how to move you out of here in the next couple of days. I'm going to need help."

He held out his hand for her to come back to him, and then he pulled her with him back to the cabin. Felicity wondered uneasily where he had hidden the body of their visitor, and she tried not to let her eyes stray from the path in front of her. Unfortunately, they were drawn against her will toward the darker patches of forest as she passed them.

Once inside, Felicity felt better – she could breathe normally. She had managed to keep Jase from realizing the full extent of what she had told her brother, and he seemed convinced that they weren't in any immediate danger. With her temporary security assured, Felicity began to watch Jase curiously. His face wore a calculating expression.

"What are we going to do?" she demanded, certain that his face spoke scheming.

"You are going to do nothing," he narrowed his eyes as if daring her to object. "I told you I would take care of you…"

Felicity pursed her lips, and she crossed her arms across her chest. "And even after what you acknowledged, I'm supposed to let it stand at that?"

"Yes," he agreed, then a twinkle entered his eye. It was strange given the circumstances. "I need you to do what you do best – look pretty."

Blinking, Felicity lost her thought. Had he just…? "Excuse me?" She glared at him. Instead of letting her scowl affect him, Jase laughed out loud.

"Since you obviously don't have the expertise to manage the spy business, then your options are limited."

"You know," she defied him. "I don't really like your attitude. I'm pretty sure I could find my way to the road. Apparently, I'm quite resourceful." She feigned a step toward the door.

Jase surprised her by moving to intercept her, and his arm formed a vise around her waist. "Go ahead and try it," he challenged, and Felicity's instincts wanted to raise on her toes to kiss him. *What?* she asked herself. How had that happened? She should want to run. The realization froze her. "You look scared," Jase quipped, his voice a bare purr, and she couldn't miss his mirth.

Fortunately, he did not try the kiss again, because Felicity's heart pounded in her chest in anticipation of it. She hated herself at that moment. Jase stood with her in the little kitchen area, and he stepped, his arm still holding Felicity's waist, over to the tiny cupboard.

With his free hand, Jase moved a can from inside the cupboard and pressed a small button hidden underneath it. A section of the back panel of the piece of furniture slid to the left, and Jase reached into a crevice, retrieving a big, blocky phone.

"Satellite phone," he explained, grinning. He seemed to enjoy her shock every time he revealed some hidden technology.

Curious, Felicity listened intently as Jase punched in a number and waited for an answer. After a few seconds, Jase's face screwed up in an unfamiliar expression. Somehow persuasive? He spoke with a flirtatious lilt. Felicity frowned. He still hadn't let her go, though she had not actually tried to get away.

"Bonjour, Amélie."

Amélie ?

"Oui, ça va? J'ai besoin de votre assistance."

Jase laughed. "D'accord. Pourriez-vous être mon épouse autre-temps ?"

Another laugh. What was he trying to pull, holding Felicity like that and flirting so audaciously with the woman on the phone?

"Je suis à ma maison. Vous pourrez dormir ici ce soir ? Ah, oui. C'est mieux. A tout a l'heure."

"Who was *that?*" Felicity queried, impressed even as she suppressed her jealousy.

"My friend Amélie. She's going to help buy some time for me to get you out of here."

"Can we trust her?"

Jase smiled a smug smile, a strange expression on his face. "She is too attached to me to risk our relationship by causing you harm."

The words stopped Felicity's internal complaint, and she stared in his face with far too much desperation. Amélie was attached? When, exactly, had Felicity grown possessive of Jase?

Especially since she refused to let him grow any more attached to her? "How long until she comes?" Felicity squeaked, her voice slightly choked.

"She's not coming here – well, not yet. I'm meeting her in town in the morning."

Another wave of jealousy. Despite her intense struggle to control herself, something must have shown on Felicity's face because Jase paused and brushed his thumb down her face.

"You don't have anything to worry about, Felicity. I'm going to take care of you, okay. That's all this is. Amélie's going to pretend to be you. I mean, not actually you, but since Bill has sent men out for recognizance, he likely suspects something. In case you were seen yesterday, I want to make sure he knows I have a woman in town. Tall, brunette. I need an explanation to offer him. She'll put in a few appearances with me around town: holding hands, the occasional kiss, laughing at stupid things. Speak with an American accent."

"Is this something you do often?" Felicity accused, masking her irritation with humor. *Something we do often…the occasional kiss.* She prayed that her face had not betrayed her. Jase could never know how close he stood to ensnaring her – because that's what he would do. Ensnare her, not win her. Not gain her affection or love. Not in any impending circumstances she could imagine.

She convinced herself that the hollow vacuum left by her husband's betrayal had rendered her desperate for a new structure, and Jase's compassion and protection offered a support. Her heart wanted her to follow her gratitude. That was all – that had to be all.

Not in these circumstances, though. Not while she stood in peril, and certainly not in competition with another woman. A stubborn pride in Felicity's mind would not compete for a man's love – especially not after her husband's infidelity. She had decided that with Brendon immediately. It was true with Jase, too. If he was ambivalent, Amélie could have him. Felicity composed her expression. She didn't need to expose the chaos in her head.

"I'm glad she's helping," Felicity leveled stoically. "It will buy us more time to enact a plan."

"Right," he shrugged. Had he realized how close he had come to conquering her? She thought maybe he had, if his disappointed countenance spoke truth. "But don't get too comfortable. I'm buying you hours, not days. Maybe 24. And I'll be

253

in town for a third of those. Amélie and I need to be seen together in a few places so we can set up the story." For a moment, all subtlety and play evaporated from his eyes, and he pierced her with his urgency. "Please, Felicity." He placed his hand on her cheek again. "Please don't go *anywhere*! Don't do anything! I can't keep rescuing you from these situations. I might slip up at some point and you would suffer."

"I won't do anything." *Not yet.* "I'll read Dickens and listen to Mahler." She took his free hand and returned his intense gaze. "I promise."

Felicity had no problem making the promise. With the revelation of the Henrys' identity, she had nowhere else to try to contact Nick. She had dropped the phone in the basement, and Jase had locked the door when they left. She didn't feel equal to more hiking just yet, and if Jase couldn't buy time for them, she would be placing herself in a more vulnerable position. What if another one of Bill's men came looking for her while Jase was gone? Felicity would rather have the semi-security of the house if she had to hide from a killer.

When Jase called her to breakfast in the morning, Felicity noticed a difference in Jase's countenance. She had gotten used to "real" Jase, and he apparently had not woken up at the moment. This "Jase" was the charmer, the performer who Felicity had seen at the parties, around his coworkers. *At least Amélie doesn't get the real Jase,* she hummed to herself before she could clamp down on the thought.

"I think I'll be back in about four hours," he informed as he placed her breakfast on the table and seated himself in the other chair. She nibbled at her food, not quite able to mask her melancholy.

"Are you not eating?" Felicity wondered, staring at the empty spot in front of him.

"I woke up early. I've already been to town and back this morning."

Felicity snickered. "So, what you're saying is that I'm a sloth." She laughed at the idea, wondering what he would think if he knew that she rarely slept past 6 a.m. because her kids woke her up to take care of them. Before the cabin, she couldn't remember the last time she had slept past 8:00.

Grinning, Jase shrugged as if in agreement. "You know what

I think of you," he countered as he stood and took her plate. He rinsed it off and turned back to Felicity, who had stood up in the meantime. "Are you going to be okay?" he crooned, anxious. When Felicity just nodded, he lowered his face toward hers. Her heart stopped, but like that once before, he just placed his lips gently on her forehead. Without looking back at her, he strode out the door.

Chapter 21

If you are out of trouble, watch for danger. S –
    Sophocles' *Philoctetes*

*I know he has done bad things, but he has been so good to me it's
    hard to remember.* – Felicity's journal, March 29

For several minutes, Felicity stood frozen next to the
cupboard in the makeshift kitchen, her fingers fidgeting with the
beads hidden beneath her t-shirt. When Jase toyed with her, flirted
and teased, she found him incredibly attractive, but she found her
defenses on high alert, and she just managed to resist him. When he
spoke with such considerate urgency, though, Felicity melted into a
cooperative puddle, a willing accomplice to her own demise. The
beads reminded her what would happen to her if she did that.

Once again, she filtered through her reasonings for rejecting
Jase's advances. His instability, his background, his character – the
consistency she owed her kids precluded an alliance with such a
man. Though it had proven a lie, her idealism demanded a man like
Brendon. Like the Brendon she had thought she had known. Maybe
no such man had ever or would ever exist.

If she demanded moral excellence and nobility, how did Jase
even continue to attract her? Was his own desire for her the magnet?
Was she so vain that her ego compelled her to reel in her catch? Or
just so desperate that any sign of affection could win her? *How
pathetic!* she thought for the second time. Who was Jase when he
was not playing the hero? A man who would kiss a woman for the
sake of a mission. A man who would sleep with a woman for a
mission? Probably. Felicity recoiled into herself at the thought, a
hurt animal retreating in her shell. She could never, even if she
trusted in his benevolence, trust someone with her heart who would
share his own with others. And whatever a "professional" may
claim, no man or woman could remain fully faithful while indulging
himself with another person. The realization calmed her, as she
recognized that she could not let herself grow possessive of Jase
Hamilton. She would let him help her, she would offer him gratitude,

and then she would leave him – whatever his ambitions.

As she had promised Jase before he left, Felicity settled onto the sofa with *A Tale of Two Cities*. She forewent Mahler for a lush piano piece by Ravel - repetition had rendered Mahler grating. Charles Darnay had just been imprisoned for the second time when Felicity thought she heard the sound of an approaching car. Rushing to the front door, she peered through the small window at the top, ready to sprint to the closet if it proved necessary.

To her relief, she spied Jase's car outside, with what looked like Jase behind the wheel. Holding her breath, she waited to relax until the car stopped, and she recognized Jase's figure rising from the driver's side seat. With determined indifference, she noted that a tall, brown-haired woman exited the passenger side – the woman was elegant and beautiful. Her perfectly manicured hair and clothes adorned a face, touched by the lightest makeup that just highlighted her almost unearthly beauty. Felicity reached to run her fingers down her own ponytail, huffing out a breath of frustration that Jase had not thought to get her some cosmetics with the clothes.

She shook her head at herself, irritated. Unlike the past several days, Jase wore the amused expression Felicity had seen him wear the first few times she had met him. The woman – Felicity assumed her to be Amélie – laughed brazenly, throwing her head back in a carefree manner. Oh, they would work as newlyweds.

Felicity moved away from the door - Sydney Carton suddenly called her name. She moved back to the couch and reopened her book. When Jase entered with his "friend," Felicity did not want to appear over-eager to see him. The book provided a good buffer for her to hide behind.

"Felicity?" his voice called after Felicity heard the click of the door. He sounded troubled, maybe even angry.

"In here," she replied nonchalantly. "Still reading."

Jase mumbled something to Amélie, who giggled, and Felicity piqued a little at the exclusion.

"Felicity, this is Amélie."

"Bonjour, Amélie," Felicity tried to smile. Her enthusiasm for speaking French had suddenly waned.

"Ah, très bien. Bonjour," the corners of Amélie's full, red lips arched upward. "*Vous parlez francais?*"

"Un peu," Felicity clarified, trying and failing to sound warm.

"Amélie has been putting in appearances around Banff. It's going well." Jase smiled at Amélie. All his former melancholy had evaporated.

"That was a great idea. Merci bien, Amélie," Felicity turned toward Amélie. "I'm very grateful that you've given us time to make a plan."

"*Avec plaisir*," Amélie returned graciously.

Felicity definitely saw an air of frustration pass over Jase's features as he took in her indifference. She suppressed her pleasure at his displeasure.

"Will you be staying long? I can sleep on the couch if we need more room," Felicity offered.

Amélie looked archly at Jase; Felicity couldn't figure out why. Did the Frenchwoman generally share a room with Jase? Or did she expect that Jase and Felicity already shared a bed? In Jase's world, Felicity guessed that would have been nothing unusual. Her eyes narrowed, and Jase finally smiled.

"I would never dream of displacing you after what you've been through," Amélie insisted. She glanced impishly at Jase. "I will sleep on the couch."

Felicity's stomach churned at the look Jase returned to Amélie.

"Sleeping arrangements aside," he smirked, "If this plan works, we may not need to leave before we have everything set in place. If anyone at ProtoComm suspected anything, I feel confident that Amélie has calmed them down."

Biting her lip, Felicity blinked away the tension in her face. She didn't know how long she could play the very un-jealous girl who didn't mind the seductress flirting with Jase. Regardless of her intentions, she worried that the competition and jealousy would draw her in where Jase's attentions had not. *That's really sad,* she thought to herself. More evidence that she could not engage with him on any level of real connection.

Amélie and Jase began a discussion – switching between French and English - of their next day's plans, detailing which locations and activities would appear most convincing and would make them most likely to encounter a ProtoComm person. They had already encountered several during their initial four-hour excursion.

Most of the management would be going home after the weekend, and only Bill, Brendon, and a few others would remain behind. Unfortunately for Felicity, Bill maintained a semi-permanent address in Banff to be near his parents and did not have any definite plans to return to Phoenix for a while. Funny how such an evil man could feel the responsibility to care for his elderly parents. It reminded her of the old mafia movies: as long as someone was "family," they "had your back."

When had she ceased to be family? she wondered, surprised at the suddenness of the wistful thought. How could Brendon have just set her aside like that? Maybe he recognized that the woman he had married had the backbone to stand up to him when necessary, and he had grown concerned that if or when she found out what he was doing, she would defy him as she always defied injustice.

For the first time in a while, Felicity smiled in genuine pleasure as she moved to her room. Despite all that she had been through, she suddenly felt a modicum of self-satisfaction. All that time, she had wallowed in the misery of Brendon's rejection, somehow irrationally blaming herself for not being enough. What if he had rejected her instead because she was too much? Because he knew he couldn't buy or coerce her to turn the other way. If that were the case, Felicity could live with that.

Gratefully, the idea of nabbing and fleeing with her kids now didn't seem entirely insane. If she could hold her head high before them, she could eventually handle explaining to them why they would have to live as they would have to. Hope spouted tentatively in her chest. Since she had married Brendon, she had doubted herself, doubted her own worth, her competence, her intelligence. Apparently, Brendon had considered her competent and intelligent enough to serve as a threat, and in her mind, that fact made her worthy.

Drifting blithely into slumber, she slept soundly for several hours under the effect of her enlightenment.

Sometime during the early morning hours before the sun, Felicity awoke, her serenity disturbed for a reason unknown to her. Through the stupor of her sleepiness, two silhouettes pressed into her mind. She seemed to see Jase and Amélie, dancing, pressed so tightly together that no light could be seen between their bodies, though the rising sun cast a long shadow around them.

The low murmur of their conversation escaped Felicity's perception, but the throaty laughs and seductive smiles wreaked havoc on her peace of mind. She wanted to bolt daringly across the space between them and pull Amélie from Jase's grasp, but when she made it to her feet, it seemed every step she took moved the couple farther away from her. A trill of laughter erupted from Amélie's mouth as Jase ran his lips up the line between her neck and chin, finally landing on the tender softness beneath her ear.

In a rush of anger, Felicity found herself sitting upright in her bed, the echoes of the laugh still ringing through her room. She rushed to dress herself and stumbled into the hallway seeking the source of the sound of mirth that had invented the dream. Low murmuring voices wafted into the hallway from the direction of the living room.

Though she had feared, expected, the voices to come from the bedroom, their location did nothing to assuage her irritation. She shuffled petulantly to join Jase and Amélie, not really caring what she interrupted. Instead of the intimate tryst she expected, however, Felicity found Jase and Amélie seated, completely appropriately, at the small breakfast table and sipping coffee.

"Did we wake you?" Amélie apologized in her thick French accent.

"No," Felicity lied. "I was just taking my time. I'm sure Jase has told you how slow I am in the morning." Her eyes narrowed in mock irritation.

"He forgot to tell me that part," Amélie laughed, more subdued than before.

"Like I could talk much with you around," Jase teased the Frenchwoman. Felicity heard, for the second time, that foreign accent hinting around the edges of his tone. With Amélie's own accent to compare it with, Felicity confirmed her earlier suspicions: it was French.

"You contribute your share," Amélie retorted pleasantly.

The familiar ease of their interchange garnered an envious pang in Felicity's stomach. Not hot jealousy, more of an ache of longing. She remembered the easy banter between Brendon and herself before they had left for Canmore, and then at the cabin. Her fingers wandered distractedly to the beads at her neck. It seemed like an eternity ago, another lifetime since she and Brendon had left their boring, normal home. Had she really complained about the tedium? She had, even as she made believe that her life was wonderful – for Brendon's sake.

Her idealized vision of Brendon – the imagined man she had

lost – was such a paragon, and not just in his own mind. From the beginning, in high school, he had made her feel like she was the most fascinating person in the world. He pursued her relentlessly, charming her and reeling her in. Once he had her, any hint that she was reconsidering their relationship sent him into utter despair.

Felicity didn't have any great need to be needed, but she couldn't stand to break someone's heart so thoroughly. She stayed. She dismissed her wandering heart as a sign of her immaturity, a childish fancy. She buckled down and learned to love him. And she had loved him. She knew every person had weaknesses and failures, and she chose not to focus on those. Instead, she kept his strengths firmly entrenched in her vision.

His generosity – mostly with others. His intelligence. His sense of humor – only at her expense about half the time they were together. His masterful and commanding nature, tempered by charm. And the intensity of his claim on her when he turned his eyes on her.

In reality, though, there were many more negatives that accompanied the positive, faults that she should never have ignored. His ability to repaint the truth into the image he desired. His sneering judgment of people who thought differently than he did. His tendency to mock people – mainly her, but sometimes the kids and often strangers – for days after an imagined slight. His marked arrogance and sense of superiority. His dismissal of Felicity and her kids. But possibly most important, the fact that Felicity had not felt an emotional connection with Brendon since the first day after they had married, the day he had communicated to her that, now that she was his, she had to live up to his image.

As if he could read her mind and wished to redirect it, Jase interrupted Felicity's thoughts with a flirtatious-sounding comment in French as he leaned over Amélie's shoulder with a confidential laugh. Displeasure flashed across Felicity's features.

"J'imagine qu'elle n'a pas passé beaucoup de temps à s'inquiéter de ce qui se trouvait sous la cabine," Amélie smiled.

"Did you say something was under the cabin?" Felicity wondered.

Amélie and Jase exchanged a look, as if they hadn't intended for Felicity to understand

"What?" Jase hedged.

"Is there something under this cabin?"

Amélie pursed her lips in displeasure.

"Not this cabin," Jase apprised her. "The one where you stayed."

"What's under my cabin…?"

When Jase didn't answer right away, Felicity scoffed in irritation, turning away toward her room. It was stupid, but she just couldn't bear watching them another second.

Jase caught up with her at the hallway.

"What's going on?" he implored, rubbing his hands up and down her arms soothingly. Felicity felt a hint of guilt over her childish response to being left out.

"I just think I should know what's going on since it affects me. You guys just babble in French, as if I'm not in the room. It gets frustrating."

Maddeningly, he pulled her into a hug – as if he had a right to comfort her. She couldn't find the will to push him away, though.

"I'm sorry," he comforted. "It's very easy for Amélie and me to talk because we've known each other for a decade, and we've been in a lot of tight situations together. But," he lowered his face to look directly at Felicity, "we have too much history to take each other seriously, okay? We take our work together seriously, but the rest of this is just a game."

"Sounds fun," Felicity snarked, but cut him off before he could answer her, "but what is under my cabin?"

Jase let go of her and paced a few steps. "That cabin is Bill's Banff area residence."

"We stayed at Bill's place?" The thought gave Felicity chills.

"Made monitoring you easy," Jase shrugged a tad guiltily. "And the plan involved impressing you. Lull you into complacency just in case Brendon couldn't pull off the lie. Bill always gives himself the best."

"No worries there," Felicity mumbled. "But I imagine," she continued, "that there was nothing strategic in keeping me at the cabin because of what's underneath it."

"You're right," Jase acceded. "What's underneath is there because it's Bill's cabin. It was strategically good for Brendon to use the cabin because it's Bill's cabin. Other than that, those aren't related in any other way."

"So, what were you and Amélie talking about?"

"The closed backup server you and I discussed is underground at the cabin. It has a consolidation of all the transactions done by ProtoComm, and I am convinced that I'll find what you need on Brendon there."

Felicity's mind went into overtime. They were physically so close, but she had no idea how she would gain access to those servers.

"What email did you contact your brother with?" Amélie called from the breakfast table.

Felicity's suspicion heightened. Were they trying to read the exchange? Not happening.

"Um, I just made a new mailman account." The more truth the easier to remember. "I think it was Felicity1245. I just had to make up a number; there were so many Felicity's."

Felicity figured she had an exponential ability to feign forgetfulness on the numbers. *Maybe it was Felicity2145,* she rehearsed mentally.

"Amélie, would you please try to login for us? See if Nick has sent anything to Felicity?"

"Naturellement."

"Why do you want to see the email?" Felicity fished, trying to sound curious instead of suspicious. "I just told him I'm okay. I didn't expect any response from him."

Jase's answer came a little too slowly, as if he had to decide what he needed to say, or maybe come up with it. His troubled tone had returned. "I thought maybe your brother could find something from the computers that would help us."

Breathing deeply through her nose, Felicity closed her eyes, determined to calm herself. Sometimes she felt so overwhelmed that she didn't know how she had a coherent thought. Much less manage complex maneuvers. Yet she was here matching wits with Amélie and Jase, and planned to challenge Brendon at some point.

"Felicity, c'est faux," Amélie asserted.

"I'm sorry, what?"

"It's wrong. The email doesn't exist."

Felicity prayed that she could carry out the deception- she had very little practice in the art. "But I was sure..." she began. "I could be wrong about the number, I guess. I avoid math at all costs." Felicity attempted a sheepish smile. Would they have believed her ruse if they had known she aced college calculus? She just stared at them, biting her lip in apology.

"Okay," Jase began in irritation, but then he seemed to catch himself, and any spark of anger diffused into frustration. Though she couldn't decipher his emotions, he didn't seem to suspect her.

"Do you remember why you picked the number you picked?" Jase asked patiently, trying to help jog Felicity's memory.

Felicity furrowed her brow. "I just used one of the ones they suggested. I could have sworn..." she continued ingenuously. "My mind is just so overwhelmed!" she sighed dramatically, playing on Jase's sympathies. Her abstraction of the morning should buttress her melancholy performance.

Jase's eyes softened a little, shedding their barely-concealed irritation. "Amélie, let's see if we can tap into Brendon's system from here. Maybe Felicity will remember later."

Amélie grimaced at Jase. Felicity couldn't tell whether Amélie felt impatience with Felicity or irritation at Jase's indulgent attitude toward her. With a little huff, Amélie turned broodingly back to her laptop. Jase moved cautiously toward Felicity, as if he feared alarming her.

"Felicity?" he tentatively stepped closer, as if he couldn't decipher her mood. Felicity almost smiled at how convincing she must have been. "Are you okay? You seem distracted this morning."

Maybe, or maybe I just can't look you in the eye because I'm lying to you. "I'm okay," Felicity hedged.

Jase took her hand, peering into her face in search of something, something that drew a smile behind his eyes when he found it. What did he suspect? Why would it make him smile?

"Thank you so much for your help, Amélie," Jase threw across to the Frenchwoman somewhat abruptly. He kept his eyes glued to Felicity's. Felicity cast hers to the floor. "I know you wanted to be seen by a few people while you're in town. Why don't I join you at Tonquin at 5 o'clock?"

Amélie responded coyly. "Our room, or the village?"

"The village will be fine," Jase replied.

The exchange drew a huff from Felicity, and when she raised her eyes in irritation, she caught Jase's broad smile. Suddenly she knew what he had seen in her eyes, and it had nothing to do with her lies. She gulped as he released her hand.

"Très bien." Amélie crossed to Felicity. "It has been such a pleasure meeting you, Felicity. I'm glad I could help you. Maybe we'll meet again under better circumstances." Amélie and Jase exchanged a look, and Amélie turned away with a roll of her eyes.

What had that meant? Was Felicity's peril so boring to the Frenchwoman? No, the boredom definitely stemmed from Jase, and Felicity looked back and forth between the pair.

She did not feel particularly ingratiated to Amélie at the moment, but she determined to be gracious. Plus she needed to break the moment that brewed between her two companions.

"Thank you so much." Felicity turned, reaching for Amélie's hand. Instead, Amélie leaned into Felicity and kissed both of her cheeks in the traditional French fashion.

Stepping away from Felicity, Amélie repeated her kisses for Jase, but instead of the platonic distance she had kept between herself and Felicity, Amélie stepped intrepidly into Jase's arms, pulling them around her. Only then did she kiss his face, lingering for a moment on each cheek. A feminine finger trailed under his chin as she stepped away, and she wore a definite smirk.

"Au revoir," she tossed flippantly back at them as she let herself out the door. "Be careful, Jase." Somehow, the words stood as an admonition to Jase, not an expression of concern, and Felicity recognized that the caution referred to Felicity herself, not to any imagine physical danger from Jase's escapades. Jase's "friend" was more concerned about his connection with Felicity than the very significant peril he placed himself in by standing against ProtoComm.

The realization stirred raging butterflies in her gut, and when she turned back to Jase, her carefully cultivated indifference liquified into molten anticipation. All of her new self-respect, all of her high internal speech about nobility, all her determined nonchalance. Somehow, Amélie proved the lie within it. Gritting her teeth, Felicity glared at the doorway through which the woman had disappeared.

"Felicity," Jase begged impishly. "Are you okay?"

When she turned to look at him, she sucked in a breath. He stood a hair's breadth away, not moving closer, but not giving her space. Electricity sizzled up and down her body from the connection that brewed between them. She quickly tried to erase her jealous expression, but she must have failed.

When Jase finally spoke, he turned so that he stood in the middle of the tiny hallway, and when Felicity mirrored his movement, her back pressed against the wall behind her. A smile played on the corner of his lips, and something seemed to warm inside of him. Felicity stared at those lips.

"What's the matter?" he repeated, raising his arm to lean against the wall above her head.

Oh, that scent, she tried not to notice, though musk and cedar and leather mingled with something floral – or spicy – in the confined space. A mix of Jase's cologne and whatever else he wore. Belt, shoes, shirt…heat.

"Nothing," Felicity insisted petulantly, though she turned her head to avoid his gaze. She closed her eyes and breathed deeply to calm herself. Despite her resolve, her voice came out breathy.

Jase inched even closer to Felicity, if that were possible, until she abruptly became aware of the warmth of his breath on her exposed neck. "Felicity," his voice caressed her name. She pressed herself further against the wall, but she didn't step away. "Amélie and I have been friends for a very long time. She is something very different to me than what you are," he insisted, his voice almost a whisper.

"Friends?" Felicity rejoined skeptically, raising her eyes to his.

An alluring smile warmed his mouth, and his eyes dropped hungrily to her lips.

She waited for her habitual protest to voice itself, but something restrained it. Without her permission, Felicity's breath became shallow and quick, matching her heart's rhythm. His hand raised slowly to her cheekbone, his eyes never leaving her lips.

Is this it? she demanded of herself. *Am I going to do this?* Nothing inside her rose to object. On the contrary, her lips parted in anticipation, charged with tense excitement. Although her mind implored her to escape, her body revolted against her better judgment.

As Jase's mouth descended toward hers, her eyes closed, her defenses failing her completely. Instead of the heat of his lips on hers, though, the gentle scruff of his cheek tantalized the sensitive skin of her face to perhaps a greater degree than the fulfillment of the kiss would have. His fingers, woven into her hair, pulsed with the anticipation that they would press her to him.

"I promised you," he whispered, warm breath caressing her face.

"Jase," she moaned. "I –" Her stomach churned with a painful fusion of regret and guilt. She couldn't let him kiss her, but she wanted nothing more than to finally taste his lips. If he had pressed her then, she would have broken, but he had withheld from her – to great effect. If she kissed him, the barrier would break, and she saw nothing to impede her descent back into utter dependency. Despite her restraint, her hands clutched his sweater and held him to her, and she could not make herself let go.

For a moment, nothing happened. He merely rested his face against hers, the tenderest of connection, and breathed as if to inhale her essence. Finally, he turned ever-so-slightly so that the corner of his mouth met hers. "When you are ready," he murmured. His actions belied his words, and though his body pressed against her, pinning her to the wall, he leaned his face away just enough that another turn held his lips just beyond her reach.

When he pressed back toward her, he aimed his lips for the tender skin just beneath her jawline. He brushed fire along her chin, and when he reached her neck, his mouth paused at the beads where they met her skin. "When you're ready," he repeated, the motion of his lips a feather touch of fire beside the cool beads. She gasped at the sensation as he finally curled away from her and the cool air rushed between them. "The choice has to be yours."

Jase caressed her hair with one hand while he lowered the arm that rested on the wall. Finally, he unraveled his fingers from her hair and stepped back until she could no longer sense him. She did not open her eyes, nor attempt to move from her position against the wall. Her knees trembled too much to be trusted.

When her breathing had slowed and her strength returned, Felicity opened her eyes to find herself alone in the hallway. She had no idea where Jase had fled, or even if he had left the house altogether. With her heart still drumming a rapid beat, she did not have the resolve to see him again. No coherent thought arose to upbraid or encourage her. Mindlessly, she wandered, dazed, into the living room and fell on the couch. Had Jase left her out of consideration of her request? Or to increase her longing?

She lay down and closed her eyes, unable to call out to him or search for him. How dangerously close had she come to giving in? She had a mission, and she would use Jase to get protection from ProtoComm and Brendon. Then she would go back to her kids. Reaching her hands to rub her neck, she encountered the beads that encircled her throat. When she remembered Jase's lips, displacing the beads, the thought filled her with warmth. The beads were yesterday's life - a life she would never again live. She slid her hands to the back of her neck and unclasped the strand, proceeding to shove the beads into her pocket. She didn't want to move just yet, but she would drop them deep in the nearest trash bin once she arose.

With the removal of the beads, Felicity felt a noose slip from her shoulders, a leash that tied her to a time she intended to leave behind her. She knew that much. She did not know what she was going to do with Jase. Unfortunately for her, using people was not really her wheelhouse. If she gave into his pursuit, if she gave in to that part of her heart, she would not be able to step away when she needed to – to leave him behind. She could not lose sight of her goal. Felicity forced herself into a restless sleep. Exhausted, she willfully rejected rational thought and dove headlong into mindless oblivion.

Chapter 22

Do not swallow bait offered by the enemy. – Sun Tzu, *Art of War*

Maybe she would have been more receptive if we hadn't entered with a million shards of glass. – Briel's text to Nessa after the failed apprehension of Felicity

Awakening suddenly, Felicity sat up and assessed her surroundings. Her rapid ascension from sleep disoriented her, and she half expected to find herself at home in her comfortable, king-size bed surrounded by 1000 count sheets and a down comforter. Her disappointment was acute.

Recollecting herself, Felicity glanced nervously at the clock on top of the little cupboard. 5:45 in the afternoon. Had she dreamed the whole encounter with Jase? Unsure, she called to him. "Jase?"

No answer.

With a groan and a stretch, she unfurled herself from the sofa and rose slowly to her feet. She felt slightly muddled, but her reason had returned during her repose, and she now became aware of a subtle pang in her gut. *Fear?* she wondered. *Fear that you've chased him away,* she clarified to herself. Had she completely lost her senses? She had a goal, and she could not compromise that. It did not matter that she wanted Jase. *I want Jase,* she suddenly inhaled. It did not matter. In fact, her emotional vulnerability had turned her into a fool.

What was she doing?

Why was she putting her fate in the hands of a man who worked for the company that sent her into slavery?

Why was she trusting a man who admitted to drugging her?

Why was she believing that a man who lived on the property of Bill Henry had benevolent motives toward her?

Most importantly of all, why did she want more than anything for him to wrap his arms around her and hold her and tell her that she would be okay?

Felicity closed her eyes, pulling in a breath to steady herself.

She was being a fool, and she needed to stop.

Glancing around the room, she searched vainly for something to do that would take her mind off of what had happened. She missed Jase; she wanted him to come back and show her that he wouldn't leave her, that his claims about Amélie were true. If she gave in for fear of losing him, she would hate herself both for her lack of character and for her stupidity.

Suddenly, she realized that Jase had gone to meet Amélie at 5:00, which would guarantee Felicity at least a couple of hours of uninterrupted isolation. Since she couldn't trust Jase, she needed to reach out to the only person she knew with one hundred percent certainty that she could trust. Nick. It had cost her before, but what had it cost her? Jase trust? At this point, she wasn't sure she considered that a loss.

After ten minutes of sifting through Jase's room and the living room, Felicity realized that Jase would never be so careless as to leave a random communication device loose in his cabin. Trying the door to the basement accomplished nothing, and she quickly returned to the center of the home, peering around her in search of inspiration.

She grabbed a bottle of water and seated herself at the little table to consider her next step. Should she try to hike somewhere again? Head east or west in a direction she hadn't yet tried? She just couldn't risk it again, and her frustration lowered her head to her hands.

A laugh burst out of her lips when she opened her eyes and realized what sat on the chair beside her.

True, Jase would never be so careless as to leave a communication device, but apparently, Amélie would. On the chair where Amélie had sat earlier in the day, a small black laptop blended in with the dark upholstery of the seat.

Suppressing her nerves and guilt, Felicity reached for the device and placed it gingerly on the tabletop. Now came the hard part. Inexperienced at espionage, Felicity had no idea whether to expect some radical security software or tamper-proof alarm system. When she thought about it, though, those things usually popped up after someone logged into their user. She was no computer genius, but being Nick's sister meant that he had run her through some troubleshooting on occasion. She pulled up the recovery panel and opened the advanced startup. When the computer restarted, she pressed the option for safe mode with networking. A moment later, she was in a browser, her breath speeding with anticipation.

nightengale: I'm on an unsecured hostile computer. Can you help me secure it?

root: Thank God, it's you. Do you have administrator privileges?

nightengale: No. I'm in safe mode. What do I do?

root: Smart. With networking. Don't worry about it. Just click this link from my server.

nightengale: What did I just do?

root: You downloaded some software. When we're done, you can specify the timeframe you want erased, and it will delete the logfiles from that period. We'll cover thirty minutes to be safe. Just install it now.

nightengale: Done. I hope you know what you're doing.

root: Look, it won't be exhaustive, but it will take someone a lot of work to find your traces.

nightengale: Fine. Have you been able to retrieve those files from Brendon's computer?

root: Just this morning, but I couldn't get ahold of you.

nightengale: How can I upload them?

root: You need some type of storage device. Do you have a disc or a pin drive or something?

nightengale: I don't, but Jase has all sorts of things hidden around here. Give me a few minutes. If I'm not back in 5, you'll have to figure out what to do with those files yourself. Turn them over to somebody who can use them. Brb.

root: K. I'll be here.

Felicity balked at the idea of an exhaustive search - she knew she didn't have time. At any moment, Jase would return, expecting, no doubt, to find her simpering helplessly under the effect of her earlier experience with him. She laughed. She kind of wanted to. *Priorities,* she smiled.

She focused her efforts on obvious storage receptacles. Rifling through the drawers in the bedroom and bathroom, glancing in the kitchen cabinet. Finally, she returned to the small cabinet that contained the stereo equipment. She moved around the few CDs then fumbled into the spaces beyond the light. Mostly, she encountered cords. Tapping along the back of the stereo, she found a long, thin protuberance of plastic. *Flash drive.*

nightengale: Found a flash drive.

root: Perfect. Just insert it into the USB port.

nightengale: Done.

root: Okay, run this test for me real quickly. I need to check your download speed.

She clicked on the link that popped up.

root: Good, you're T3.

A bunch of words flashed rapidly across the screen, and Felicity recognized all the computer programming that she never had taken the time to care about. In her current situation, she regretted ignoring Nick's offers to teach her.

root: This guy has nice specs.

Felicity snickered.

nightengale: Rethinking your relationship with Briel?

root: Very funny. This shouldn't take long. Just click this link, and it will download to your laptop. Do me a favor and change your download location to the flash drive.

nightengale: Done.

root: This is a fairly sizable file. It will take a few minutes. While it's loading, go ahead and download this other program for me. I can start cleaning up.

nightengale: I'm not an administrator, remember.

root: Please, like that matters. Remember who you're talking to?

nightengale: Okay, Mr. Know-It-All. Sorry.

From the front of the house, Felicity heard the tell-tale sounds of an approaching vehicle. She ran to the door. *Jase*, she distressed. He had only been gone for an hour and a half. Because of her big city conditioning, Felicity expected driving to take much more time than it did in small-town Canada. She sprinted back to the computer.

nightengale: Gtg. He's back!

root: I need two minutes. Stall him.

Ugh! she complained to herself. Her heart began battering her ribcage. Sprinting to the door, she adopted a face which reflected her internal discord and ran, panting onto the front porch.

"I'm so glad you're back!" she breathed, throwing herself into his arms.

"What's wrong?" he asked quizzically. No doubt her lack of restraint shocked him.

"I heard a sound outside. I didn't dare investigate without you."

"What kind of sound?" his tone had relaxed – he obviously assumed overreaction on her part.

He wouldn't feel the need to search out an animal sound, so she made up something definitely manmade.

"I'm not sure. Maybe a motorcycle or a four-wheeler? At first, I thought it was you, but when I went to the door, I didn't see anything."

He scoured the visible forest with his eyes, apparently seeking some evidence to support her story and elucidate their situation.

"Wait for me inside," he commanded, shoving her gently toward the door. "And lock everything."

"Do you want to give me the keys for the basement?" she whispered.

"No, whoever was here has apparently left. I didn't notice anything on my way in, and I haven't seen anything since I got here. I'm just going to double-check."

"Thank you." She hoped her tone sounded sincere.

Turning to her, he reached reassuringly to touch her face, "Everything's fine. I'm going to keep you safe."

Stop! Stop it! Stop it! she complained silently. Every time he showed tenderness, concern, he distracted her. He was probably trained for it, and Felicity would not let him hypnotize her into blind following. True, Jase had taken care of her. And also true that after she had trekked to the Henrys', Jase had reacted with unexpected understanding and patience. Certainly, the only time he seemed to intrude on her agency was when he was literally fighting for her life.

But she had to lie to him. On the off chance that he did intend to protect her, that didn't mean that his priorities aligned with hers. Since hers were nonnegotiable, and since they were intended to save her children, she would do what she needed to do.

Locking the door behind her, Felicity dashed across the living area to the laptop. Instinctively, she glanced around her, intensely aware of the large, uncovered window a few feet from her. She could not see Jase, but the light inside reflected back at her from the glass. She knew that anyone outside would have a clear view of her.

Hoping that she could explain her action to Jase, she hurried to switch off the lights. Fortunately, the laptop had hibernated while she diverted Jase, so its glow did not disrupt the darkness. She carefully crept with it into the bathroom so the computer's light would not have access to any window. Opening it, she briskly typed a closing message to Nick, popping out the disc simultaneously.

nightengale: I have one minute.

root: Okay. Just clear your browsing history here and your cache, and I should be able to handle the rest. Btw, I think this computer might give some good info. Re-download the remote access program again after you clean the computer? I'll still have remote access as long as no one detects the program, which they shouldn't unless they know to look. I'll be careful. Take care of yourself.

nightengale: Love you.

Felicity removed the thumb drive, erased her trails, and set Nick up for remote access. When Jase finally entered, Felicity had just flopped, relieved, onto the couch, her breath rapid and shallow. She hoped she could pass it off as fear.

"Felicity?" his voice rang out in the darkness.

"I'm right here," she called from her spot on the sofa. She was sure he could hear her breathlessness.

He strolled casually into the room, flipping on the light. Felicity blinked against the glare.

"Sorry," Jase chuckled, leaning against the doorframe.

"Did you figure out what I heard?" she queried with feigned agitation.

His face screwed up in thought. "No," he appeared slightly skeptical. "I can usually find some trace of a person's presence. The only signs I saw were from you or me."

"Well," Felicity hoped she could convince him of her artless candor. "Maybe I heard an animal. I don't think so, but I've lived in the city my whole life. And this experience is completely new to me. I'm sorry I sent you on a wild goose chase." Her guilt made the last sentence believable.

"Really, with what you've been through and the gloominess around this house at night, I'm surprised you've remained as sane as you have."

Stop being so understanding! she chastised him silently. The more she fought to distance herself, the more pull his kindnesses held.

Fortunately, he couldn't ever lay down his own suspicion, and when a look of realization flashed through his eyes, Felicity returned to defensive mode. "Why did you turn out the light?" he queried. "I didn't tell you to do that."

"I didn't like feeling blind to the outside." That was easy; she didn't even have to lie. "If someone came up to look in the window, I wanted to see them before they saw me."

His expression relaxed. "That makes sense." Twisting his lips, Jase gazed intently into Felicity's eyes. "I'm afraid we can't stay here much longer. Amélie was able to lay a fairly convincing trail, but Bill always seems most relaxed when he has something up his sleeve. Like playing dead before he pounces. All day today, he just sat calmly at his desk, rarely engaging in casual conversation, absent from his usual politics. I think you might want to pack up tonight for an early morning hike. I have a four-wheeler waiting not too far away, and we can use it to traverse the rest of the woods. I'm not waiting here for Bill to find you. There's no telling what may happen next."

When an otherworldly sense of elation came over her, Felicity forced herself to suppress her enthusiasm. Her time alone with Jase was beginning to grow dangerous for her, and not because she thought he would do anything. His dual identity, the tenuousness of her circumstances, her desperation to share the burden: everything was conspiring against her to make her act like an idiot. She began to imagine the next morning's egress, the last time she would close the door of the tiny cabin. The beginning of the trek back to her children.

Except, it wouldn't wait until morning.

Jase could not possibly have foreseen the prescience of his words. ...*no telling what may happen next.*

When his hand came out of nowhere, he shoved her to the ground with irresistible force as the giant picture window exploded into a shower of glass that rained down around her.

Without a word, Jase erupted into a blur of action.

Felicity had lived in constant fear of Bill Henry. Felicity had not thought to expect Briel.

Apparently, neither had Jase.

Felicity instinctively slid underneath the sofa as far as she could go, glad that it had a ten-inch clearance. She watched as Jase ducked into the hallway and out of sight of the intruder. No gunshots rang out like she had seen in the movies. No barrage of noises echoed into the usual peace of the idyllic woods.

Instead, as the tinkling of the glass quieted, the sound of a familiar voice called to her from the darkness.

"Felicity, I'm here to help! Jase is lying to you."

Chapter 23

All of our reasoning ends in surrender to feeling. – Blaise Pascal, *Pensées*

The voice stirred many emotions in Felicity, but the woman's words mattered little. How had Briel found her? The woman who claimed to work for Felicity but really worked for the man who sent Felicity to slavery. The woman who had smiled and laughed with young children then gone home and assaulted a man in her apartment building.

Carefully lifting the upholstery flap, Felicity peered around the room for the source of the voice. She could see no one, which seemed strange with the shards of glass that spelled Briel's presence so clearly. After a moment, though, Felicity spied Jase where he stole around the edge of the room before sliding behind the sofa near her. Instinctively, Felicity reached for him once he had entrenched himself in the narrowest corner behind her. She scooted out from her hiding place and hugged his arm with both of hers, leaning her face against his sleeve and breathing in his strength. Confidence poured from him, and Felicity began to calm.

"I'm telling you the truth," Briel insisted from somewhere near the window. "Nick is the only person you can trust right now, and he told me how to find you."

Even with Jase bolstering her, Briel's words left Felicity hollow. "…he told me how to find you." Only then did Felicity realize the profundity of her error. Instead of recognizing the danger in communicating with Nick, Felicity had held onto the communication as a lifeline. She had left the computer open to remote access and in so doing had provided a virtual homing beacon for her brother to follow. Felicity now realize that everything she had told Nick had made its way back to Briel. How could Felicity not consider the ramifications? Innocent, naive, brilliant Nick. Just dumb enough to trust a woman he carried a flame for. Just intelligent enough to trace Felicity's location using a computer connection.

Jase interrupted her self-recriminations, leaning his mouth down to her ear. "I'm going to divert them," he informed her. "You run to the car. Do you think you can reach that backpack as you run by?"

Dazed, Felicity raised her head from his arm, glancing into his penetrating gaze before she peered around for the backpack. Since it was on the path to the door, she nodded stiffly.

"Get into the driver's side. If I don't make it, leave without me. There's money in the center console and supplies in the bag. Go!"

Unable to move, Felicity stared, open-mouthed at Jase. Leave without him? Of course, she would. That had always been the plan, hadn't it? To get away when she could? Unexpectedly, her body refused to move, held in place by fear. Not fear for herself, though – for Jase. The thought of what he would face if she left arrested her egress held her to him. She shook her head violently.

"Go, Felicity!" he mouthed, but she just met him glare for glare. She could make out the whisperings of Briel and the other operative, but they sounded far away, as if still beyond the shattered window, and she spoke low enough that she knew they could not hear.

"No, Jase," she contradicted. "I'm not leaving you to this. Why would you put yourself in Briel's path when she doesn't even want you? She wants me. If I turn myself in to her, you can get away."

As if Briel had heard the words, the woman spoke from across the room. "You can still salvage this, Felicity. Let me help you. You don't know who Jasc is – you can't trust him." Felicity almost laughed at the sentiment coming from Briel. Between Briel and Jase, which one had lied to her? Which one had offered her freedom, and which one stood determined to detain her? She shouldn't trust Jase? Well, she trusted Jase a hell of a lot more than she trusted Briel.

Still, Felicity wondered why Briel and her partner did not just rush in and overtake her – Brendon would probably be just as happy if Felicity were dead. Maybe they held back for fear of Jase, but Felicity could do nothing. It would be two against less than one. They would have her back in captivity in minutes. Yet, they didn't attack.

"Look at me, Felicity!" Jase reach for her face, sliding his hand to direct her eyes to him and leaning so close that his breath warmed her face. "Never, do you understand?" His voice hummed low and focused. "You get away. You are the priority here. Whatever happens to me happens – I'm trained for this, and it's my choice. You go while you can. Take the money. If the phone is in the car, take it. I'll find you if I get out of this. Get to your kids, and get them out of town."

Get to your kids. His words broke the spell. Her noble intent to protect Jase at her own expense. But it wasn't her own expense. In light of immediate danger, Felicity had lost sight of the most important thing. Somehow, Jase had not. Felicity had to protect herself above all else because she needed to be strong to take care of her kids.

And she would leave Jase behind. If she needed any further proof of Jase's care for her, she was a fool. He had sacrificed his own happiness and security to make sure she wouldn't. Gratitude swelled in her chest – gratitude and guilt. If she could figure out a way to get him to safety, she would. If her life went the way she expected, that would involve eventually convincing him to leave her – if he didn't die in his own living room, protecting her from Briel.

Steeling herself, she turned from Jase and scurried in a crouch to the far end of the couch. She could almost reach the backpack. She glanced back at Jase, and he nodded. She sprang at the backpack, arching her path so she could clutch it on her way to the small entry hall. As she moved, Jase shoved the small sofa at the pair that lunged toward her, and they dodged, off balance, to avoid the huge projectile.

Felicity tried not to think about what she left behind her as she let herself out into the front clearing. The sound of the scuffle reached her ears just before the front door closed. She started toward the car, and her pocket snagged on an errant nail that stuck out from the porch railing. Not her pocket, she realized, but what she had stashed away after her earlier encounter with Jase. When she saw what had happened, she tried to stop her forward momentum long enough to grab the beads, but she could not slow enough, and the string snapped, scattering shimmering blue spheres across the porch and the grass in front of her. She couldn't move for a moment, staring numbly at the flashes of light where they tumbled and rolled.

Even though she had known for weeks that her marriage was dead, the beads where they spiraled to the ground spoke a finality that she could not pass by unaffected. Not only was her previous life over, its death proved a relief. The scattering beads fell as a final shovel of earth thrown onto the grave. Her life before had been at death's door for far longer than she knew, and though she had hidden for a few days in a fantasy world that somehow kept her from facing reality, once she stepped out into the wide world, she would have no choice but to look the truth squarely in the face.

She realized with elation that the thought did not sadden her. It did not even scare her. Strangely, even as she ran for her life, her breath floated, lighter, into her lungs than it had since the day she had seen her husband and his lover entwined in the library. Felicity recognized the truth that she really, honestly didn't care what he did from now on. Felicity was free.

A thump against the inside of the door jerked her to awareness, and she glanced up through the little window to the sight of Jase and the white-haired op, seemingly engaged in battle once again. She could not see much below their shoulders, and she could not tell if Briel was participating in the fight. If not, the diminutive op had probably gone back through the window to come after Felicity alone.

The thought sent Felicity into a lurch that cross the remaining space to the car. By the time she reached the car, she was shaking, but she threw herself into the driver's seat and fished for the keys. Quaking, she fought to control her hands so she could successfully fit the keys into the ignition. At that moment, the front door burst open.

Mesmerized, Felicity stared motionless at the two figures that toppled onto the porch. Jase had obviously escaped the man, who was getting up slowly from the ground just inside the door, but Briel still advanced on Jase. A steady barrage of punches rained down on Briel from what Felicity now realized were very skilled hands. Equally as impressive, Briel dodged and averted blow after blow, obviously determined to get past Jase to where Felicity sat mindlessly in the car.

Jase, with a swift move that Felicity could not quite

comprehend, flipped Briel into the air and sent her rolling toward the edge of the clearing. Somehow, she jumped to her feet quickly, but Jase had bought himself time enough to reach the car. Felicity couldn't escape the sense that Jase had aimed the move exactly so that Briel was uninjured but was disoriented enough to lose her advantage.

"Go!" Jase shouted to Felicity. "Go, go, go!"

Shaking herself, Felicity forced her hands and mind into motion. She turned the keys in the ignition, but she started at the noise of the engine. Felicity threw the car into reverse and backed frantically toward the narrow gravel drive. She knew she had to turn around, so she swung the car alongside the trees at the edge of the clearing until the nose pointed the right direction. She tried not to take time to register her surprise at the success.

In the second that the car stopped reversing to initiate its forward momentum, Jase wrenched the passenger door open. Felicity's foot had just completed its course toward the gas pedal, so Jase jumped agilely into the moving vehicle. Of course, the maneuver offered no real difficulty for Jase, and Felicity could see that a moment's hesitation would have given Briel time to reach the car. As it was, Briel managed to bang on the back bumper with her hand as they sped away.

She couldn't help but celebrate that Jase had gotten away from her pursuers, but the fact that he had joined her in the car really messed up her plans. His presence fully undermined Felicity's intention to free him before his loyalty to her could cost him too much. Somehow, she had to lose him on the flight.

"Where are we going?" she prodded.

"Just follow this road around. You'll turn left after about two miles." Jase glanced behind him. And then, as if Felicity needed the reminder, "Drive fast." She almost laughed at the ridiculously obvious statement.

The density of the trees and the curve of the roads obscured any view Felicity might have of the way behind her. Though she thought she might have heard the gun of an engine, she could not sacrifice any attention to what lay behind her. She had to keep her eyes ahead to avoid precarious bends in the road. Twice, she looked up to see that the car headed directly toward a copse of trees, but she managed to avoid any major hazards.

Luckily, Felicity could delegate the predicament behind her

to the capable eyes of Jase, and she concentrated on the road before her. "Are they following us?"

"I'm sure they are, one way or another. If they didn't try to follow us in their car it's probably because they stuck a tracker on this one," he shrugged exasperatedly at Felicity.

"Were they there when you were searching in the woods?"

"Most likely," he glowered into the darkness. "If it had been anyone but Briel, I would have found them then. She is not someone you want to mess with, Felicity."

Felicity shivered. All those times that Felicity had left her children alone with Briel! Unable to restrain herself, Felicity's mind wandered back to pictures of Briel pushing her children in the swing. *Would that be before or after you betrayed me?* Felicity speculated bitterly to herself.

"Once we reach the end of the path, we will have to abandon the car and go on foot. The good news is, you and I will be easier to conceal than a one-ton car."

Reaching across her, Jase killed the headlights and pointed to a narrow break in the trees. "Pull in there for a minute."

Felicity obeyed.

"Switch with me. Quickly." Felicity was vividly aware of Jase's hands on her waist as he easily lifted her from her place and, raising her over him to the passenger seat, he rotated swiftly into the driver's. "Hold on," he commanded.

As they reversed onto the road, the bumpy terrain that she had easily navigated going forward jostled her violently.

"Sorry," Jase apologized without taking his eyes off the road. "Buckle your seatbelt."

He did not rekindle the headlights. Instead, he sped at breathtaking speeds through the impossibly black woodland roads. Felicity closed her eyes for a moment, petrified every time they rounded a bend that Jase would crash them into the next tree. Rather than alleviate her discomfort, however, the lack of visual input brought on a wave of new sensation: motion sickness.

Breathing deeply, Felicity reopened her eyes just in time to see Jase tear what seemed to be blindly onto an impossibly narrow path. It looked more like a walking trail than a road. The action radically increased the turbulent motion of the car. After several minutes of jouncing along the trail, Jase stopped the car and turned off the engine.

"We walk from here. They should be miles behind us by now, but we can't stop moving. With the morning light they will, no doubt, easily find our trail. Briel will have no trouble with that." His mouth twisted sardonically on the last sentence. Felicity studied his expression by the light of the full moon overhead, which cast its glow through the tangled branches above.

Once again, Felicity felt nauseated, but not from any physical stimulation. Instead, the very near possibility that Briel might lie behind the next tree gripped her by the chest, and the dancing shadows sent shivers down Felicity's spine.

Jase's warm hand where it found hers reassured her, and he tugged her forward, hiking as swiftly as her clumsiness allowed him down the path the car had navigated before. As they maneuvered around trees and over roots and rocks, Felicity saw no evidence that Jase paid attention to their course. His carelessness worried her. Would even he be able to find their way out? As if to increase her suspense, something large – *probably a bear*, she fretted anxiously – darted from the path in front of them.

While they trudged through the dense forest, Felicity became aware of a steady incline to their steps. She had never been physically inept, and her awkwardness surprised her as she stumbled over tree roots and stones along the way. After several minutes traveling with the trail, Jase turned from the relatively easy terrain before them and launched them directly up the steep mountain slope.

Felicity's breath sped, whether from anxiety or from increased exertion she couldn't tell. A pain in her side made walking more difficult and worsened her sluggishness. In response, Jase turned to her and, taking her shoulders, directed her to a fallen tree onto which he positioned her and pushed her down.

"You can rest for a few minutes."

Stepping into a patch of moonlight that filtered through the trees, Jase pulled the backpack off of his back. Felicity had not noticed when he grabbed it from the car. Consulting the GPS that had directed them days before, Jase nodded, seeming satisfied.

"Where are we going?" Felicity begged probingly.

"Train station."

The train station. Felicity's mind began to whir – If they got on the train, the entire situation would just reset and begin again. Where would Jase take her now? Would she ever get back to her kids? Would he have to fight Briel again? Fight ProtoComm? Place himself in danger by standing between Felicity and the weapons aimed at her?

"We'll have to sweep around north of town to approach the station without spending too much time on the roads." He seemed to deliberate. "Are you okay to walk a little more right now? We have several hours to kill until the train comes through, but I would like to be closer before we stop. Plus, we can throw Briel some false trails with the time we have."

Felicity had assumed that she would have to move again soon and was grateful for the length of rest she had already had. "Sure," she agreed easily.

"We're going to sweep near your cabin," he informed her. "It's on the way, and the presence of other people should throw Briel off a little."

Shivering, Felicity tried to steel herself. Brendon was probably back at the cabin, probably with Aimée. It didn't hurt Felicity as much as it made her kind of ill.

Gently, Jase took her hand, rubbing it as if to warm it, and he turned to watch her face. "I'm sorry," he offered. "It's an idea I have. It should buy us some time. I thought about sweeping around to avoid it for you, but I think it will serve us better if we can throw Briel off the trail before I get you to the train station." He sat next to her in silence for a few minutes, lacing her hand in his and watching his fingers as they twisted around each other. "I wish you didn't have to do any of this."

"I'll be fine," Felicity suddenly declared, her tone unconvincing as she rose to her feet.

"Come on," Jase urged, following her lead and standing beside her. "We'll find some place less visible to rest for a couple of hours – we should have time."

Felicity glanced around at the crowding trees and wondered how any place could be less visible. Suddenly she shivered, the moments of inactivity having cooled her enough to make her susceptible to the damp cold surrounding her.

Jase grimaced and began removing his jacket. "Put this on," he insisted, and then turned to repack his backpack, muttering something to himself about his being "inconsiderate."

Felicity smiled a weak smile despite her stress. How had she ever doubted his kindness?

For what seemed a couple of hours, he led her farther up the mountain, allowing her an occasional rest when Felicity appeared indisposed. Abruptly, Jase stopped them next to a thick overgrowth of bracken. The rising sun had lent the sky a mild glow, but it was not yet beaming into the trees overhead.

"We can rest here for a while. I want you to get a couple hours sleep if you can. You'll need your strength to hike back to the train station," he informed her. Then he commanded, "Come here."

Leading her by the hand, Jase walked to the right of the underbrush and headed directly at an expansive spruce tree, larger than any she had seen. Just as it looked like they might smack into the side of the tree, Jase ducked to their left and entered a concealed alcove behind the bushes: bushes which, she could now see, created an exterior barrier to the path they had traversed.

Jase swung his free hand in a wide arch to remove the spider webs which seemed well established in their refuge. Felicity tried to hide her squeamishness. She didn't relish the idea of sleeping for a couple of hours among arachnid roommates.

Letting go of Felicity's hand, Jase dropped his backpack and again dug around in search of something she couldn't predict. He pulled out a small silver aerosol can. When he sprayed it, Felicity wrinkled her nose in displeasure. The odor smelled slightly sulfurous, but she thought she caught a hint of something spicy or floral.

"Spider repellent," he grinned, and kicked some leaves and needles aside from the great spruce before dousing it in the spray. Felicity shuddered as several spiders scuttled to escape the offensive chemical. Reaching into a side pocket of his pack, Jase removed a tightly wound object from its spot. It reminded Felicity of a poster or picture, wound up so as not to create creases in its surface. When Jase opened the object and began to shake it out, she recognized it as a small vinyl tarp which Jase then placed on the ground near the trunk of the tree.

"Come here," he commanded again, and seating himself on the tarp, he leaned back against the tree. Hesitantly, Felicity ambled toward him, crouched awkwardly beneath the protruding branches of the brush. Falling to her knees, she crawled shyly toward Jase, her reserve balking at the intimacy of the situation. As she inched toward him, he reached back into the pack and pulled out another tightly wound bundle, a thin wool blanket she saw as he shook it out. Felicity laughed.

"Is there something you're *not* carrying in there? Or are you going to produce a five-star resort in a minute."

He smiled wryly, and, finally impatient at her reluctance, reached out and lifted her to him, turning her so that her back rested against his chest.

"Get some sleep," he insisted.

As she closed her eyes, settling against his chest and letting the heat of his arms protect her from the chill of the air, her mind began to flash images across her vision that battled against rest. The image of Jase at the bed and breakfast, battling that dangerous-looking man, the imagined sight of the operative in the forest coming after Jase with some deadly weapon before Jase dispatched him, the memory of how Jase jumped instantly between her and the pair at the cabin, rushing her to safety as he stood in the gap for her. Felicity recognized what he was doing – it was what she would do, had been doing, for her children for years. It was even what she had done for Brendon in the early days, before he turned his claws against her.

Whatever doubts she held about Jase, the realization of his self-sacrifice communicated the depth of his connection to her in a way all of his reassurances never would have. And she would leave him in the end, for her kids. How could she let him keep throwing himself into peril for her? Wouldn't it be better if she could convince him to leave her? She didn't know how she would survive without him, but that was her eventual ambition regardless, so why not make it happen before she and Jase grew too attached to each other? Shifting her hips, Felicity scooted to where she could look at Jase, her legs crossed perpendicularly across his. He tilted his head at her in confusion.

"I need to talk to you," she stammered. Even though she knew why she was doing what she was doing, nerves fettered her tongue. She was hardly adept at getting people to do what she wanted.

"What is it, Liss? You look serious."

"You mean more serious than people chasing me and trying to sell me into slavery?"

Jase pursed his lips. "You know what I mean. What's going on?" He grasped her hand in his, gently massaging the back of her hand with his thumb.

Damn! she complained internally when her gut thrummed in pleasure at his touch.

"Now that we are out of your cabin, now that the immediate danger is over, it doesn't make sense for you to stay with me. We've lost Briel – you should point me to the train and get away from her and Brendon's groupies. It's the perfect time."

Jase quickly reined in the flash of injury that passed his brow at her suggestion, obviously suppressing it under genuine concern. "Liss!" He raised his hand to brush her hair out of her face. "Do you think I could rest before I am sure you are safe? With Briel out there hunting you? I can't just 'point you on your way.' She will find you, do you understand? And I don't intend to leave you to her. If you want any guarantee that you will get back to your kids, it will either involve my traveling with you or stopping Briel here."

No, she insisted silently. Neither of those was an option. The reason to get him away from her was to keep him safe. If he were just going to leave her alone so he could run into some deadly battle? "If you insist on helping, give me the money you offered, and I will use it to get away. You don't need to fight Briel to make me safe."

"How, exactly, is money going to make you safe?"

"I'll use the money to get back to Phoenix. I won't go home – I'll go to my parents and tell them we have to move. If there's no money left from what you give me, they can spare a little to rent a bed and breakfast while we put their house up for sale. It will be complicated, but it will work."

"Stop, Liss. Felicity…there is no reason for you to go through all that."

"There's no reason for you to go through all this.," she contradicted.

Raising his hand to her face, he held her gaze to his. "I'm not going to just abandon you.."

"It's not abandoning me – " Her plan was not working, largely because the two halves of her psyche could not unite in the effort.

"No, you can't convince me," he pressed. "I am incredibly stubborn, and when I start something, I finish it. I understand that you are having trust issues…" Jase sought her eyes with a smirk. "And it would make total sense if you are thinking this is a good chance to take back control of your situation, but Liss…"

So, he was chalking her wish for separation up to trust issues; she could work with that. Felicity bit her lip, holding herself tightly in an upright position, hoping to reinforce an impression of discomfort – the complete opposite of reality. "I'm going to get away from you eventually," she insisted, not fully able to restrain a melancholy note to the words.

"This is not the place," he continued, "and this is not the time for you to strike out on your own – not when we have come this far." As his ebony eyes riveted to hers, they bore more determination than Felicity had ever encountered. "I have told you from the beginning that I was going to take care of you, and I meant it. I will keep you safe for as long as you'll let me, and when you won't, I'll make sure you have resources so you can manage it yourself."

Manage it herself? His words finally pulled her back from her ambitious intent – did she really think she could outlast a trained agent? One Jase considered formidable? She had to, but she didn't know how. Exhausted, Felicity turned her face into Jase's sweater, grabbing the material and pulling herself in to bury her face in the soft cloth. Who was she kidding?

"I'm sorry," she moaned. "This is so confusing, You are confusing." Despite her words, she melted against him, her head under his chin.

"You don't have to explain anything to me," he soothed. "You have been through more than anyone should have to bear, and you have handled it with incredible strength. You've been pursued by something so much bigger than you, and you've been pursued by your would-be rescuer." He smiled, pulling her more tightly against him. "You are completely justified in never trusting anyone again. I just want you to let me get you to safety, and then whatever you choose to believe about me, you probably won't be far off from the truth. Until then, though, I have one purpose, and it is to make you safe."

The physical relief of repose began to creep over Felicity's tired, sore muscles as she lost the will to fight against the comfort he offered. With her mind at war with her instincts, she did not have the internal fortitude to maintain a battle she did not really believe in.

She soon felt herself slipping out of consciousness. If he seemed to inhale the scent of her hair, what did it cost Felicity? If she let his warmth envelope her, what danger did it entail? She was not going to run, and she now realized that fact. A moment later, she remembered nothing more.

Chapter 24

I ask one thing only: I ask for the right to hope, to suffer as I do. But if even that cannot be, command me to disappear, and I disappear. You shall not see me if my presence is distasteful to you. – Alexei Vronsky, *Anna Karenina*

It's lunacy to send a lone woman to confront a criminal mastermind with an entire organization behind him. – Nick Alexander, September 14.

Predawn, March 30

Gradually, Felicity grew aware of light brushing softly across her face, an occasional brilliance flashing somehow around her sealed lashes. Echoing in her slumber-dulled ears, a chorus of soft flutterings confused her, and a sweet, piercing scent pervaded her steady breaths. Inhaling deeply, she stretched her arms wide and high, and slowly opened her eyes.

To her surprise, everything around her reflected varying shades of green off the filtered light of the sun. A low chuckle behind her brought her to her senses, and she sighed, not willing to expend enough strength to be irritated.

"Rest well, sleepyhead?" Jase teased.

"What time is it?" she rejoined, avoiding his question. With the sensation of his arms still around her, she didn't want to admit to him how completely comfortably she had slept.

"It's about 8:30. I hated to wake you, but we need to move if we're going to make it to the train before Briel finds us."

"I don't think you woke me. I always feel tired and sore if someone wakes me suddenly."

"Maybe you've been sleeping in the wrong places, " he teased. "Besides, I'm pretty sure I woke you."

Felicity felt the heat of embarrassment rush to her face. His amusement made her uncomfortable as she imagined means he might have used to draw her gently out of her slumber. Certainly, she had felt only pleasant sensations. The fact irritated her.

"Let's get this over with," she snapped, trying to rise.

His arms restrained her. "Please," he crooned. "You know me, Liss. You woke because you had slept enough, and though you feel wonderful in my arms, I can't believe you were entirely comfortable sitting up on the floor of the forest while you slept. Relax. There will be plenty of time for rushing and anxiety. Enjoy the slower pace for a few minutes."

Teasing. She remembered the concept from the time before her betrayal, and Jase seemed to have utilized it to offer some levity. It had been far too long since she had encountered teasing without the accompanying mean-spiritedness. Now she realized that Jase had often teased her, but he only did so by including her in the joke.

I guess I'm not offended, she reasoned. And with a sigh of concession, she stopped trying to rise. Holding her with one arm, Jase reached for his backpack and placed it in front of her. He peered over her shoulder. "See if you can find the GPS."

Distracted by her curiosity, Felicity began digging through the bag in search of the GPS. She spied the familiar silver spray can, two pine green parkas, and several of the energy bars that Jase had divided between them throughout last night's trek. An intimidating knife lay folded at the bottom of the bag, its folded length running the entire width of the backpack. Somehow, the GPS had managed to squirm to the bottom of the pack, and, gingerly pushing aside the other contents, Felicity removed the device.

"Thanks," Jase said, his face brushing against hers as he looked over her shoulder at the GPS.

Biting her lip, she tried to turn to hand it to him, but he reached along her arm to restrain her wrist.

"What *is* this thing?" she asked. She had used the GPS in her car, but the little black device looked more complex.

"It's just a GPS. Hold on to it," he insisted lowly, his voice in her ear. "I want to teach you how to use it."

She brought the GPS up into her view and stared, somewhat intimidated, at its inexplicable screen. Though technology had never particularly scared her, she had absolutely no experience with trekking through forests, and she felt no confidence that the machine she held could offer any assistance.

"Press menu," he commanded, releasing her wrist and pointing to the right side of the device.

As she did so, a list of options appeared on the screen,

including an internet browser, she noted.

"See the compass, the barometer, the maps, the homing beacon: it has everything you need so you don't get lost. And it's not traceable."

Could have used that when I went searching for a computer, she mused.

"Now, move down to the map application. See? That's where we are, within a few feet." He reached around her and showed her a small icon in the corner. "If you zoom out, you can see the city of Banff and the train station." He touched something else and the screen went blank.

"Easy enough," she allowed, slightly abashed at her earlier apprehensions.

"This shows you which direction you're going. You want to keep the arrow in line with your destination."

As she stared at the arrows, an idea tried to form in her mind, but she couldn't quite grasp it. Finally, it solidified into comprehension. "Why are you showing this to me? Aren't you just going to do it for me?"

"Felicity," she felt his head drop as did his voice. "Between here and the train station I can almost guarantee that we will run into Briel again. She's the best. When we do, there is a chance you may have to go on without me while I slow them down."

Go on without him? *Stop it!* she commanded him silently. Did he have a death wish? Her mind raced, grasping for a solution that would get him away from her but not offer him as a sacrificial lamb.

"Don't say anything, Felicity," Jase commanded, misunderstanding her silence. "I promise I will do what I need to when the moment comes, but until then, you don't need to say anything. I won't hold you back, and I won't make up reasons to keep you with me – you have my word."

"So you are going to leave me, even though you said you wouldn't abandon me?" she retorted. She was undermining her own intentions, but what else could she do? If he was determined to sacrifice himself, maybe the only way to save him was to keep him with her.

Jase's head shot up, shock apparent in his face. "I'm not abandoning you, Felicity. I'm giving you enough of a head start from the people after you that you can get to your kids and get away.

I wanted to be more involved in getting you set up in safety, but it's looking less like that will be an option.

"I just don't see the point in your leaving me before the train. If something happens to you before then, Briel will just hunt me down anyway."

"So I'll make sure she doesn't." He peered intensely into her eyes. "I will do what I need to do to stop her, and I'll be fine."

Felicity pursed her lips. "But if you're not, you'll leave me unprotected. You'll basically be ensuring that I am caught."

As if he could see every detail of her thoughts, Jase smiled warm appreciation. What did he think she was about?

"I'll get you to that train, one way or another," he resolved, ignoring her assertion. "By this time, there's a good chance that Briel will have reported back, and more of Brendon's men will be looking for us, so I need to get you closer."

"So you're going to take on even more of Brendon's people?" Felicity demanded. "Yet you're promising me you'll be fine?"

Jase offered no answer, just zipped up the backpack and made to rise.

Frustrated at his obvious avoidance, Felicity huffed a complaint. He was so stubborn! She scrambled off of him and out the opening of the little hovel, heading back toward the path. If he wasn't willing to protect himself because he had to protect Felicity, then she would just take the option away from him – she would just leave him before the confrontation with Briel. Though she hadn't figured out how she would survive a trek through the woods without him – he had made a valid point there.

She had expected Jase hot on her heels, but he just sighed and eased his way out after her. "Felicity, wait."

"This is not happening," she muttered, increasing her speed toward the gradually brightening path, skipping in preparation to run.

Rapidly approaching footsteps informed her of her stupidity only seconds before Jase gripped her arm, spinning her back toward him. "What is this about, Liss?" he demanded. "You're not hiking these woods alone, with or without Briel on your tail."

"You told me I was free to leave any time I want," she spat. "Well, I want it now."

"No, you don't," he countered. "This isn't you asserting your freedom."

"It is," she insisted petulantly. "You've had me cooped up in that hole of a cabin for so long I forgot that I could leave you. Well, I just remembered."

"No, this is some notion you've gotten in your head because of something I said. I've upset you." His accent had thickened, and she could easily pick out the French quality to the words. Strangely, the effect softened her resistance – though only a little.

"I know you don't want to be alone, but you would do it if I told you it was the best way. So, why are you resisting me so strongly now?" He ducked down, trying to meet her eyes. "It was when I said that I would turn back and slow them down...*Tu t'inquiètes pour moi*."

"I'm not worried about you..." She shook out of his grip. "In fact, I agree with you – you should go back to intercept Briel while I get to the train."

Jase narrowed his eyes at her. "What are you trying to pull?" he demanded.

Reverse psychology? "I'm doing what you want. I'm letting you go have your little fight with Briel, and I'm going to get away." If he left her now, though, chances were he would not need to fight Briel and the others, so just maybe she could trick him into a safer plan of action.

"It's not the right time for that," he countered. "This path lets out just outside the boundaries of your cabin, and even if I manage to find and intercept Briel, Bill has easily a dozen more flunkies there who would love to catch you for him."

Though the thought terrified her, she suppressed a shiver and pressed on. "That's good – at least I won't get lost. I stayed there for a week. I know the lay of the land, and I can avoid discovery."

"Felicity, you're not thinking clearly. You cannot place yourself within reach of Bill Henry. Of the two, Briel is definitely a much less dangerous option."

Rolling her eyes, Felicity pressed deeper into the woods. "So you're saying that Briel is not that dangerous?" she spoke to the air before her. "Then why am I running from her? Nick says she's safe – maybe she will help me."

He gripped her arm again, spinning her so he could face her. Defiantly, she glared up at him, but softened when an expression passed over his brow that was the closest Felicity had ever seen to fear on that handsome face. Guilt clutched at her chest.

Still, when he tried to slide his hand down to grip hers, she stepped away. He didn't try to pull her back, but what he said next spoke both to his self-doubt and to his honesty. It didn't help her guilt issues. "Look, I've known Briel a long time. I could be wrong about this whole situation. It's possible that she is just after the information you have, and then she will release you. In the past, I think she leaned toward the more ethical."

"In the past…?" Felicity demanded.

"She was always ethical – certainly more so than I am. But I went to her for help when I found out about you, and she basically shut me down. It was completely unlike her, and since it's been so long since I worked with her, it's possible she's changed – life can be hard. And for her to come in like that at the cabin? Guns blazing? I'm not feeling like I trust her in this. Not with you."

A sudden epiphany paused Felicity's tirade, and she lost sight of her attempts to steer Jase into her desired outcome. "It was you!" she exclaimed, and her last bastion of resistance evaporated as her heart warmed.

"It was?"

"In Briel's hallway! Talking to her. She did some movement and sent you to your knees. I knew you could have gotten out, but not without starting a brawl. That was you!"

Jase ran his free hand through his hair, abashed. "You saw that? I'm sure it was hard to figure out what was happening there. It was horribly awkward, and then we were speaking in code. I can't imagine how that looked. But I came to her at a disadvantage. I had no right to ask her for a favor, though I thought she would be moved more by your plight. I wronged Briel – a few years ago – and I know she has not forgiven me. And going to her was a risk, but I had to try something…"

"But you were talking about me. You said you wanted to help me. You were…desperate."

Smiling, Jase succeeded in grasping her hand. "I did, and I was. And you were crazy to spy on her."

Felicity stared at him, completely unable to stir. With his disclosure, her entire paradigm of Jase Hamilton altered fundamentally. Everything he had said from the beginning – all his claims about his concern for her – they were true. From even before she had known him, he had been trying to protect her. If Jase was really what he claimed to be, Felicity didn't need to hate herself for caring about him, to see it as weakness that she had fallen into something beyond her control. If Jase was who he claimed he was, Felicity had trusted the right person. With Jase, she was actually safe.

And she had wronged him so many times.

"I didn't know – Jase there's something I need to tell you."

Taking in her expression, Jase used their hands to pull her close. "You look guilty, Liss. Whatever it is, you don't have to worry about how I'll take it."

"But I've been lying to you. For quite a while now."

For several breaths, Jase just blinked. Felicity could discern his calculations that weighed what she would say, and her guilt swelled again, though he spoke with understanding. "I knew you were holding back, but what do you mean, you've been lying. I have tried to adjust for whatever you felt you needed to withhold, but you're pretty good at keeping a tight lid on your thoughts."

"Just…I lied to you about what Nick and I talked about, and I contacted him again – from Amélie's computer."

Despite his obvious chagrin, Jase smiled a crooked smile. "Amélie, huh? Serves her right, I guess, the way she tormented you. But it's pretty natural for you to want to talk to your brother. Why did you feel the need to lie to me about that?" he queried, and Felicity watched his mind kick into high gear.

"I've told you for weeks that I needed to contact Nick," she sputtered, "and I could tell you were dragging your feet. It made me doubt…" Felicity cut herself off, not quite willing to admit what her mind had supplied of his motives, and she watched as hurt flashed across Jase's brow.

"It made you think I was isolating you, that I wouldn't let you go."

"It's been a long couple of weeks, and things have changed even in the past few of hours. Before that, I had lots of reasons not to trust you. You drugged me. You have been in constant contact with my kidnappers since the day I was taken, and you were holding me on Bill Henry's land."

"Holding you?"

"Sometimes it felt like it, but no. I know that wasn't what the cabin was about. It was a refuge, but I was alone, and I hardly knew you, and there were so many strange aspects. And I –"

A motion of his head interrupted her babblings as he yanked up his eyes and focused on something Felicity couldn't see. He placed his arm in front of her and pushed her back into a little grove of trees, spinning behind her and wrapping his arms around her, his hand over her mouth. Her heart was pounding from the emotion of the past few moments, and his sudden action brought the thuds to a rapid thrum. She wanted to complain, but she read his anxiety. A moment later, she heard the voices.

"The signal disappeared somewhere over there," the male voice stated.

It was answered by a female voice, slightly closer to Jase and Felicity's hiding place. "Quiet, Liam!" it snapped in a tense whisper.

Felicity's breath sped, and Jase lowered his hand, no doubt secure that she understood the need for silence. In contrast to her earlier thoughts, she closed her eyes and melted against Jase, desperate to borrow his strength while she could.

Though she still saw no one, she sensed footsteps moving quietly through the forest. Had Briel and her companion found them? Or were there more people who wanted Felicity dead? Considering the unlikelihood that anyone would want her dead, she wouldn't feel surprised to find more improbabilities heaped upon her life.

Only a couple of yards on the other side of the tree, Felicity finally heard the motion of her hunters. A snapping twig revealed the clandestine footsteps. Jase tensed, and Felicity opened her eyes to prepare for action. She caught her breath and held it, stealing shallow draughts of air when she couldn't refrain.

After several minutes of silence, Felicity nearly sighed in relief as Jase relaxed his arms. She spun toward him, burying her face in his sweater while she waited for her fear to ease. He gingerly caressed her hair, his warm voice assuring her she was fine.

It was the worst thing he could have done. Her mind went into full meltdown, confused and disoriented. Did she want him to leave her, or was she going to force him to stay with her?

Jase leaned back and placed his hand on her cheek. "Come on, Liss," he urged, stepping back and lowering his hand to hers. "We really need to move, okay? I'm going to get you to that train, and then I'm going to make sure Briel stops going after you – whatever that takes." He turned and began to lead her out of the copse and toward a path a few yards away.

"Stop saying that, Jase! Stop setting yourself up as some kind of sacrifice!"

Unfortunately, Jase would have none of it. He stopped his forward motion, and his shoulders rose and fell. "I don't think it's very likely that we can lose Briel, so I am going to have to stay behind."

"And leave me alone while you get yourself killed."

"Briel won't kill me."

"Maybe. Or maybe she will. Either way, you'll leave me alone."

Jase ran his fingers through his hair. "I don't like that part either."

When she stopped walking and tugged her hand away, he turned back to her.

"Especially when it doesn't make sense," she pressed.

"It does make sense, Liss. Because I'm going to find every person who is after you and either lead them away from you or kill them."

Just like that. "Which is just another way of saying you're going to abandon me." She knew her protests were circular and almost nonsensical, but she had run out of rational arguments and had reverted to more emotional tactics.

"Felicity, I'm going to take the target off your back, or at least redirect it temporarily. I'll get you as close to safety as I can, so you can make it far away from these people who are after you. I made some plans this week. It's all in here." He lifted the backpack, and Felicity dragged her step. He was actually going to seek out Briel and her conspirators, just so he could stop them from coming after Felicity! "Don't slow down," he pressed. "We have to get across this span, and then you can ask me anything you want."

She wanted to protest, but when she looked around at the exposed terrain all around them, she ceased pulling against his hand. Whisperings of motion brushed across her ears, and she didn't know how to discern whether it sprang from the wind or from her phantom pursuers. How could she possibly make it alone?

After traversing a short but vulnerable trek across an open clearing, he directed her onto a trail that ran behind a low row of exposed igneous rock. The location provided a visual buffer between them and any pursuers, but it also hemmed Felicity in. The stone was not just an outcropping – it was a crevice, somehow cut into the surface of the mountain and ridged with twelve feet of stone on either side. It was either a refuge or a trap – *like most attempts at safety.*

Jase glanced around them, his eyes on the ledge above them, and Felicity thought for certain that he heard the whisperings she had imagined before. If she didn't lead them away from him, he was about to find himself inundated by attack from more than one front.

"Can I have a second?" she tried to turn to him, but he deftly redirected her shoulders so she could not turn. "I just need to rest a little." She needed to plan, but forces were converging more quickly than she could manage. If she could just make it to the end of the ridge, she could use the forest for cover. She could hide herself from both Jase and her pursuers. She could leave Jase before he became collateral damage in the war against her.

"Push yourself for a few more minutes," Jase insisted, and she realized that her anxiety had spilled over into physical reticence. "This is either the best or the worst way to go. No trees for cover, but the path, there is no way to happen across us unless you know about the path. You would have to be above us to see us. So as long as they don't know..."

"I don't like it – it's like a trap," she voiced her thoughts. "We should stick to the trees."

Without pausing, he shoved her between the stone ridges, and his speed propelled her forward almost against her will. She let him press her on for far too long, and with every step, with every hint of sound from above, her desperation grew. After all her pleas had fallen on deaf ears, she couldn't let it continue. Maybe it was the isolation of the spot, maybe her growing frustration at her failure, but she had to get away from him. The pressure in her chest threatened to explode into a screech of frustration, and she knew the result would prove treacherous for them both.

She dug in her heels, forcing a halt under the shadow formed from interlacing branches that created a canopy overhead.. "Stop, Jase," she stammered. "I need you to stop! I can't do this anymore."

His reply came almost inaudibly, and both his tone and his urgency confirmed Felicity's earlier suspicions that there was a presence haunting the woods above them. "I promise, Liss. This is the best way. I just need you to push yourself a little farther, and you'll be on the train with all of this behind you. I know you're tired."

"This is not because I'm tired!" she hissed, yanking her shoulders back and away so he couldn't prevent her from turning. "I'm…you've got to leave me, do you understand? You can't take on Brendon! You can't take on Briel! You can't take on Bill Henry's machine! Not for me. It's too much… You need to let me go."

Locking his eyes on hers, he gripped her shoulders so she couldn't look away. "I am not letting you do this alone. You know who I am, what I've trained for. I can and will take on these people, but I need you to make it to safety."

"I just – " Her voice choked on the lie. She saw no other way to cut the tie, and if she didn't, she wouldn't just lose him. In effect, she would kill him.

"I can't stand pretending anymore; I've toyed with you for too long, and I'm not the kind of person who can let you risk your life for a lie. All of this, playing along with your little infatuation with me – it's playing pretend, don't you understand? You are nothing to me! I needed you to get back to my kids. I recognized the advantage that you could offer me, so I used you to figure out how to crush Brendon, so he couldn't hurt my kids. That's all you are – a tool. I didn't mind using you, but you shouldn't put yourself in danger for me. Let me leave you behind as soon as I'm safe."

At least she meant the last sentence, though the other portion of her diatribe tore her heart to shreds.

Abruptly, Jase's energy shifted, and all of his urgency subdued under a somber melancholy. Her words had hurt him. Though she couldn't regret it, Felicity could sense a sheen of tears that suffused her eyes at the effect of her words.

"I never expected anything from you," Jase insisted in a somber tone. "Wished, hoped, but never expected. I did all this because you deserved it, not because I expect to get something out of it."

Felicity swallowed. Fortunately, Jase's eyes were downcast so he didn't see when the tears started to fall. Heartlessly, she pressed on, hating herself but encouraged by her progress. "I don't deserve it, though. Not from you." *Counterproductive,* she reminded herself before shifting tactics. "I don't want to take anything from you, not even help. You sought me out at that party. You put cameras in my house. You drugged me. You sent your friend after me. Once you had me, you took me back to a cabin owned by the man who wants to send me into slavery. You toyed with my mind, tried to make me jealous with Amélie. You poured whatever meaning you needed to into Brendon's actions – maybe he's not even as bad as you claim."

When he finally looked up, she jerked away, turning her face so she could wipe away the damp trails from her cheeks. She had caught the look in his eye for just an instant before she turned, and she recognized danger in their depths. He stepped up behind her, gripping her shoulders and holding her to him.

She sucked in breath at the shimmer of heat that rippled from where his fingers pressed into her sweater all the way to her toes. Jase's urgency had returned when he responded, but its direction seemed to have changed. "I don't believe you, Liss," he murmured. "I can believe you think me a bad man, but I know you don't think your husband is good. No matter what you think of me, you cannot go back to trusting him. Your life depends on it. Just stay with me long enough to get on the train."

"No," she stammered. "I can't. I won't."

For a moment, Jase stood frozen, suspended in some thought. Finally, he spun her around and scrutinized her face. She wanted to look away, cast her eyes to the ground so he couldn't read the ghosts of her tears. His intensity, though, riveted her to the black depth of his stare. Something in her expression transformed his own. "You're a horrible liar, Felicity Miller," he asserted, still barely audible. "You said it before; you want me to stay safe. You're trying to get rid of me before I am put at risk." He reached up and brushed his thumb across her cheek. "But Liss…" He shook her shoulder gently, trying to force her to reason. "…you can't leave me – I won't let you. You can't push me away until I am ready, until you are safe. I am better at this job than anyone you have ever read about or met. I can get you where you need to go, and you're going to let me."

Her words gushed out against her will. "I can't let you put yourself in danger for me anymore. Don't you understand? That part wasn't a lie. You're not getting out of this what you hope to get. Once I am safe, you will never see me again." Her voice broke, and her resistance deflated. "How can I let you take the risk when I only intend to abandon you?"

"You have no choice," he replied in a hushed tone, and he reached down to pull her to him by their clasped hands. "Whatever your plans for the future, my plans don't change. I do whatever I have to do to keep you safe. What you do after that is, as it has always been, your decision."

The utter stillness of the air charged with energy as she raised her eyes to his.

Every determination she had made dissolved as she stared into the spark that lit the ebony orbs of his gaze. Stubborn determination, unflinching strength. Unexpectedly, her hands raised to his face, and shock flashed across his visage. She understood, but she couldn't figure out how to stop herself. He had finally overcome her, and the pain of her false accusations had wakened a deep need in her chest to reconnect what she had just tried to sever.

When she slid her hand behind his neck and pulled herself up to her tiptoes, something broke inside Jase. His arms slipped behind her, lifting her off the ground as his mouth crushed onto hers. One of his hands wove into her hair, and when he pressed her against the cold stone of the mountain, Felicity exploded into a thousand shards, more fractured than Jase's colossal window after it was blasted with munitions.

From the moment his mouth pressed onto hers, time ceased to hold meaning, and she had no idea how long his body crushed her against that stone. Her hands roamed over the ridges of his back and his hands slid just beneath his jacket that still draped over her shoulders, underneath to the thin softness of her T-shirt. When his lips brushed down to her neck, her collarbone, her head fell back in abandon for several moments, before he knitted his fingers into her hair and pulled her mouth back to his. Felicity was on fire. Briel and Brendon and all of Bill's men could have stormed down the side of the chasm where she stood, entwined in Jase's arms, and she would only have realized when they pulled her away. Too soon, she sensed his release, his arms extending as he stepped back and gently lowered her to the ground. She could not wrench her eyes from his face, his downcast face that shuddered with the rising and falling of his breaths.

What had she done? She had as good as signed his death warrant.

Certainly, Jase seemed as confused as she, and when she spun on her heels, his attempt to grab her hand fell short. If he had held half of his normal ability or if less adrenaline had pumped through her system, she never would have gotten away. But she had to get away.

She did not know where her strength came from as she

sprinted away from the most terrifying experience of her life. More than being laid in the car in Banff, more than waking in the back of a truck, more than running from the white-haired man at the cabin, losing control of herself to Jase terrified her. Placing him in danger destroyed her. She ran through a literal stone tunnel, but her mind had entered a tunnel its own, and she would look back with only a vague impression of the ground over which she passed as she fled from him.

Her energy finally waned. Though Jase had called her name several times, she had managed to evade him, some animalistic survival instinct activated in her mind that let her accomplish more than she normally could have. The sun had risen high overhead and begun its descent by the time she settled onto a little boulder that stood several yards off the path. For all she knew, she had just lost herself in a vast wilderness, had sentenced herself to freeze and starve and become food for wild animals. Stilling her mind, she dropped her face into her hands. Jase had sounded so miserable as his desperation grew, and even through her mental echoes, his voice reverberated.

Not that she regretted running.

Now that she had escaped the pull Jase wrought on her, now that she had all the information, a new truth was gradually awakening in her mind. She had spent so much time afraid that Jase was a danger to her. Somehow, it had never occurred to her that she could be a danger to him. He was prepared to throw himself in the fire for her – a woman who could not, because of duty owed to others, prioritize his well-being? The best she could do for him was get away from him. It was the only sacrifice she could make on his behalf, to strike out on her own and not risk his life for her.

A few minutes of rest pulsed energy back into her limbs, though not the adrenaline-filled rush that had brought her to her refuge. Unfortunately, she could not wait for more strength to return. Like in Quido those several weeks before, thirst drove her forward, and she forced herself to her feet.

Somehow, she had ended up close to a path, though she had twisted and turned several times to disguise her route from Jase. She returned to the path in hopes that it would lead her somewhere.

Never in her most errant thoughts would she have imagined where it would lead.

After less than half a mile, she tumbled out of the path into an all-too-familiar stretch of space, and Felicity instantly regressed to a much darker place and time.

Chapter 25

Break what must be broken, once for all, that's all, and take the suffering on oneself. – Fyodor Dostoyevsky

A catharsis is great, and God knows that I needed one. – Felicity's Journal, April 5

Midday, March 30
When the crash came, Felicity felt herself pulled back into her mind, Outer-Felicity slapping her feet against the terrain while Inner-Felicity slowed the world to a pace she could handle.

Come back, she tried to upbraid Inner-Felicity, but there was no response. Instead, Felicity found herself watching the trek across the familiar grounds as if already a passenger on the train. Maybe the strange déjà vu of the location had set her off as well. She stared to her left at what resembled an avalanche of stones which could have occurred naturally. Out of the center of the stones flowed a waterfall which tumbled haphazardly between the crevices and pooled into a small pond at the bottom. Though Felicity had spent little time outdoors since arriving in the area, she definitely recognized that fountain.

I stayed here with the husband, Felicity noted without emotion.

Though Outer-Felicity strategized how to skirt the perimeter of the property in a way that put her on the path to town without exposing herself, Inner-Felicity trembled with every step closer to the cabin. Trembling Inner-Felicity unleashed all of her anxieties on her external shell. *Jase works for ProtoComm,* it warned her. *You should never have trusted him. He knew you would come this way. He sent you here.*

When she recognized the silhouette of her cabin, Inner-Felicity went silent, finally terrified into a stupor. Felicity's motion slowed, and she halted easily within sight of the windows. Despite the potential for discovery, she could not move.

Her eyes swept slowly over the sight that had held her last

illusion of normalcy, and her haunted mind sought for some revenant remnant of that life. Of course, she would find nothing. Brendon Miller had spent years creating a false reality to sell to Felicity – did she believe that truth would miraculously appear from the midst of that delusion?

It was true for me, she lamented, and the emotion managed to carry a semblance of thought back to her rational mind. The moment resonated with reverberating clarity, the moment she had let herself see the reality of her imagined life: *He had lied...He lied to her...She would not lie to herself.*

The memory of her deluded self wrenched a laugh from her lips, and the sound shocked her into awareness. Wasn't she standing, exposed, within range of her psychopathic husband? Outer-Felicity lifted her feet again, pressed her way slowly forward, as if through viscous gel rather than air, and around the perimeter of the property. By the time she had reached half way around, she had developed enough presence of mind to obscure herself in the trees.

That was when she heard him.

"Felicity!"

The sound came from a dozen yards away, far enough that the caller had to yell, and Felicity spun dumbly to see what her husband needed.

When her mind processed what she had done, her heart began a thrum of dread. Brendon had called her name. She reached for the non-existent beads at her neck.

Suddenly, the weight of her feet disappeared. Instead, she flew through the air, and she couldn't imagine how she had made herself move so fast.

That was when she realized the world was upside down.

As the cabin flew out of sight, Felicity pulled herself upright, suddenly aware that her speed was not her own. From nowhere, Jase had appeared and had literally thrown her over his shoulder to carry her away from Brendon.

"So mindless!" he complained, and Felicity winced at herself.

"I'm so sorry," she squeaked, the sound barely escaping from her vice-gripped lungs. They had started panting the moment she had seen Brendon, vivid terror finally overtaking the strange, death-like fear that had entranced her since she had stepped foot on the property. "I panicked."

"Not you," Jase corrected, lowering her as gently to the ground as he could at his rapid rate of speed. Apparently, the fact that she had spoken meant she could also walk on her own. "I should never have set you on this path. I expected to be with you. I didn't consider what it would do to you."

"What it would do to me?" Felicity wondered, her voice still hollow.

Jase had to slow to push through some dense brush, and he took the chance to enter a deeper explanation. "I kissed you," he explained, raising his hand to cup her cheek. "I broke your mind open, and then left you to stumble back into the most dangerous place for that vulnerable mind – the place of your greatest injury."

Finally, up ahead, Felicity saw the light brighten through the trees. Just before they stepped into a clearing, Jase turned and stopped her.

"Listen to me: you're going to be okay. I'm going to keep you safe. But if I leave you here for a few minutes, do you promise to stay?"

I'm leaving you, she contradicted silently, but she knew she didn't have the strength for it at the moment. She would be lucky if she could walk to the other side of the clearing in her current state, so she just stared vapidly into Jase's eyes and nodded.

"It will just be a few minutes," he assured her, placing a tender kiss on her cheek. For the first time since she had seen the cabin, she found herself able to breathe. *Literally a drug,* she smiled back lazily. "I can still get you to the train, so don't move until I'm back," he commanded.

After what seemed an hour, Felicity realized that she had waited for much longer than she had anticipated. She spied Jase's backpack nestled under a nearby bush, and she stepped over to it, pulling the GPS to check the time. 11:20. Not five minutes, she realized. Almost thirty. Nervously biting her cuticles, she began mulling over in her brain what she would do if Jase did not come back. She dug through the backpack to determine her assets. With his backpack, she had the GPS, the compass, and lots of money for the train. But then where would she go? Flexing her leg muscles, she prepared to run.

"What are you doing?"

Briel's voice came from so close beside her that Felicity thought she had been found. When she heard the response, she quickly relaxed her legs, retracting her command to them to move.

"I'm trying to follow these footprints," a hushed male voice responded. "They appear to have split up. Look."

From where Felicity crouched, she had a fairly good view of Briel and her partner. The man pointed to the ground about ten yards from where Felicity hid, and Briel glanced around her, eyes narrowed, as if searching for a clue to Felicity's whereabouts. Though she held her breath, Felicity sensed that her path lay only inches from discovery. She stared, eyes wide with fear, as Briel started toward the copse that obscured Felicity.

Fortunately for Felicity, Briel seemed to find no hint of her prey. Instead, the determined tracker kept her eyes trained on the ground, examining, Felicity supposed, the trajectory of the footprints.

"Should I follow Jase?" the man interrupted from behind Briel. When Briel turned to answer him, Felicity eased gently backwards, farther into the clutch of trees and bushes. Maybe it would be better to make a break for it when she had the element of surprise. Tensing her legs, Felicity prepared to sprint for her life.

Before she could move, though, an unexpected barrage of bullets sprayed at Briel and her partner from behind the shed and the row of hedges. Felicity darted behind a tree, heart battering violently inside her chest. The noise of the shots seemed to have camouflaged Felicity's movement as Briel's eyes darted toward the bullets' source. Conflicted, Felicity considered running again. Maybe Jase had sent the shots as a desperate attempt to free Felicity. Of course, she'd never seen a gun on Jase. If Briel had to dodge gunfire, it meant Felicity could flee through the confusion. Jase wouldn't hit Felicity. If someone else had shot at Briel, though, Felicity might get caught in the crossfire. Her mind quickly realized the conundrum.

Why would Brendon's men shoot at Briel?

"Back here, Liam," Briel commanded, her voice listing toward Felicity's hiding spot. Felicity tensed, trying covertly to peek from behind the tree in Briel's direction. She spotted Briel and Liam, dashing behind a tree trunk only a few feet from Felicity. Unlike Felicity, however, Briel and Liam slinked along the bushes and toward the danger rather than away from it.

Keeping to the treeline, Briel and Liam darted from tree to tree staying as low to the ground as they could in the space between. Eventually they made it to the thicker forest that abutted the row of hedges from where the shots had rung.

For one moment, Felicity stood frozen, appalled that Briel would purposely approach gunshots. Her instincts wanted to cry out to them in warning. Her reason prevented her, however, and Felicity sprinted in the opposite direction from Briel and Liam as fast as she could, dashing partway across the clearing to another copse of trees. The arms that grasped her from the shadow of the brush nearly brought a scream to her lips, but an iron hand clamped over her mouth, and a familiar voice whispered urgently in her ear.

"It's me," Jase reassured her. "We've got to get out of here."

"Who was shooting? Was that you?"

"No, not carrying, remember? Those are hired guards."

Pulling her along behind him, Jase crashed through the forest on the east side of the property.

"Will we make the train?" Felicity inquired.

"We will, but we'll have to drive to do it. We'll never make it if we try on foot."

"Drive what?" she worried.

"I found an older-model four-wheeler, the kind I can start without a key."

"Is that what took you so long?"

"No, I ran into a guard, the one who shot at you."

"They were shooting at me? It seemed they were shooting at Briel."

"Maybe," he acknowledged. "I didn't stop to ask."

With her hand in his iron grip, Jase started to run, dragging Felicity behind him. For some inexplicable reason, she turned and stared back at the cabin, and she ended up stumbling as she shuffled backward. Briel and the other man broke into the clearing, the armed guard not far behind.

"Felicity!" Jase commanded her, and she spun back to him.

Awakening as if from a dream, Felicity turned to look into the eyes of Jase, the eyes that had, for the past three weeks, directed her into the path of safety.

"*Fuis*!" he insisted urgently. "*Fuis, ma petite*! I'll stall them. You've got to get to that train!"

Slow to process, Felicity hesitated.

"Run!" Jase commanded again.

Felicity turned to comply and tore single-mindedly across the clearing and into the trees on the other side. Briel's voice called out,

"Felicity!"

Felicity ignored her.

From behind her, she absorbed a torrent of sounds.

"I'm fine," she heard Brendon say. "Go after Felicity."

"Stop them!" Jase commanded to someone; Felicity couldn't imagine who.

The sound of bodies tearing through outstretched branches echoed loudly in her ears. Glancing back, she saw Brendon on her heels, a volley of gunfire following after him. More than any time during her entire ordeal, she felt abject terror. Brendon was after her.

"Stop!" Jase bellowed. "You might hit *her*. Just stop Brendon!

Who could Jase be talking to? Felicity's mind spun with confusion, but she couldn't let herself slow to figure it out. Not with guns at her heels. Not with Brendon after her. She ran full tilt toward the town, oblivious to anything around her. Eventually, the noise of breaking bracken that pursued her faded into the distance. She hadn't known she could run as swiftly as she did, but adrenaline had, no doubt, shot through her with the fear. The noonday sun beating upon her, she burst through the cover of the trees into the relative exposure of the street.

When the forest spit Felicity, exposed, into the street, she at first thought she would duck into a shop and ask for directions to the train station, perhaps hiding until Brendon or Briel and Liam passed her.

The sun beat down on her more directly than it had since she had arrived in Banff, where she had spent the majority of her time under the cover of trees, and she had no time to play around with the GPS. Unfortunately, asking directions would leave a witness for whoever would come after her. Felicity decided to try her hand at the complicated handheld device.

Glancing around as she started forward, she headed toward what looked like a more populated section of the street. After several minutes of plodding up the pavement, Felicity spied what she had sought. A sign announced the presence of a gift shop ahead of her to the left. Having glimpsed behind her for pursuit, Felicity slipped into the shop and immediately threw her backpack on the ground.

First thing, she pulled out the GPS and looked at the time. 12:22. Felicity had next to no time to cross town and arrive at the train station before the train left at 12:45. According to her map, the gift shop stood almost a mile south of the train station. She needed to get to the main thoroughfare, and head so she could cross the bridge toward the station. Sensing someone's presence, Felicity looked up to see the proprietor of the shop eyeing her suspiciously. So much for avoiding potential witnesses.

"Hi," she said weakly.

"May I help you?" he offered, skeptical.

"Um," *To plan B, then,* she shrugged silently. "I'm trying to get to the train station. Do you know the best way?"

"Another lost tourist," she heard him mutter, though his volume made her think he hadn't intended her to hear.

"Well, the fastest way is to, once you cross the bridge, head west on Buffalo and straight north on Lynx. You'll run into the station after about a mile and a half."

"Thank you so much," Felicity gushed sincerely. *Better than a GPS,* she thought wryly.

As she exited, she heard the owner muttering again, "Wish they'd buy somethin' sometime. Can't make a livin' handin' out free advice. Maybe-"

She couldn't hear the rest because the door swung shut behind her. Glancing up and down the street, Felicity still saw no sign of Briel or her companion. Had they given up so easily? The streets of Banff were not exactly complicated. Surely, they would have known how few options she had for hiding on the south side of town. Felicity remembered Jase's saying that Briel could find their trail in the woods. Not likely the streets would prove more difficult to navigate.

Still, Felicity didn't wait to figure it out. At her best, she had run an eight-minute mile in high school, and she had been in peak condition at the time. She knew she could run a mile at home, but it took her twelve minutes there, though she never ran for speed, and the air in Banff felt considerably thinner than at home. She had to try.

Setting a steady pace, Felicity jogged hurriedly up the road, trying to run as fast as she could while breathing normally. She remembered the time she had collapsed during a race in school because she hadn't paced herself. *It's hard to pace yourself when you're running for your life,* she realized with defeat.

The road she navigated proved even and straight, only zagging slightly west then east as it approached the station. By the time she reached the bend in the road, she could easily see the train station, and she could breathe more easily in spite of her exertion. As she approached the station, Felicity swept her eyes over the small crowd that had gathered on the deck. No sign of any of her pursuers.

Not wanting to draw attention to herself, Felicity slowed to a brisk walk, skirting the building across the street from the quaint railway building. If Briel were anywhere near, Felicity would see her. Just as Felicity started for the building, a small cluster of what appeared to be tourists began crossing the street as well. Felicity hid behind them, smiling gregariously when they shot her confused glances. She felt grateful that the dry mountain air had minimized her perspiration. As group entered the train station coffee shop, Felicity stepped directly to the train counter and pulled out a wad of bills.

"Can I still make the train?" she asked desperately.

"Well, hurry. You got two minutes to spare."

"Thank you!" Felicity gushed, throwing down the money without seeing how much she gave. She had ten times more in the backpack.

Running, Felicity hurdled herself onto the train just a few seconds before it started to move.

Rather than fall into the first seat she found, Felicity climbed a short flight of steps, searching out isolation. She found a seat and breathed a sigh of relief. Though she had no security of her future, she felt an abatement of the agonizing tension that had followed her since she had awakened before the sun.

Felicity would not have purposely picked the train for travel, she realized. Though she had no experience with motion sickness outside of her earlier drive, she decided the train's rocking could easily have turned her stomach. Above her, glass windows spread all along the roof, opening expansive views of the blurring landscape as it flashed by. Still, though visually open to the scenery, the car felt confined. Crisscrossed metal supports that resembled spider's legs stretched just out of reach of her raised hand. A low wide beam split the ceiling down the middle, and it seemed like her head would touch it if she stood.

Outside, the world whizzed past her at a dizzying speed. As the train pulled out of the station, Felicity stared back at the expanding distance between herself and her home of the past several weeks. At the distance between herself and Jase. *Stupid, selfless man!* she complained.

Exhausted, Felicity couldn't block out the astonishing speed with which the landscape near her blurred past. The mild nausea returned, but she didn't know if it sprang from the train's motion or from the memory of the bullets zinging past her, and the realization that Jase had run back toward them.. She tried to concentrate on the vast mountains which stretched along the horizon; their size and distance rendered them relatively motionless, and their immovability stemmed some of her disorientation.

When she finally felt settled, Felicity closed her eyes, willing herself to sleep. She had, at no time in the past few weeks, felt so assured of her personal safety, and the sprint through the forest had sapped her strength. She needed slumber to block out her worries for Jase. For the first time in too long, Felicity slept hard.

The gentle motion of the train should have relaxed her, but it instead focused her attention inward, and images stirred in her mind that her sleep couldn't filter out. She saw Brendon, emerging as a specter from the murky shadows in the forest. His eyes filled her vision, a strange green fire, and her dreams supplied fear her waking mind suppressed. Brendon was furious, desperate.

Awake, she had reveled in the realization that what he had done to her no longer created a sense of injury, just a diffuse disgust at how pathetic he was. In her dreams, the disgust couldn't block out how dangerous his piteousness made him. Once the vision disturbed her sleep, the next jostle of the train wrenched her from slumber.

She sat up, stretched, and shook off her worries for Jase. This was for the best. She needed to separate herself from him, but at the cost of his life? *He said he would be fine.* She wanted to wallow in her anxiety over Jase's safety, but what could she do either way? Would she go back and try to find him?

If not for her kids, she would have, but her time with him had been a fantasy, and since she couldn't bring him back from the dead if he were gone, she had to let it go. Obsessing over something she could do nothing about now that she had time and space to figure out the kids? It would be utterly irresponsible.

Felicity said a quick prayer for Jase and pulled her backpack from under her seat. Tugging down the zipper, she jostled the contents until she uncovered the GPS. Her fingers caressed the plastic casing, replaying the sensation of Jase's fingertips brushing against her own. She extinguished her memories and glanced at the device's digital display: four o'clock. Not that it mattered.

Time held no real import at the moment, but she felt hungry. Since the sun had risen that morning, she had eaten nothing. She scrounged in the bag for an energy bar, pushing past the cash that would buy her kids' safety, until her fingers felt the crinkle of the plastic wrapper. She stopped herself, though, thinking better of it – she might need the bars when she did not have access to other food.

Besides, she needed to move. Rising gingerly from her seat, she stretched again and turned to take in the rail car. She had hoped she would see an attendant, but she saw none. Sighing in exasperation, she turned to her left to descend the stairs. Surely, a train that traveled for hours had food of some sort. *People have to eat,* she reasoned.

As she started down the stairs, a familiar voice froze her in her steps.

Briel.

How could Briel have made the train? Felicity asked herself as she scrambled back up the few steps she had descended. Felicity herself had barely made it, and she had left Briel behind in the woods. For one moment, Felicity could not move, but she gathered herself quickly. Though her heart still stuttered in her chest, her mind grew clear. She needed to find a way out.

Moving to the other end of the car, Felicity searched for a second set of steps. She did not find any. Instead, she found nothing but seats, though some sort of small door blended in with the metal panel at the bottom half of the wall. What would happen if she opened it? Would an alarm sound and give her away? Then again, maybe an alarm would bring attendants to the car and keep Briel out.

The next moment decided her. Glancing behind her, Felicity spied a mousy blond head of hair break the surface of the stairs. Felicity crouched down, and her fingers searched frantically for a handle of some sort on the door. She spied a panel, about three inches square in size, with a groove in it. Placing her fingers in the groove, she slid it to the right and revealed a circular mechanism. She had seen similar in movies or hospitals.

Since the door sat at the far left side of the railcar, the seats blocked the center aisle from her view, but she thought she heard quiet footsteps gliding her direction. Her fingers quaking, Felicity fumbled with the handle until it finally turned, and she quickly yanked the small door open. The rush of wind slapped her in the face, and her courage faltered.

Gulping, she braced herself firmly and stuck her head out the opening. Metal rungs, soldered to the side of the car, descended in steep intervals from the tiny door to a platform below. As long as she could remember, she had suffered from only one true phobia: fear of heights. Though the distance wasn't far, the speed of the ground beneath her compounded the effect and fifteen feet to the platform seemed twice as high. She recoiled from the possibility, and pulled her head back into the car.

"Felicity!" she heard Briel's voice. Turning toward the sound, Felicity spied Briel, only a few feet from her. The sight decided Felicity. Spinning quickly, she lowered her legs out the narrow opening and felt for the nearest rung. *Don't look down,* she quoted too many movies to count. She hoped the advice was wise.

"Wait, Felicity," Briel pleaded.

For one dizzying second, Felicity hung, suspended blindly over the speeding earth below. Then her foot found the rung. As Briel lunged for her, Felicity lowered herself out the door and scuttled heedlessly to the platform below. She gazed up into the horrified eyes of Briel.

"Felicity, stop! You'll kill yourself."

"Like you care!" Felicity spat back, turning to view the span to the other railcar.

Felicity knew that if she stopped as requested Briel would most likely kill her, or at least imprison her. Felicity had no intention of making the job easy. Her temporary sense of victory evaporated as she took in her surroundings. No door to the next railcar graced the facing wall, only another set of metal rungs. Felicity groaned.

She would have to climb back up to the top of the other car. Still, she saw no alternative. Hesitantly, she began to traverse the expanse. Even though the train was not moving too rapidly as of yet, the wind whipped wildly against her on the open platform, tearing at her sense of balance. She doubted whether she could stay upright long enough to cross the eight feet between herself and escape, but she forced her feet to move forward.

An upward glance strengthened her resolve as Briel's nimble feet began the descent toward Felicity. Concentrating on the rungs across from her and ignoring the rushing ground, Felicity leaped across the distance. Her fingers gratefully found a metal brace.

Without looking behind her, she pushed off of the platform

with all her strength, skipping the bottom three rungs altogether. The sound of Briel's landing behind her prodded Felicity to unexpected agility. Glancing below, Felicity saw Briel reach the bottom rung and begin her ascent. Felicity had just cleared the top rung and scurried over the top edge of the car.

In front of her lay a smooth silver surface, easily navigated, but with no comforting braces for her hands. Fortunately, the car did not have the elevated glass compartment, so it was a good eight feet closer to the ground. Plus no one would notice her trek across to the other side.

She instinctively sensed the drag that crawling would be. Still, she couldn't risk standing. Her acrophobia wouldn't allow it. A scream ripped from her throat as she felt Briel's fingers close on her left foot. Without looking back, Felicity scrambled as quickly as she could toward the other end of the car.

Here, she could see, was the protected platform intended for passenger use. How could she penetrate that barrier? She didn't let herself waste time wondering. Briel would be slowed by her climb over the top rung, as Felicity had been, but Felicity couldn't delay. By the time Briel hoisted herself onto the top of the train, Felicity had reached the other side of the car.

No easy metal rungs offered themselves on this end of the car. Felicity's stomach clutched in unbridled fear. Behind her, Briel crept closer with every breath. Below her, an impossibly narrow lip extended from either side of the flexible gangway between cars. She started to lower herself, unsupported, toward the platform.

"Felicity, don't be stupid." Briel's accent thickened with some distress. "I don't want to have to tell Jase that I dropped you under a train. Please." She held out her hand.

For a suspended moment, Felicity stared at the hand, willing herself to reject the lifeline and take her risks on her own ability. Briel had likely killed Jase.

Something in Briel's expression restrained Felicity, however. Felicity remembered Jase's words when discussing Briel's heartlessness: *It was nothing like her.* When Felicity focused on the intense concern in Briel's eyes, heartless seemed far from the smaller woman's sentiments. Faced with almost certain catastrophe if she continued forward, Felicity chose the temporary refuge of captivity with Briel. *Surely, I can find some way to survive,* Felicity reasoned. She just needed time. After glancing at the speeding ground one last time, she turned back to accept Briel's outstretched hand.

Once back in the railcar, Felicity perched herself, fuming, into the first seat available. She glared at Briel, perhaps not the best way to endear herself to her captor, but Felicity couldn't bring herself to kowtow to someone who worked for Brendon. Briel pulled a cell phone from a pouch on her hip and pressed a button. A second later, the phone beeped at her.

"What?" the voice demanded.

"I've got her. We're in the observation car."

Turning to face Felicity, Briel seated herself and stared, eyes narrowed, into Felicity's face. "Felicity," she drawled slowly. "I can honestly say you have surprised me these past few weeks." Briel wore a marked expression of irritation, and Felicity couldn't imagine the reason behind it.

Still, Felicity would not try to assuage her curiosity because that would require talking. She wouldn't give the operative any more information than she could manage.

"We have a problem," Briel's phone interrupted whatever she had planned to say to Felicity.

"Go ahead."

"One of them made it on the train."

An exasperated sigh escaped Briel's lips. "Can you make it up here?"

"Not without exposing us. Do you want me to risk it?"

Briel's eyes narrowed in thought. "No," she decided. "Felicity's not going anywhere until we get to Prince George. Better not to let him see us. If he heads this way, create a diversion."

Briel turned back to Felicity, and Felicity decided she could risk some minor communication.

"How did you get to the train in time?" she demanded.

Briel laughed. "Four-wheelers. While you plodded at a snail's pace down the roads of Banff on foot, we sped through on wheels in under ten minutes. We were settled on the train before you even arrived."

"Why didn't you just capture me in Banff?"

"And risk running into Jase again?" Briel huffed. "No thank you. We wanted to put some space between you two. He really mucked things up for us. Until he came, we were frustratingly close to our objective."

"He was important to my objective!" Felicity exclaimed.

315

"Jase was the only thing that kept me alive!"

"He's quite the piece of work," Briel asserted, and Felicity decided not to reply. "I thought you were smarter than that."

Felicity tried not to thrill at the word "he's." He is. Present tense. Briel had implied it earlier, and there it was again. Maybe the diminutive woman and her companion had not pulled the trigger on him. Slightly mollified, Felicity decided not to fight any more for the time being. "Can I have something to eat?" she sulked, ignoring the insult. "I haven't eaten since before sunrise." She had her own backpack, but she didn't want to reveal its presence to Briel.

Briel pulled an energy bar from some hidden pocket. "Here," she said, and tossed it to Felicity.

Probably crumbled, Felicity complained to herself. Wryly, she noted that Briel had same brand of bars as Jase. *Must be spy fodder,* she thought ironically.

"Thanks," Felicity finally muttered, sarcasm flattening her tone.

She opened the foil wrapper; inside, the bar was intact, and Felicity inhaled it hungrily.

Without being asked, Briel pulled a bottle of water from a harness on her back and handed it to Felicity...*nothing like her*...Felicity hated to admit it, but Briel was as considerate once the masked was removed as she had been playing pretend.

"Um, thanks," Felicity allowed. She hadn't realized her level of thirst.

Pregnant silence filled the car, and Felicity wondered if Briel knew how it grated on Felicity's nerves. *Probably,* Felicity hissed silently as she glared at Briel's face reflected in the window. Her physical needs subdued, Felicity began to slump in her seat. Despite her precarious situation, she felt no imminent danger, and fatigue from her attempted escape crashed down on her. At first, she fought the sleep – she had awakened only half an hour before! But dreams had disturbed her rest, and remembering Briel's words that nothing would happen until Prince George convinced Felicity that a nap would be relatively safe.

At least it would be better than the anxiety of being awake and trying not to stare at Briel. They were four hours from their next destination. As sleep gripped her, Felicity had a brief comprehension of Liam's words over the phone.

"One of them made it on the train," he had said. One of

whom? Who made it on the train? Not Jase – the man would have just said that. Not Brendon. "…one of them…" One of Brendon's guards? The thugs with guns? That was the only "them" Felicity knew of. But why would that bother Briel? They were one and the same. Felicity shivered as she faded into slumber.

Mumbled voices aroused her from her repose – she had no idea how long she had slept. For a moment she considered opening her eyes, but her mind clicked, and she remembered her circumstances. She pressed her lids shut.

"How will we get her off of the train?" a male voice asked.

The now familiar murmur of Briel's voice responded, "It shouldn't be too difficult. I've noticed that she can usually be persuaded to follow." Amazing how different this voice sounded than it had when Briel cared for Felicity's children. In Phoenix, Briel had somehow adopted a sing-song voice, pleasant and lilting. Though still smooth, Briel's voice had fallen to a low, serious pitch, more monotone and intense.

"Yes, but persuaded how?"

Felicity wondered that they could have this conversation in such a public place, but she stifled her curiosity.

"Relax, Liam. We have no need for your methods. I am sure she will cooperate."

"But we have no leverage against her. Maybe she's a sucker for a hot guy," the male voice leered. "I wouldn't mind trying to persuade her like Jase did."

Felicity wanted to punch the man, but she kept her breathing even and restrained herself from movement.

"No need, Liam, and she wouldn't respond to that kind of persuasion anyway, not from you. You're not her type. She apparently goes for the hopeless romantic. Jase almost got himself shot – almost got me shot – when he started barking orders at us at the cabin. No, the only way to get her to comply is to mention her children. Mention them, and she will cave to any demand we make. I have watched this technique work for months when her husband used it."

Felicity tried hard not to betray her awareness. In her mind, however, a tempest raged. Brendon had manipulated her using their children? To think that he would use Alex and the boys to redirect her for his sleight of hand! Felicity had intended, when compelled to leave with Briel, simply to refuse. What would they do in front of so many people? Nothing.

Still, Briel was right. Mention Felicity's children, and Felicity grew fully compliant. *Not fully,* she tried to disagree with herself, but then she could think of literally nothing she wouldn't do to spare her children from harm. Although uncertain of what Briel could threaten, Felicity would go with her if pressured.

Briel and Liam lulled into silence. Unsure of how long she should wait, Felicity began counting seconds in her head, waiting for what she hoped would be a long enough time. She wondered idly how Liam had made it past the guard they had wanted to avoid. Fortunately for her, after about five minutes, Liam began murmuring to Briel again. Though Felicity could not hear the words they spoke, Liam erupted in a harsh laugh after a couple of exchanges between them. The clamor would be a good excuse to wake up.

Groaning, Felicity stretched and raised her head. She blinked confusedly out the window beside her and slowly looked around, trying to appear puzzled.

"You awoke just in time," Briel declared, seemingly convinced by Felicity's deception.

"Where are we?" Felicity replied, feigning disorientation.

"We are almost to Prince George. We have someone waiting there to escort us back to Banff."

The revelation surprised Felicity. Why not just kill her, or deliver her directly to Mexico? She didn't want to go anywhere near Brendon. If she could live until her dying breath with her last glimpse of Brendon's face in her mind, it would be more than enough.

When she returned to Banff and Brendon, she would have new visions to replace the old, pictures of him in his implacable cruelty. As if the trauma of the past few weeks wasn't enough.

"Don't even consider resisting us," Briel threatened. "If you cooperate, we may have you back in time to see your children return home. If not, they will find no parents when they come home."

Felicity's mind burned with perplexity. What did Briel mean? Had Brendon changed his mind? Would he let her live and continue caring for their children? But Briel had said they would have *no* parents? Had Brendon decided to abandon the children completely? Felicity chewed her lip in her anxiety.

Under her feet, Felicity could feel the train slowing. Suddenly, she remembered about the man that Briel and Liam had spoken of, the one who "made it to the train." How would they pass him without initiating an altercation?

Maybe I should initiate an altercation, Felicity pondered. Though the prospect of returning safely to her children enticed her, she worried that returning with Briel's or Brendon's help would hold stipulations that she wouldn't accept. Felicity would not agree to raise her children in the shadow of a criminal. No, if she could gain her freedom, she would contact Nick immediately and make him clear out their parents and her children.

As resourceful as Nick could prove, Felicity felt certain that he could accomplish such a task even with ProtoComm at his heels. She hated to uproot everyone she loved, but if she didn't insist that they leave Phoenix, Brendon would no doubt use them to manipulate Felicity. Nick was single and brilliant – he would have no trouble relocating. Though Felicity's parents would resist leaving their home, they had both retired and could easily move if persuaded.

The sudden jolting jerk of the train aroused her from her considerations, and Felicity's mind went into overdrive. Briel gripped her by the shoulder and raised her to her feet, heading with Liam toward the staircase. With every step, Felicity scoured her surroundings for an opportunity to escape.

"Should we wait until the train clears?" Liam queried to Briel.

"It might otherwise have been easier, but not with Bill's man here. He would just wait outside and find us when we exited the train. We should blend in with the crowd while he is still hindered by them."

Bill's man?

Felicity closed her eyes for a brief moment to gather her thoughts. Briel worked for Brendon. Brendon worked with Bill. Briel wanted to avoid Bill's man. But weren't Briel and Bill's man working for the same side?

When Felicity's mind wandered back to the forest by the cabin, her confidence faltered. Her mind replayed the events in slow motion, and she could not make sense of what she saw. Briel and Brendon had exchanged glances, as Felicity would expect, and Briel had subsequently pursued Felicity with a vengeance. But Felicity had been confused that Bill's men seemed to shoot at Briel, and Jase had allowed the possibility. What if Briel didn't work for Brendon anymore? What if Nick was right all along? " Briel had complained that Jase had almost gotten them shot "barking orders" at them. Was Briel on Felicity's side after all?

As she reached the bottom step, though, Felicity's questions lost their priority. Suddenly alert, she recognized an opportunity for escape. Briel still gripped Felicity's shoulder, but more lightly than she had a moment before. Instead of focusing on Felicity, Briel seemed preoccupied by scanning the cabin, no doubt for "Bill's man." Twisting her body, Felicity stumbled across the aisle at the bottom step and cried out in mock pain, as if she had lost her footing.

Briel eyed her warily and opened her mouth to reprimand Felicity, but a middle-aged woman had stopped, concern apparent on her face.

"Are you okay, sweetie?" the woman asked.

Felicity glanced at Briel's expression, petulantly amused. Briel snapped her mouth shut, her nostrils flaring in a furious breath.

"I've twisted my ankle," Felicity complained in her best helpless manner. "Those steps were so steep." She reached down and began rubbing the offending ankle. A young man squeezed into the seat in front of her.

"Would you like me to get you some ice? And a steward, too. I imagine they have a wheelchair or crutches."

"Would you?" Felicity batted her eyes at him hopefully. "That is so kind of you." She was laying it on thick, using the drama to draw even more attention to herself.

Risking a glance at Briel, Felicity took in a red face and clenched jaw. Briel glared meaningfully at Liam who made his way behind Felicity. Felicity's heart sped. Where was the man they wanted to avoid? Surely, he had to come by eventually! When he did, Felicity would make her move.

The pain in her neck was instantaneous and intense as Liam's hand clamped down, but it did not cause her to cry out. Instead, it took her breath away. Behind her, Liam began to murmur in a low voice.

"Why don't you let me carry you out?" he recommended, his finger pressed firmly on a point between her shoulder and neck.

Though the pain was intense, Felicity refused to budge. Liam dropped his hand, glaring at her with significance. "Don't make me do it again," he seemed to say. *I've been through childbirth,* Felicity challenged silently. *You'll have to do better than that.*

As if he had heard her, Liam raised his hand and placed it

menacingly on her shoulder again. To any passersby it would seem a comforting gesture. Felicity closed her eyes, preparing for agony. Though she determined not to buckle to his pressure, she did not relish the thought of the pain. She held her breath.

Before the pain had erupted, Felicity heard Briel hiss at Liam.

"Watch out," she warned, darting her eyes once over Liam's shoulder.

Felicity smiled. Her plan had worked.

Without first looking behind her to see the man, Felicity dove across the aisle and scrambled to the seats on the other side of the stairwell. She didn't wait to see the expressions of the startled passengers. As quickly as she could, she clambered over the seats, moving to the back of the train, against the flow of passengers. She disregarded the pulling of her muscles and the bumps against the frames of the seats. To her left, the unknown assailant began pursuit, his progress frustrated by the oncoming passengers.

A collective scream broke out behind Felicity, and glancing over her shoulder, she spied a raised gun in the hands of a large, muscled man. She didn't take time to assess his appearance beyond his size and his gun. Had she been foolish to leave the relative safety of Briel? *Too late now,* she concluded.

"Get out of my way," the man with the gun demanded.

Felicity heard his lumbering footsteps pounding behind her. The cleared aisle opened up for her as well as for him.

"Don't let him get her," Felicity heard Briel's furious command. "He'll kill her."

Felicity sprinted out the back door of the car and rapidly entered the next. It was almost empty.

"Watch out," she screamed as she tore past the few passenger's startled faces. Behind her, she heard the door bang open and the renewed screaming as her pursuer entered the car.

"Stop now," the familiar voice of Liam commanded.

Felicity couldn't tell if he spoke to her or her pursuer, but she didn't wait to find out. The next car was an open platform, and she would risk the five-foot jump to the ground if she could make it out the door. The sound of an ensuing scuffle lasted the few seconds that it took her to reach the door to the open gangway, and Felicity sighed in relief as the door began to close behind her.

"No, you don't," a gruff voice assailed her, and she suddenly felt her shirt cinched tightly around her torso. Her breath fled her, and her scream choked impotently in her throat.

"Please don't," she begged as her unknown pursuer wrenched her around to face him. Her voice came out weak and small.

Instead of answering, the man grabbed her around the waist, almost stashed her under his arm like a package, and whirled to face the approaching Liam. She wondered tacitly why the man didn't pull his weapon. For one moment, Felicity stayed obediently beneath the man's arm, but the second Liam raised his hand to strike, Felicity began squirming violently, trying to free herself from the brawny man's grasp. Liam was forced by her unpredictable struggle to attack his enemy with caution. *If I can just break free for a moment,* Felicity lamented.

The man grew irritated, tired of trying to hold on to Felicity. He felled a blow directly to Liam's jaw which caused Briel's companion to stumble a step back. With lightning speed, the man released Felicity from under his arm, grasped her by the hair, and swiped her, open-handed, across the face. She recoiled from the pain, unable to move for at least a minute while her mind processed the sensation. Her jaw pulsed an agonizing throb.

In that moment, the man replaced her, stunned into immobility, under his arm and laid more viciously into Liam. For several long minutes, Felicity thought that her captor would prevail over Liam, until abruptly, Briel burst through the door.

Without pausing his attack, Liam spat a reprimand at Briel, "Where have you been?"

A definite note of amusement colored Briel's tone when she responded, "I went to get this."

Felicity gasped as Briel lowered a large, black handgun into her view.

"Let her go," Briel demanded.

Instead of the calm assent that Felicity hoped for, the man pushed her violently to the edge of the platform. Her scream burst from her lips and seemed to echo in her ears as she hung, suspended, from Liam's outstretched hand. Seeing the man's intention, Liam had grabbed her by the wrist.

The man seemed to guess at Briel's reluctance to use her gun. Despite his marked disadvantage, he wrapped his arms constrictingly around Liam, using him as a shield to defer Briel's shots. Felicity's scream had drawn a small crowd from the deck below, and they watched with shocked faces as she dangled precariously from the gangway. Using all her strength, Felicity turned to grasp Liam's hand with her other and walked herself up his arm as if using a rope until she stood securely on the platform.

Finally, all that held her to her captivity was Liam's outstretched hand. She had never, to her knowledge, injured another human being, and the thought bothered her greatly, but Felicity would not let Liam's iron grip rob her of her impending liberty. Leaning down, she sunk her teeth as firmly as she could into the flesh on the back of his hand. He howled in pain. "Briel, I can't hold on!" he warned. Felicity sunk her teeth a millimeter farther, and his hand retracted from her wrist involuntarily. She was free.

Turning quickly, Felicity leaped from the platform she had been so afraid to fall from, not looking as she spat the taste of Liam from her mouth. The rising ground jarred her teeth and caused her bones to collide painfully with one another, but Felicity didn't pause. Standing as quickly as she could, she sprinted from her landing place and dashed across the tracks toward another motionless train.

Briel was upon her at once. Stumbling over the tracks, Felicity fought to right herself before she fell completely. Briel needed no such caution. Adeptly, Briel dashed toward Felicity, drawing her gun as she closed the distance.

Though she did not look behind her again, Felicity could hear the footsteps almost upon her. She made one last, desperate search for an escape, but to no avail. If she had possessed the strength, Felicity would have cried.

"Stop, Felicity," Briel warned dangerously. Behind the threat, Felicity noted that inexplicable tone of compassion.

Felicity could not continue. She could not outrun Briel. The adrenaline that had carried her away from the man on the train had faded, sucked from her by her extended exertion and uncontrolled fear. Without turning, Felicity tripped forward a few more steps before coming to a halt.

"Felicity, please," Briel begged.

Her best efforts exhausted, Felicity succumbed, despondent, to her renewed captivity and turned back to face her captor.

Chapter 26

At this time, your contract at ProtoComm is null and void due to your failure to perform your duties and responsibilities. We will retain your final paycheck to mitigate our losses. – Martha Patterson, Administrative Assistant to Bill Henry, accompanying the pink-slip for Jase Hamilton. April 6

How is Felicity? We haven't heard from her in a few weeks, so she must really be enjoying herself. – Email from Margaret Alexander to her son, Nicholas. April 7

Evening, March 30

Sitting alone in the makeshift cell, Felicity began to steel herself for what would come. Panic would accomplish nothing, she knew. If she had doubted her survival, her course would have been different, but she had no reason to expect impending death. Briel and her lackey would have just killed her and disposed of her if that was their intent, not stuck her in a cell. Since Felicity was still "displaced," there was no reason to hide her demise with any great care.

She rested her head in her hands. Even with all she had been through, the moss creeping down the concrete walls and the drip of the water made her head swim. Though cold, the moisture was stifling, the air thick and stale. She breathed through her nose slowly to calm her heart rate. She pressed Jase out of her mind.

Just as she felt in control of her breath, the crackling noise of the door's opening restarted the palpitations of her heart. Felicity would not, however, let her abductors see her fear. She hated the thought that she would give them any pleasure by seeing her afraid. With the steeling thought in her mind, Felicity felt a marked suspicion at the conciliatory tone of Briel's voice as it floated through the grey light of the cell.

"Felicity, it may seem that we are on different sides, ," Briel began matter-of-factly. "But you've been lied to. We need your help, and we might be able to help you, too." When she spoke next, she dropped her voice, her gentle accent lilting smooth and pleading. "I know you're confused, but I can explain everything."

She shouldn't believe Briel, but the potential for compassion managed at least to unlock Felicity's tongue.

"I feel honored that you came to interrogate me yourself," Felicity hummed sullenly. "You didn't send your personal bully from the train."

Something like guilt flashed across Briel's countenance before she buried it with a slight smirk. "We need information from ProtoComm."

Felicity stared at Briel with a blank look. "Why are you asking me? I'm sure Bill would give you whatever you wanted."

"I appreciate the sarcasm," Briel smirked. "But Brendan never provided me the kind of access I needed."

"Wh-what are you talking about?" Felicity stuttered.

The calculation returned to Briel's tone. "Felicity, don't act stupid. We know full well how complicit you are in all this. I saw what you have on your computer, besides the fact that you chose to stay with Jase long after you could have left."

Felicity gaped at Briel. "Jase was the only thing protecting me from Brendon! You certainly wouldn't!"

"Right now, Brendon is being held captive at your cabin. And you just jumped willingly into the long train of women who have corrupted themselves for Jase."

Incredulous, Felicity shook her head at Briel. "I don't know where you're getting your information…"

"We put together what we found on your computer with the events of the past few weeks. We extrapolated the rest."

"Well, you might want to interpolate right back to three weeks ago and start over. Someone has pointed you in a very wrong direction."

Without admitting the possibility, Briel pursed her lips. "What is your version?

"It's not 'my version.' I didn't have to take evidence without context and try to piece it together; I was there. And after all that time you spent in our house. The time you spent in Brendon's company. I thought you were professionals!"

"Fine," Briel shrugged. "Then enlighten me."

"I know Nick told you I had been kidnapped by ProtoComm."

"He told me you woke up in the back of a truck. He told me ProtoComm – Jase's company – was into some bad things, and that you claimed Brendon was involved."

"Not Jase's company. Brendon's company, in a very real sense. What Nick didn't tell you – what I didn't tell him…"

Felicity trailed off for a minute. Once she started talking, she realized that she had not actually had to tell her story to anyone before. She had purposely withheld details from Nick so he wouldn't freak out, and Jase had lived it with her.

"Start talking, Felicity. You're not going anywhere until you do."

"Hold on," Felicity hedged. "Why am I believing you? You work for ProtoComm."

"Not ProtoComm. My company has been engaged to investigate the disappearance of a Mexican businessman's daughter. She has been missing for two months, but no request has been made for ransom. A, uh, disgruntled, employee from ProtoComm provided a lead to her location. Did you ever hear of John Mitchell?"

"John Mitchell? So, he's alive?" Felicity couldn't keep the joy out of her voice, and Briel glanced up at her in confusion. Almost immediately, Briel's other words sunk into Felicity's brain. "Wait, if you knew where John Mitchell was, why did ProtoComm let him live?"

"Felicity, I never worked for ProtoComm – my cover with Brendon was to access ProtoComm for a Mexican businessman, who hired us just a few days before I came to work in your house. We think the man's daughter was kidnapped by the same people who were taking you to Mexico."

"The slave trade?" Felicity couldn't mask the sudden compassion that swelled within her for the girl.

"We think so. She's young and pretty, and that kind of victim usually carries more value alive than dead."

"How did you end up working for Brendon? He's the one who gave you access to ProtoComm's information."

"He 'gave' us nothing. We were watching Brendon for about three weeks before you left. He seemed to be a peripheral player, someone who had access but not knowledge. We figured we could exploit his position without compromising him until we found evidence. I induced Brendon to hire me. It looks like someone at ProtoComm had been watching you as well, and for some time.

What set this trip in motion was when Bill discovered that I was working for you. Something, maybe my presence, induced Bill to come after you, but when their agent got close to your house, one of our men took him out."

Brendon induced Bill, Felicity lamented before she processed the words. A lump rose in her throat. "The car wreck?"

Briel looked surprised at Felicity's quickness. "Yes," she agreed. "Liam followed the man, and when he arrived on your street, Liam pushed the man's car into the ditch. Then, he dragged the man, unconscious, into his own car and drove him away from your house."

"Someone was coming to my house, with my children? For what purpose? Briel, how could you?"

Belying her complicity, Briel looked truly regretful, even guilty. Her answered spewed out defensively. "Jase came to your house, too, God knows why! And this man wasn't our fault. All information points to the fact that someone had targeted you, apparently Bill, before I came on the scene. We saved you and very possibly your children."

Felicity peered skeptically at the diminutive woman who stood before her in the cell.

"We're the good guys, Felicity," Briel insisted.

If it was the truth, Felicity felt grateful that Briel and her cohorts had protected her family. But where did that possibility fit into the explanation of events that Felicity had developed over the past few weeks? She had seen no proof that Briel was who she said she was, so Felicity offered no direct reply.

"If you're the good guy, why the dismal prison cell?"

"Because you're with Jase, and Jase is not a good guy..." Finally, Briel sounded like she doubted herself. "He works for Bill."

"You know that's not true, not the way you mean it."

"I don't know," Briel countered, "because you changed the subject before you explained."

Breathing deeply, Felicity steeled herself. "Please understand," she prefaced, "this is really hard for me. It's the first time I've had to say it out loud."

Briel nodded, a tacit promise of patience.

"I went to Canmore thinking I would have a long, luxuriant vacation with Brendon. I wasn't as excited about the 'with Brendon' part as the 'long and luxuriant vacation' part, but I was willing to give it a try. Thing is, he told me he would be with me all the time, but he kept disappearing for hours on end, no explanation. It took my running into Jenna Whitfield finally to figure out that ProtoComm was there."

"And that was enough to make you run off with Jase Hamilton?" Briel demanded scornfully.

Felicity glared at her. "Let me finish, and you'll see. You've known Jase longer than I have, I imagine, but you have misjudged him in this. He explained why you don't trust him, but I have had evidence that he intends good for me and my kids."

Hugging herself, Felicity rubbed her hands up and down on her arms to warm and calm herself. Every time Briel went off on Jase, Felicity wanted to scream at the younger woman.

"Right after I ran into Jenna, I watched her go into a huge glass building, and when I went closer, I saw a sizable ProtoComm gathering. Some kind of convention."

Closing her eyes, Felicity tried to concentrate all of her memories into words; black and white letters moving through her mind – no images. "I was furious. Why had he felt the necessity to lie? He could have told me I was a tag-along. No, it wouldn't have seemed as generous, but I could have had a wonderful time. I was just so angry with him – the first time I had let myself go there in years."

Standing to her feet, Felicity began to pace. "I ran away from the building as fast as I could, and I sought out somewhere I could distract myself from his unkindness. Unfortunately, I ran to the wrong place." Felicity stopped talking, stopped moving, and stared unseeing into the dark corner of the room. She only continued when prompted by Briel.

"I can tell that's not the whole story," the younger woman pressed.

"I went to the library. He was there, with his administrative assistant, Aimee. They were not engaged in professional activities."

Felicity had to stop, and Briel didn't push. If Felicity read the expression right, Briel believed Felicity and was trying to fit the new possibility into her parameters. Finally, she made herself keep going.

"I waited until he came back to the cabin to confront him, but he just made excuses about why he was justified, how everything was okay, how it didn't really affect me. I mean, I guess pretty typical stuff. I couldn't be in the room with him anymore. We were scheduled to go to a party that evening, and I insisted we go. I guess he would have insisted if I hadn't – his plan depended on it. And I went. Like an idiot."

"And that was where Brendon kidnapped you?"

"Well, I mean, it's not that simple." Felicity huffed out a breath. "Jase drugged my drink."

"Jase drugged…"

"So, he had been working for ProtoComm, doing security stuff, and Bill had told him to install surveillance at my house. That's how he found out about the plan."

"Found out about the plan, or made the plan?"

Felicity shook her head. "It was Brendon's plan. You should have seen him when they put me in that car. Standing there in Aimée's arms, glaring at me like he wished he could have strangled me with his own hands." A sob gasped out of her, not fully formed. "And the next thing I know, I wake up in the back of a pickup truck, only a few miles from the Mexican border."

"What you're saying," Briel summed up sardonically, "is that Jase drugged you, Jase grabbed you from New Mexico, Jase basically held you hostage in his cabin in Banff, but you're believing him and condemning Brendon?"

"When you say it that way…" Felicity allowed.

"I have to think about this. One way or another, ProtoComm is currently holding an innocent man: Brendon or Jase."

"Brendon is not innocent." Felicity insisted.

"We can discuss your opinion on the character of men who have affairs after you help us figure out where they are holding my client's daughter. But I think it's safe to move you out of this cell."

"If you're simple-minded enough to believe that this is about my hurt feelings over an affair, than you are dumber than I thought. As soon as I realized what he had been doing with the company, I realized that I had a lot more to fear than a broken heart."

"I'm not convinced that you really believe that, but if you do, I guess it makes sense why you would feel the need to get away from him. You're reaching, though, Felicity. And it makes no difference to me whether Brendon or Jase is the bad guy other than who to have you call."

"How can you expect me to talk to him again?" Felicity begged, her tone enervated by sudden anxiety.

Rather than answer, Briel called to the guard outside,

instructing him to "take her to the executive office."

Felicity only had to wait a couple of minutes before the door creaked open again. A large, muscular man grabbed Felicity by the elbow and led her, none too gently, through a parking garage and into what looked like an office building lobby. At the lobby doors, Briel met her and accompanied her the rest of the way into the elevator and up to a spacious, executive-looking office. "Adam," Briel nodded her thanks to Felicity's escort.

After so much sparsity, Felicity couldn't help but appreciate the luxury afforded by her new "cell." A shaggy, beige carpet lay atop dark wood floors. The velour sofa cushions enveloped and caressed her skin which had felt tight and drawn since her leap from the train. With no idea of the time or how long she might have to wait, Felicity opted to take advantage of the luxury. It had been several hours since the train, and the sun had set long before she reached her prison. Sleep crept irresistibly over her, and she settled into another restless slumber.

Her mind supplied the image, far more vivid than she could have born were it truly before her: Jase, turning away from Felicity and into a barrage of bullets, his body collapsing onto the cold dirt of the clearing, and Brendon, gripping Felicity and dragging her from the spot where she had gazed into Jase's lifeless eyes.

The tears running down Felicity's cheeks awoke her, and she realized she had passed the night in sleep. No one had disturbed her when the morning light beamed directly into her eyes – no human. The ghosts in her dreams had ripped her well-being to shreds.

Forcing herself to redirect her thoughts, Felicity began to assess her surroundings. The building where they held her couldn't be in Banff. In Banff, she had seen no building over three stories tall, and this building had five, if the elevator buttons indicated correctly. In the chic tourist trap of Banff, the general architecture reminded Felicity of an Alpine village. The room where she now rested boasted sleek floor to ceiling glass, very modern. Outside the window, exposed wooden beams extended beyond the building face giving the facade an angular texture. Again modern.

Briel must have been watching her from somewhere, because as soon as Felicity rose to peer out the window, the door behind her opened.

"Did you rest well?" a pleasant voice inquired.

Surprised, Felicity spun to face the unknown intruder on her solitude.

"Who are you?"

"I'm Nessa. Can I help you be more comfortable? Briel provided you with some clothes." Felicity heard an almost identical accent to Briel's.

"Are you serious?" Felicity felt like laughing at the solicitous tone of Nessa's voice. "I'm being held prisoner. Are you the good cop?"

Nessa's face folded in consternation. She seemed genuinely chagrined. "Please allow me to help you. I know what you've been through. Briel doesn't understand..." Nessa cut off, deciding against continuing.

Felicity glared incredulously at Nessa.

"Briel wanted me to offer you anything you needed for your comfort." Nessa informed Felicity, her tone turned cold. Felicity got the distinct impression that Nessa wanted to offer more than just comfort: maybe help or information. "She doesn't want you to live in squalor while you are here."

"Where am I?" Felicity softened slightly. "We're not in Banff. I can't see the town at all."

"We are nearer Lake Louise, several miles north of Banff."

"Is this a house?" Felicity remembered the parking garage the man, Adam, had led her through.

"Not exactly. It was a lodge. Our client bought it to serve as our headquarters while we are here."

"He *bought* it?" Felicity's mouth dropped open.

"He wanted to make sure we did not have any problems with functionality."

Felicity's mind swam at the magnitude of the players who now controlled her life. Until she had left Phoenix, her grandest adversary had come in the form of local police officers who loved to write tickets to the suburban moms. The man who now held her fate had bought a *lodge*. A *hotel*. Amazing. And she already knew personally the scope of ProtoComm's influence.

"What does Briel want me to do?"

Nessa thought for a moment. "I'm going to let Briel tell you herself." She wore that same look of distaste that she had worn several times during the conversation. With that declaration, Nessa walked toward the door. Over her shoulder she repeated, "Let me know if you need anything."

The now familiar beep of the woman's cell phone sounded. Felicity had heard the same tone from Briel's and Adam's. "She is ready to talk to Briel," Nessa declared into it as the door closed behind her.

Only minutes later, the door reopened. With Briel came a small woman pushing a room service cart laden with fruit and bread. The smell of fresh coffee accompanied the entourage. Despite herself, Felicity sighed.

"Are you hungry?" Briel inquired as the woman pushed the cart to within Felicity's reach from the couch. Felicity didn't answer, but reached for a croissant and began nibbling. "I have decided how you can help us."

Felicity said nothing. She just gnawed on her croissant and stared blankly at Briel.

"I need you to reach out to Jase."

Thrill blossomed in Felicity's chest, and she set down the croissant.

"Do you know how to reach him?"

Briel glared at Felicity's enthusiasm. "I have something I could try, an old number he has kept for years, as far as I know."

Controlling her breath, Felicity tried not to reveal her anticipation as Briel tapped in some numbers. The message came on, and Jase's voice crackled through the speaker. Felicity's heart leapt, but disappointment soon followed. "You've reach Jean Paul's Bait and Tackle. Leave a message, and I'll get back to you." Briel pressed in a series of numbers, but the responding messages spoke similar nonsense, all in Jase's voice. He obviously hadn't left a way to reach him – or he wasn't alive to reach.

"So, that didn't work," Briel allowed, "but you've given me a new option worth trying. If what you say is true, then you can talk to Brendon and accomplish the same thing."

"I can't. I can't talk to him."

"Look, if what you think is true, reaching out to him will give us so much information, and you can prove your theory. First of all, if he can answer his phone, then he's probably okay. And if he's okay, then he is probably the one in with ProtoComm."

"He is. What else will it do?"

Briel seemed to think. "If Brendon is involved, it will send him into motion. ProtoComm knows they've lost you, and they can't have you around to expose them. They will come after you to wrap up their loose end."

The thought gave Felicity pause. "What in the hell am I supposed to say to him?"

"Nothing. Just cry."

"Cry?"

"Yeah, cry, then beg him to take you back or tell him you were wrong, or you miss him. Whatever you think will stroke his ego."

Horrified, Felicity shook her head. "Do you understand what that will do to me?"

"You're stronger than you appear, Felicity Miller. You'll be fine. Besides, according to you, Jase needs help."

"Not necessarily,' Felicity countered. "He could have gotten away from them. He got away from you. Or he could be dead."

Briel smirked at her. "Jase isn't dead – I almost believe he can't die. Besides, he was standing there with the guards while Liam and I were sending bullets back at them to clear a way out."

"So, you might have killed him? Though I guess I might as accurately say I did, since I stood there like an idiot while Brendon's men and you rushed me.." Jase's shout in the woods made more sense now. He was yelling to Briel not to shoot, not to hit Felicity.

"Don't beat yourself up for it. If he's caught, his captors are just as likely to be in danger as he is. "

Felicity managed a smile at that.

"So, will you do it?" Briel pressed.

"How does it help get Jase out?"

"Eventually, I bring down ProtoComm. Maybe it's soon enough to save Jase, if he's innocent, maybe not."

Not good enough, Felicity complained internally.

"You don't know Jase any way well enough to be so defensive of him. Before you get too choked up about Jase's dilemma, I think you ought to see some things we have dug up about him during this investigation. He may have done some nice things for you – he may even have taken good care of you. But he is not a good guy."

"Not a good guy, like, he's a bad guy? Or not a good guy, like, not a good person?"

Briel shrugged. "I'll let you decide." She placed a laptop on a free spot on the food cart and lifted the screen. "And after you see this, you may change your mind about him."

The screen gradually faded on, and Felicity recognized her own face.

"What is this?" she whispered. She recognized her darkened room at Jase's cabin on the monitor. On her bed, she could just make out two reclining silhouettes.

Instead of answering, Briel clicked the play button.

Jase's voice floated out to her from the tinny computer speakers, and Felicity's heart clutched. She missed him so badly. "*Felicity*," he murmured.

A momentary pause.

"*What is it?*" came Felicity's quiet murmur.

"*Someone is here. Not in the house - outside.*" His form rising onto one arm, leaning over her. "*I need you to come with me.*"

The screen cut away roughly to the basement view.

Jase's longing expression as he raised his hand to cup her face. "*Please don't do anything. Don't try to solve this yourself.*" A sigh. "*I told you I would take care of you.*" Felicity reined in any reaction lest she reveal any sentiment to Briel.

Another cut. Felicity burying her face in Jase's shirt. "*I'm so glad it's you,*" she had gushed warmly as his lips found her face.

How long would Briel force her to watch this? How did Briel have this footage?

"Where did you get this?" Felicity hissed.

"What's wrong, Felicity? Didn't you know that you were exposing yourself when you entered a relationship with a criminal?" Briel didn't even try to hide her acrimony.

Felicity's anger burned. She repeated her question with more vitriol, "Where did you get this?"

Briel's lips curved in a knowing smile. "ProtoComm's servers, of course. It looks like Jase was sending back footage of you to Bill."

Completely confused, Felicity shook her head, her breath hitching with pain.

"Please, Briel," her expression tormented. "I…I need to understand."

The look on Felicity's face seemed to melt Briel's sarcasm. Her question came out hesitantly. "What is it you don't understand?"

Felicity's eyes unfocused. She seemed to search the floor, her hands, the landscape outside: searching for some elucidation to her perplexity. "You said you work for a Mexican businessman. I thought you worked for Brendon."

"I did, to an extent. My client wanted me to use Brendon's connection to ProtoComm in order to retrieve the information about his daughter. But my secondary purpose had always been your protection."

"But you refused to help Jase protect me." The room spun as Felicity wrestled with Briel's assertion. "I thought you were supposed to finish the job that Jase had interrupted, get rid of me forever." She dropped her head in her hands, her breath a shallow, jagged pant.

"No, Felicity, I would never do that. And I knew Jase always has an angle – I had no reason to trust him this time." Briel reached a hand out and touched Felicity's arm. It felt sweet but awkward, as if not normal for the younger woman. "And if what you say about Brendon is true, maybe your husband thought he could hire me for something like that, like I was a common mercenary, but that is not me."

Felicity peered into Briel's eyes for the truth. Even with her own self-doubt, Felicity believed she saw sincerity in Briel. Jase had said it – Briel leaned toward the ethical. She had only become the enemy when she thought Felicity had betrayed Brendon. Instead, Briel should have praised Felicity for standing up to a criminal.

"I'm going to try this," she informed Briel. "I'm terrified, but I'm going to try."

She did not know how long she sat frozen, unbreathing on that sofa, once Briel handed her the phone.

"Felicity...Felicity," Briel's insistent voice urged her to awake from her trance. Briel shook her gently. "Felicity, I need you to call.

After staring at the phone for a full minute, Felicity opened the screen and dialed in the number.

When she finally heard the voice on the other end, everything within Felicity quavered.

She had always experienced her mind as a uniform substance. Thoughts dug through it and found direction like an earthworm through the earth, and they could go from any point to any other point without too much effort. Now that she had been through the destruction of her external world, she started to see her mind as a scaffolding, a framework that held her mind together. Her thoughts were a webbing or a net that flowed through and around the framework, anchored along various points, suspended and dependent on the framework.

Brendon's affair had hit her framework like a 6-point earthquake, her infrastructure weakened and shaken and uncertain.

Brendon's attack, the kidnapping, the knowledge that he was literally willing to end or destroy her life? Now every time she experienced him again, thought about him, heard about him – it was a wrecking ball directly to her framework. Hearing his voice? It was TNT at the base of every load-bearing column that held her mind together. Twice since she had made it to Banff, her framework had neared collapse: once at the coffee shop and once as she had neared the cabin she had inhabited with Brendon. Both of those times, Jase had reached out and steadied the beams, throwing her a rope to stabilize the tremors.

When Felicity sat on Briel's couch, holding the phone with an arm she couldn't feel, there was no Jase to hold her together.

"Who is this?" came Brendon's intense tone, as strident through the phone as in her presence.

Felicity balked. She couldn't move. The dynamite detonated, and faster and more thoroughly than had happened before, Felicity's mind crumbled. Fortunately, Outer-Felicity – the robot version of herself – proved unexpectedly adept at performing whatever tasks Felicity needed to do. Inner-Felicity, crumbled into a miasma of worthless rubble, heard her mouth speak.

When Briel shook her by the leg, Felicity said, "It's me, Brendon."

Inner-Felicity trembled. She wept in terror. She scratched at an imaginary door that would let her run away. She dug under the rubble in hopes that she could shut out the voice.

"Felicity?" the tone changed, strange and soft and suspicious and prodding.

"It's me, Brendon. I'm okay."

Silence met her ears for several seconds, so soundless that Felicity realized Brendon must have muted her.

"I'm so glad," he finally came back. "Where are you? Can I come get you?"

Instantly, all of Felicity's alarm bells rang, and even Outer-Felicity went into protective mode. There was no way Brendon could find her.

"I don't know exactly where I am," Felicity responded truthfully. "I'm somewhere in the forest. There are a few buildings around, but I don't recognize them."

More silence, and Felicity wondered if ProtoComm could trace her location through her phone.

"You and I really need to talk. There are so many things that you don't understand. When I told Bill that Jase – his employee - had kidnapped you…"

Felicity glared over at Briel and mouthed, "I told you so!"

"I was so worried," Brendon continued. "I know you hate me right now, but I would never want anything to happen to you."

Smooth as always. Says whatever he needs.

Muting the phone, Felicity turned to Briel. "I can't do this anymore. Get me off."

Nodding, Briel prompted her. "Tell him you think you're near the cabin. Tell him you're going to try to make your way there."

"I'm not going back there!" Felicity insisted.

"No, you're not," Briel assured. "But I would like him to think you are."

"You're the boss," Felicity shrugged, unmuting the phone. "Are you there?" she hedged. "I couldn't hear you for a second."

"I'm here, Felicity. Reception is spotty in the forest. Whose phone are you using? Does it have a map? Can you send me your location?"

"It's a landline," she covered quickly. "I found this nice couple who have a house out here. I think I'm near the cabin. I'm going to head that way and try to find it."

"That's really dangerous, Felicity."

"No, I swear I am really close. I can see a drive through the trees, and it looks like the one leading up to the cabin. If I'm wrong, I can just turn around and come back here."

"Wait, Felicity. How did you get away? How are you safe?"

"I'll tell you at the cabin. I don't want to be here anymore."

"No, Felicity, tell me…"

"Soon. I'll see you soon." Felicity flipped the phone shut as quickly as possible, so glad to close the curtain on any contact with him.

For several seconds, she just breathed. The framework shook, but it did not collapse. The network of her thoughts cooled and organized into coherent and discrete units. For the first time in a while, she knew she was going to be okay. She had survived the impossible.

"You did well," Briel smiled eagerly. "This will be great. I don't think he will pass up the opportunity to get you back."

"So, he's definitely with ProtoComm…" Felicity prodded.

"Don't get ahead of yourself," Briel insisted. "But it certainly looks that way."

"And Jase had nothing to do with it."

"I would say that's overstating the facts, Felicity. You admit that he drugged you."

Felicity stood to her feet, pacing around the sofa. "It's not that simple."

"So, what's your excuse? Make me believe."

"Brendon had Jase install cameras at my house. Until then, Jase didn't know anything about it. When he realized what Brendon was scheming, he started making his own plan to stop it – that's why he came to you, but when you wouldn't help. He made an alternate plan. Maybe it was harsh, but I understand why he did it the way he did it. And somewhere along the way, he started to care about me."

"Got infatuated with you, you mean."

Though she wanted to protest, Felicity couldn't deny that she enjoyed the sound of those words almost as much as her own version. "Either way, he is not ProtoComm. He is innocent."

Rather than answer, Briel reached for the laptop where she had shown the videos from Jase's cabin. Why was she so dead set against Jase?

"Jase is far from innocent. You passed over those videos of his pretty easily. I would think it would bother you that he had those cameras in his house at all, much less that he would have sent them to ProtoComm."

Felicity said nothing, but the words punched her in the gut. She had passed over that, and it was very disturbing. Still, without some nefarious explanation, she was willing to give him the same doubt as the law – until her belief passed a reasonable doubt.

"I'm going to leave this here with you," Briel pushed the computer toward Felicity. "It has no internet access, but you can look at the videos in Jase's file. I think you need to watch some of his other videos." After plodding through several folders, entering an administrator passcode each time, Briel right clicked a folder labeled "Jase."

She typed in the administrator password again, which Felicity tried and failed to see, and then opened whatever server held the folder. She finally clicked a folder labeled "Source," revealing about 20 videos inside. Raising her eyebrows at Felicity, Briel turned and walked out of the room.

In order, Felicity clicked through each video, watching a minute or two to get an idea of the subject of each. Most of them were of her house, and it disturbed her to see how consistently the camera followed her around. Still none of the material was particularly concerning, or out of character with what Jase had told her.

Some of the later videos were not of her, and Felicity found these highly disturbing. One showed a rundown neighborhood – some major city – and a large box truck. A man stood behind the truck talking to several teenagers, young people who were obviously under the influence of some drug. The man called the teens over and handed them each a small packet, and one by one, the kids stepped into the truck. Felicity was sick. One showed an even more horrifying sight: a low warehouse with dingy, unkempt beds lining the walls. Strung out women lay sprawled on top of the flimsy coverlets, eyes unaware of their surroundings. Hadn't Jase claimed he didn't know anything about ProtoComm's activity?

How much more could Felicity take? If seeing what she was seeing didn't traumatize her more, losing her faith in Jase would. *Why is that?* she asked herself. Hadn't she known what kind of man he was? Hadn't she ignored her better judgment to accept him? Because having anyone would do?

Clicking down the video, Felicity leaned back and closed her eyes. She had no idea how she could get back to her kids. Get them to safety. Figure out a plan. She had counted on Jase to figure that out for her.

With the thought, she sat back up, staring at the screen and wondering if she could use the computer to contact Nick. The files on the screen came into focus, and she realized something: the filenames were dates. The files Briel had shown her – the files of her – were in February and March. The files she had just seen had been in the past twenty-four hours – after she had left him. If they were truly Jase's. it meant Jase was alive. It might also mean that Jase was digging deeper into ProtoComm's computers, where he would have found the videos of the crimes.

What if he had found something? Intrigued, Felicity studied the other files in the folder, and she realized that the files Briel had shown her were missing. What had happened to the videos of her and Jase in the cabin? There were the videos of her in Phoenix and in Banff with Brendon, and there were the files of Bill's trafficking victims, but where were the files of Jase and her in Banff? Felicity clicked up a level on the folder. The main folder was labeled "Jase." Briel obviously had something other than these videos of Jase's. There was only one other folder in Jase's file. It was labeled "Subject."

Opening it, she clicked on the first video, dated in mid-March, around the time she would have been in his cabin. In fact, the videos Briel had shown her were in the "Subject" folder. Not in the "Source" folder. *Jase didn't record us in the cabin,* she realized. *Someone recorded him.* He wasn't the "source" of the videos of them together. He was the "subject." There were several others, videos of Jase on his phone, mostly. Turning up the sound, Felicity leaned in.

Jase sitting in the same coffee shop where he had taken Felicity. *"I know you're not a chemist, but you have to have a guess…I don't need exact numbers. I won't have time to measure."*

He stood in what appeared to be one of the back halls if the glass hotel in Banff. Same colors and materials. The clip picked up mid-conversation. *"I've sent you the route…No, I want you to wait until she's in New Mexico. Gotta go!"*

Through the lens of a low quality camera, he could be seen walking along the street approaching the hotel, stopping a few buildings before and entering a small, two-story restaurant and lodge. With him walked a beautiful brunette – Amélie. They smiled and laughed, arm in arm. It was a security feed from some nearby building.

Before she closed the computer, Felicity clicked on the last video in the "subject" folder. The date was March 31 – only a few hours before. Jase was alive, or had been long after he had held Felicity escape. She couldn't contain her elation, and a huge smile spread across her face, though it fell a bit when she took in his expression.

Jase sat in the cabin alone, staring out the shattered picture window with his chin in his hand, looking a little like a child. Definitely, he seemed sad – if not outright depressed. After a moment, Jase sat up in his chair, suddenly alert, and Felicity mirrored the motion, catching his anxiety. Dashing across the room,

Jase popped open the kitchen cupboard, no doubt to access the panel behind. He didn't have time. At least six armed soldier-types flooded through the front door, pistols raised. To his credit, Jase took out two before the others subdued him.

Felicity bit her lip, standing to her feet before she shut the computer. Running to the office door, she started to beat at it with her fist. No one responded at first, but then the door swung out, and the man, Adam, blocked the threshold in front of her.

"I need to talk to Briel!" she begged.

"Not an option," Adam shot her down.

"You don't understand; I have to talk to her. It's about ProtoComm." Felicity had a feeling that Briel wouldn't care about Jase, but ProtoComm lay in her field of interest.

When Adam just shook his head, Felicity grunted in frustration.

"Let me talk to her, Adam," a familiar voice commanded.

Adam stepped out of the way, and the woman, Nessa, stepped through the door.

"What is it?" Nessa inquired.

"ProtoComm has Jase. They nabbed him out of his cabin this morning. They might kill him. Why would they keep him alive?"

"Calm down, Felicity. Start at the beginning."

"ProtoComm has Jase. You need to tell Briel!"

Nessa shook her head. "Briel is gone, Felicity. She left ten minutes ago."

Her heart sinking, Felicity turned from the doorway, her mind whirling. Briel was gone. Who else could Felicity appeal to? As far as Felicity knew, no one else in the place had a heart.

"Would it be okay," Felicity turned back to Nessa, "if I call my brother? He hasn't spoken to me in days, and since Briel left Phoenix, he probably hasn't had any updates." An idea had begun to form in her mind.

Since she was basically a prisoner in the lodge, Felicity knew no one. She had no resources. Even if some of her captors knew Jase, as Briel did, most likely none of them would help him. Apparently, he had a reputation.

But Felicity owed him. And Felicity cared about him.

And Briel could abandon Jase, but Felicity wouldn't.

Fortunately for Felicity, the woman, Nessa, had decided to show some compassion.

"This will only make phone calls," Nessa informed. "No texts, no internet access."

"Old school," Felicity quipped. "I understand."

Once the door shut, Felicity flipped the phone open, trying to remember Nick's number.

"Hello?" his familiar voice queried.

"Hi, Nick," Felicity breathed.

"Man, Felicity. Every time I talk to you in recent history, I'm just so grateful you're alive."

"Me, too, Nick. I'm just hoping this is almost over."

"Is there some hope of that?" he wondered. "I mean, it's not like they've arrested Brendon yet."

"About that," Felicity fished. "Have you found any new information off of Brendon's computer?"

"It's been days" He sounded indignant. "Of course I have. That other thumb drive I gave you is worthless compared to what I have now."

"That's fine, because I left it behind when Briel came busting through the window to capture me."

"Lissie, I'm sorry. Briel doesn't work for ProtoComm, so I thought she would be a safe option to help you. Are you okay? Was I wrong?"

"Well, I don't think she's patently evil like the ProtoComm crowd. Maybe crosswise to my own plans, but you couldn't have known that. You were misinformed and stubborn, but that's a hell of a lot better than where I misplaced my faith in humanity. I'm not one to judge."

"You can't blame yourself, Sis."

"I can, and I will, because it will teach me not to make the mistake again. But I won't let it stop me from doing what I need to – the kids need me to get over myself and make up for what I have cost them. Which brings me back to leverage – can you think of any way you could get me the new information you've found?"

"Do you have a computer?"

As a matter of fact, I do. "Give me a minute."

Moving to the laptop, Felicity glanced around the room for cameras. She had no idea what to look for, so she decided just to keep going until they stopped her. Rushing over to the side console, she rummaged through the contents. One drawer entirely filled with pens, another with pencils, another with notepads sporting "The

Lodge" across the top. Finally, in the bottom drawer, in a small cardboard box, she found six thumb drives, also with "The Lodge" in the same design.

She placed it in the port on the computer, and it ran automatically, flashing a marketing video across the screen that promoted "The Lodge" for "your next business event."

"I don't know if I have internet access on this computer," she complained, glancing around again. No one had made a move to come in.

"Check the wifi connections and see if you see any broadcasting."

Felicity found none, but as she glanced around the room, she thought about the desk on the side of the room. When she approached it, she noted the little blue ethernet cord coming out of a hole on one side. Sliding it into the port on the laptop, she hunched over the desk waiting for the computer to detect the new connection.

"Got it, Nick! Ethernet."

"Good, that's faster. Will it let you download the file from the other day? The one giving me remote access?"

Felicity pulled up a browser and typed in the address. After clicking through, a dialogue box popped up. Fortunately, it didn't ask for an administrator password.

"Okay, I'm in," Nick informed her.

A knock on the door brought Felicity upright.

"Felicity?" came Nessa's voice as the door opened.

Felicity quickly placed the laptop on the desk chair, stepping around and looking concerned, pacing as if it were her natural state.

"I just wanted you to know that I sent your message to Briel. Did you get your brother?"

"I did. My call just dropped. I was about to call him back." Felicity hoped Nick would hear her, take the cue, and work fast. She didn't know if she was going to be able to call him back, and she had no idea what he would send her, but she hoped it would prove useful.

"Sorry," Nessa frowned. "We need the phone back. It's a mission burner, and we have to send some people to meet Briel."

Fortunately, Felicity did not have to feign her disappointment. If anything went wrong with the file download, she would have no idea how to fix it.

"When can I get out of here?" Felicity complained.

Instead of answering, Nessa checked her watch. After tapping at it a few times, Nessa shook her head.

"Briel needs you."

Felicity did not like the way that sounded.

"You told Brendon that you were going to the cabin. Briel needs you to show up there."

"No! Absolutely not!" Felicity basically yelled. "I can't see him. I can't."

Not that she tried, but her mind imagined the scene. Felicity, surrounded by a house full of ProtoComm operatives, professional traffickers. And Brendon with the mask off; no more need to pretend that Felicity mattered. No more need to act like a good person. But he would, she knew. He would act like he had done and was doing nothing wrong even if he had handcuffs on and was being led up to prison. And if they never caught him, he would go on pretending. With the whole world believing him. *As he has proven time and again, Dr. Miller can work magic where few others can.* Humanitarian of the year.

"Jase is there," Nessa intoned, her face deathly serious. She didn't know why, but Felicity got the feeling that Nessa did not share everyone else's ill opinion of Jase, and it made Felicity like the woman better for it.

"So he's still alive – again…But Briel won't help him," Felicity countered.

"But he can take advantage of the distraction to help himself."

"And what about me?" Felicity demanded.

"You're mine, Felicity," proclaimed Nessa, and determination painted her expression. "I can't interfere unless you're in danger, but I will be taking personal responsibility for getting you back safely."

With Nessa's promise, Felicity felt strangely up to the task. Briel seemed much more intimidating than Nessa, but Nessa carried herself as a paragon of stability, loyalty, determination. She seemed kind of immoveable, and Felicity could use that kind of framework to buttress her own.

"You know he's not what they say he is," Felicity insisted. She needed to know that Nessa would help Jase if the opportunity arose.

"Who?"

"Jase. I know he has a past. I imagine it's a variation of most of the people in this building. But I have seen him at his best, most generous, bravest. I have a unique perspective in that I can compare it with the façade of goodness and generosity and bravery. I have seen both up close and personal. And Jase is the real deal. The human, damaged, real deal. In my opinion, we're all damaged. We're all a mix of our own demons and those thrust upon us by others, but the choices we make show what we love. And Jase loves the right things. Some people fake goodness so they can get away with evil. Jase is the opposite. He fakes his indifference, but in reality, he cares so much, it threatens his ability to do his job."

What Felicity said seemed to affect Nessa, and the operative nodded her head. "I will help him as long as I can keep you safe while I'm doing it."

Felicity took the other woman's hand in both of hers, gratefully squeezing it. "He deserves it." Felicity insisted.

Chapter 27

Remember that he is the consummate salesman. It is his job to believe what he is selling you even as he makes it up. Then he counts on his boundless energy and determination to deliver what he has promised, however unrealistic it may be. If he doesn't deliver, then the burden is on you for misunderstanding what he had promised. – Felicity's handwritten note to Briel about Brendon, tucked into Nessa's bag, March 31

"We are not defined by where we are from, but by whom we love." – Quote from movie watched by Felicity with her children. March 3.

Afternoon, March 31

"We'll drop you off at the edge of town. You still have Jase's GPS, so you can use it to help you find your way. We're going to have to make it believable that you have been wandering in the forest for several hours." Apparently, Briel or her partner had grabbed Jase's backpack from the train.

Felicity played with the thumb drive that rested in her pocket, her insurance policy if Briel and her crew failed to free Jase or Felicity. Though she listened to Nessa's explanation, Felicity only took in half of it. Who cared about a little dirt going up against what loomed before her?

After the SUV came to a stop in a small clearing a few hundred feet from the road, a man planted himself in front of Felicity and began sporadically swiping dirt onto various places on her body. He sprinkled some in her hair and matted it down.

"Is this seriously necessary?" Felicity sighed, irritated.

"The more realistic your cover, the more time we will have to get what we need and get you out. You fell asleep behind a gazebo at 100 Mountain Avenue. Don't give him the address – he doesn't need the particulars. He'll be suspicious if you know trivial facts. We just want you to be able to provide a story if you need to. It's about half a block from the intersection with Park Avenue. That would be a natural location for you to end up if you were trying to find the cabin."

Nessa pulled out the backpack she had brought with her. "Here's the GPS. You're here. Your cabin is over here. See? It's marked. We will be watching you from a distance."

Felicity did not respond. Without looking behind her, she began the march to the cabin.

For the first portion of the trek, Felicity observed her surroundings, praying that she could find a way to escape and get back to her kids. It was lunacy for her to go through with this while she had three children who would need her. If she failed, Brendon would never be found out, and he would have full reign over the kids. The occasional slip of a step or crackle of a branch confirmed for Felicity that she would not have much success with the idea. Briel's group had Felicity firmly in check.

Her deja vu disoriented her. The familiar filtered light cast lace shadows on the ground in front of her. As she ran through the trees, she tried to prepare herself to face Brendon. Since the last time she had seen him, so many things had changed, especially her opinion of him. She needed to consolidate her thoughts before his presence rattled her emotions, a fact which irritated her to no end. If she'd had her way, she would have been able to process coolly whether with him or not, but instead, cowardly Inner-Felicity turned her into a pathetic mush pot of a human.

When her foot stepped onto the pebbled drive, she halted her forward progress, darting aside into some brush for concealment. It may not last, but she needed the two halves of herself to stay cohesive for the next few hours. Glancing down at her hand, she noticed the ring that still banded the fourth finger of her left hand. She had intended to take it off after her trek to the Henry's, but Jase's sudden appearance had distracted her.

Well, now that she would face her husband again, the man who had thrown her away – if she were to pretend to trust him or to appeal to him – she would make one very clear statement to herself. With the cabin in sight, where the illusion of her marriage had unraveled, she slid her wedding ring off of her finger. She glanced quickly around her and spotted a sturdy twig, and stabbing it into the ground, she jostled it side to side until she had created a small crater a few inches deep. Into the crater, she dropped the plain gold band before sliding the soil back to its spot and covering the ring.

This is what you wanted, Brendon Miller, and this is what I give you. You have done with me, and now I have done with you. Ashes to ashes and dust to dust. If she could have burned the band, she would have done so. Whatever Jase had accomplished in the past couple of weeks, he had helped her see that her life with Brendon was dead, but that her own life would go on. Though the realization released her, it left her weak with spent emotion.

She could not falter, though. If everything worked out okay, she could go cower to her heart's content, back in the safety of her home. If everything crashed, she would probably retreat to her inner sanctum for a long time – or forever. Reaching into her pocket, she reassured herself by rubbing her fingers over her insurance policy. Maybe the professionals would execute everything perfectly, and maybe they wouldn't. But Felicity was prepared to do what she needed

Despite herself, Felicity's mind flashed to the cold seclusion of the stone passageway. She remembered Jase's warm breath as he leaned in to kiss her, how alive she had felt. The idea of Jase, trapped in that house, pained her. Almost enough to make her want to go forward despite her fear.

Briel had warned her that she would need to enter the property from the northwest. If she had hiked from Mountain Avenue, her trajectory would have taken her there. Most likely Brendon wouldn't notice a discrepancy, but Bill's men very well might.

Rather than creep up to the house nervously, which her caution told her to do, Felicity stumbled into the clearing as if fleeing from a battle. She called Brendon's name, timidly at first, fearing that he would hear her and come outside, but knowing that was exactly what needed to happen. Only silence replied. From a distance, she could hear the various twitterings and buzzings of the woodland creatures that inhabited the forest, but she felt as if a barrier separated her from their song. Utter, lonely silence.

Felicity stepped nervously behind one of the front pillars, daring to peer in the front window. Inside, she could make out the empty dining room, and beyond that, the profile of two men in the living room. Instead of drawing attention to herself, as Nessa had instructed her, Felicity eased across the porch to the side of the house, squinting through the slits of the blinds into one of the secondary bedrooms. Only darkness. Stepping down from the porch, she glided around the side of the house to another window and immediately recognized Brendon's muffled voice. Pressing her ear to the glass, she strained to hear what he was saying.

"She will be here soon, and you can prove to Bill whether what you say is true."

For several seconds, Felicity could only make out a low muttering, but then she heard it. Jase's voice.

"...hasn't left town," Jase was saying. "I told you she would call, and she called."

The two men's voices, in conference, resurrected every suspicion Felicity had held from the moment Jase had lain her in the car all those weeks before. She had felt such elation at the sound of Jase's voice, alive and seemingly unhurt, but his words took away all her joy.

Jase and Brendon? Talking about Felicity? Jase informing for Brendon? Though her insides churned, the raw wound of recent betrayal raked with renewed injury, Jase, too? She had misjudged Jase? She was an utter failure! How could she ever trust anyone again? Brendon, Briel, Jase – *I need to make sure not to trust Nessa.* Felicity was developing an abysmal track record.

"Which makes it even more suspect," Brendon's voice brought her back, and Felicity had to wind back to remember that they were speaking of her earlier call.

"No, it means that I intended this. I found out that she doesn't have anything from the computers, she doesn't know anything, and she's not a danger."

With the words, Felicity's breath evened out. Maybe – just maybe – not betrayal. If he was covering for her, as his words implied, he had handed her a lifeline.

"I convinced her that you had no idea what Bill was doing with her. You thought they were taking her to the hospital. You don't have anything to fear from her except her hurt feelings over the affair. Since you're the person she has looked to for direction all these years, I'm sure that's why she called you now."

Snuffing out her remaining anger with a deep breath, Felicity processed Jase's words. She told herself that he was not only a captive, but a trained operative of some sort. Of course it was possible that he was just trying to save his own skin, but that didn't exactly gel with the words. It almost sounded as if Jase wanted

Brendon to believe that Felicity was harmless. Of course, if that were the case, it would change her game plan significantly.

"Felicity?" the low voice behind her demanded, and Felicity felt a rugged hand pressed across her mouth. Her heart pounded with fear at the man's unexpected appearance, but her mind quickly offered an explanation that calmed her emotions as he let her go. She recognized him – Adam – and he was one of Briel's. Felicity had gone off plan, and the man was there to get her back on it.

"You need to knock on the western window into the kitchen. Briel needs the security focused there."

I didn't forget, she countered silently. Aloud, she just acquiesced. "My mistake. I'll go there now."

It didn't matter. She had gotten lots of helpful information, the most important being that she had a role to play according to Jase's version of events. And a lot of it would just involve what she had been doing for the past fifteen years anyway – stroking Brendon's ego.

As she hiked to the opposite side of the house, her heart rate steadily climbed. She was definitely walking a tight rope; falling off on either side would prove catastrophic. Still, if she had to fall to one side or the other, she knew Briel's group had some form of a conscience – they wouldn't sell her into slavery, at least. Felicity, though, would at least try to manage a third option, one where she didn't die or end up a slave or turn into a pawn in someone else's maneuver. One where she got Jase to safety and got back to her kids in one piece.

Felicity knocked on the glass.

One of the men she had seen through the front window snapped to attention, spinning to assess the noise. When he saw her, he barked a command, and people whipped into action. A moment later, an armed guard of some sort stepped around the edge of the house, and Felicity put on her best look of distress.

"Mrs. Miller," the man offered politely. "Mr. Miller is waiting for you inside."

Once he showed her through the door and she saw Brendon's face, she didn't have to pretend anymore – genuine distress blossomed in her chest. With a deep breath, she dispelled most of it. Glancing around, she noted with relief that Aimée had not made an appearance. *At least I don't have to fake connection with Brendon with her around.*

"Brendon!" she gushed, stepping toward him with measured steps. When no one interfered, she moved more rapidly, into his arms.

After a brief embrace, he moved away from her, skeptically studying her face. "Where have you been?" he wondered, delicately touching the dirt smudges on her face.

"There's so much…" she buried her face in her hands, formulating her story carefully.

"Just start from the beginning," he urged before supplying her with the story he wanted her to believe. "You passed out at the party. You were upset with me and drank too much. Bill had his men drive you to the hospital."

He was literally so incredibly gifted. If she had not had the memory of the pebbled missiles embedded into her mind, she might have doubted her own version of the story.

I was upset with him? Like he had said something impolite instead of having me kidnapped? Bastard!

"I remember being laid into the car," she stared at the floor, working her imagination rather than her memory. "I don't really remember anything after that until I woke up in the passenger seat of that guy from your work, Jase?"

"You woke up there?"

"I mean, I vaguely remember a pickup truck? I was somewhere in the US. It looked kind of like Arizona, but I didn't recognize it. And I wasn't very aware for a while. Like I had been drugged or something." She stared up at him as pathetically as she could manage.

"How did you get back here?"

"It was that guy, Jase. First thing I remember clearly was sitting in his car as he drove me back to a little cabin near here. I was in and out the whole car ride, like I was in a chemical haze, and I didn't protest because my addled mind thought he was going to bring me back to you. Instead, though, he took me to the middle of the woods and I didn't see anyone for days. There was food and basic necessities at this place, but I didn't know how to escape. I played along with the guy to stay safe, but I grew impatient to get back to the kids. When that Jase guy left his little house yesterday, I climbed out a window and headed here. I just hoped there wouldn't be anyone else here with you when I got here…"

When she looked up at Brendon, his features wore a mixed expression. Pleasure at her compliments, no doubt. But even a hint at his indiscretion raised his hackles. Felicity bit her lip and said nothing.

When he reached out for her, she did not pull away. She had never experienced such a schism inside her body: not when she had felt the disorientation from the drug, not when she had retreated inside herself. All of the things that were supposed to feel amazing – the grip of his arms on her skin, the heat of his body, the pressure of the embrace – rather than stir her to any form of ecstasy, they erupted revulsion within her. She had to squeeze every muscle in her body to stay in place.

"Someone, get her a drink," Brendon commanded, gently pushing her away. "Felicity, I think you should go lie down in our room. You look like you have traveled through a hurricane."

"Who are all these people, Brendon?" Felicity queried, as if confused by their presence.

A slight hiccup in his thought wrinkled his brow, but he recovered quickly, as he always did when lying. "After you disappeared, Bill decided that someone had targeted me. Why else would someone kidnap my wife? So, he hired guards to stay with me."

"They certainly seem to know who's boss," she quipped, and Brendon glanced askance at her. "You're so adept at taking charge when you need to."

Mollified, Brendon turned to take the drink from one of his goons.

Felicity wondered at how easily he could be manipulated – it actually frightened her. Never did she want to resemble him in any way, and manipulation was his forte. Even if she could justify it, she would not do that again.

When one of the men approached her, Felicity looked to Brendon for direction. The act came so easily to her it made her sick. Brendon nodded, and she took the drink and turned to leave.

"Did you call the police? Don't they want to talk to me?" She was interested to see how he reacted.

Without missing a beat, Brendon supplied the lie. Probably a partial truth at least. "This is bigger than police. Bill has contacts in the government that helped look for you. Did you go to the police?"

She was surprised when the lie rolled off her tongue with similar ease. "I was in a daze for a while, and then Jase didn't want me to call the police. I didn't have a phone, so I didn't think I had much choice in the matter." *Partial truths, just like Brendon.*

Breathing deeply, she followed the man out of the room. When would Briel and her crew arrive? Felicity wanted to get out of there as soon as possible.

When she walked into the room, her stomach dropped. There were several of her items still on the bedside table, but there were also a bottle of woman's perfume, a sleep mask, and a folded woman's robe. To her surprise, Felicity didn't retreat inside herself. She just felt an inexplicable pity for the woman. *Don't be naïve,* she reprimanded herself. *The woman is an adult and knew what she was getting into.*

She had noticed the man take up position by her door, and she knew she would not be able to get out until Briel did something. After twenty minutes of staring at the door waiting for it to open, she stood to her feet and began an investigation of the room. If she didn't find some way to occupy her mind, she would go crazy.

Though there were a few other items that obviously belonged to Aimée, most of the room looked identical to Felicity's time there. *Is it really that easy to swap me out for someone else?* The idea haunted her. Standing in the middle of the room, she suddenly felt flimsy - insubstantial. Part of her just wanted to disappear. Before she could withdraw again, though, she notice her carryon case where its corner protruded from under a desk.

She tugged it out, pushing aside her sweater and first-aid kit to reveal the little spiral notebook she kept there. For the first time in several days, her heart swelled with longing for her children. The little book held some of her greatest treasures. A few years past, she had started the concept with Alex. Whenever either Alex or Felicity wanted to say something nice to the other, she would write or draw a message in the little book. Alex had requested that they expand it to include Noah at some point, and even little Michael had added some of his scribbles to the pages.

Flipping through the book, Felicity realized that there now stood a very real possibility that she would not see her children again. It had been true the entire time, but she had not let herself consider it. With their beautiful drawings and sentiments on display before her, Felicity couldn't stand the idea that they would grow up without her. That they would never really know her heart

She pulled open the drawer in both nightstands and found a pen in the second one. Moving back to the desk, she seated herself there and raised the pen.

My Precious Children,

I sit down today to write you a letter because life is unpredictable. We never know from day to day if we will live to take our next breath or see the ones we love one more time. It's easy to forget this because our lives are so full: full of fun, full of activities, full of struggles. But the truth is, man is but a breath. We will all, at one point or another, pass from this realm of life's activities and beyond the reach, temporarily, of those we love the best.

You are so young. You may have seen a sampling of the struggles, but no one can truly comprehend the struggles and sorrows life will bring us, nor the joys and beauties.

When I was young, I had visions of the wonderful things I would do, of the dreams I would achieve, and worlds I would conquer. Never, in my wildest thoughts, did I see what God would choose for me instead. I vaguely thought that I would have some kids, some ethereal, unreal ideal that would somehow bring me fulfillment without interfering with all of my lofty ideas.

If I had known before what lay ahead of me, I might honestly have chosen differently. This life I lead is not the utopian picture I had envisioned. And guess what. If I had chosen differently, I know that when I had arrived in heaven, God would have taken me to His side and given me the little crown I had earned through all of my great deeds.

But I wonder if He might take me aside and let me see the life I had missed, the life with you, my beloved children. I would see these struggles and joys, I would see what I had sacrificed for my insignificant dreams, and I would weep. Because no goal or dream, no matter how grandiose or noble, could possibly compare to one of you children. There is no sacrifice I could have made for the good of humanity that would compare to what I have made or would make for you.

You are beautiful.
You are truly beyond my wildest dreams.

I write this to you now because, although I face death every day that I am alive, as do we all, an event has occurred that increases the likelihood that I might not see your beautiful faces again on this earth.

And though I can offer you nothing that will remove the emptiness that my absence would bring, I hope that I can soften the bitterness that you might feel. We all go through things that we didn't plan on – a lot of them we don't like or think are fair. And we have the choice to either let our bitterness eat at us and consume us, or to cry our bitterness out to God and let Him heal us. You may feel doubt, but continue believing nonetheless, that God is watching over you. I remember that every day, and it gives me hope.

Love forever,
Mom

It had been a long time since she had spent more than a few minutes thinking about her kids – she hadn't been able to afford that kind of emotion. Now she understood why. Before she had written half the letter, the tears were streaming down her cheeks. She couldn't think for several minutes, and because her mind had shut off, her fear level rose up the back of her head. Doubling over, she forced herself to breathe.

When her mind took back control, Felicity rose to her feet and paced the room. She strode in a square along the rug at the foot of her bed, but as she neared the door, a sudden terror struck her. The voice of ProtoComm's CEO muffled through the wood of the door, and Felicity realized that her time was likely nearing its end. Reaching in her pocket, she rubbed the thumb drive reflexively. Maybe she would write down her thoughts to clarify them. Even better, she would thank her brother for the thumb drive. If she survived, it would be largely thanks to him. If she didn't, she owed him an apology. She seated herself back at the desk, poised to stash the book away if she heard the door behind her.

Hi, baby brother.

First of all, let me just start out by admitting to you that it was really stupid of me to refuse your help. You are the only person on the planet I can trust without qualification. Add to that the fact that you are brilliant and literally a giant, and I think I would have been home with my kids by now had I called you.

Secondly, I know we are not big on the emotional stuff, but I want you to know that I adore you. I think you are the best little brother a sister could have. Everyone knows you're funny and a computer genius, but not everyone knows you have character beyond most humans. You work hard, you care about people, and you are beyond respectable.

I'm praying that I will be seeing you before you see this letter, but it's kind of just in case. I want you to know I love you and am pulling for you in everything you do.

Help mom and dad take care of my kids, if it comes to that.

I know it's a copout that I'm not writing our parents, but I couldn't possibly put everything in a letter for them. Just tell them I am beyond grateful for everything they've done, and I'll see them sooner than anyone else anyway!

Don't hate me for being an idiot. I love you!

Felicity

Of course, she had no idea how she would get the letter to him, but she felt better having written it. She tore it out, folded it, and put it in her back pocket.

Since no one had disturbed her, Felicity rose and walked to the door, pressing her ear to see if she could hear any signs of Briel's entrance. Nothing. Felicity began to doubt herself, to wonder if maybe Briel and her crew worked for Bill, too, and the trip to the cabin had all been a ploy to get Felicity back. *Stupid*, Felicity realized. *They would have just bound me and thrown me in the back of a car and taken me to Mexico if they worked for Bill.*

Felicity knew it was childish to risk it, but she could not stand to sit still anymore.

Chapter 28

What do bad guys look like? Do they wear black? Do they speak in sinister tones? Do they tent their fingers and stare at you in disdain? Or do they look like the good guys? Do they know they're crossing a line? Do they struggle with themselves, justifying their actions to themselves so they can do what they want? Do they try to persuade others, because if they can, they feel more confident of their choices? Do they reprioritize their lives to allow themselves liberties, so they can take what they want? Do I? Do I do any of those things? Do I test myself, not against other people, but against what I know to be right? I have seen myself. I know what I could be. And if I don't fight against it, I will be the same as he. – Felicity's Journal, April 17*

Dear mom, We miss you. Come home soon. Love, Alex, Nicholas, and Noah. – Undelivered letter to Felicity from her children, April 9.

When she stood to her feet, Felicity paused to consider. The French doors that led off the master bedroom onto the private patio beckoned to Felicity, but rather than move directly to them, she kept peering around the room. Her room. Her clothes in the closet. Her suitcase stuffed in a corner. She moved to the closet and saw that most of her things were lying in a basket in the corner.

A few items remained on hangers, mixed with new clothes, and Felicity fumed at the thought that Aimée had taken possession of them. Felicity headed to the bathroom, and she saw something that made her heart stop. Somehow in the façade of making her believe she wasn't a prisoner, Brendon had forgotten to be careful. On the portable table she used for her laptop when she was in the bath sat her laptop and her phone.

Her heart racing, she tucked the computer under her arm and the phone in her pocket, and she and peeked out into the bedroom.

No sign of life.

To avoid unwanted eyes, she ensconced herself in the closet before pulling up her text on her phone. Desperate with hope, Felicity shot a text to her brother. True to form, he responded immediately.

Felicity: *Nick, it's me.*

Nick: *Who is this?*

Felicity: *It's Lissie.*

Nick: *Why do you have your laptop but you can't call me?*

Felicity: *Your wonderful Briel forced me to come back to my cabin and talk to Brendon.*

Nick: *That's my sarcastic Lissie.*

Felicity: *I don't know how much time I have – that will depend on Briel – but remember the blackout site I mentioned? I'm pretty sure it's here. Can you access it from my wifi?*

Nick: *I seriously doubt it. It's probably isolated. Might be able to tell if you can get me to the security station, though.*

Felicity: *Security station?*

Nick: *Trying to speak non-Geek for you. Should be a server they have cameras hooked up to. Usually off site, but close enough for underground cable. Have you seen anything like that?*

Felicity: *I didn't go outside much here. I was just about to break out, though. I can look around for it.*

Nick: *If you can break out, get out!*

Felicity: *Not good enough, bro. If I run off, Brendon comes back to town and comes after me. Did you have good enough evidence on Brendon to put him away?*

Nick: *I had more on Bill Henry.*

Felicity: *That's what I thought. Brendon wouldn't need to keep leverage on himself on his computer. Look, I won't be stupid. If someone comes after me, I'll run. But if I think I can find this room without being caught, I'm going to try. I may not have this opportunity again.*

Nick: *Can't you leave that to the professionals? Where's Briel?*

Felicity: *Wish I knew. She was supposed to be in here by now, and I was supposed to have what I need. Keep this window open.*

Nick: *Believe me; I will.*

Felicity: *Love you.*

Nick: *You, too! Be careful!*

Felicity shut the laptop and peered out the closet door. Still her big, empty room. *Bill's room,* she shivered, disgusted. Sliding to the door, she listened again. She could no longer hear Brendon, but Bill and Aimée were in some deep discussion. Everyone seemed to have forgotten Felicity. Her return had probably not been in their list of contingency plans. *Because only an idiot would come back here,* she snickered.

If she were going to get out the patio doors, she would need a tool of some sort – either real of makeshift. She had done it at home. Had to open her French doors to move furniture, almost always without Brendon's help. She just had to wedge something under the secured door and pop up the latch, and once the latch was disconnected from the door, both doors would push open easily.

With new energy, she made her way, laptop in hand, to the double doors. She could see no guard, though about a third of the patio stood in shadow. She began to scrounge around the room for a screwdriver. When she found nothing, she moved to the bathroom and finally found a breakfast-in-bed tray that had a dull knife. Even better.

She took the knife to the door, lowering to her knees and sliding the tool beneath the brass bracket that bolted the immovable door to the floor. After a few seconds of maneuvering, she felt a pop, and she pulled the door toward her with a jerk. Climbing on a chair, she performed a similar procedure on the top of the door, and a moment later, she was able to pull both doors inward, slipping the deadbolt out of its slot in the moveable door until both doors were open. It wouldn't do much to protect her, but she slipped the knife into her jacket pocket just in case.

Though she planned to escape straight away, she left the doors slightly ajar on the off chance that she would need to return. *Now I get to climb,* she grumbled internally.

Felicity made a complete circuit of the patio, and, using her elevated position, she scoured the grounds for guards outside the house. Her earlier assessment proved accurate, and she saw no guards within view. Quickly, she wedged the laptop between two rails and scurried over, resting her toes on the small ledge on the other side.

She was able to hold the slats and lower herself to the ground a few feet below without too much difficulty, and she grabbed the laptop. Glancing around, she spied an older model four-wheeler parked at the edge of the clearing. It had been a decade or more since she had driven one, but she thought she could manage if she could get it started.

For a few seconds, Felicity considered just taking the vehicle, hoofing into town and calling her brother to come get her. She had to try to get the information, though. She grabbed the laptop from its wedged position and eased past the room where Jase sat, all the way to the treeline to the north. She spotted the fountain, and she considered it for a moment, but it seemed counterintuitive to put computers near water. Between the fountain and her, though, she noticed a small shack that she had seen before. She had subconsciously associated it with the pool equipment, but when she approached it, she noticed a heavy-duty chain on the door. Even though they were far from civilization, Felicity had expected better security. Instead, she realized with a laugh that she only had to unscrew the plate that held the lock from one side and the door would open. It was so simple, in fact, that until she stood in the temperature-controlled little space, she doubted herself. Apparently, Bill Henry felt confident enough in his power that he was careless.

She pulled out her phone to text her brother, but she had no signal. *Wi-Fi* only, she realized, since she had transferred her number to the phone Jase had crushed. *No wonder they didn't think it was dangerous.* Of course, the realization didn't bode well for her computer, either, and sure enough, when she opened her laptop, checking to see if she had signal, she had none. She stepped one step outside the building, and the signal came back weakly. The phone still didn't register. She didn't like the idea of working with the door open, but it would have to do. Glancing around at the many panels, she realized that she was hopelessly lost. She turned to the laptop.

Felicity: *I'm here. How do you get in?*
Nick: *Just give me remote access to the computer.*
Felicity did so.
Nick: *Okay, turn the laptop around so I can see the equipment.*
Felicity obeyed.
Nick: *Do you see that cable on the bottom left?*
Felicity searched and found the cable he requested.
Nick: *Plug it into your USB.*
Felicity obeyed.

Nick: *That's just a video feed. Pull it out from the server and plug it into that big box past in the second row.*

Felicity reached past the first row of boxes to a large box behind, stretching the cord to its full length to reach the laptop.

Nick: *Got it! Now I need about five minutes to dig around. Are you secure?*

Felicity: *I think so.*

Glancing around her, Felicity could not see another soul. The evening had started to grey out the atmosphere, though, and her eyes were not the best with the lack of contrast. Still, she saw nothing that concerned her. She stared back at the cursor on the computer, trying very hard not to stare at the clock in the bottom right corner. Eventually, the cursor blinked to life.

Nick: *I got it, sis! I created a file on your desktop. Copy it to the flash drive, and with the stuff I already have on there, you should be in pretty good shape. It won't be enough to send them all to prison, but it will make them afraid. And if I'm right about what is on these servers, we'll manage some incarceration in short order.*

Felicity: *I can't even, Nick. You have really saved the day. And I know the drill: leave the computer plugged in because you can find more cool toys. Maybe you can backup my content for me, too, since I'm losing this laptop forever.*

Nick: *Lol. I can do that.*

He paused for a minute, and Felicity thought he might have stopped typing. Then the message appeared on the screen.

Nick: *Don't die, sis.*

Felicity: *I'll try, Nick, but I need you to do something for me.*

Nick: *"I'll try" is not a good response to "don't die."*

Felicity: *I need you to get to mom and dad. I know it's a lot to ask, but you need to pack them up, pack up my kids, and get out of town. Someplace safe. If something happens to me, I need to know you guys will all be safe.*

Nick: *I will get the kids out, but Lissie, if something happens to you, I will not be safe. I will be out for blood.*

Felicity: *I love you, Nick, but chasing revenge won't buy you peace, and my kids will need support. Promise me you'll take care of them. Promise me you'll stay safe.*

Nick: *I'll try.*

Felicity: *Touché*

Nick: *Be careful. I love you.*

Felicity: *You, too. Love you.*

After pacing the perimeter of the little shed, she found a spot in the southeast corner where the Wi-Fi reached. She shut the door with herself inside to test, and it still worked, so she set it down and eased out, shutting the door behind her.

Now that she had evidence, she could leave. Brendon, though, seemed to have relaxed his concern now that he had his two greatest threats in captivity – or so he thought. Most of the guards, it seemed, were positioned in the house. Felicity glanced back at the room where she had heard Jase. She could leave him there. She owed it to her kids.

She owed him, too, though, as much as she wanted to deny it. Following the treeline, she crept as close to the house as she could manage before sprinting the distance to the eastern wall. She glided to the window where she had heard Jase, listening for more conversation. She heard none.

Guess I'll go old school, she shrugged. Felicity picked up an acorn and chucked it at Jase's window, quickly concealing herself in case someone besides Jase stuck his head through the opening. She saw and heard nothing for a full sixty seconds, but then she detected a quiet click followed by the scraping of an opening window. She peeked out from her hiding place to see Jase's face where it searched for the source of the sound.

"I don't see anyone," he called inside, and Felicity quickly darted back behind the tree.

How could Jase come to the window if he were a prisoner? Her mind reeled, terrified that she had proven a fool once again. *No, it's not possible,* she insisted, but since she couldn't figure out how Brendon had managed all of his deception, she knew she couldn't make any claim to savvy about the ways of criminals.

Even the idea threatened to devastate her – *not twice! I can't be a fool twice!* She took two steps back so she could lean against a tree, and she clutched her arms across her stomach to hold herself together.

"You should check the other bedroom and see if anything is off in there," Jase's voice carried to her as he addressed an unknown person in his room.

She closed her eyes. Not only had he lied to her, he had sicked one of Brendon's goons on her, sent the man to check on her room to see if she had escaped. She waited for the sound of the scraping window, and then started a mad dash toward the ATV. In a matter of seconds, the guard would discover her empty room, and she would have Brendon's people in hot pursuit of her.

"Felicity," the harsh whisper barely carried over the scuffling of her feet. "Felicity, wait!"

She glanced over her shoulder for a second, not slowing her motion toward the vehicle.

"It's your kids. Brendon has your kids. I couldn't leave!"

When she tried an instant stop, her feet slid several inches on the soil and leaves that carpeted the forest. Jase hung out the window, motioning her back, and she found herself rushing as quickly toward him as she had run away.

If he was lying to her, she would have just run back into captivity for no reason, but she was not willing to take the risk that he might be telling the truth. A few seconds later, she stood only a few feet from him, furious and terrified.

"You need to get back to your room! The guard will be back to me in less than a minute."

"I can't go back there!" Felicity countered, furious. "You sent him to my room! He'll be telling Brendon that I escaped!"

"Liss," Jase soothed, "I sent him to the other guest room. It's where Aimée has moved her things in, and she has been told to stay there unless she's with Brendon. Brendon has made her feel like a princess, all protected and coddled, but I'm pretty sure he doesn't want her knowledge to get out if he gets arrested. Now that you're caught, there's no danger."

My stupid, stupid naïve cynicism! she lamented. She didn't want to be wrong again, to trust Jase only to be proven a fool. But she couldn't outright dismiss him, and she was about to walk back into a trap based on his questionable testimony.

"Where are my kids?" She inched her way back toward Jase's window.

"They're still in Phoenix," he explained, "in a safe house. Brendon had someone pick them up from your parents – who had no reason to suspect anything strange, I imagine – and take them to a secure compound on the grounds of Bill's mansion."

"They must be terrified," Felicity worried, and when she reached the house, Jase reached his hand out to grip hers.

"Likely not," Jase countered. "I'm sure they're using Bill's toys and pool to entertain themselves. I'm sure Noah has a fulltime nurse." Jase glanced behind him. "I'm sorry, Liss. You need to go; I'm going to fix this. It's why I'm still here. I could have escaped a day ago otherwise."

As he turned away from her, Felicity's heart gave a lurch, guilt replacing her suspicion of Jase. Not only was he uninvolved with Brendon, he had stayed in captivity to save her children. As she rushed back to the patio railing, she heard the window scrape shut, and she pulled herself back onto the railing – with considerably more difficulty than she had found descending from it. No one seemed to have noticed her excursion.

Felicity sat back down at the desk, only then realizing that Nick's letter had fallen out of her pocket. She prayed it would blow away unnoticed. After another half hour, Felicity heard a commotion outside her room through the French doors. She ran to them to see what had happened. Unfortunately, a guard doing a round outside had found the paper. She prayed that Jase had heard the ruckus, too, because she was going to need some help when they came for her.

A moment later, she heard a thud hit the wall of her room on the other side. Within thirty seconds, her patio door was being jimmied open, and Jase stepped through.

"It's going to have to wait for another day, Felicity," he insisted. "I don't know what they saw out there, but they're coming for you right now. We'll figure out how to get your kids."

Behind him, a clamor arose from the other room, and he quickly but quietly shut the door.

"Patio, now!" he commanded, and he grabbed her hand, dragging her to the French doors and out to a crouch behind a wicker sofa. A handful of guards stood near the front drive, probably assuming that she had gone the easy route.

I'm not that stupid, she smiled smugly, proud that she had picked a route that would have tricked them.

Jase pulled her closer, wrapping one arm around her waist.

"You're alive," he purred, but then his tone hardened. "But why are you here? Don't tell me you came back with some crazy plan to save me?"

"Maybe I would have," she smiled. "I thought they had shot you…" Emotion stopped her voice for a second, and Jase's eyes softened.

"I'm fine, Liss. And now we're back where we started. Why

are you here?"

"Briel," Felicity explained. "Briel had me, and she wanted to use me as a distraction so she and her team could raid the cabin. But they haven't made their move, and I don't understand why. They basically had me captive, and since I didn't know how to fix the problem at home, and I knew that Brendon had you, I didn't fight too hard against her."

His grip around her waist tightened for a second, but then he pushed her away, taking her face in his hands and looking directly into her eyes. "I told you, never try to save me!" he chastised, turning immediately back to the guards without waiting for her protest. "Come on!"

Again, he grabbed her hand and pulled her with him, standing and scurrying over the rail. She had a feeling that he could have hurdled the thing if he hadn't held her hand. He finally let go, pointing to the four-wheeler, and making a quick 360 to assess everyone's position. The guards still had not seen them. Sprinting as fast as she could manage, Felicity made it across the clearing to the vehicle without hearing any evidence they had seen her. By the time she had straddled the machine, Jase had reached the back end of the vehicle.

Still no shouts, and Jase began to push the ATV. He aimed for a section of the ground that sloped slightly down, and after traveling twenty or thirty feet, he barked, "Kick the pedal down!" The vehicle sputtered to life, and he climbed on behind her. He pointed the direction where Felicity knew Banff lay, and she steered as he desired.

They directed the vehicle toward the town, but after traveling only a few hundred feet, a jeep loomed up in front of them. Felicity barely pulled up without flipping the four-wheeler, and Jase hopped off cursing, ready to fight whoever exited the car.

"Wait!" Felicity jumped off and grabbed his arm. "It's Briel."

Though Jase relaxed a little, he did not seem less ready to fight, and Felicity stepped partially in front of him before turning back to the SUV. Jase grabbed her to pull her behind him, but the maneuver had given Briel time to hop out of the vehicle and train her gun on Jase.

"Cool it, Jase," Briel commanded. "Listen to me before you start throwing punches."

"You sent Felicity in there," he growled, and Felicity thought he might launch himself at the small – but intimidating - woman operative.

Felicity turned to face him, stepping toward his body. "She has a gun and five of her team with her. Please don't try to fight them all."

As Felicity spoke, the rest of the crew stepped down from the jeep and aimed their weapons, some at Jase and some at Felicity.

"Triggers off!" Briel commanded, and six guns lowered their muzzles toward the ground. "Give me a second, Jase. Let me explain."

"Explain how you sacrificed Felicity for your other mission? I don't think so."

Though Felicity wanted to speak up in Briel's defense, she really couldn't find the heart to. If Briel had just let Felicity go, maybe her kids would be safe with Nick, and not held by Brendon as collateral.

"Why didn't you come in after I did what you asked?" Felicity continued Jase's tirade.

"Jase, this was supposed to be an easy in/easy out mission. Felicity would have been back with us in half an hour. But, Felicity, we didn't expect you to go in without some kind of commotion happening. How did you manage it?" Briel wondered.

"I tricked Brendon," Felicity shrugged. "He has so little respect for me, it wasn't hard. And I heard you, Jase."

"Heard me?"

"You told Brendon that I didn't know anything. You made out that you had grabbed me once the guys reported me missing, which made me mistrust you for a minute, but then I realized you had thrown me a lifeline. I would never have considered playing dumb. I would have blurted out accusations and accused him to his face. You offered me a plausible story to keep me safe."

Reaching behind him, Jase grabbed for her hand again. "I did," he agreed, "but I never dreamed you would do such a great job, especially because I didn't know you had heard me. And it further shows," he took a step backward until his back pressed against Felicity, "that you expected her to be stepping into a very dangerous situation."

"I'm telling you," Briel insisted, "we would have had her out."

"Would have?" Jase demanded.

"Bill showed up! Bill wasn't supposed to be there! We wanted a witness; we wanted Brendon. If we went in with Bill there, he would shut us down before we could find anything out.

"Brendon has my children," Felicity leveled at Briel.

"Damn it!" Briel hissed, her stance turning almost as defensive as Jase's, though toward a threat not present. The reaction instantly made Felicity like the younger woman better. Anyone who felt that protective of Felicity's children got the benefit of the doubt. "Then we need Felicity to go back in," Briel insisted.

"No!" yelled Jase.

"Jase, if it will help her grab Brendon and free my kids, I have to."

"Let me do it!" Jase suddenly demanded. "I can come up with something that will get them off of Felicity's trail, and something that gets Brendon isolated for you."

Briel scowled at him, dubious.

"You know I can," Jase proclaimed.

"I know you can, but can I trust you?"

"I don't know if you can trust him, Briel," Felicity interrupted. "Because he may not care about your agenda, but I can trust him. And he wouldn't let my kids get hurt if he could help it."

Felicity felt Jase's hand tighten on hers, and she tried to read his thoughts through his profile. Definitely some strong emotion, with the addition of surprise. Her chest constricted, but she continued to pin her gaze on Briel, ignoring the rising tension she felt from Jase.

"Fine," Briel agreed. "But we will come in if it helps our mission. Don't expect us to help you if you get stuck."

"No need," Jase assured.

"How are you going to give us directions when you figure out a plan?" Briel challenged.

"Just give me an earpiece and a two-way," Jase shrugged, and Briel turned back to the jeep, retrieving the small device and handing it to Jase.

"I swear," she warned as she passed off the earbuds, "if you compromise my mission, I will come after you. And Felicity is staying with me until I have Brendon, so I guess she'll find out how trustworthy you are."

"She will," Jase agreed.

He turned to Felicity, taking her elbow and leading her away from Briel's crew. Once they were out of view of the team, Felicity gripped Jase's arm

"Jase…" She forced herself not to choke up when he turned to face her, though her voice constricted on the words. "I was so confused. I thought you had lied to me when I heard you send them to my room, but I was still so relieved to see you. I had been afraid you were dead."

Releasing her arm, he cupped his hand behind her head and pulled her to him "I told you I would be okay," he murmured, massaging the small of her back with his other hand. "I told you I am good at this job."

"But they were shooting at you and you were yelling, and all I could do was run away." Her stomach churned at the memory, and her breath hitched in her chest.

Jase stepped back and leaned down, taking her face in his hands. "It's what you needed to do. It's what you always need to do. There is no shame in hiding from a stronger adversary. Even I do it on occasion, okay? Your job is to stay safe for those kids. You owe them. You don't owe me."

"I do owe you," she raised her hand to caress his cheek. "But I don't just owe you; I care. It would destroy me if I was responsible for something happening to you."

Brushing her hair out of her eyes, Jase pulled her back to him. "It won't destroy you, because you don't have that option, Liss. I will be fine, but you will go on regardless. That is what you owe me, more than anything else. I'm going to go get Brendon, I'm going to make you safe, and I'm going to find out where your kids are. And then you will take your kids some place safe and live. That's what you owe me."

For several seconds, Felicity could say nothing. She just inhaled the now familiar scent of Jase, and reveled in the feel of his arms. She was grateful for the moment, even if there might not be another. Finally, she sucked in a steeling breath and pushed away from him.

"So, now that I am thoroughly conquered," she smiled up at him, and his eyes pulsed a somber pleasure, "I'm going to let you tell me how to proceed. Can I trust Briel? I just get the idea that she would sacrifice anything for her mission."

Jase shrugged as Felicity watched him regroup into his

professional mien. "She would, within some pretty broad bounds. Her mission is important. I can't say I blame her. But I'm going to make it right for both of you. I've been too lazy for too long."

Confused, Felicity peered up at him quizzically.

"I'm trained to do things other people aren't trained to do. Briel is, too, in a sense. But she left our job and became what we always should have been. I left our job and used my knowledge to make money. It was a mistake."

"And what you 'should have been' sends you into a pit of vipers?" Felicity pouted.

Jase grinned. "Exactly!" Then more seriously, he pulled her back into his arms.

"But you're going to make it out, right?" Felicity begged.

"I've gotten out of worse scrapes."

She pushed him back and scrutinized his face. "You didn't answer my question."

Narrowing his eyes, he smirked, but didn't answer. Instead, he leaned down, lifting her face to his and covering her mouth with his. The trees around them shut out the view of the cabin, the noise of Briel and her team, any thought but Jase. For just one moment.

Then it was over.

Sighing, Felicity removed herself to a respectable distance. There were so many scenarios in which that kiss was their goodbye. He seemed to understand that whatever the outcome, she would leave him. That she could not fight what she needed to fight nor be what she needed to be if she deferred to her desire for him.

Mirroring her demeanor, Jase stood erect, smiling broadly.

"*Adieu*, Felicity."

Her eyes widened in shock. The word spoke finality. Did he expect to die inside? Or did he intend to walk away once she was safe? It was what should happen – she knew it, and he seemed to as well. Still, when he turned to march back to where Briel stood with her team, Felicity had to suck back the tears that threatened to fall.

Chapter 29

I always thought that people were meant to live their lives in pairs, picturesque couples who would walk hand in hand through the perils and travails of life. Now I've found out that two are never truly made into one. They become closer or not. Friends. Companions. Compatriots. Fellow travelers. But at best, we are twisted branches, sometimes intertwined and growing as if from the same source. One in purpose. One in direction. One in aspirations. Not one in essence. Thank God. Because even though I have been extricated from a tangled configuration, I continue to exist. I am still whole. Maybe battered and bruised, but not crushed or snuffed out. I go on. – Felicity's Journal, April 21

Do you know if something is wrong with your little brother? He's been so closed off for the past couple of weeks, ever since you left. I'm worried that he might be into some shady business. Apparently, you have a stabilizing effect on him. – Email to Felicity from her mother, April 3

Felicity stared after Jase's retreating form as he strode casually into the cabin where certain danger awaited him. Part of her wanted to yell after him to come back, but she had meant what she told Briel. Felicity trusted Jase to do what he could to help Felicity, and he certainly had more expertise than she could even pretend to have. Still, "sending" him in to a deadly situation felt akin to abetting a murder. Hard enough with a stranger, but sickening for someone she cared about. *Just another contrast between Brendon and me,* she mused sardonically.

As he approached the cabin, Jase headed toward Felicity's patio, hurdling the rail with one smooth motion. Felicity realized that she could hear the whispered conversation between Briel and her crew. They seemed as uncertain about what to expect from Jase as Felicity did, and the fact brought a smirk to her lips.

"You used to work with him, though," Adam insisted to Briel. "Don't you know how his mind works?"

Briel shook her head. "Jase doesn't know how his own mind works," she countered. "In training, he used to manage things instinctively that we all had to spend weeks of repetition to make our own. Because of that, he thinks several moves ahead of everyone else – but also in an unorthodox manner. Usually, his different thinking means he wins. When he doesn't though, he can fail spectacularly."

The thought brought a shiver to Felicity's spine before Briel's two-way radio sparked to life.

"Look," Jase was saying, "I didn't see her. I had nothing to do with her escape."

Looking up, Briel nodded toward Felicity. "Get her in the car," the operative commanded.

At least it was true that he hadn't helped her escape. If anything, Felicity had saved Jase, though Jase didn't seem to want saving at the time. More accurately, he had left with her because she needed protection – a probability proven true when they ran into Briel and her team. And now he was back where she had found him, back with ProtoComm,

"And you expect me to believe," Brendon's voice came through the radio, "that you saw no sign of her."

"I saw signs of lots of people. Could have been her. You have women on your team. She lived here for several days before we sent her south. I don't know what she was wearing today, what kind of shoes, whether she was wearing perfume. I can't track someone without knowing I'm tracking them – "

"Likely story," Adam mumbled.

"But Brendon doesn't know that," explained Briel. "He has no training. It sounds reasonable."

Felicity agreed – it did sound reasonable. She certainly would have bought the story.

" – not letting you in," Brendon was saying. "Bill still thinks the verdict is out on you, but I decided a long time ago."

Jase laughed. "At the party, when I met your wife?"

"Met?" Brendon complained. "You practically seduced her."

"It was my job. Bill wanted a profile. I needed to talk to her to get a sense of how to proceed. Besides, you were literally done with her, about to throw her away. Why did it matter to you?"

"A man who could do that to another man's wife – there's something broken about him."

As opposed to a man who would do that to his own wife? Felicity seethed.

"True," retorted Jase. "You only do things like that to your own wife – much better."

Felicity snorted. Apparently, she and Jase thought alike in this at least. Awakened by the noise, Briel reached over and shut the door to the jeep. For the next half hour, Felicity could make out almost nothing that was said. Until Briel's crew started running, Felicity had no idea what was happening. Once the dirt started to fly, Felicity's heart sped. Something had happened. Could be good; could be bad.

Because they rushed to the cabin, no one bothered to lock Felicity in the car. She threw open the door. Nessa, the woman who had helped Felicity most, had stayed behind to keep an eye on her, and Felicity began to hound the other woman with questions.

Finally, "Is Jase alright?" elicited a nervous headshake from Nessa. Felicity could read the tension on her companion's face, and the concern of each mirrored the other.

"We heard gunshots," Nessa lamented. "We have no idea who shot or if anyone was shot, but Briel had to go in."

"To save Jase?"

Nessa scoffed. "Not likely. She wants Brendon. He's the key to ProtoComm, and if she saves one of them, she saves Brendon."

"Saving a criminal…"

"To nab a worse criminal. Brendon is a pretty face. He knows a lot, but he doesn't do a lot. That's all Bill and the system he has built up around him."

Felicity gritted her teeth. "And so Briel will leave Jase behind."

"It's the nature of the business." Nessa did not sound like she appreciated that nature.

A moment later, the cabin exploded with resonating cracks that rang artificial in the arcadian woods. Nessa and Felicity both stepped toward the cabin, but Nessa pulled up short, restraining Felicity by the arm.

"You can't go in there, Felicity! You are as likely to get Jase killed as to help him."

"I'm not going to sit here!"

"You are," Nessa corrected, and Felicity suddenly found her arms pinned behind her, the surprisingly strong Nessa shoving her to the open door of the jeep.

"Don't do this," Felicity begged.

"If I let you go in there, Jase will never forgive me. And I'm not comfortable with that."

"If you don't let me go in there, it may be a moot point. I can distract Brendon."

Nessa scoffed, digging under the seat with one hand as she held onto Felicity with the other.

"You can distract Jase and Briel, which might undermine everything they're trying to accomplish. Including save your kids."

Felicity felt the fight leave her, and a minute later, Nessa had latched Felicity's hands to the wheel of the jeep with a zip tie.

As Nessa started toward the cabin, Felicity fanned the flame of her irritation, a buffer against despair. She had no desire to sit fused, immobile, to a car.

Nessa seemed to think better of it for a second, though, and spun back toward Felicity.

"I know you hate being stuck out here, and I don't blame you, but it can't be helped."

"But it can - "

"No," Nessa interrupted. "And I did not come back to argue with you. I want to know: would it make it better to hear what's going on inside," she held up the radio that she had worn on her belt, "or not to hear?

"To hear it, please!" Felicity begged. "I would rather know if you guys lose so I can know what to expect."

Rolling her eyes, Nessa set the radio down on the center console of the vehicle. "Thanks for your vote of confidence." She shut the door and sprinted up the drive and around to the front of the building.

The initial burst of gunfire had ceased, and Felicity had heard nothing from the house since. Nessa had stood too far away for Felicity to make out the words spoken after the guns discharged.

Now, though, Felicity could hear everything clearly.

"...seems Bill isn't so concerned about you when his own skin is on the line," Briel charged.

"Why would he be?" Brendon replied. "I didn't get into this business for the altruism."

Even though you want to look altruistic, Felicity fumed.

"Works for me," Briel continued. "He's not the one I came in for."

From what Felicity could make out, Bill had somehow gotten away from Briel and her crew. They still had Brendon, though, and Felicity let a small seed of satisfaction blossom in her chest with the thought. At least until she realized that she hadn't heard Jase's voice since the gunfire.

Felicity pushed the radio dialogue to the edge of her consciousness while she concentrated on getting her hands free. At home, she would have reached into her purse and clipped the zip tie with her sewing kit scissors. How would she manage it when she couldn't reach into anything? Instead, she turned primitive and started to gnaw at the plastic with her teeth. She could tell right away that the task would take a while. What else did she have to do besides listen to the radio, a passive observer. It was like torture. Better to find a way to do something proactive.

After 30 seconds of chewing, her jaw started to ache. Still, she had made a small nick in the plastic. If she could manage another 30 seconds, she might weaken it enough to break it.

"How is he?" Briel demanded, and Felicity went stiff so she wouldn't miss what came next.

Nessa's slightly heated tone answered tersely. "He'll live."

Felicity read between the lines that Jase had been injured. For whatever reason, Nessa had a connection with Jase. *It's hypocritical for me to be jealous, right?* she asked herself. She shook her head. Jealous or not, longing or not, Jase was not hers – because she wouldn't have him.

When she felt the impact, time stopped. Her entire body floated upwards and sideways toward the passenger seat, until her shoulders felt ripped from their sockets, arrested in their momentum by the steering wheel and the adjoined zip tie. Her right elbow wrenched and twisted, and she feared something had torn. After an eternal moment, her body settled down into the seat again.

The force on the zip tie had, after its initial resistance, snapped it in half, and Felicity's right arm fell to her side. Any attempt at moving even her fingers sent stabs up her arm all the way to her shoulder. Her right hip was bruised from where it crashed into the center console, and she had banged her ankle against the gas pedal as she lurched sideways. Once her mind processed the state of her body, it turned its attention to the source of the explosion. The source of danger.

A sedan, black and unassuming, was wedged partially under the driver side door of the jeep. Standing nearby, a hulk of a man leered at Felicity, stalking up to the sedan and climbing across its hood to Felicity's door. Finally waking up, Felicity pushed her body, as well as she could without the use of her arm, up and over the console. The wedged car was partially blocking the jeep door, and the hulking man was forced to scrape the metal doorframe across the car's black hood. It slowed him down enough to let Felicity make it over the console.

With her left hand, she twisted and grabbed the handle, throwing the door open and trying to get her legs out to catch her when she tumbled out. They mostly performed their job, though she stumbled, painfully dashing her injured shoulder against a treetrunk. By the time she recovered from the pain, the goon had slid around the jeep and barreled to within a few feet. Felicity rolled around the tree and started across the path of her pursuer, just out of his reach. Her change in direction surprised the man, and he stumbled as his fingertips brushed her jacket.

Running proved painful, the impact of her feet jarring her arm with every step. The run to the main road was a full half mile, and she knew she would never maintain her speed for that long. She would have to lose the man among the trees.

Maybe the idea would have worked, but just as she entered the treeline, a clatter arose on the patio of her room. The noise pulled her up short, giving her pursuer time to catch up and wrap her in his grip. Still, her capture didn't rip the scream from her throat. It was the sight on her patio.

Two men held Jase, his sleeve soaked in blood, down on his knees, a gun to his head. When he turned toward the cry, though, his eyes sparked to life. Felicity's captor began to drag her, kicking and scratching, back toward the front of the cabin. She tried to watch Jase, terrified at what she would see, but the spark she had seen in his eyes seemed to stir a fire in him

Dropping to his uninjured side, Jase rolled onto his back. His hands were bound behind him with tape, but he somehow kicked out, and next Felicity saw, one of his captors lunged inexplicably toward the other, both stumbling away from Jase before recovering. In the meantime, Jase had regained his footing, and he lowered his uninjured shoulder, lurching toward the closer captor with incredible speed and strength. The captors had not had time to recover their balance, and Jase finally knocked them to the ground. Felicity watched him leap over one of the men's outstretched arms before rushing back into the bedroom.

Though Felicity felt grateful that Jase had escaped, the distraction his capture had provided her evaporated as soon as he disappeared through the door. She abruptly realized that she had quit struggling against the arms that pinned her, and the man had only to mount the few steps to the front door to finish her imprisonment. Swallowing her fear, she breathed a steadying breath as the man pushed open the door.

The scene inside stood frozen, a standoff moment between soldiers.

Briel held Brendon on the ground, her knee forcefully in his back while she pointed a gun at his head. On the other side of the room, a large man had forced Adam to his knees and held a gun on Briel's right-hand man. While Felicity had run from the damaged jeep, Bill seemed to have returned, and he and Aimée stood on one side of the room. Seemingly unused to the chaos, Aimée gaped in obvious shock, and Nessa and Briel's white-haired teammate stared grim-faced at the scene before them. Jase had just stumbled into the room, his exhaustion palpable, Felicity could hear his overthrown pursuers rushing toward the room.

Once everyone saw Felicity, the room erupted into motion. Adam took advantage of his captor's distraction, dropping to his back and kicking at the hand that held the gun. The weapon discharged toward Bill and Aimée, and Brendon's assistant screamed in terror. Felicity's captor released her and lunged toward Bill, obviously trained to protect the CEO at all costs. Jase ran at Felicity, knocking her to the ground behind the sofa. She could no longer see anything that was happening, but Jase rolled back to his feet, prepared to reengage.

Considering her options, Felicity let herself breathe for just a moment. Bill would not hesitate to shoot or kill anyone on Briel's team, and Felicity could not deceive herself that she could effect any great benefit to them or to Jase. She did have one ace, though. Pulling up her phone, she typed off a message to her brother. He answered a few seconds later, and she quickly dialed back to him for a phone call over Wi-Fi. She carefully placed the phone on the ground and pushed the speaker button, turning it to full volume just before a motion drew her attention away.

"No!" she yelped, angry at her distraction, but Jase had already stepped out and established himself in some kind of aggressive stance. Felicity couldn't stand the blindness of her position, and she crept to the edge of the couch to peer around the corner. Jase's captors had made it into the room, and the numbers no longer favored Briel's team, especially not with the bleeding Jase.

Briel had not moved – Felicity doubted anything would convince Briel to give up her prize.

The large guards who had lost Jase redirected their efforts upon entering the room, and one had Nessa by the hair while the other tussled with the white-haired operative.

"Let me leave with Brendon, Bill," Briel suddenly shouted. "My team and I will leave you and your crew alone." Nessa stopped struggling, and the white-haired man managed a headlock on his combatant. Jase still stood at attention, and Adam had moved out of reach of his opponent.

Bill glared at Briel, somehow still seeming superior. "Do you think I'm an idiot? If you walk out the door with Brendon Miller, my company won't last a week."

"If you don't let me leave," Briel countered, "I shoot him here and come after you next."

Shocked, Felicity tried to glance at her children's "nanny." Felicity had heard Jase's assertion about Briel and her cold professionalism, but hearing it first hand was still shocking.

"You shoot him, and your friend is dead," Bill smiled smugly, his arm sweeping to the guard who held Nessa. Briel's confidence faltered, and Felicity's stomach dropped. The problem with having morals was that it limited one's choices. Where Bill would sacrifice life without a qualm, Briel would hesitate, and that would likely cost her.

Apparently, Jase had the same concern.

Felicity didn't even see him move. Before anyone could react, Jase held his bound arms around Bill Henry's neck. Felicity had seen similar situations in the movies, but they had never stolen her breath. It was one thing to threaten someone with a gun or a punch, but Jase looked as if he could snap Bill's neck like a twig. As automatons, every one of Bill's gang transferred his attention to where Jase held their boss in a death grip. The ones who weren't

377

restrained trained their guns on Jase.

"Take him, Briel," Jase commanded.

Utilizing the guards' inattention, Adam glided over to Briel and helped her haul Brendon to his feet. The two moved toward the front door, and the white-haired op dragged his captive with him as he backed toward the exit.

"Shoot him!" Bill instructed, and a couple of the men seemed to twitch in preparation.

"Don't!" Felicity screeched, standing to her feet from behind the couch. She heard Jase curse under his breath. It was her leverage. It was supposed to get her to safety and back to the kids. But she couldn't let Jase die, not when she could save him. Not after everything he had done for her. "Nick, now!" The room froze as the garbled sound of a recording playing through a phone and from under a couch. Still, the words were clear.

"That is you, papa…" gasped Aimée, suddenly coming alive. The room sucked in a breath with her, their shock at the revelation seizing everyone so that they missed several seconds of the recorded conversation. *That explains so much,* Felicity snickered to herself. *Sleeping with the boss's daughter…*

"…supply-side issues," the voice on the recording was saying.

"There is never a shortage of slaves, Jack. Get in contact with that Nigerian chairman. His LGA has a pipeline through Tunisia to several European countries, and you can use my Tunisian contact to move the cargo into the Balkans."

"We'll lose inventory in the passage."

"Just the weak, the sick…the elderly who can't work anyway. Acceptable loss, within the margin."

Jack's voice growled to someone near him before he addressed Bill again. "I'm sorry I had to involve you in this, Bill. I just know you don't deal in children, and the Somali contact sent nothing else. I needed a solution for our buyers."

Felicity hadn't heard the recording before Nick played it, and she thought she would vomit. Everyone on Briel's team, Jase, and even several of the guards wore expressions that matched her own. Still, she had to move. "And there's more, right, Nick?"

After a pause, Nick replied. "A list of folders I've named the Who's Who of ProtoComm: Bill, Jack Buckley, David Farnham, Anna Waters, Brendon Miller." Everyone grew even more still, if that were possible, and the sound of breathing ceased. That was when people began to notice Bill's choking gasps.

"I appreciate it, Nick," Felicity offered. "Now you guards know who you are working for, if you didn't already. If you let us go, you will probably have time to get out of here before this team calls in law enforcement. I doubt they checked your ID when they busted in."

Several of the guards backed toward the exits, and within a minute, the numbers had evened again. Felicity paused, glancing at Briel who seemed to rein in her shock and reengage her mind.

"Now if you're left, I suggest you lower your guns," she instructed, "and my team is going to back to the door with Brendon Miller. Jase is going to hold onto Mr. Henry until he releases him to Aimée at the door."

"Do what she says," Aimée commanded, and Felicity noticed a sudden movement in her peripheral vision.

"Aimée!" Brendon gasped, obviously surprised.

Felicity had almost forgotten about Brendon, and the realization brought a grin to her mouth.

"Apparently, you're not as important to her as you thought. Maybe it wasn't true love. Maybe she chose Daddy's money over substance."

With almost comical caution, Aimée followed Felicity to the main doorway, obviously intent on not spooking anyone. Once they had passed the couch where Felicity had crouched before, Jase stood beside her with Bill, and Felicity noticed a bloody smudge on the older man's shirt where the bullet wound had slowly leaked blood. Releasing Bill, Jase wrapped his good arm – the tape that had bound it ripped through – around Felicity, pulling her backwards and toward the door after Briel and the others. He shoved Bill toward Aimée, and using the distraction, Jase yanked Felicity outside.

Without a pause, Jase twisted around and dragged Felicity to the waiting jeep. The crew had arrived in two vehicles, and with three people added to their party, they had to cram into a single jeep. The white-haired operative jumped in the driver's seat, and Nessa and Briel crammed into the front seat together. They had no time to worry about seating arrangements, because by the time they reached the vehicle, shots had begun to ring out behind them. Adam had taken over Brendon, and he shove Felicity's husband into the car before climbing in behind him. Jase handed Felicity up, scrambling in behind her as quickly as he could with his injury. Once inside, he shut the door and pulled Felicity onto his lap.

"I don't trust him," Jase murmured, and Felicity stifled a giggle.

"He once said the same thing about you," she smirked into the dark.

As they raced away from the cabin, Brendon turned to his wife. "Felicity," he began.

"Don't talk to her," Jase leveled. "And if you touch her, I kill you."

Reprimanded, Brendon leaned away, turning his attention to the road outside Adam's window.

Despite the awkwardness of the situation, Felicity found herself forgetting about the man who had taken up the majority of her energy and attention for the past fifteen years. Instead, she settled comfortably into Jase's embrace, lulling into sleep for the half-hour ride to Briel's headquarters. Felicity awoke to the hulking angular shape of The Lodge.

Chapter 30

I've got them. - Nick's communication to Felicity through Briel's cell phone, April 2.

Belize. – Felicity's response to an email from her mother, April 2.

Once they reached The Lodge, the front seat emptied, its inhabitants forming a semicircle outside Adam's door. Briel then opened the door, and Adam descended, pulling Brendon out behind him. Liam pointed a gun at Brendon, and Adam – who had managed to zip tie Brendon's hands some time on the trip – yanked Brendon toward the corridor leading to the basement cell where they had held Felicity for the short while before.

"Make sure you find something better for his hands," Felicity called out after them. "Those zip ties are pretty easy to bite through."

Jase gently tugged her elbow, leading her to a small lobby that led to the elevators. Other than Adam, who stood guard over Brendon, the rest of Briel's team trudged up the stairs. With a start, Felicity realized that did not include Jase.

Once in the little lobby, Jase pulled the two modern chairs until they faced each other and almost touched. He led Felicity to one and seated himself in the other, taking her hand in his.

"You are crazy, Felicity. You gave me a heart attack back there."

"Well, you gave Bill one. And I think the effect will last longer."

Though he smirked, Jase said nothing for a moment. "I think you're wrong about that," he murmured, and the sadness in his voice tore Felicity's heart to shreds. Apparently, the time had finally come. "First of all, I want you to know that while you were sleeping, Briel called in a favor with some of her coworkers who went and retrieved your kids from Bill's compound. Your brother has them now."

Felicity had felt so relieved to be out of Bill's hornet's nest, she had almost forgotten that her children were held hostage. The guilt of her forgetting warred with her relief at their rescue. Once her emotion at her children's plight passed, Jase took a deep breath to go on. "It was well done," Jase assured her, "and Briel has set up a really nice place for you guys once you are back with Nick and your parents. Your parents are prepared to move wherever they need to keep you guys safe."

"I guess it makes sense to move," Felicity frowned, slightly troubled.

"You wouldn't want to go back to that house," Jase shrugged. "I mean, of course you can go back, but I have paid movers to stand by for your instructions. Nick is ready to manage it when you are ready. If you don't ever want to go back, you don't have to."

Strangely, Felicity found that she liked the idea of never going back to that house. It was like a pretend world, an illusion that had bound her in lies and deception for fifteen years. Going back felt like entering a faerie world, ephemeral and dark. Maybe someday, when someone else had moved their very different things into the property, Felicity would knock on the door and see if the myth had shattered once new spirits had invaded it.

"No, you're right," she nodded to Jase. "You can tell the movers to pack it up. I think it's probably best for the kids, too, if they can have a clean break."

"I also thought you should know that Brendon has already asked for a deal. He will corroborate everything on those files if the government will shorten his prison sentence. White collar. Briel has enough connections that I feel pretty confident she will deliver him what he wants."

Felicity pressed down her rising anxiety. "How long do you think he'll go to jail?" she queried as dispassionately as she could manage.

Obviously attuned to her, Jase leaned in forehead to forehead, his injured hand joining hers. "It will be at least a year," he comforted.

"Only a year," she whispered. "Then my kids will have to go back to him."

"A year is a long time," Jase comforted. "Your kids will be older and wiser, and so will you."

Despite his assurances, she did not feel entirely consoled. Still, there were so many unknowns, she decided not to try to solve them all just yet.

"There's something else," he leveled, his tone raising the hairs on Felicity's arms. "I'm going back to my old occupation."

"Government work?" Felicity wondered.

"Like it," Jase admitted, "and it works out, because you and I were going to be separated soon anyway."

"'Be separated'?"

"We talked about this before," he explained, leaning back to look out the glass walls of the lobby. "I don't fit with your kids, and they don't fit in my world. And you owe them first love."

Felicity reached to touch his face with her uninjured hand.

Looking back to her eyes, he mirrored her move, reaching for her face. He brushed his thumb gently over her lips. Despite the sadness of his tone, Jase smiled at her. "You made things very clear from the beginning."

"But I was just scared!" Felicity insisted. "I didn't want to make a mistake. I didn't want to go further than I could pull back from."

"And you were right, Felicity," he continued gently. "It was – well, maybe not a mistake, but a temporary fix."

Felicity thought back to her drug analogy, a sob rising in her chest.

As if sensing her misery, Jase pulled her onto his lap, encircling her with his arm. For several minutes, neither of them said anything.

"I was right," she finally allowed, lowering her head to his shoulder.

"You were. And now you're free…" As he said the words, he gently gripped her left hand raising it to their eye level as he stroked his thumb over the pale ghost of a ring that encircled her fourth finger. "You're free."

Raising soft eyes to his, her lips curved up at the corners. "*Tu l'as régler*," she smiled, and Jase's eyes warmed at her use of the familiar tongue.

Instead of answering, Jase entwined his fingers in hers and lowered his face until his lips brushed her temple. Unable to bear it, Felicity turned to him, wincing as she gripped his face with her other hand, but not letting the pain of her arm deter her. Her lips found his, and he seemed to light on fire. He released her hand, instead weaving his fingers through her hair with one hand and tugging her closer with the other, as if he couldn't stand the space between them.

Tears began to run down her cheeks, and Felicity found herself dizzy with lack of breathing.

Finally, Jase gasped, as if he, too, hadn't breathed for too long.

It was a release, a dismissal, and goodbye. Wiping the tears from her cheeks with his thumbs, Jase brushed the warm skin of his cheek against hers before leaning away.

"Don't say anything," he whispered, and Felicity knew she couldn't have spoken anyway. He gently stood to his feet, sliding her to her own.

Her tears flowed anew, and he brushed her hair out of her eyes, gazing into them with a strange ecstatic melancholy. He again stroked his thumb over the pale circle where her ring had been. "I won't say it either."

Turning from her, he stepped through the door and strolled out beyond the glass walls of The Lodge. Once he had faded into the grey light of dawn, Felicity sat down in his chair and wept.

Chapter 31

Finally! – Felicity's Journal, April 3

Punishment and place of confinement: 10 Years, ADC –
Correctional Institutes Division. Sentence of confinement
suspended to one year in minimum security facility followed
by 8 years probation. - Brendon's sentence, June 25

"We have a plane waiting at the Calgary airport," Briel explained. "I'm sure our client wouldn't mind an extra passenger, especially in light of how much you have helped us."

"And when you land," Felicity interjected, a sudden mirth turning the corners of her mouth skyward, "you can get the rest of the files from Nick."

"From Nick? What does he have to do with this?" Despite her apparent resolve, Briel seemed curious about the man she – perhaps futilely – had determined to reject.

"You didn't think I got the files by myself?

"I just assumed that you had told Nick how to get them off of your computer."

"Nope. Nick found them on ProtoComm's computers. He hacked them, and sent them to me." Felicity smiled widely as she watched her words sink in to Briel's brain. A look of undisguised fascination flashed across the young agent's face before she recovered her professional demeanor.

"Well, I'll be sure to find him, then, and thank him," Briel hedged, obviously trying to hide her pleasure at the thought. "There was some good intel on our client's daughter on there."

"And Nick will likely be able to help you find more."

Briel nodded before Nessa came and escorted Felicity to a waiting car.

"Is Jase okay?" Nessa wondered.

Felicity bit her lip, that hypocritical jealousy scratching at the door of her psyche.

"I wish I knew," Felicity admitted. "He's stronger than I

could imagine, so I'm not sure how much touches him."

"You'd be surprised," Nessa sighed.

The operative seemed somber, and Felicity knew that her own envy was a selfish indulgence. "You know him well."

Smiling, Nessa huffed a laugh. "No, no one knows Jase well. He is a closed book, but that doesn't mean things don't touch him."

Felicity found her breath constricted, and after a few seconds' struggle, she finally found her voice, asking a question that pained her by the surrender it implied.

"You'll take care of him?" Felicity begged, trying to keep desperation out of her voice.

Surprised, Nessa smiled up into Felicity's face. "I know how much you care about him. Maybe it's a consolation to you or maybe it's a curse, but I care, too. I will take care of him as much as he'll let me. We've brushed shoulders over the years, but he doesn't invest in relationships. Jase has a history with everyone he has met, but he may or may not know it. Not that he will forget you, of course. But Jase is just the kind of person who has an impact on the people who know him but he may never see it."

Felicity nodded, repressing her discomfort. "I'm glad he has friends to look after him."

"Friends," agreed Nessa with a hint of sadness. "And you take care of your family. Briel seems all business, but she's not all that different from Jase – tough on the outside, but a heart of gold. She loves your kids."

Despite a slight pang of fury at the memory of Briel with her kids, Felicity shook off her childish sentiments. Briel had done Felicity right in the end, and if nothing else, Briel had given Felicity the really pleasant memory of Brendon pinned to the ground by the knee of a woman just over half his size.

Epilogue

Closing her eyes, Felicity steadied herself as she unfolded the damp paper she held in her hands. She had forgotten about it completely. She had found it in her suitcase after her flight out of the Phoenix Airport to her new home. The Belizean humidity had rendered the letter musty and frail, but that did not lessen Felicity's fear of its contents. Weeks of peace had pushed thoughts of that tumultuous time to the recesses of her memory, but the unassuming leaf of paper guaranteed to stir memories she had worked hard to forget.

Felicity, it began simply, and her stomach clutched as her mind spoke in his voice.

There are so many things that I never got to say to you, and things that have missed their moment so will remain unsaid.

Still, there are some that I think you ought to know.

First of all, I recognize how completely messed up I was in even attempting to win you. I had spent so much of my life with a myopic perspective, totally focused on the tiny lens of how my choices affected me.

I saw that in you which had never wakened in me before: selflessness. You lived it every day of your life, and I saw it lived out in a way that broadened my lens significantly.

Can you forgive me for falling in love with that?

I was an inconsiderate, self-focused fool who could believe that, in your weakest and most vulnerable moment, it was okay for me to try to sway you to love me. In my defense, that portion of me that pursued you really believed that I was uniquely able to care for you. That part of me was newly birthed and very immature, and so I beg you will offer lenience for it.

Fortunately, you were much more experienced in that one part of life. Your love is a mature and wise love, and there is a part of me that believes you held me in that circle despite my immaturity. As if you could give me credit for my motives and intentions.

I know you hate it when I point out how amazing I think you are, but that is just one of many reasons I believe it.

You were right from the beginning to refuse me. You would have continued in the right if your compassion had not softened you, and compassion is not the kind of love I pursued with you. It was a good love, and I see the value, but I saw that it was not the same for you as I had wanted for myself.

There is not a day that goes by that I do not miss you, that I do not curse you for leaving me and praise you for refusing me. I am a child and a lunatic. And I can adore you and revere you while knowing with everything within me that you were never to be mine.

All I can ask is that when you think of me, you place me back in the confines of your compassion. You have changed me forever, and I cannot lose that which you awakened.

Because of you, I will walk a different path. One with more compassion and mindfulness. One that subdues my own selfish desires under the needs of others – at least more than it had before you. I have not become a saint because of you, but I have known what a saint looks like.

Thank you for waking me up. Thank you for breaking my heart. And thank you for, rather than letting me corrupt who you are, shining your light on the darkness that had confused me for far too many years.

Someday, I hope to find my own light. In the meantime, thanks for letting me borrow some of yours.

Jase

For several seconds, Felicity didn't move. She had let his time with her pass into that same illusory portion of her mind as the lie of her time with her husband, though her time with Jase held an entirely different hue than her time with Brendon.

Felicity couldn't regret Jase.

She had opened her heart just enough to hold incredibly tender impressions of him, but she had protected her mind – as had he – from believing the impressions to be concrete reality. Still, a tear escaped her eye before she folded the letter and set it down.

Through the open window, an intricate mix of guitar and marimba floated in with the salty breeze. Felicity wanted nothing more than to join her family on the nearby caye, and, shuffling to retrieve her keys, she turned to walk out the door.

Thinking better of it, she returned to the side table where she had placed Jase's letter. She picked it up and crossed determinedly to the small, open-flamed coconut fire which repelled the manifold insects that would otherwise invade her island home. For one infinitesimal second, Felicity hesitated. Then she dropped the letter onto the embers and watched as it flared up and smoldered into oblivion.

Immediately, she strode out the door and past the dusty courtyard to the boat which would unite her with her family.

"Time to go back?" the pilot asked pleasantly.

"Yes, thank you," Felicity replied.

The breeze cooled as it flowed across the ice-blue waters that flew by beneath her - the boat could not move fast enough. Finally, after ten long minutes, Felicity spied the caye and smiled contentedly as the boat docked, and she leaped lightly onto the wooden planks. Felicity watched as her mother tied Noah's shoe and mussed his hair playfully before scooting him back onto the make-shift dirt dance floor before them.

Though the band played loudly, her children, having nearly lost her once, seemed preternaturally attuned to Felicity's approach. Little Nicholas's smile turned to greet her, and he rose quickly to bridge the distance between them.

"Missed you," he said in a soft voice.

Felicity laughed. "I was gone thirty minutes," kissing his cherubic cheek. "I'm never leaving you again, not until you're ready to leave me," she assured him.

"I'll never leave you, mommy," he insisted, and Felicity let the innocence statement rest.

Alex coolly sauntered up to her mom, Noah wheeling beside her.

"Hi, sweetheart," Felicity hugged her daughter, who flinched in her embarrassment for only an instant. Felicity bent to kiss Noah's golden curls. "Watch them for a minute while I go wash my hands, would you?" Felicity smiled at Alex. "I'm going to get a drink, too. Do you want something?"

"A Coke, thanks."

Felicity nodded. "Be right back."

Felicity rounded the corner into the low, thatch-roofed café, smiling to herself at the sight of her kids where they laughed lightheartedly. Scattered around the room Felicity entered, citronella torches mingle with the dim light of the white strings which twinkled along the eaves. The effect was relaxing and soporific. Though the sun had not set, its rays could not penetrate the low windows which faced every direction but west.

In the restroom, Felicity quickly scrubbed her hands, drying them on her jeans in her hurry to return to her brood. The barman called out to her with a cheerful greeting.

"How are you, Miss Felicity?"

"Great, thanks, Milton. How are you?" As she spoke, Felicity approached the bar to order her drinks.

"Wonderful, Miss. What can I get you?"

"I need a Coke and an iced tea."

"No problem."

Felicity smiled pleasantly at Milton while he prepared her drinks, and he returned her smile as he handed them to her. "Thanks," she said and, keeping her eye on the full glasses, she turned slowly toward the main exit and started across the room. As she passed the window that opened onto the courtyard, she caught sight of her children and set the tray on a tall table so she could lean against the window sill to watch them. Noah perched next to the musicians and clapping to the beat, Nicolas ran around on the dancefloor, laughing and running away from his big sister, and Alex hovered protectively over her baby brother, corralling him away from the little road that ran beside the restaurant. Felicity's heart lifted, and gratitude tugged her to join them as quickly as possible.

"Watch out, Miss!" Milton called as she began to spin toward the exit. In an instant, her body registered new information, and she sensed the heat of a presence which stood entirely too close behind her. Her pulse rate sped, and every instinct awakened by her new life experiences jumped to full alert.

Though she had sworn to herself that she would never use it, her hand flew – almost without her permission – to the small pistol she now wore strapped to a belt at her waistband. Adrenaline pumped speed into her motion, and with one swift turn, the gun rested against the brow of the last man she ever expected to see. If she had not that day read his letter, Felicity had no doubt that she would have screamed. Instead, her breath hitched in her chest, and her hands began to shake as he threaded his arm around her waist and lifted his hand to push the gun toward the ceiling.

"You'd better learn to take the safety off," Jase offered with a subtle and heart-stopping smile. "But that was an impressive move."

Everything in Felicity quavered at the vision before her, at the warmth of his arm around her as he gently tugged the cold metal from her hand.

"Jase," Felicity barely whispered, her heart thundering as she considered how close she had come to hurting him.

"Liss," he hummed, setting the gun down on her tray of drinks before raising his hand to her face.

Forcing herself to calm, Felicity stared into his eyes for a moment. "Why are you here?" she demanded, her tone finding strength as she registered the lack of danger.

Hurt flashed across Jase's face, and he loosened his grip on her waist before stepping back and resting his elbow on the table. "I just wanted – have you heard about Bill?"

"Bill?" she managed. "Hopefully thrown off a four-wheeler on his flight from the cabin."

Jase smirked, and Felicity found herself smirking back at him.

"Bill had a stroke two weeks after his flight. He's lying in a hospital in Switzerland, an invalid, unable to feed himself. You're pretty isolated out here, and so I thought you would want to know – to get some peace."

"Well, I guess there is some justice in the world after all." Felicity leveled, her eyes finding a fixed spot on the wall as she considered the ramifications. When they found their way back to Jase's face, Felicity peered at him, searching for the new determination he had promised. "So, have you made it to someday?" she wondered.

For one instant, Jase's practiced performance melted into vulnerability, and his tone softened to match. "*Tu as lu mon lettre.*"

Abashed, Felicity stared at the ground, remorse enveloping her as she thought of the ashes of the note. When she finally looked up, he had stood straighter, stepping toward her with a gaze that stopped her heart. She couldn't move.

"Liss –" His voice kissed her name. "I'm sorry..." Still, before she could process what he said, his arm had wound again behind her waist, and he was pressing her to him.

Without a word, Felicity raised on her toes as he lowered his lips to hers. She closed her eyes and breathed in the scent of him.

"I was wrong to come here," he whispered against her mouth. "I have to leave you now, or I never will."

Though she wanted to beg him to stay, Felicity just nodded,

and she kept her eyes closed as he released her and his warmth evaporated from before her. For several seconds, she didn't move, fighting the massive bout of dizziness his presence had wrought.

It wasn't real, she told herself, *it was a dream.* In answer to her willful thoughts, when she opened her eyes, he was gone, though she caught a familiar scent in the air where the dream had stood.

She retrieved her drinks from the table, noting the slight amusement on Milton's face when she peered back at him through the dim light of the cabana.

Not really a dream.

Collecting herself, she pressed forward, the loss palpable but not regretted. Both of them had known, and the last kiss had not provoked regret – it had offered resolution. God had brought Jase into Felicity's life as a knife, to sever her connection to the myth she had lived before.

Once Jase had served his purpose, he withdrew beyond her reach. Whether Felicity herself had served a similar role in Jase's life or someone else would present to give him peace, she prayed that God would offer Jase a similar resolution to her own.

With somber assurance, Felicity turned back to the light that waited for her outside – the light that had freed her from years of illusion. Even with its imperfections, she knew that the beautiful reality of her life, outside in the tropical sun, had proven the best reality she could imagine.

As if in confirmation of her thoughts, her kids rushed to her as soon as she rounded the corner, dragging her into the gold of the setting sun, to the music and the beauty of the life she had chosen – of the life that she loved.